# THE QUEEN'S HUSBAND

Victoria and Albert have been destined for each other since birth. However, the passive Albert is well aware that marriage to a quick-tempered, demonstrative young woman like Victoria could result in unnecessary scenes and stormy court feuds. He is right. The young queen, as well as having to endure her constant pregnancies, is in constant revolt against anyone encroaching on her position – and Albert is doing just that. Despite attempts on her life and political crises, her family remains her prime concern, but who really holds the power behind the throne – the queen or her husband?

# THE QUEEN'S HUSBAND

# THE QUEEN'S HUSBAND

*by*

Jean Plaidy

**Magna Large Print Books**
Long Preston, North Yorkshire,
BD23 4ND, England.

British Library Cataloguing in Publication Data.

Plaidy, Jean
    The Queen's husband.

    A catalogue record of this book is
    available from the British Library

    ISBN   978-0-7505-3335-5

First published in Great Britain in 1973 by Robert Hale & Company

Copyright © Jean Plaidy, 1973

Cover illustration © Jill Battaglia by arrangement with
Arcangel Images

The Estate of Eleanor Hibbert has asserted its right to have Jean
Plaidy identified as the author of this work

Published in Large Print 2011 by arrangement with
Arrow, one of the publishers in the Random House Group Ltd.

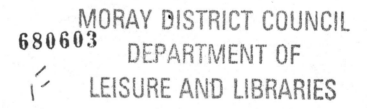
Magna Large Print is an imprint of Library Magna Books Ltd.

Printed and bound in Great Britain by
T.J. (International) Ltd., Cornwall, PL28 8RW

# Contents

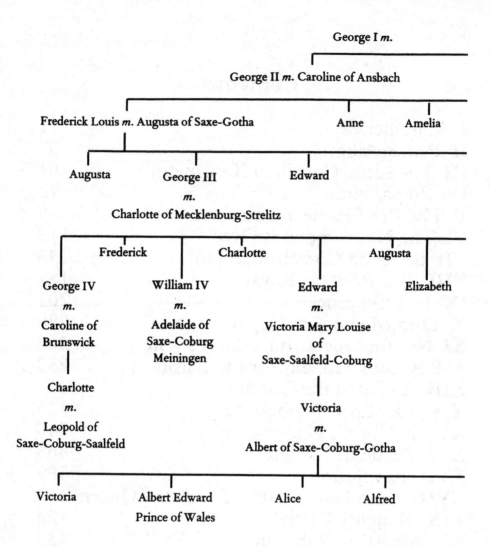

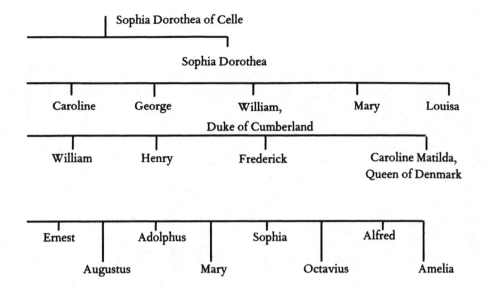

Sophia Dorothea of Celle

Sophia Dorothea

| Caroline | George | William, Duke of Cumberland | Mary | Louisa |

| William | Henry | Frederick | Caroline Matilda, Queen of Denmark |

| Ernest | Adolphus | Sophia | Alfred |
| Augustus | Mary | Octavius | Amelia |

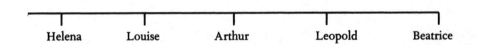

| Helena | Louise | Arthur | Leopold | Beatrice |

# Chapter I

## ALBERINCHEN

The family were in the summer residence, the charming little schloss called Rosenau, some four miles from Coburg; and the two Grandmamas had come to visit them. The first thing they did when they arrived was to hurry to the nursery for both Grandmama Saxe-Coburg and Grandmama Saxe-Gotha doted on the two little boys, Ernest aged five and Albert, fondly known as Alberinchen, just a little over a year younger.

Alberinchen was the favourite. He was such a beautiful child with his big blue eyes and dimples. 'More like a girl than a boy,' said his nurses. Ernest was bigger than his year's seniority warranted; he was brown-eyed and more physically energetic than his brother, and although they quarrelled constantly and fought now and then, the children were miserable when separated and because of the closeness of their ages they did almost everything together.

Alberinchen knew, though, that he was the favourite of the grandmothers and what was more important, of his mother, for the happiest times of his life were when she came to the nursery; she was beautiful and different from anyone else Alberinchen had ever known. Life without Ernest would have been inconceivable, for Ernest was almost always there, but his feelings for Ernest were made up of rivalry, companionship and custom; his mother was as beautiful as his conception of an angel; she laughed all the time and her suffocating caresses filled him with bliss.

'Where are my big boys?' she would cry, peeping round the door of the nursery; and they would both run forward, Alberinchen pushing Ernest aside, knowing that Ernest would not retaliate because if he did Alberinchen would cry and the precious half hour of Mama's visit would be spent in consoling him. Alberinchen's tears were notorious; when they came it was everyone's desire to stop them as soon as possible.

Alberinchen would sit on his mother's lap and Ernest would lean against her; she would place her arm about him and they would talk about a new game she had thought of. It was very different from other people's visits. *They* always wanted to know about lessons; and the two little boys would be expected to read their books or repeat the verses they had learned; but with Mama they would be playing the new game which involved a good deal of fun.

On this occasion the door was opening and there was Mama, Duchess of Saxe-Coburg-Saalfeld, looking so beautiful and excited that the two little boys, shrieking with delight, ran to her and clung to her gown.

'So my two little boys are glad to see me?' she asked unnecessarily.

'Alberinchen's here,' Alberinchen reminded her.

She lifted him up. Beautiful little Alberinchen, she thought; my consolation. What a lovely child and how he depended on her. 'And Ernest too,' said Ernest.

'My precious darlings,' cried the Duchess.

'What shall we play?' demanded Ernest.

'Your grandmamas will be here at any moment. I was surprised that at least one of them is not here already.' Mama grimaced. 'So perhaps we should not be discovered crawling round on the floor. We'll have to play a word game instead.'

Ernest wailed and Alberinchen was about to cry when it occurred to him that he was more likely to win at a word game. But that game was never played because just at that moment Grandmama Saxe-Coburg came in.

Ernest pouted and Alberinchen was disappointed but he wanted Grandmama Saxe-Coburg to go on loving him so he did not betray the fact that he was disappointed.

'How are the little boys today?' asked Grandmama Saxe-Coburg.

'Well and happy,' said their mother.

She caught up Alberinchen and held her face against his. 'The resemblance is remarkable,' said Grandmama Saxe-Coburg.

'Well, why shouldn't I be like my own son?' said the Duchess.

'And Ernest is just like his father.'

Alberinchen smiled smugly; it was of course far better to be like his mother, who was gay and beautiful, than like his father who had lines on his face and pouches under his eyes; although Alberinchen, in fairness to Ernest, could not see that Ernest was in the least like him.

'I daresay we shall see the Saxe-Coburg coming

13

out in little Alberinchen in due course,' said Grandmama.

'I am sure you will search most assiduously for a resemblance.'

There was something strange about the way in which they were speaking to each other. Alberinchen was only faintly aware of it; he wished Grandmama Saxe-Coburg would go, so that he could be the centre of attention.

'And how are they getting along with their lessons? I was speaking to their governesses...'

Mama grimaced, which made her seem as though she were a child in the nursery; Alberinchen gripped her hand tightly. He would be ready to cry if he could not answer the questions Grandmama Saxe-Coburg asked him.

'They are a little young for so many lessons,' said the Duchess. 'Little Alberinchen is only four.'

'They can't start learning *too* young,' said Grandmama, 'and if properly taught, lessons are a joy like games and sports.'

Alberinchen could not agree with that so he kept close to his mother; but he realised that she was ineffectual against Grandmama Saxe-Coburg so the lesson books came out and he had to spell out the words; and as he did better than Ernest there was no need for tears.

While they were thus engaged Grandmama Saxe-Gotha (the young Duchess's step-mother) came in and sat listening, nodding with approval; and this went on until Mama said she was going riding and must leave them to get ready.

Alberinchen's face puckered, but she held him

tightly against her and kissed him fervently.

'Darling Alberinchen, I'll see you later on. And you too, my precious Ernest.'

So they were left with the grandmothers.

There was something rather alarming in the air; Alberinchen was not sure what. Was it the manner in which the grandmothers looked at each other?

'Now, Ernest, read from here.'

Ernest with his rather imperturbable good humour began stammering out the words.

'Can it possibly be true?' whispered Grandmama Saxe-Coburg.

'I hesitate to say, but I very much fear...'

'She could not be so ... *criminal*...'

'Ernest I fear has not been...'

'But Ernest is a man ... and that is different. But if this is true ... I tremble...'

'I always thought her frivolous.'

'You heard what she said about my looking for the likeness to his father?'

'Why is there always trouble in the family?'

'Hush. The boys.'

'They wouldn't understand.'

'Little ones have big ears.'

Alberinchen touched his ears which made the grandmothers gasp.

'You see.'

'I do. Alberinchen, my darling, show me your drawings. I'm sure Grandmama Saxe-Coburg would be delighted to see them.'

He was so excited by his drawings that he immediately forgot the conversation he had heard; but he remembered it later.

The young Duchess of Saxe-Coburg-Saalfeld hastily changed into her riding-habit. What a relief, she thought, to get out of the palace for a short while. She could not bear the censorious attitude of her mother-in-law and her step-mother. She knew they were discussing her now.

I don't care, she thought. I must have some life or I'd die of boredom.

Her marriage had been a failure from the start. How she had cried when at sixteen they had married her to the Duke. He had seemed so old and she was so inexperienced; of course if he had been different, a little tender, if he had tried to make her love him, it might have been different. But like his ancestors he was crude and sensual; and he had no intentions of giving up his mistresses because he had acquired a wife – for the sole purpose of course of getting heirs. No one could deny that she had done her duty in that respect. She had given him first Ernest and then Albert; and he was pleased with the boys. And so was she. She loved them dearly, but she was too young and too pleasure-loving to be able to make them all she asked of life. Perhaps some women would have been able to – but not Louise. She hated her husband, who was parsimonious and, although he indulged his sensuality, could scarcely be called gay.

She had tried very hard to be a good wife, but after Ernest's birth she had begun to look round for some means of making life more amusing – and she had found it.

Of course she should not be riding out alone:

she should be with a party. He goes his own way, she told herself defiantly. Why shouldn't I go mine? And in any case how could she take a party to meet her lover?

The Dowager Duchess of Saxe-Coburg went to her son's apartments when she left the children. She was very uneasy.

'I must have a talk with you, Ernest,' she said, 'about you and Louise.'

The Duke's expression hardened, 'There is a good deal to be said on that matter,' he agreed.

'It is all so unfortunate.'

'I believe that I am on the verge of discovery.'

'So these rumours...'

'Of her misconduct? Yes, I believe them to be true. I am having her watched.'

'And you suspect that someone here is her paramour?'

He nodded. 'Szymborski.'

'Never.'

'Well, he's a handsome fellow.'

'Is he Jewish?'

The Duke nodded.

'Oh, Ernest, and how long do you think this can possibly have been going on?'

'That's what I intend to find out. I suspect that she had been unfaithful before Albert was born.'

'Ernest! This could have terrible implications.'

'Oh, I believe Albert to be mine.'

'It could not be otherwise. But it is criminal of her.'

'I agree with you. That is why I am determined to bring the matter to a head.'

'She was always frivolous and she is little more than a girl now. Ernest, what will you do?'

'It remains to be seen. So much will depend on what we discover.'

'If there were other children...'

'I know you are thinking that we could not be sure that I was their father. Even so...'

'No, don't say it. Don't even think it. Ernest is you in miniature and I am convinced that darling little Albert is your son.'

'I feel so, too. But how could I be sure of any others?'

'It is a scandalous situation.'

'And will become more so.'

'Does Leopold know?'

'Not yet.'

'He will be horrified.'

The Duke felt faintly resentful. His brother Leopold was his mother's favourite son and regarded in the family as something of an oracle since he had succeeded in marrying the Princess Charlotte which, had she lived, would have meant that he was the husband of the Queen of one of the most important countries in the world – very different from the little dukedoms and principalities of Germany. But Leopold was far too ready to interfere in family matters. It was not as though he were an elder son either. Fortunately he was in England where he was paid a good income even though his position there was somewhat invidious. King George IV had never liked him and had not wanted him as a son-in-law. But Leopold was so good-looking and clever that Charlotte had insisted on marrying him, and by accounts – Leo-

18

pold's at any rate – she had been so enamoured of him that he had easily been able to subdue her will to his. What a glorious future it would have been for Leopold – and the house of Saxe-Coburg – if Charlotte had lived to be Queen.

Still, Leopold had not lost hope of governing England, for a very significant event had occurred at Kensington Palace three months before young Albert had been born. Their sister, who was Duchess of Kent, had given birth to a daughter – Alexandrina Victoria – and if the King did not marry and produce an heir – which was scarcely possible considering his age and condition – and his brother William did not either – and he seemed in no state to do so – that little girl, Leopold's niece, his own niece, would be Queen of England.

So Leopold stayed on in England hoping that since he had failed to be the husband of that country's Queen, he might one day be her uncle.

Very clever of Leopold, but that was no reason why he should be considered an oracle who could solve the problems of Saxe-Coburg.

Of course his mother believed he could.

'I think,' she was saying now, 'we should write to Leopold and ask his advice.'

'Mother, this is a matter for me to settle.'

'When he came over four years ago, he did mention that he thought Louise a little frivolous. He noticed, you see.'

'We all knew the character of my wife, Mother. It was obvious.'

'He came all the way from England then just to find me a house in Italy for the winter,' said the

19

Dowager Duchess fondly. 'I am sure he would be willing to come on this far more important mission.'

'I am of the opinion that I can deal with this affair.'

'What do you propose to do?'

'To bring the matter into the open. I may find it necessary to rid myself of her.'

'Ernest, be careful. This could reflect on the children. You remember when Leopold was here, how taken he was with little Albert.'

'They were taken with each other, I think.'

'It is true. Albert could just toddle at the time, but although just a year old, he was very *forward* for his age. He followed Leopold everywhere. I remember how he sat on his knee watching his lips as he talked.'

'I remember how enchanted Leopold was by such admiration.'

'He said to me, "I have a dear little niece in Kensington Palace whom I love as much as I could love this little fellow." And he went on to say that as soon as he had set eyes on our little Albert he had thought of his little niece in England. "She could be Queen of England," he said. "And would it not be a wonderful arrangement if these two children could be brought together." He said that, Ernest.'

'No one makes plans for the family like Leopold.'

'Oh, he is clever, so wise and so eager to bring good to the family. Just think – our little Albert could be King of England. It's a possibility, Ernest. So you see, my son, how careful you will

20

have to be. There must be no whisper against little Albert.'

'I'll see that there is not. At the same time I have no intention of allowing my wife to deceive me under my very own nose.'

'I just cannot believe it of her.'

'You will ... when I produce the evidence.'

'All I ask you, Ernest, is take care.'

'You may rely on me to do that.'

She sighed. She hoped so. But all her children of course could not be as wise as Leopold.

The book lay on Grandmama Saxe-Coburg's lap and the two boys listened entranced as she read to them.

'These two little boys you see here were Saxon Princes and one was named Ernest and one named Albert.'

'Those are our names,' cried Ernest.

'Which one was Albert?' asked Alberinchen.

Grandmama Saxe-Coburg showed them.

'They were your ancestors, my darlings, and they lived in the Castle of Altenburg. Their father was Duke Frederick.'

'Our Papa is Ernest,' said Alberinchen.

'That's quite right,' said Grandmama. 'There are a lot of Fredericks in our family and Ernests too.'

'And Alberts,' put in Alberinchen. 'There are a lot of Alberts too, Grandmama.'

'There is one here now,' said Grandmama, kissing him, which made him hunch his shoulders and laugh delightedly.

'There's a bad man coming in,' said Ernest,

placing a plump finger on the page.

'Yes, there is a bad man. Now the Duke Frederick had a chamberlain named Kunz of Kaufungen and because Duke Frederick had made him give back land which he had stolen he decided to have his revenge. So one night he, and some wicked men who were helping him, crept into the castle where the two boys were sleeping and they seized Ernest.'

'What about Albert?' cried Alberinchen.

'Well, there was another little boy, an attendant of the Princes, who was sleeping in a bed near that of Albert and they mistook him for Prince Albert and took him instead.'

Alberinchen's face puckered. It seemed that Prince Albert was going to be left out of the adventure and he didn't like that.

'Albert was clever,' said Grandmama quickly. 'He saw at once that a mistake had been made, so he said nothing and when little Graf von Barby, the boy they had mistaken for Albert, was dragged away, he hid under the bed in case they came back.'

'And what happened then?'

'They discovered their mistake and came back for Albert. They found him under the bed.'

'But he was clever to hide there,' said Alberinchen.

'It was very clever. Well, the good Duke Frederick was not going to allow his sons to be kidnapped, so he sent his trusty soldiers after the villains and they caught them and the boys were restored to their father. Now, that is a true story and it happened in the year 1455 .'

'I like that story,' said Ernest.

'So do I,' Alberinchen laughed. 'I liked it when Albert hid under the bed.'

'It's history,' said Grandmama Saxe-Coburg. 'Now you know how exciting history is you must pay great attention to your lessons.'

'I like history when it's about us,' said Alberinchen. 'That wasn't about us was it, Grandmama?' asked Ernest.

'It was about our family. And as most royal families are connected with each other, history is about us.'

'I like history,' said Alberinchen. 'I wish Mama would come. I want to tell her about how Prince Albert hid under the bed.'

They were playing the capture of the Princes. It was a good game because they could each play the part of a prince, but there were other exciting roles. They both wanted to be the wicked Kunz at the start of the game and Duke Frederick at the end. Ernest thought he should have the choice as he was the eldest, but Alberinchen did not agree with this and it seemed as though the game was going to end in a fight and the inevitable tears when their mother put her head round the door and said: 'Are my boys pleased to see me?'

The game was forgotten. They dashed at her.

'My darling, darling Alberinchen. Dearest Ernest!'

'Oh, Mama, how beautiful you look.'

'That's because I'm pleased.'

'Why are you pleased, Mama?'

'Let's sit down and I'll tell you all about it.

We're going to have a children's ball.'

'What's that, Mama?' asked Ernest.

'We're going to dance.'

Alberinchen's face puckered.

He didn't like dancing, he said. It made him tired.

'Tired!' cried Mama. 'Why I could dance all night and not be tired.'

'So could I,' said Ernest. 'It's only silly Albert who can't.'

Alberinchen's lips trembled and his mother hastily embraced him. 'Albert is not silly, are you, Alberinchen?'

'I'm clever like Albert who hid under the bed.'

'Oh, that story, yes. It was interesting, wasn't it, my pets? Now you're going to love my ball and we're all going to dress up. What would you like to be, Ernest?'

Ernest could not think but Alberinchen wanted to be Prince Albert who was nearly kidnapped.

'Well, I don't think so, darling. I've got a lovely idea for you.'

'What is it, Mama?'

'It's a surprise. You'll learn all in good time.'

'A surprise!' The little boys danced around joyously.

'Now,' said Mama, 'who doesn't want to dance? Look at Alberinchen.'

The surprise was his costume. He was to be dressed as Cupid.

'Who was Cupid, Mama?' asked Alberinchen.

'The God of Love. He carried arrows with him and when he shot them into people they fell in love with each other and married.'

'Like you and Papa?' asked Ernest.

Alberinchen watching her face saw a strange expression flit across it. It frightened him but he did not quite know why.

'Like people who fall in love,' said Mama.

'Shall I have arrows?'

'Oh, yes.'

'You can shoot them,' cried Ernest. 'Mama, I want arrows too.'

'No, darlings, you won't shoot them. Alberinchen will just carry them and he will dance with the pretty little girls.'

'I don't like little girls,' growled Alberinchen.

'Oh, my dearest boy. You are not very gallant.'

'What is gallant?' asked Ernest.

'It's something nasty,' Alberinchen said, confident that it must be if he was not it.

'Well, it's something Princes must learn to be.' Mama laughed and hugged him. 'My precious little Cupid!' she added.

So there he was in satin costume and Ernest was similarly garbed.

'What darlings they look,' said the grandmothers to each other; and their fearful eyes were on the Duchess Louise who was rather hysterically gay as though she knew that there would not be many more such balls where she would be able to dress up her children and join in the fun.

All the young guests were lined up together.

'You know the steps,' whispered Ernest to his brother. 'They're those you learned yesterday.'

'I don't like those steps,' said Alberinchen.

But Ernest wanted to dance; he liked the look

25

of the pretty little girls who were placed opposite them, and it was interesting to be with other children.

Ernest took his partner's hand and they danced along the line of children as they had been taught to do, while the grown-ups looked on and were enchanted.

'Ernest is quite the little gentleman,' said Grandmama Saxe-Coburg.

'A real little Prince,' agreed Grandmama Saxe-Gotha.

Alberinchen stood sullenly. He did not like being dressed as Cupid. He wanted to be dressed as Prince Albert. He did not want to dance with silly girls but to hide under the bed and then fight and scream when the wicked Kunz came to take him.

They were waiting. The music was playing. The little girl was standing before him, smiling. He hated her; he hated all little girls. He stood sullenly, his eyes lowered.

'Albert.' Grandmama Saxe-Coburg was calling to him. But he remained, his eyes lowered.

His mother came over. 'Alberinchen, darling, it is your turn to dance.'

He would not dance. He hated dancing.

He began to cry. He was aware of the shocked dismay all about him, so he yelled; soon his screams were drowning the music. His face was red; they were always afraid when he screamed like that and he knew that they wanted to stop him at all costs.

One of his nurses came forward at a sign from Grandmama Saxe-Coburg, seized him and hurried him away.

In the room he shared with Ernest he stopped screaming. Once again his tears had brought him what he wanted.

But that was not the end of the affair.

Grandmama Saxe-Coburg came into the room. He stood eyeing her defiantly.

'Albert,' she said, 'I wish to speak to you.'

The fact that he was called by his proper name was a sure sign that he was in disgrace.

The tears started to fill his eyes.

'Your conduct in the ballroom was not what I would have expected of a Coburg Prince,' said his grandmother.

'I didn't want to dance,' said Albert.

'But what about the little girl, your partner? *She* wanted to dance.'

'But *I* didn't.'

'And because of you, she couldn't. Was that kind?'

'It makes me tired,' sad Albert pathetically.

'What, you, a Prince ... too tired to dance with a little girl!'

'I don't like dancing. It's silly.'

'It's a necessary social grace, and that is something you will have to learn, Albert, social grace.'

He wondered about social grace. Was it as exciting as history and stories of his ancestors?

'One day, you will grow up and you will marry. You won't be able to cry then, you know. I wonder what Uncle Leopold would have said, if he could have been in the ballroom today.'

At last the child looked contrite. What power

Leopold had! It was three years since Albert had seen him but so impressed had he been that he remembered still and was eager for his uncle's good opinion. But perhaps Leopold's name had been kept alive by constant references to this god-like uncle.

'You must not think, Albert, that this is an end of the matter. That was a disgraceful scene and you will hear more of it.'

As Albert was about to burst into tears, his grandmother left him.

Albert was silent. There was no point in exercising his lungs on unresponsive silence.

Duke Ernest was in his study and his younger son stood before him. The Duke was holding a long thin cane which fascinated Albert.

'Now, Albert,' said the Duke, 'I am ashamed of you. You have insulted a lady. I have heard all about your conduct in the ballroom. Your partner in the dance, a little girl of nobility, stood before you and you refused to dance with her and screamed so much that you had to be carried struggling from the ballroom. That is conduct which I cannot tolerate in my Court.'

Albert continued to stare at the cane.

'Therefore I am going to punish you. I am going to beat you with this cane and you will still feel the effects of this beating for days to come. Now don't start to cry. Is that the way princes behave? You can scream to your heart's content but Ernest is gone for a walk and will not hear you; your mother will not hear you either. As for your grandmothers, they agree with me that what

I am about to do is necessary. So Albert, take your punishment like a man and remember that when you are about to behave badly in future the cane will be applied with even more severity than I shall apply it now.'

His father seized him. 'No!' screamed Albert.

'But yes,' retorted the Duke.

Albert's screams were deafening.

'I won't be defied,' shouted the Duke.

Albert screamed the louder. His face grew red; he was gasping for breath. The Duke raised the cane but Albert's piercing screams grew louder.

The Duke hesitated. The child would do himself an injury; he had heard of Albert's screaming but had never realised how alarming it could be.

It grated on the Duke's nerves; he felt he had to stop it at all costs; at the same time the sight of that small face suffused with blood and growing more purple every moment alarmed him.

The boy would do himself an injury; and the Duke knew that if he applied the cane those terrifying screams would grow worse. 'Stop it, Albert,' he commanded.

Albert continued to scream.

The Duke could not bear the sound; it seemed to pierce his eardrums. And then suddenly the child started to cough.

The Duke put the cane down. Albert, they said, was delicate. That was why he didn't like dancing. It tired him. Albert went on coughing; he found he couldn't stop.

The Duke said: 'If you promise to behave better next time, I shan't use the cane now.'

That quietened Albert.

'I think,' went on the Duke, 'that we have come to an understanding.'

It was true. Albert understood that his screams were as effective with his father as with others.

The cough had helped too. He started to cough again. He went on and on making an odd noise as he did so.

His father went with him to the nursery and the grandmothers came in for a consultation. Meanwhile Albert discovered that Ernest, returned from his walk, was coughing too.

The brothers had contracted whooping-cough.

They must stay in the nursery, said the grandmothers. Everything that could be found to amuse them was brought to them. There were not so many lessons and more picture books; and Albert studied the drawings in one of these picture books which told the story of the two Saxon princes who had been kidnapped.

He did not mind being kept in the nursery because Ernest was with him; they could play and fight and listen to accounts of the treats that had been planned for them when they were better.

'Why does Mama not come to see us?' asked Albert.

Ernest couldn't answer that; and when they asked the grandmothers they talked of something else.

The young Duchess was imprisoned in her room. She was frightened. Everything was known now. They had spied on her. She had been seen with her lover; they knew that she had visited his house.

What would become of her? What of her little boys? They were confined to the nursery now with whooping-cough and she longed to be with them.

They were cruel, these German Princes – cruel and crude. There was one law for the men and another for the women. Why should Ernest be so shocked because she had taken a lover? She wanted to laugh when she thought of the hosts of mistresses with whom he had humiliated her. Yet she was supposed to ignore that side of her husband's nature; to remain coldly virtuous and await those occasions when he deigned to share her bed for the purpose of getting children. Her part of the bargain had been kept. He would have to understand that.

She would never forget – and who else would? – the terrible case of their ancestress, Sophia Dorothea. How very like her own: a crude boor of a husband from whom no female was safe, be she lady of the court or tavern woman; and poor tragic Sophia Dorothea had loved romantically the Count of Konigsmark. The discovery of their liaison had brought about the murder of Konigsmark and the banishment and divorce of Sophia Dorothea. Poor sad Princess who had languished in her prison castle for more than twenty years while her coarse husband went to England to become George I. And she had had two children – a boy and a girl. How heart-broken she must have been to leave them!

And here she was ... she, Louise, married to Ernest, mother of two dear little boys, her Ernest and little Alberinchen. Poor darlings, if I am sent away what will they do without me? she asked herself.

The door was unlocked and her husband came in. He looked at her with contempt and her expression became one full of loathing.

'It's no use making any attempt to deny it,' he said.

'I was unaware that I was attempting to do that.'

'Szymborski is leaving the country.' She was silent. 'We have put no obstacle in his way. We think it better to have him out of the way with as little scandal as possible.' She nodded. 'As for yourself, you may go tomorrow. You shall go quietly and without fuss. There has been enough gossip.'

'You and your women have created a fair share of it,' she retorted.

'I have behaved as a natural man is expected to behave.'

'By crude peasants, perhaps.'

'Whereas you have behaved in a manner which is intolerable to me, my family and the people.'

'Why should what is shameful in me be so natural and commendable in you?'

'I did not say commendable ... only natural. And the difference is, Madam, that you are the mother of the heirs of Saxe-Coburg. How long have you been consorting with your Jewish lover? Was it before Albert's birth?'

'How ... dare you!'

'I dare because we are here in this room alone. I would not have the boy's future jeopardised by voicing these fears outside.'

'Albert is your son.'

'With a wanton for a mother how can I be sure

of that?'

'A mother can be sure.'

'I can conceive circumstances where even she might not be sure.'

'You are making me an object of your insults. Pray don't.'

'You are an obvious object for insult. How can I know that you have not brought a bastard into my house?'

She ran to him, her eyes blazing; she would have struck him but he caught her wrist and twisted her arm till she screamed with the pain.

'Albert is your son,' she said.

'I believe you,' he said, releasing her. 'If I thought he were not, I would kill you.'

'Always be good to Albert. He is not as strong as Ernest.'

'Albert is my son and shall be treated as well as his elder brother.'

That placated her to some extent; but she felt desolate. She knew that she would be sent away, but for the first time she realised how wretched she would be when she was unable to see her children. Perhaps she would never see them again.

'Yes, Ernest,' she said, 'Albert is your son. Never doubt it. I swear it.'

He looked at her searchingly and there was still a niggling doubt in his mind. His impulse was to seize her, to throw her to the ground, to beat the truth out of her. But Albert *is* my son, he assured himself. He *must* believe it. It was unthinkable that he could accept anything else. He had feared that under stress she might confess that Albert was not his son. What if Ernest were not also?

Then he would be a man without sons. That was unthinkable. He loved the boys in his way. They were his. Ernest surely was, there could be no doubt of that. Ernest had his looks. And so was Albert. It was true those fair delicate looks were inherited from his mother but many babies resembled their mothers and bore no likeness whatsoever to their fathers.

He could not afford his suspicions. Albert was his son and no one must doubt that in the years to come.

He looked at his wife with hatred.

'You will not take the boys away from me,' she said.

'Are you mad? You play the whore and then think it would be pleasant to be the mother for a while. You will never see the boys again.'

'That would be too ... cruel ... wicked.'

'What a pity you did not think of that before.'

'Ernest, listen to me, I beg of you. I'll go away. You can divorce me ... never see me again. I admit I have done wrong, but please ... I beg of you don't take my babies from me.'

'It's a pity you did not think of your children when you were with your lover.'

'I have thought of them constantly. Only they made my life worth while.'

'They ... and Szymborski?'

The Duchess broke down and wept.

'Be ready to leave the schloss tomorrow morning early,' said the Duke. 'I want no one to see you go. You will just disappear.'

The Duchess, thinking of her little boys, began to weep silently.

The boys were recovering. Grandmother Saxe-Coburg stayed with them and she was constantly in and out of their room.

'Why doesn't Mama come?' Alberinchen asked Ernest.

Ernest thought she might have whooping-cough too.

Grandmother Saxe-Coburg said that fresh air was good for the boys while they were getting better, so they were taken out into the pine forests. They played games and pretended they were the kidnapped princes. But Albert could not forget his mother and made up his mind to ask his grandmother what had become of her.

One day when she was reading to him he put a finger on the page and said: 'Where is my Mama?'

The Dowager Duchess hesitated for a moment and then she said: 'She's gone away.'

'She did not say goodbye.'

'There was no time.'

'Was she in a hurry?'

'Yes, she was in a great hurry.'

'When is she coming back?'

'I can't tell you that.'

'Tomorrow,' said Alberinchen and his grand-mother did not answer: and when she saw the questions trembling on his lips she said: 'I'll tell you a story.'

That quietened him; his enormous blue eyes were fixed on his grandmother while he waited for her to begin.

'Three months before you were born another little baby was born right over the sea in a place

35

called Kensington.'

'Over the sea?' repeated Albert.

'Yes, in England, which is a big country. There are many in our family as you know, and the little baby girl who was born in Kensington three months before you is your cousin. Her name is Alexandrina Victoria. She is a little mayflower because she was born in May.'

'What sort of flower am I?'

'Boys are not flowers. You are an August baby. But one day you will grow up and so will the little girl at Kensington. Then you will meet because that is what your Uncle Leopold wishes. And I'll tell you a secret, little Alberinchen. If you are very good when you grow up you shall marry the Princess in Kensington.'

Albert's eyes were round with wonder. He was not sure what it meant to marry; but that story about the baby girl of Kensington was his story too.

There were changes in the household. The nurses were dismissed.

'The boys have to grow up and learn to be men,' said the Duke. 'Now that their mother has gone there shall be no more pampering. Albert particularly needs a man's hand. He will have to stop this crying habit.'

Herr Florschütz came to be the new tutor; he immediately set about discovering what standard the boys had reached and found them to be rather forward for their ages. Lessons were going to begin in earnest now. Alberinchen was not dismayed for he was a little brighter than Ernest and he enjoyed coming in first with the answers.

He was constantly asking when his mother was coming back and began to wonder because the answers were always evasive.

The two grandmothers disagreed as to the desirability of Herr Florschütz's taking the place of the nurses.

'Poor mites,' said Grandmama Saxe-Gotha. 'They need a woman's tender hand.'

But Grandmama Saxe-Coburg was of the opinion that Herr Florschütz would make a much better attendant than the nurses for he was expected to combine these duties with those of a tutor, the Duke's income being inadequate to his position and his necessarily large household.

'His mother was a bad influence on Albert,' was her verdict. 'He was growing too much like her. A man's firm hand is what he needs.'

The grandmothers seemed to be the only women who came into close contact with the boys. Albert screamed less but dissolved into tears at the least provocation. Herr Florschütz was immune from tears. He just allowed Albert to cry; and Ernest said he was a bit of a cry baby.

Albert cried sometimes quietly in his bed when he thought of his mother. Sometimes she had come to tuck them in. Why had she gone away without telling him, without even saying goodbye? Why did his grandmothers look strange when he asked about her? When was she coming back?

He had a little gold pin which she had given him. She had used it once when a button had come off his coat.

'There is a nice little pin, Alberinchen,' she had

said. 'It will hold your coat together until the button is sewn on and after that you must keep it and remember always the day I gave it to you.'

So he had and he would take it to bed with him and put it under his pillow; and first thing in the morning he would touch it and remember.

It became the most precious thing he had.

Once Grandmama Saxe-Coburg came into the bedroom and, bending to kiss him, saw that he was crying quietly.

'My little Alberinchen,' she said, 'what is it? Tell Grandmama.'

'I want my Mama,' he said.

'You mustn't cry,' she said softly. 'Only babies cry. You must be brave and strong. Otherwise you won't be able to marry the little Princess of Kensington.'

## Chapter II

## PRINCE ALBERT

Albert had passed his tenth birthday. He no longer screamed to get his own way and had become rather solemn. He was inseparable from his brother Ernest and, although they fought now and then, the bond between them had grown stronger with the years and neither could be really happy out of the company of the other. They were as different in character as they were in appearance. Ernest was tall; Albert shorter; Ernest robust, Albert alarming his grandmothers by his delicate looks. Ernest had bold black eyes and a pale skin; Albert was pink and white with very fair hair and blue eyes. Ernest already had a roving eye and liked to joke with the prettier maids in their father's castles; Albert had no interest in the women; he enjoyed the company of their tutor and his brother. The only women he was really comfortable with were his two grandmothers.

He had never forgotten his mother. He had a vague idea now of what had happened, for Ernest had discovered and told him.

'She had a lover,' Ernest had explained, 'and so she had to go away. Our father divorced her.'

Ernest gave his version of what this meant and Albert could not forget it. Something terrible and shameful had happened in his family; he knew this was so because of the manner in which no one would explain it to him. Looking back he could see the little Alberinchen who had loved his mother more than he had loved anyone else except himself. She had been so beautiful – more beautiful than anyone else, more loving. No one had conveyed to him in quite the same way how precious he was; no one had made him feel, merely by being close, happy and secure in the same way as she had.

Something had happened when she went away. He was not sure what, but it was for this reason that he had accepted Herr Florschütz so wholeheartedly and was glad the nurses had been dismissed. He did not want to look at women; they reminded him of his mother and something shameful. He loved her as he always had. Whatever she had done, and Ernest implied that it was terrible, he believed that he could never love anyone as he had loved her. He kept the little pin she had given him and he looked upon it as his greatest treasure. But his discomfiture in the company of women persisted because they made him think of vaguely shameful things.

He was happy, though, in the woods and mountains; and his father wished him to excel at all manly sports so he and Ernest spent a great deal of time fencing, riding and hunting. He began to love the beauty of the countryside and became an expert on flora and fauna. There was plenty of opportunity to study these, for their father's pleasant little castles were situated among the magnificent scenery of forests and mountains. Rosenau, his birthplace, would always be his favourite, but he also loved Kalenberg, Ketschendorf and Reinhardtsbrunnen: and, provided that Ernest was with him, he was happy in any of the family residences. Sometimes they visited one grandmother, sometimes the other. These ladies vied with each other for the affection of the boys; and when Albert could forget his mother, he was happy.

In the early days following her departure she had been constantly in his thoughts, but because of the attitude of those about him he had not spoken of this. Often he complained of pains to the grandmothers and they would hustle him to bed and send for the doctors. He knew that his illnesses terrified them and, as they gave him such importance, he enjoyed them.

'Oh, Grandmama,' he would pant. 'I have such a pain here...' And it was a great joy to see the alarm leap up into Grandmother's eyes.

He knew there were conferences about Albert's health. He was known to be 'delicate' – 'not robust like Ernest'. Ernest was inclined to despise Albert's delicacy until reproved by his elders for this attitude. Somewhere at the back of Albert's mind was the thought that if he were ill enough his mother would have to come back to him.

The situation did not persist because at the early age of six he started to keep a diary and, when this proved to be little more than a detailed account of his ailments, shrewd Grandmother Saxe-Coburg felt that they had been unwise to worry so much about his health.

'The child is obsessed by illness,' she declared to her son. 'He appears to take a pride in it. If this goes on when he grows up he will make a point of becoming an invalid.'

It occurred to her then that a good part of Albert's fragile health might be due to his imagination.

'Get them out into the fresh air,' she advised. 'We'll let him see that Ernest's rude health is more admirable than his delicacy. We'll watch over him as usual but we won't let him know it.'

The Duke soon began to realise the wisdom of his mother's council, for although Albert would never be quite the sturdy boy Ernest was, he was fast forgetting about his illnesses and in spite of a weak chest and a tendency to catch cold his health immediately began to improve.

The fresh country air agreed with him and, as the Dowager Duchess said, to see those two boys coming in from the forest after one of their riding jaunts, chattering away about what they called their specimens, one's fears for their health could be happily forgotten.

Herr Florschütz was good for them too. From the first he had been quite unmoved by Albert's tears. Once he had startled the little boy during one of the grammar lessons when Albert had been told to parse a sentence and did not know which was the verb – in this case 'to pinch' – Herr Florschütz gave young Albert a sharp nip in the arm so that Albert should, he said, know what a verb was. Albert, who had been in tears because he could not find the verb, was startled into silence. Herr Florschütz hinted that he did not think very highly of tears as a means of extricating oneself from a difficult situation, and as Albert had a natural aptitude for learning why not exploit that, and then he would be so proud of his achievement that he would want to crow with pride rather than whine in misery.

So Albert applied himself to learning and Herr Florschütz applauded; so did his father and the grandmothers. 'You're the clever one,' said Ernest. Yes, it was much more pleasant to crow with pride; but only inwardly of course. He was learning very much about life.

He asked Ernest what he wanted to do when he grew up. Ernest thought for a while and said: 'To govern like our father; to ride, to hunt, to feast, to enjoy life.'

Albert had replied: 'I want to be a good and useful man.'

Ernest called him a prude which angered Albert, who struck his elder brother. Ernest retaliated and in a short time they were rolling on the grass in a fight.

Herr Florschütz, coming upon them, ordered them to stop and said they should copy out a page of Goethe for misbehaving.

As they did it, Albert apologised. 'I started it.'

'Is that what you call being a good and useful man?' taunted Ernest. 'Fighting your brother.'

'I was wicked.'

'Oh, well,' laughed Ernest, 'it's better than being a prude.'

They laughed together, secure in the knowledge that nothing could change their devotion to each other; and as soon as they had finished their task they were off into the forest to collect wild plants for the collection which they had called the Ernest-Albert museum.

So passed the years until Albert was twelve years old.

The memory of that day in the year 1831 stayed with the Prince throughout his life. It had been an ordinary day. He and Ernest had been at their lessons all through the morning studying mathematics, Latin and philosophy, at which as usual Albert excelled. Ernest was longing for the afternoon when they would get out into the forest. He was anxious to add a special kind of butterfly to the 'museum' and hoped that he would be the one to capture it before Albert did. Meanwhile Albert was producing the answers required by their tutor and the lessons were running on the usual smooth lines.

At last Herr Florschütz shut the book before

him and glanced at the clock.

'I should like to hear the song you have composed,' he said to Albert. 'I wonder if it is up to the standard of the last.'

'It's even better,' said Ernest, 'Albert and I sang it last evening.'

'Then I shall look forward to hearing it this evening.'

Albert hoped the hearing would not be too late; he liked to get to bed early, unlike Ernest, who preferred to sit up half the night. Albert could not keep awake. He would if possible retire after supper on the pretence of reading history, religion or philosophy and Ernest, guessing what was actually happening, would creep up to the room and find him asleep over his books.

Nothing could keep him awake; as soon as supper was over the drowsiness would attack him. What he would have enjoyed would have been to study, to take exercise in the forest, to shoot the birds and collect the butterflies for the museum, to hunt for rare plants and rocks and stones and to study music, compose his pieces, to be tried out with Ernest; and then supper and bed. The trivial social life of the evening tired him; he could be painfully uncomfortable, finding it impossible to hide his fatigue. There had been an occasion when he had actually dozed at table and only Ernest's constant prodding had kept him from slumping over the table in deep sleep.

Ernest taunted his brother in his good-humoured way; but he would always watch over Albert on special occasions to make sure he did not disgrace himself by falling off his chair and continuing to sleep on the floor – which he had done once when they were alone.

The brothers understood each other. Albert had never had the physical energy of Ernest; Ernest had never had the mental ability of Albert. They were different; they respected the difference; and the bond between them grew closer as the years progressed.

Out into the beautiful forest they rode. They were at Reinhardtsbrunnen, the home of their maternal grandfather. He was dead but his brother Frederick had inherited the title and estates and the boys were always welcome there. How Albert loved the forest, with the sunshine throwing dappled patterns through the leaves of the trees; and riding on and on to where the trees grew more thickly, he recalled the fairy stories their grandmothers had told them and which invariably were set in forests such as this.

'That was a long time ago,' he said, speaking his thoughts aloud. Ernest shouted: 'What?'

Albert told his brother that he was thinking of the stories about the forests where gnomes and trolls, woodcutters and princesses and witches had abounded.

'You always enjoyed them. They used to tell them to keep you from howling. You were a little howler, Albert. Always in tears. I can remember your screams now. What a pair of lungs you must have had!'

'I must have been a horrid child.'

'You were. But one thing about you, you did know how to get your own way. I salute you, Albert. You always will, I'm sure.'

'Ernest, have you ever thought that we shan't always be together?'

'Good God no. Why shouldn't we be?'

'Our grandmothers would not care to hear you use such oaths.'

'Prude!' Ernest jogged Albert with his elbow and almost knocked him off his horse, then he broke into a gallop and Albert, spurring his horse, went after him.

Ernest pulled up and waited for his brother. 'What did you mean by that?' he demanded, 'Of course we shall always be together. Who'd stop us?'

'Circumstances,' suggested Albert. 'When I marry the Queen of England I suppose I shall have to live there.'

'Marry the Queen of England! Who says you will? Suppose I marry her instead?'

'*You!* But she has been promised to me.'

'Royal marriages.' Ernest scoffed. 'What's suggested in our cradles doesn't always come off. Surely you know that? And this queen ... she's not a queen is she?'

'I follow what is happening over there. The old King George is dead and his brother William is King. He is old and half mad and his wife is sterile.'

'Hold it a minute,' said Ernest.

'What an expression!' chided Albert.

'My dear old prude and pedant of a brother, old men often surprise the world with their virility. What if your little Alexandrina Victoria is not a queen after all? Then what, eh? If you marry her she'll have to come to Coburg and I shall be the

Duke remember. I *am* the elder brother.'

'Perhaps Uncle Leopold wouldn't want me to marry her if she isn't a queen.'

'There you are. Too many "ifs". You stop fretting about this cousin until she *is* the Queen. Now what about tying up the horses. I believe this is a good spot for the butterflies.'

'I was only saying, Ernest, that if she becomes Queen and I marry her and live in England I should expect you to come and visit me ... often.'

'Well, thanks for the invitation. My equerry will accept it in due course.'

'As Duke of Coburg you might not have one. Father is always complaining about the expense of keeping up his Court.'

'Don't worry about that. My brother, King Albert of England, will send me one. That would be amusing, an English equerry.'

'What nonsense you talk.'

'Why I am only being amiable and sharing in yours. Don't think too much about this marriage. The grandmothers were only romancing.'

'And Uncle Leopold?'

'Everyone knows he has plans for marrying the family all over Europe. You'll probably end up in Spain or Portugal. Imagine that. It would be very hot in the Peninsula. You'd fall asleep at midday instead of after supper.'

'Of course it's true that one can never be sure what's going to happen,' agreed Albert. 'You remember when we had whooping-cough.'

'A trying time,' said Ernest.

'And when we were better everything was changed. It was like a dividing line neatly drawn through our lives; all the nurses went and Herr Florschütz came. Our mother went...'

Ernest glanced at his brother and his glance was sober. 'Let's tie up here, Albert,' he said rather solemnly.

They did, and Ernest threw himself down and, plucking a blade of grass, started to chew it.

'What's wrong?' asked Albert, stretching out beside his brother.

'It's about our mother,' said Ernest. 'They didn't tell you because they thought it would upset you.'

'What about her?' asked Albert.

'She's dead.'

Albert did not speak. He stared up at the sky through the leaves. He felt the sudden rush of tears to his eyes as he thought of her looking round the nursery door, showing him the pictures in a book, giving him that fierce sweet-scented hug. He had never given up the hope that she would come back; when he had talked of the future he had unconsciously seen her there, for when he was a man and the King he was certain he was going to be, he would have brought her back to be with him. And now Ernest was saying that she was dead.

'Why did they tell you and not me?'

'I am the eldest,' said Ernest.

Albert sprang to his feet in sudden anger and Ernest said quickly: 'No, I'm teasing. It was because they feared it might upset you. They told me to break it to you gently.'

'They didn't ... kill her.'

'Kill her! What a notion! She had been ill for years.'

48

'They should have told us.'

'Of course they shouldn't.'

'She was too young to die.'

'She was thirty-two and she was very ill.'

'She would have been thinking of us at the end, Ernest.'

'Perhaps.'

'But of course she would. We were her sons.'

'We couldn't have been important to her or she wouldn't have left us.'

'She didn't want to leave us. I am sure she cried and cried.'

'Everyone doesn't turn on the tears like you did, Albert.'

'She loved us.'

'You were the favourite.'

'I know,' said Albert softly.

'Well, she's dead and she was unfaithful to our father. That was very wicked and she had to take her punishment.'

Albert was silent. She had been wicked, he admitted; and because of that, she had left them. What a terrible thing wickedness was! Every time he looked at a woman he would think of the wickedness which had separated him from her and had brought her to her sad and lonely death.

'She lived in Paris,' said Ernest, 'which we all know is a very wicked city.'

Albert shivered, but Ernest had jumped to his feet.

'Come on,' he said, his relief obvious because his duty was done.

But Albert could find no pleasure in the forest that day. His thoughts were far away in the past with his beautiful mother; he could not get out of his mind the belief that temptation was lurking everywhere and if succumbed to could ruin lives. He would never forget what had happened to his beloved mother who had become a bad woman. Wickedness had its roots in that subject which Ernest found so interesting but which filled him with abhorrence: the relationship between the sexes.

Death was in the air that year. Grandmama Saxe-Coburg did not pay her usual visit to Rosenau, nor was she well enough for the boys to visit her. Duke Ernest was called to her bedside one day and the boys stood at the window watching him and his little party ride away. 'They say she is very sick,' said Ernest. 'And she is old.' Albert shivered. But one did not have to be old to die. He was thinking of his mother as he had last seen her and now when he thought of her he must imagine her lying in a coffin ... dead. And the nails which were driven into that coffin were like her sins.

It was impossible to imagine never seeing Grandmama Saxe-Coburg again; Albert kept thinking of how she had looked after him and had meant more and more to him since his mother had gone.

Each day he waited at the window for a sign of the returning party. He would know as soon as he saw them what news they had brought. Ernest would stand silently beside him while they both watched the road.

'Perhaps Father will bring Grandmama back

with him,' suggested Albert.

'How could he if she were very ill?' demanded Ernest.

'Perhaps she is not so ill. Perhaps she has recovered. If she comes back I will sing my newest song to her and I am sure she will like it.'

Then they began to talk of what they would do to entertain Grandmama Saxe-Coburg when she came to Rosenau to get well.

And one day they saw their father returning and they knew that he came in mourning.

He sent for Albert and when his son stood before him he laid his hand on the boy's shoulder.

'She was my mother and your grandmother,' said the Duke, 'and she has gone from us now. It is a great sorrow for us all. And you perhaps more than any one of us. You were her favourite.'

The tears flowed down Albert's cheeks; he brought out a handkerchief and dried them.

'Death is terrible,' said Albert.

'That is at least a lesson you have learned, my boy.'

'Only a little while ago she was well and there was no sign that she was going to leave us.'

'These things happen, my son. She was not young and she would say that she had lived her life. But I have sent for you because she talked of you particularly at the end.'

'What did she say of me, Father?'

'She said she had every confidence in you. She said you had good moral qualities and she believed you would grow into a good man.'

'It shall be my earnest endeavour to do that,

51

Father. I want to be both good and useful in the world.'

'She was ambitious for you, Albert. There is not much here for you. You are a second son. A good marriage is what you need. It was her dearest wish that you should marry your cousin. I hope that wish will be fulfilled.'

'If my cousin is agreeable I shall be.'

The Duke laid his hand on his son's shoulder again.

'Always remember that it was the wish of your grandmother – her last wish.'

Albert swore solemnly that he would.

The brothers were going on a journey and they were very excited because it would be the first time they had left Germany.

After the bustle of preparation and many excited conferences they set out with a very small entourage.

'It's all I can afford,' said the Duke, 'and my brother Leopold will have to understand that.'

At least Herr Florschütz was with them, for lessons would continue as usual and that very useful gentleman did service as an attendant as well as tutor.

It was very interesting travelling through the little German States and visiting relatives en route. The changing scenery was a constant delight to the brothers and they were able to collect many unusual pieces of rock and stones for their museum; stopping at inns was a great novelty and it was an adventure to mix with ordinary people, particularly when they were sometimes incognito and at others those they met had never heard of the Coburg Princes.

What a pleasure it was to be reunited with Uncle Leopold, whom Albert had never forgotten. Indeed Uncle Leopold had not intended to be forgotten. He wrote frequently to members of his family, especially to those whom he considered to be his protégés and Albert was certainly one of these. Although a younger member of the family he had long placed himself at its head and was already busy arranging possible unions for every marriageable young Coburg.

Uncle Leopold, very good-looking, in fact not unlike Albert himself, very careful of his clothes – he liked to consider himself the best-dressed King in Europe – rather vain, wearing three-inch soles on his boots to increase his height, victim of numerous not very clearly defined illnesses, had such an assured high opinion of himself that his nephews felt it must be well deserved. Such was Leopold – warm-hearted it seemed, overflowing with affection, displaying a great dignity and making sure that everyone observed it; the most distinguished member of a family which he had determined was going to straddle Europe. From the moment of the meeting he and Albert were immediately aware of an accord which the less sensitive Ernest could not intrude upon. Albert was Leopold's boy, and Leopold immediately decided that he was his favourite nephew. There was only one member of his family who could bring a warmer glow to his scheming avuncular heart and that was the little niece now living at Kensington Palace – Alexandrina Victoria.

Uncle Leopold lived in much grander style than they did in Coburg; and in any case Uncle Leopold's personality would have made the humblest cottage seem grand. He had very recently married and they met Aunt Louise, a charming young woman, completely overawed by Uncle Leopold, which pleased Uncle Leopold who clearly thought that he had done her a great honour by marrying her. She was cultivated, and spoke, as well as her native French, English, Italian and German; as she was the daughter of Louis Philippe, the King of France, they were in very exalted company indeed.

Ernest really preferred Aunt Louise to Uncle Leopold, but then Ernest was beginning to show a tendency to admire pretty women and Aunt Louise was pretty with her fair hair and light blue eyes and small figure. She had rather a large nose – 'the Bourbon nose' Uncle Leopold called it affectionately – but that was a good thing to have because it proclaimed her royalty.

Uncle Leopold was anxious to show the boys something of Court life.

'This is a great kingdom,' he reminded them, 'rather different from the little dukedoms of Germany, eh?'

He liked to walk with Albert and leave his wife to entertain Ernest, to Albert's great relief for he would have hated to have been left to the mercy of a pretty young woman. Uncle Leopold talked at great length about his illnesses, and how his good friend Baron Stockmar had advised him to take this and that remedy. 'Stockmar is in England just now but one day I want you to meet him. He was my doctor and then my adviser. Stockmar is a very clever man.'

'Why is he in England now, Uncle?'

'My dear sister, your aunt, the Duchess of Kent is there, and she needs as many friends as she can find to support and advise her. She is in a rather uneasy position at the moment. I should like to be there but my duty of course is here in the country which I govern. Stockmar tells me what is happening there. I must know this,' he added roguishly, 'because my dear niece, your cousin, is a very important little person over there.'

'Uncle, is she the one I am going to marry?'

'Yes. But it is a secret so far. A few are in my confidence, but we do not want it to spread too far.'

'Does she know, Uncle Leopold?'

'Not yet.'

'Do you think she will want to marry me?'

'When I tell her that I want her to, she will.'

'I would rather she had chosen me without being told.'

'That would have meant that she was somewhat bold. No, it is well that when she is told of my wishes she will want to obey them. That is her character. It is because she is sweetly docile that I love her. And that, my dearest Albert, is the quality I prize in all my little nieces and nephews.'

That was how the conversation went whenever they were together. Leopold would always bring it round to the little girl of Kensington. Albert wished that he could see her. Uncle Leopold's description sounded delightful; but when he discussed the matter with Ernest, his rather cynical elder brother remarked that Uncle Leopold could be prejudiced in his descriptions of the young lady of Kensington; he believed that this was a common practice with royalty when marriages were being arranged.

Albert suggested that his brother might be jealous because he, Albert, had been chosen to marry a queen – if she became one. This made Ernest explode into laughter. No, he wanted no queens, thank you. He would make the right sort of marriage but that would not prevent his having 'friends' whenever and wherever he wished.

Leopold questioned Herr Florschütz closely about the boys' studies. He said he would consult Baron Stockmar and plan out a schedule for their education.

'Will our father agree to that?' Ernest wondered when the boys were alone together.

'Agree,' cried Albert, 'of course he'll agree. Uncle Leopold is the most important man in Europe.'

'He has bewitched you,' said Ernest.

'Bewitched! Who's bewitched? Now *you're* thinking of the grandmothers' fairy stories.'

'You do seem to think he is the most brilliant, magnificent, clever...'

'Oh, shut up,' said Albert. And then: 'But he is.'

'There, I told you so. No wonder Uncle Leopold loves you. You flatter him so innocently.'

'How could one flatter innocently? Flattery in itself suggests something false.'

'There you go, Herr Florschütz's model pupil. No wonder Uncle Leopold decided you should have the prize.'

'What prize?'

'The Queen of England, idiot.'

The visit passed all too quickly for Albert. It had been a wonderful experience. The dream uncle of his childhood had taken on flesh and blood and was every bit as godlike as Albert remembered. The Court at Brussels was grand. 'You should have seen that of my late father-in-law in England,' Uncle Leopold told the boys. 'I never liked him but he was considered to be very artistic. Carlton House was absolutely splendid and the Pavilion at Brighton – well, it had to be seen to be believed. Then of course he got to work on Windsor Castle and Buckingham Palace.'

'It must have been very grand to be grander than Brussels,' said Albert.

'Ah, my boy, you have seen nothing of the world. We'll change that. We've got to get you educated along the right lines. One of these days you must go with Stockmar on the Grand Tour.'

'We should enjoy it,' said Albert, underlining the fact that Ernest would be there too. 'But I don't think our father would be able to afford it.'

'There are some things which it is false economy to go without,' said Uncle Leopold.

So it seemed very likely that when the time came the boys would go on the Grand Tour.

'Of course,' said Uncle Leopold, 'you are young as yet. Thirteen. Boys still. But another six years, eh? Time soon passes. Have no fear, I shall write to your father. It is very important that you should be prepared. Do you speak English, Albert?'

Albert said that English was not included in his studies.

'An oversight,' said Uncle Leopold, 'which shall be remedied.'

How he enjoyed those talks with Uncle Leopold. He avoided Aunt Louise, because he felt embarrassed in her company. She was pretty and when Uncle Leopold was not there, inclined to be gay. His uncle did in fact have to reprove her on one occasion for making a joke.

What a good man Uncle Leopold was! thought Albert. When he grew up he hoped he would be a little like him.

It was an exciting visit and Albert enjoyed it thoroughly, except for the evenings, when Aunt Louise organised entertainments for them and Albert was hard put to it to hide the fact that he was almost asleep.

When at last it was time to say goodbye, Uncle Leopold embraced his younger nephew fondly. There was an understanding between them. Uncle Leopold was going to make sure that he was prepared for his future, which was to be the husband of the little girl in Kensington.

When they reached home it was to find that their father, after having been a widower for more than a year, had married the Princess Mary of Würtemberg.

Having a step-mother did not inconvenience the Princes in the least. After their return from Brussels they continued with life just as before, and as the Princess Mary of Würtemberg was amiable, more like an older sister, life was very pleasant. It was true that Albert was more aware of what was happening in England than he had been.

When he heard that Queen Adelaide had 'hopes' he was downcast because he knew Uncle Leopold would be; and when those hopes came to nothing he rejoiced. There were periods when he was completely unconcerned by the future; that was when he was composing a new song, or when he and Ernest went off on one of their expeditions into the forest together; the 'museum' was growing and each exhibit held some particular memory for him. It was a pleasant, happy life and he had no desire to grow up. Mornings were spent in study, long afternoons out of doors; riding, fencing, shooting, walking and long nights of sleep. No one, commented Ernest, enjoyed sleep as much as Albert and he didn't confine this state of somnolence to the night either. 'I am constantly prodding you to wakefulness,' complained Ernest.

Ernest laughed at his brother for his increasing solemnity and rather against his will Albert indulged in an occasional practical joke which was the only sort he could see any point in.

Once he and Ernest filled the cloak pockets of one of their father's guests with soft cheese. This was a lady, which rendered the joke doubly hilarious in Albert's eyes. They made a point of being in the cloakroom when she was helped into her cloak and had the satisfaction of seeing her plunge her hand into the mess in her pocket. Suspecting them, she had berated them angrily, and, while Albert remained regarding her with big reproachful eyes, Ernest was almost choking with laughter.

That was a period when they played practical jokes whenever they could think them out. Their indulgent step-mother told their father that it was a phase most boys went through and it was in a way a relief to see Albert slightly less of a model boy.

But Albert was really much happier at the more serious activities. He was developing a great dignity, and practical joking did not really fit in with this. Music was his most pleasant relaxation; he played the piano and organ with skill and composed a little; he had a good voice which he liked to air; he could draw and paint tolerably well; he was interested in science; he wrote a little and confided to Ernest he would like to write a book – a very serious one, on German thought and philosophy. In addition to all these intellectual achievements he could fence and give a good account of himself in forays with Ernest; he was a good swimmer, and could manage a horse with skill. The one exercise he did not enjoy was dancing – not so much going through the motions but because it usually meant touching hands with people of the opposite sex and as he said to Ernest there was something erotic in the procedure.

'Now that,' said Ernest with a chuckle, 'is exactly what I like about it.'

His step-mother noticed that when he was introduced to ladies his manner was awkward.

'Oh, that'll pass,' said his father. 'He's a boy yet.'

When Ernest was seventeen it was time for his confirmation and, said Herr Florschütz, Albert was so advanced, so serious in his inclinations and in every way as forward as his brother that there seemed no reason why he should not share in the ceremony.

So on Palm Sunday in the Chapel of the Palace at Coburg, the boys were catechised for an hour. Albert's responses made a great impression on the spectators, and when asked if he would steadfastly uphold the Evangelical Church he answered in a resolute voice not simply the 'Yes' which was expected but added: 'I and my brother are firmly resolved to remain faithful to the acknowledged truth.'

Albert at sixteen had indeed grown into a model Prince; and few in Coburg seemed to think that his lack of social graces was of great importance.

## Chapter III

## THE LITTLE COUSIN OF KENSINGTON

It was almost a year later when a letter arrived from England for Duke Ernest; when he had read it he summoned his sons and told them that he had had an invitation for them.

'It is from your aunt, the Duchess of Kent, who asks me to take you both to visit her. There is also a letter from your Uncle Leopold. I suspect he has arranged the whole thing.'

Ernest was excited; Albert a little apprehensive. He knew what this invitation meant and he had to face the fact that he could not be young for

61

ever. He was nearly seventeen, a marriageable age for royal people. Could this visit mean that the pleasant life he had led for so many years with Ernest as his companion was over?

There would be a great many preparations to make, said their father. Uncle Leopold did not want them to visit their English relations like paupers.

The forest had taken on a new beauty; Albert spent many happy hours examining the specimens in the 'museum' and recalling how they had come into his or Ernest's possession.

'To leave all this!' he cried.

'Childish relics,' said Ernest. Albert looked at his brother sadly. If he himself was the more learned, the more serious of the two, Ernest was in a way the more grown-up. 'Just think what this visit means,' went on Ernest. 'We shall see your little paragon of Kensington.'

Albert shivered. 'Perhaps she will prefer you, Ernest.'

Ernest said he thought that very likely.

'I am sure Cousin Feodore does, and she is half sister to the Kensington cousin.'

'I think women do prefer you, Ernest.'

'That's because I'm far nicer to them than you are. You just try a little flattery and you'll find they succumb at once to your beauty.'

'That's something I can never do.'

'The trouble with you, Albert, is that you're too solemn, and too good. Women like something a little wild and wicked.'

'Then I think they are too stupid to bother with.'

'And so they will go on preferring my pale

62

cheeks to your pink ones and my wicked dark flashing eyes to your angelic blue.'

'I wish we need not grow up. I'd like us to remain boys together like this for always.'

Ernest's eyes rolled wickedly. 'Ah, there are pleasures in adult life, Albert, of which you have yet to learn.'

Albert did not believe it and he was very uneasy.

'I can't wait to see Uncle Leopold's little angel of Kensington,' said Ernest.

But Albert felt he could very happily wait for a long time. The family party, at the head of which was Duke Ernest, left at the end of April. 'A good time,' said the Duke, 'for crossing the Channel, which can be something of an ordeal for those unused to being on the water if the sea is rough.'

Albert *knew* that he was one of those; and he was right. The sea was rough, the crossing long, and Albert, very sick, heartily wished that he was at home in the forests of Germany; in fact death seemed preferable to the sufferings imposed by that stretch of diabolical water.

At last – and a very long last – they arrived and what a pleasure it was to be on dry land.

'You look as if you have faced death,' said Ernest jocularly.

'That was exactly what it felt like,' said Albert, 'and when I think that we have to endure that again before we get home my spirits sink.'

'It'll pass,' said Ernest. 'Think of the pleasures ahead.'

He had seen her. She was tiny and imperious and

was called Victoria – the Alexandrina having been dropped, presumably as unsuitable for a British Queen. She was gay and very affectionate. Oddly enough she did not embarrass him as he might have expected. Was it because he had been conditioned by Uncle Leopold? Did he feel that he had to like her – more than like her, admire her – just as he had to accept that terrible crossing as inevitable?

She spoke in German very fluently and what he called excitedly, emphasising certain words as though to give special points to her meaning. She was *so* delighted to see her cousins. She had looked forward to the meeting for a long *long* time and she knew that their visit was going to be such a *happy* time for her. She considered she was very *lucky* to have so many cousins. They came over now and then and she spent *hours* planning treats for them. She believed she was going to enjoy this visit very *specially*.

She was not exactly pretty but there was something very appealing about her. Her colouring was similar to Albert's – the same light brown hair and blue eyes; there the resemblance ended; she had a rather big nose – an arrogant nose – and slightly prominent teeth. When she laughed she showed her gums, which would not have been very attractive but for the fact that her laughter was so spontaneous and unaffected. Her demeanour fluctuated so speedily that it was difficult to keep pace with it. At one moment she would seem to be playing the Queen and the next she was a modest young girl not yet out of the schoolroom. She was not exactly arrogant, just sublimely and unconsciously aware that she was destined for a great position.

Albert clicked his heels, bowed and kissed her hand. He hated kissing hands, but managed to do so fairly graciously. She did disarm him, because she seemed so determined to like him – and Ernest too; but he noticed that her eyes were more frequently on him.

She insisted on showing them to their rooms, chattering all the while, while her mother looked on indulgently, for she was clearly very happy to see her brother and his sons.

'And you must meet my darling dog Dash at once,' said Victoria, and the dog seemed to take a particular fancy to Albert, which pleased the Princess. When he looked up from patting the dog he saw her prominent blue eyes fixed on him and as their eyes met she blushed charmingly. He decided that, for a girl, she was very agreeable.

'Victoria has been planning all sorts of treats for you,' said the Duchess. 'She and her governess, the Baroness Lehzen, have been making arrangements for weeks. There is to be a visit to the Opera, because she understands you are particularly fond of music.'

'It is *Puritani*,' cried Victoria. 'Oh, I *do* hope you will like it. And there are to be balls. I am sure you love to dance.'

Albert wilted a little but Ernest said nothing would enchant them more.

'And you sing!' cried Victoria. '*That* is something I love to do. Do you like duets?'

Albert was able to say with enthusiasm that he enjoyed singing and duets.

'This is going to be a very happy visit,' said Victoria.

The Duchess of Kent said that she thought the Princess's cousins would like to go to rest awhile as they must be very fatigued with the journey. Victoria seemed a little surprised but Albert said quickly that he would indeed be glad of the opportunity so they were conducted to their rooms and Albert stretched out on his bed and was soon asleep. But Ernest came in and insisted on waking him. He stood at the window and described the park to him. He could see an enormous round pond, almost like a lake, and the trees were beautiful. 'And this is not the King's residence. We shall meet him, of course. I wonder if he is as people say.'

Albert sighed. He could see his brother was not going to allow him to rest and he was so tired.

'He is very eccentric and has a head like a pineapple, so I've heard,' went on Ernest. Albert yawned.

'And what did you think of little Victoria?'

'She is indeed little.'

'I liked the way she looked up to us. I think she has a certain charm. Do you, Albert?'

'Yes,' said Albert.

'Well, I think we can make up our minds that she will be for one of us. I shouldn't mind if I were the elect.'

'You are very flippant about a serious subject,' said Albert.

'You are never flippant about any subject, brother. But I've been keeping my ears open. I heard what our aunt had to say to our father. The

Prince of Orange is here and he has brought his two sons, William and Alexander, with him. The *King* is entertaining them. You know what this means.'

'You mean that his sons will be suitors for Victoria?'

'Suitors with the King's blessing, it seems. Oh, we have fallen into a den of intrigue, brother. The Duchess and the King are arch enemies; and the Duchess is determined that little Victoria shall marry a Coburg cousin (one of us) and the King wants to spite the Duchess – at least that's what she says; therefore he is against a Coburg bridegroom. You see you can't afford to sleep your time away; you have to go out and win the lady ... or one of us does. She gave *me* some admiring glances.'

Albert did not answer. He knew that Uncle Leopold wished him to be the bridegroom and that was good enough. He was sure that even the King of England could not stop Uncle Leopold's desires.

'Now, Albert, I don't think you should have come up here to sleep so soon. It appears that you are not as eager as you should be for the company of your dear little cousin. Don't forget the King favours Oranges. It is not going to be as easy as we thought. You – or I – have to go in and win.'

'Stop it, Ernest. I don't care for such jokes.'

'Well get up and we will join the Princess and say that we needed only a little rest. You show her the tricks your greyhound does and train her Dash to do them. Or you can sing a duet with her. You really must wake up.'

Albert allowed himself to be persuaded.

The pace was great. The little cousin seemed indefatigable. She never seemed to stop still for a moment. It was not very restful, thought Albert, and he was nostalgic for the pine forests and the quiet life of Rosenau. He must not allow Victoria to see this. He remembered his interviews with Uncle Leopold. 'You are a younger son and Ernest will take your father's title, but you, of course, will have to make a place for yourself.' That place could be here in this rather strange country, whose language he could not adequately understand; he had had a few English lessons and although he had done well on paper, when these people spoke he could not very easily understand them. Victoria obligingly used his language; he would have felt happier if he could have spoken in hers. He would ask Uncle Leopold what should be done about this. So ... he was interested in his cousin. Not as a woman; there was no question of what Ernest would call falling in love. This was his future if all went according to Uncle Leopold's plans; and Victoria was eager to please them and win their approval; she was delighted to have her cousins with her; so, if she became the Queen of this country, as her husband, he would be King; and there could be no doubt whatsoever that the King of England would be a far more powerful man than any little king, prince or duke of one of the German States.

Therefore he must please Victoria. It was gratifying to realise that he did. At breakfast time he could feel in good spirits and amuse her with remarks which she considered extremely funny; he could play with Dash in a way she found amusing. Her loud laughter rang out continually.

'Oh, Cousin Albert, you are *so* amusing.'

Then there was music. She really did have an understanding of it. 'I have *always* loved it. One birthday we had a concert in the palace. I have *never* forgotten it.'

She must hear Albert sing one of his songs. 'But, Cousin Albert, how *very* clever of you to compose that. Could we sing my favourite duet together?'

Their voices harmonised. The Duchess sat tapping her foot while they sang with Duke Ernest beside her looking very pleased.

There was a visit to Windsor to call on the King, who received them rather coolly although the Queen was kind. Albert noticed that the King was very old and by no means in good health. It seemed possible that in a short time Victoria would be Queen. Albert was impressed by Windsor; his spirits rose and he immediately felt better, more alive, to be in the country. The chestnut trees were magnificent, and the may blossom was just about to break out, and the forest reminded him of home. In such surroundings he would feel well and perhaps not be so tormented by his desire for Coburg as he had imagined. And the castle was magnificent. The elaborate state-rooms amazed him; there was nothing like those deep-piled carpets and rich velvet gold-fringed curtains in his father's houses. All this would be hers one day if the present King had no children, which was now almost a certainty.

Albert began to feel excited by his destiny. He felt sure that he would be able to guide his gay little cousin.

Oh, but the energy of the little creature! Albert's greatest problem was to keep his eyes open while she chattered away. She wanted to dance every evening; nor was she content if they retired before two o'clock. It was not only that he had to fight the terrible drowsiness which beset him, but his fatigue almost bordered on illness. His stepmother said he had grown too fast, for as a child he had always been much shorter than Ernest; now he had shot up suddenly and was as tall.

The day before Victoria's birthday, which was to have a very special entertainment, he felt so tired that he could not stay awake. The Duchess of Kent, who was very kind to him, noticed that he was looking delicate and suggested that he should retire early. He blessed her. How kind she was, how thoughtful! Victoria's blue eyes were round with dismay. *Dear* Albert. How very concerned she was! He *must* be well by tomorrow because she could not *bear* him to be ill on her birthday. Oh, the joy of being in bed, to sleep and sleep and sleep.

On her birthday there was a ball at St James's Palace. Another of those interminable balls. When I marry her I shall make it a rule that we rise early (for the early morning is the best time of the day) and retire not later than ten o'clock, he promised himself. But he was not married to her yet, and as Ernest had said, it would be for

70

her to choose. Perhaps she would choose Ernest, whose gay temperament was more like her own.

He was at present too tired to care.

It was unthinkable that he, as one of the principal guests, could sit out during the dance. He had to get on to the floor to bow and prance, as he thought of it. He felt giddy and feared he was going to faint. It was her hand that steadied him; and those big blue eyes looked tenderly up at him.

'Albert, do you feel ill?'

He swayed and she led him to a chair.

The Duchess was beside him. 'My dear Albert, you are not feeling well?'

He sat down and closed his eyes.

The Duchess said that he must go back to Kensington and that she would arrange this without delay.

So while Victoria danced at her birthday ball, Albert slept as the carriage took him through the streets and he was relieved to reach his bedroom.

But of course this was no way to impress his future bride.

He could not help being pleased when it was time to return home, although that dreadful sea crossing had to be faced before they could reach that haven.

Ernest was now certain that the Princess Victoria had chosen him.

'Never mind, Albert,' he said. 'I shall rule England but I'll let you have Coburg as a consolation prize.'

Albert was not so sure. He remembered the

way she had looked at him when he had nearly fainted on the ballroom floor. She was a very affectionate little person and everyone must admit that he was more handsome than Ernest. Moreover he had quickly discovered the kind of conversation that she found amusing and she had laughed very readily even when he had not been exactly witty. Yes, she had laughed more readily at his jokes than those of Ernest; and then he had been so good with her dogs who clearly meant a great deal to her.

She was a very warm-hearted girl and one, he believed, who would be easy to mould. He would have been feeling very hopeful but for that incessant fatigue which he could not overcome however much he tried. They had music in common. She really did love it and she became quite beautiful when she listened to some particular pieces. She chattered animatedly about the famous singers she had heard and he was impressed, for such people never came to Germany. The fact that Albert had actually composed songs delighted her. 'But how *clever*. But *that* is wonderful.' And then their voices had harmonised charmingly.

When they said goodbye she wept openly. Her emotions, he told himself, were superficial. There would be a great deal which he would have to teach her, but he could look forward to the task; and having met her, marriage was no longer repugnant to him, which he had feared it might be.

It was not long after their return that news came from Uncle Leopold. The visit had been a great success, and to Ernest's astonishment and

Albert's delight, Albert was the one who had pleased her best.

She had written to Uncle Leopold that Albert possessed every quality that she could desire to make her happy. She did mention though that she wanted special care taken of the health of 'one now *so dear* to me', which was an oblique reference to his exhaustion in the ballroom. Even so Uncle Leopold was pleased. Now plans must be set in motion in earnest.

## Chapter IV

## PREPARATIONS

Living in Coburg was Leopold's old friend and adviser Baron Christian Friedrich von Stockmar, whither he had retired some two years before.

Stockmar had at one time lived in England and had personally known not only Leopold's first wife, the Princess Charlotte, but the young Princess Victoria as well. It was Stockmar who had advised Leopold not to take the Greek crown but to accept that of Belgium. He had been Leopold's doctor in the first instance; they shared an interest in their ailments, vying with each other in recounting their sufferings; they had enjoyed each other's company and Stockmar's great concern had been Leopold's advancement. For the last two years Leopold had asked Stockmar to keep an eye on Albert in an unofficial manner. In a small court such as that of Duke Ernest this was a simple matter and Stockmar had been able to report on the two brothers from time to time.

Albert was of special interest to Leopold and Stockmar was able to report that Albert was 'a fine fellow with agreeable qualities'. He even had something of an English look. As to his mind, Stockmar heard glowing reports of this but he must remind Leopold that they were somewhat partial. Stockmar had seen too little of Albert to give a personal judgement, and he added that if the young Prince were going to qualify for one of the most influential positions in Europe (which marriage to the Queen of England would surely be) he must have more than a studious nature, discretion and caution (and Stockmar had heard that he possessed this to a great degree); he must have ambition and great will-power. He must be made to understand from the outset that this was a 'vocation of grave responsibility' and not to be lightly undertaken and that his honour and happiness would depend upon the manner in which he was able to fulfil his duties.

Now, the Prince could clearly not be fitted for this great future in Coburg. In the first place he must have a command of English. It was no use being able to write it adequately; he must be able to express himself fluently in that language and understand what was being said to him. He must not only have English lessons but have them from an *English* person. Stockmar did not think Berlin was the right place for the Prince, but if he came to Brussels his uncle could keep an eye on him. Let him have a few months there studying history and modern languages; and then Leopold could come to a decision as to the future plans. But these would need serious and immediate consideration.

Thus it was that almost immediately after the return from England, the brothers were on their way to Brussels.

It was pleasant to live in Brussels, for it meant being close to his uncle. Leopold was of course a very busy man; he had a kingdom to govern, but his great desire was to see members of his family in important positions all over Europe and as he said often to the brothers, there could not be one from which it was more possible to influence Europe for *good* than England. Leopold's heart was set on a marriage between Victoria and Albert.

When they were alone together he talked of that brief period when he was married to Charlotte and had believed that he would be in a position which he now hoped would one day be Albert's. 'A Queen Regnant needs a husband to guide her. How well I should have done that for Charlotte! And you must learn to do for Victoria what I should have done for her.'

'I should want to influence her for good,' said Albert.

'That is what I hope. You would guide and advise and, my dear Albert, you would have one of the most important tasks in the whole world. You would have to teach Victoria her responsibilities to her country, to Europe and her family. I shall not be far away and able to guide you both. We shall be in constant touch with each other.'

Albert's eyes had begun to sparkle at the prospect. He was discovering that he was ambitious.

He studied so earnestly that his tutors expressed delight in him. He was far in advance of his brother Ernest. Leopold smiled. 'All well and good. There's a great difference in governing a European power like England and in governing a little Coburg dukedom.'

In correspondence with Baron Stockmar Leopold decided that the Princes should attend a university and Bonn was decided on; so there was another move and the brothers settled in to university life, where Albert's aptitude and nature continued to delight his tutors.

They had been at Bonn for only a few weeks when important news arrived via Uncle Leopold.

'I have heard today,' wrote their uncle, 'news which is of the utmost importance to us all. King William is dead and your cousin Victoria is Queen of England. You will of course wish to write to her.'

Albert was trembling with excitement. The more he had travelled, the greater his ambition had grown. He saw now how right his uncle was and this marriage was the best thing that could happen to him. Only through marriage could he achieve a position of any great importance; and his long-sighted uncle was preparing him to receive one of the greatest prizes in the world. He must not fail.

He wrote to Victoria, 'his dearest cousin'. He must congratulate her on the great change which had come into her life. He reminded her that she was the mightiest Queen in Europe and that the happiness of millions lay in her hands.

'I hope that your reign may be long, happy and glorious and that your efforts may be rewarded by the thankfulness and love of your subjects.'

He hoped too, that he might be able to share that throne with her. King Albert of England. It sounded a wonderful project. He must prepare himself even more thoroughly than before. He worked harder; and he waited for news of what would happen next and when he might begin his courtship in earnest.

During the autumn holidays the two Princes made a tour of Switzerland and northern Italy. It was as well, said Uncle Leopold, to see something of the world. The two months of September and October were taken up by this and it had been arranged that this should be a walking holiday. Albert was quite happy; he loved the fresh air; the mountains of Switzerland exhilarated him and the art treasures of Milan and Venice enchanted him. He was quite content to spend his days walking, providing he could go to bed at about nine o'clock. He would immediately sleep heavily and be awake at six o'clock, ready to spend another day of exploration.

Albert wished that holiday could have gone on and on. He discussed his feelings with Ernest for they understood each other well.

'You know what will happen when we have finished with Bonn,' said Ernest. 'You will go one way and I another.'

'I have often thought of it,' replied Albert sombrely.

'We have to face it. If you are going to England and I to Coburg, we shall be parted.'

'Eighteen years is a long time for two people to be together.'

'Most brothers and sisters are.'

'We are more to each other than most.'

They were silent for a while. Then Albert said: 'That is why I wish I could make time stand still. Here am I on this stimulating and most enjoyable holiday with the best companion in the world, with the possibility of a grand marriage before me. If only we could be as we are forever ... happy, together, everything waiting to fall into my hands.'

'Who would have thought to hear you talk like this! It is quite fanciful. We have to have our separation and that is going to be very painful to us both. I fancy you will remember me sometimes, brother, when you luxuriate in the glories of Windsor and Buckingham Palace.'

'I am happy now here in the fresh air with you, Ernest.'

'It is nothing to the happiness you will know as King of England with little Queen Victoria beside you ready to love, honour and obey.'

Albert looked so sad that Ernest sought to change his mood by warning him that Little Victoria appeared to him to have quite a temper of her own so he need not think it was going to be very easy.

'All the more reason,' said Albert, 'for me to wish this happy time never to end.'

'Well, if you can make time stand still, brother, you're a cleverer man than I am.' Ernest grinned at his brother. 'Which,' he added, 'is as it should be. Only clever Albert is good enough for Victoria.'

Albert was right. The parting came very soon. After a brief spell at the university Ernest was to go to Dresden to undergo a course of military instruction and Albert was to take a Grand Tour of Europe in the company of Baron Stockmar. There was another member of the party, Sir Francis Seymour, a young soldier whom Leopold had requested to be Albert's companion and to converse with him always in English.

The brothers were heartbroken at their parting but for Albert at least there was a good deal to interest him. He loved the arts, and in Rome and Florence found much to his taste. He was aware of the Baron's critical eye but at the same time the old man seemed to have an affection for him; and Sir Francis Seymour in some ways made up for the loss of his brother. Travel was exciting; and this exploration of the world's art treasures, plus new and magnificent scenery, was indeed an education. During the tour he continued to study. It was a life which appealed to him, getting up at six in the morning and working until dinner which he took at two o'clock; he rarely drank wine and took water at all meals; he was in bed by nine o'clock. He played the piano and organ whenever possible; he sang and composed his songs. It was a good life. If Ernest could have shared it he would have been happy.

Stockmar, in spite of his growing affection, was not entirely satisfied with his protégé. He wrote to Leopold that the young man was intelligent, kind, friendly; his intentions were good but he rarely exerted himself. It was not so much that he was lazy but that he seemed incapable of physical effort; he was not sufficiently interested in politics to please the Baron and this would have to be rectified; his manners too must be improved for he was a little ungracious in the company of women. He would always have more success with men than with women, and in the society of the latter he seemed indifferent, awkwardly shy, and he failed to exert himself to such an extent that he appeared ungracious. Another point was that his constitution was clearly not very strong which might account for his desire to be in bed by nine and his failure to exert himself.

Leopold frowned over the letter when he received it. They would have to watch Albert's health. He would write to Stockmar asking him to superintend his diet. Of course this lack of grace was due to his having been brought up without a mother and with no really cultivated women, except his two grandmothers, near him.

There was more to worry Leopold. He had had a strange letter from his niece. He was getting rather uneasy about Victoria. Since her accession she had changed. She had more or less told him that she did not expect him to meddle in English politics and that she must refer his suggestions to her Prime Minister, Lord Melbourne, and her Foreign Secretary, Lord Palmerston. This was a blow considering that he had thought he would be the one to whom she would turn for advice.

Now she was writing that she was not at all eager for marriage. She wanted to know whether

Albert was aware that a marriage between them was being discussed by his father and their uncle Leopold. Albert must be made aware, she insisted, that there was no engagement between them, because she was not at all sure whether she would like Albert as a husband. She might like him as a brother or a cousin but that was not the same as a husband, and she must remind everyone that if she decided not to marry Albert she would not be guilty of any breach of promise because she had never given a promise. She could make no final promise that year and at the very earliest would not wish to marry for two or three years hence. She wanted Uncle Leopold to know that there was no anxiety in *her country* for her marriage.

Leopold cursed softly as he laid down the letter.

He was disappointed in his little Victoria. How she had changed! He had little doubt of his ability to persuade her, but she was very impressionable, young and romantic, and there should be no further delay in bringing about a meeting.

After all Victoria was now twenty and Albert on the point of becoming so. That was old enough for marriage.

He was disturbed about Stockmar's comment on Albert's behaviour with women. Albert was really very good-looking; he had a fine figure, was tall, and his features were exactly like those of his mother. He was, in fact, a little like Victoria to look at. She *must* like his appearance. But he must be warned that he should not appear to be over-confident. He had to woo Victoria. And the sooner he began the better.

81

The first thing to do was to warn him of Victoria's unwillingness to make up her mind, which would prevent his being too confident.

Albert's reply alarmed him at first. He would, he told his uncle, be prepared to wait providing there was a definite promise and a certainty that the marriage would take place.

If, he pointed out, after waiting for three years he should find the Queen no longer desired the marriage, he would be put in a very undignified position, and it would perhaps ruin his prospects for the future.

This reply did not displease Leopold and Stockmar.

'He is becoming ambitious,' said Stockmar. 'And that is what I hoped for.'

Leopold's answer was: 'There must be no more delays. Albert and Victoria must be brought face to face as soon as possible.'

It was arranged that the meeting should take place in October.

'Ernest should go with Albert,' commanded Leopold. 'If by any chance Victoria should decide *not* to take Albert, it would be as well to have an alternative choice.'

It seemed to Albert that September, when the leaves began to change, that they had never before been so beautiful. It was a wonderful month and he was happy to be home, but poignantly so, for soon he must leave. The great test was coming nearer; sometimes he welcomed it, sometimes dreaded it. It hurt his dignity that he should have to present himself for the Queen's approval; if she were to decide against him he would be a laughing-stock; and on the other hand if she still remained undecided and wanted to keep him dangling, that position was almost as undesirable.

He talked it over with Ernest as they stalked deer in the forest or shot wild fowl or collected pieces of rock for their 'museum':

All Ernest would say was wait and see; and at the end of September they were ready to make the journey to England.

The wretchedness of that sea crossing was even worse than he had imagined it would be. He lay groaning on his bunk thinking, as he had on a previous occasion, that death would be preferable to such humiliating suffering. It did not make him feel better to realise that his brother and others of the party did not share his sickness, and he believed that the crew secretly jeered at him.

The terrible rocking of the boat, those high grey waves, the fearful nausea ... oh, how he longed for the peace of Rosenau! To go back there, to live in obscurity, to be poor – for he should be as a second son; and even Ernest, the future Duke, would not be affluent – anything was better than this. Indeed the peace of the forest and the simple life seemed very desirable.

The crossing at last came to an end, and pale and feeble he staggered ashore. Ernest was beside him, ready for adventure. Surely, thought Albert, she will choose Ernest.

The baggage could not be found but they decided to go on without it.

'It's fortunate,' said Ernest, 'that the Queen is

at Windsor. You'll recover during the journey and the country air will do you good.'

Albert, though still pale and wan, felt better as they rode through the fresh green fields. He saw the castle – grey and seeming impregnable before him – and his spirits rose. If he were a king in such a castle with its vistas of green fields and forests, he could be content, he believed.

So much would depend on Victoria, of course.

They had arrived; the grooms had taken their horses and told them: 'Her Majesty is ready to receive you.'

So they entered the castle.

She was standing at the top of the staircase, a diminutive figure with flushed cheeks and sparkling blue eyes.

'My dear cousins,' she cried, holding out her hands.

Ernest first because he was the elder. She smiled up at him. 'Dear Ernest, I am so happy to see you. And Albert ... *Albert...*'

She glowed with delight; her gaze rested on him.

'*Dear* cousin Albert, welcome to Windsor.'

It was on Albert that her gaze lingered. His heart leaped in triumph, for he was almost sure that he was the chosen one.

# Chapter V

## THE BRIEF HONEYMOON

It was indeed triumph. The Queen was too candid by nature to hide her feelings and she made it clear to all about her, including Albert, that she found him fascinating.

She confided to the Baroness Lehzen that Albert was all she had hoped for. Did not Lehzen find him handsome? He had such beautiful blue eyes; his nose was quite exquisite; his mouth was *pretty*.

'Does one expect a man's mouth to be pretty?' asked Lehzen; and was told sharply that with so many ugly mouths in evidence it was a pleasure to see one which was charming.

It was clear that Victoria would have no criticism of Albert.

The Baroness was a little apprehensive. Having been the Queen's governess and closest companion since she was five years old, she had considerable influence with her and did not wish to lose it now. The influence had come through affection which was the only way in which it was possible to guide Victoria. Since the Queen was not on good terms with her mother she had come to regard Lehzen in that light; Victoria's affections overflowed; she loved and hated passionately; there were no fine shades of feeling. She loved her Prime

Minister, Lord Melbourne, unswervingly; she hated his opposite number, Sir Robert Peel, and would hear no good of him; the Baroness Lehzen, who had been, as she said, a mother to her, she loved passionately, whereas although she would not admit that she disliked her mother (Victoria had a keen sense of the proprieties and no good person could dislike a mother) she was very critical of everything she did. This antagonism had been aggravated by the palace factions – that headed by the Queen and the other led by her mother the Duchess. It was an unhappy state of affairs, but as Lord Melbourne, the witty Prime Minister, had said, it was an old Hanoverian custom for parents to quarrel with their children.

Two years ago, when Victoria had become Queen, there had been great changes in the palace. She had quickly shown that she had no intention of being persuaded to do anything she did not wish. She had immediately fallen under the spell of charming Lord Melbourne and the relationship between the young Queen and her ageing Prime Minister had given rise to some speculation. She had found him extremely handsome and she was very susceptible to good looks particularly in men, although quite a lot of her ladies had been chosen for their appearance. Beauty appealed to her in every form and her first comment on those who came in contact with her would invariably be of their physical assets or defects. The handsome Lord Melbourne, with his fatherly air and the manner in which his eyes filled with tears as he contemplated her, completely won her heart from the day of her accession; and with that whole-hearted affection which she generously and rather impulsively gave, she was ready to accept almost everything he put before her simply because he had suggested it.

These two people had had her affection up to this time: Melbourne, her worldly, cynical (in spite of the effective tears) Prime Minister who knew that his position could be changed if his government fell and therefore realised how precarious it was; and the Baroness Lehzen who had no thought of anything but her imperious young mistress and whose life would cease to have any meaning if she relinquished her hold on her affections.

Marriage, of course, could change the situation at the palace. If Victoria fell in love she would do so whole-heartedly and the affections she had for any other than her husband would be in great danger of being usurped by him.

So the Baroness was uneasy because she was aware of how deeply Albert's good looks had impressed her mistress, and the slightest criticism of that young gentleman would arouse the Queen's temper, which Lehzen had often declared to be, in her best nursery manner, 'Very big for such a small person.'

Now Victoria went on to extol the virtues of Albert.

'He is *much* more handsome than Ernest.'

Lehzen admitted this was so. 'Although Ernest looked the stronger of the two.'

'Stronger!' cried Victoria. 'In what way?'

'In health, I meant.'

'Oh, Albert is so much more *refined*.'

'I remember last time he came. Remember, he nearly fainted on the ballroom floor.'

'He was growing too fast. You see he was quite short then. He is tall now. What a fine figure he has. His shoulders are broad and he has such a fine waist.'

'You have a sharp pair of eyes,' said Lehzen.

'You always said that.'

'Yes, my precious angel, and it's true.'

'Well, anyone would notice Albert. He stands out in a crowd.'

'It was hardly a crowd. I must say they travel light. Their baggage hasn't come. They won't be able to change for dinner.'

'That will make it all delightfully informal.' Victoria giggled.

'You've changed quickly,' said Lehzen. 'Yesterday you were dreading their coming.'

'It's different after having seen Albert.'

'You don't have to rush into anything.'

Victoria was immediately the Queen. 'I do not have to do anything I don't wish to,' she said. 'Unless, of course,' she added hastily, 'it was for the good of the state.'

'Some might say marriage was for the good of the state. As the Queen you have to give the country its next King or Queen.'

Lehzen watched her mistress obliquely. The shaft had gone home. Victoria could never hide her feelings. Since the death of Lady John Russell in childbirth Victoria had thought a good deal about bearing children. She had referred to it as the 'dark side of marriage'. It was horrible, painful and could be dangerous. Dear Lady John had been young, happily married, she already had children and could well have done without another, and she who had been well one week was dead the next.

But Lehzen could not bear to see her darling unhappy, so she put an arm about her and said: 'Why, dearest, you're only twenty. You could wait three or four years for marriage if you wished. Didn't Lord Melbourne tell you so?'

'*Dear* Lord Melbourne.' Victoria thought of those happy meetings in the blue closet, the long chats about any subject Lord Melbourne liked to introduce. Little titbits about the ministers and members of the household, about his childhood (though never about his scandalous past), his witty comments on life and the sudden way in which he would introduce some state matter and explain it in the most amusing way. Yesterday she would have been happy for the old way to go on and on. Although she knew it couldn't because Lord Melbourne's Whig government was very shaky and Sir Robert Peel's Tories could overthrow it at any moment and a new Prime Minister would never allow the Leader of the Opposition to be on such intimate terms with the Queen.

There had to be change; and it had come as soon as she looked into those beautiful blue eyes and noticed the good looks of her fascinating cousin.

Although she had deplored the prospect of change she could not help being elated because Albert had come.

She knew what this meant.

She had fallen in love. And Lehzen, who knew

her so well, was aware of it too.

Albert's fears were rapidly disappearing because she was so enthusiastic about everything he did that he could not help knowing that he was a success. He was glad he had brought his greyhound with him, for she was devoted to dogs and had several, the favourite of them being Dash, who took a fancy to Albert. She did seem rather childish, betraying her feelings so easily, and she was simple in her tastes. She would shriek with laughter when he joked. Not that he was given to joking but she was so easy to amuse and it was pleasant to make her laugh. She would race through the gardens with Dash at her heels and she would pick him up and explain to him that Eos, Cousin Albert's greyhound, was so called because that meant Dawn, and because he was black with a silver streak he had reminded Cousin Albert of the first touch of light after the darkness of night. 'It was *such* a clever name,' she said admiringly.

Music was a passion with her as with him, and this was a great interest in common. She loved to listen to the two brothers playing together and was in ecstasies when she and Albert sang a duet together. There was one thing which caused Albert a certain uneasiness; that was her love of dancing. Every night she wished to dance. Albert had been warned by Leopold and Stockmar that his social manners must improve and, with this in mind, he had forced himself to master the necessary dancing steps and with his usual thoroughness he had become a tolerably good dancer, though he felt no enthusiasm for the exercise. Victoria however was enchanted with his dancing.

'You see, Cousin Albert,' she explained, 'I could never take part in the waltz before unless we had royal visitors.' She blushed rather charmingly. 'The waltz is such an *intimate* dance, the gentleman having to put his arm about the lady and of course as I am the Queen ... it had to be a royal arm. But, Albert, don't you *love* the waltz?'

He wanted to say that he disliked the waltz and that love was not a word he would apply to such a thing as a dance, but he had been warned. He was doing very well and he was certain that once they were married he could guide her to such an extent that she would quickly lose her frivolous ways.

'I think the music of Strauss delightful,' he said.

'Oh, I am so glad. I *love* the Strauss music. Particularly the waltzes. They make me want to dance and dance...'

The late nights were rather tiring but he must not show fatigue this time. He had seen Windsor Castle; he understood all that this marriage would entail. It was the greatest opportunity which would ever come his way, and there was no doubt that the little Queen was already in love with him.

Five days after the arrival of Albert and Ernest at Windsor he and his brother went out riding in the forest. From a window the Queen watched their return and as soon as they entered the castle sent for Albert to join her in the blue closet.

When he came she held out her hands to him.

'You know why I asked you to come,' she said,

frank, happy, and only faintly embarrassed because she had to reverse the usual custom and propose to him. 'It would make me *too* happy if you would consent to what I wish.'

He understood. He kissed her hands. Joy shone in his face and she was too enchanted to differentiate between ambition and love.

After all the fears and anxieties he had won.

She threw her arms about him and her warm-hearted affection was very appealing.

'I am not worthy of you,' she said, astonishingly.

He protested that this was untrue.

'Oh, but it will not be easy to be the husband of a Queen. It is a great sacrifice on your part.'

It was not so, he insisted; and he was determined that it should not be so. Sacrifice! To accept the greatest prize in Europe, together with such an affectionate young girl, who was so whole-heartedly in love with him!

'This is the happiest, brightest moment of my life.'

What bliss indeed. With love and ambition walking hand in hand into the future.

So elated had Albert been by that brief visit that he had scarcely noticed the crossing; alas, though, Ernest had to go straight to Dresden while he returned to Coburg. But his mind was so full of Victoria and his future that he scarcely missed his brother. He was already very fond of his future bride; her absolute devotion to him made her so fascinating. How impulsive she was, but that could be curbed; she was so whole-heartedly natural that she was disarming. He wished that he had been her senior instead of the reverse but their natures remedied that. It was clear that he was the sober one, the one meant to control.

He was going to regret leaving Coburg, of course, and he was going to miss Ernest, but there would be great compensations. He could almost feel sorry for Ernest – Duke of a tiny territory while he would be virtually King of England.

Disillusion quickly followed. He learned that it was not Victoria only with whom he had to deal and it was clear as Victoria began to hint in her letters (she wrote copiously and her letters overflowed with her love for him) that the English did not greatly care for foreigners.

First there arose the trouble about his title. Uncle Leopold thought he should be made a peer but this was not acceptable. Those 'dreadful Tories', as Victoria called them, were determined to be difficult. She herself wished him to be the King Consort but apparently even Lord Melbourne would not agree to that, and declared that it was a dangerous precedent for Parliament to be allowed to make a king, for might it not then feel it was permissible to *unmake* one. He was a prince and must remain a prince. Victoria wrote to him:

*The English are very jealous of any foreigner interfering in the government of this country, and have already in some of the papers (which are friendly to me and you) expressed a hope that you would not interfere. Now, though I know you never would, still, if you were a Peer, they would all say, the Prince meant to play a political part...*

Not interfere! But he wanted to play his part in the country! He wanted to advise and guide Victoria! What did they expect him to be? A royal stud!

He was humiliated. While he had been at Kensington she had been quite humble and had talked about the sacrifices he was making in marrying her. Did she mean by that then that he was to be a nonentity?

He had hoped that in his household he would install a few German friends to whom he would be able to talk in his own language, which would make him feel less alien in a strange land; and the most important post would be his secretary.

To his dismay Victoria and Lord Melbourne had chosen the man to fill this post. It was to be the Prime Minister's own secretary, Mr George Anson.

*I am very much in favour of it because he is an excellent young man and very modest, very honest, very steady and very well-informed ...* wrote Victoria.

Albert threw the letter aside. How dared they treat him like this! Surely he was entitled to choose his own secretary! He wrote at once to Victoria telling her that he wished to do this. All he knew of Mr Anson, whom he had seen during his visit, was that he was a good dancer, but he did not wish to choose his household because of their prowess in the ballroom.

This brought a loving reproach from Victoria.

*Regarding your wish about your gentleman, my dear Albert, I must tell you quite frankly that it will not do.*

*You must leave it to me to see that the people of your household will be people of good standing and character.*

Yes, it was a reproof. It meant: I love you dearly, but please don't forget that I am the Queen.

Perhaps most distressing of all was the matter of his income, because this was debated in parliament and it was such a public humiliation. Previous consorts of reigning Queens had been granted £50,000 but he was to have only £30,000. To do her justice the Queen was incensed and did her best to get the larger allowance for him. He knew what was being said in England: the people disliked him already, chiefly because he was German and they did not like the Germans. Even Lord Melbourne had thought it wise not to make a major issue of the Prince's income and to accept the £30,000 for him.

So he did not match up to previous consorts such as stupid old George of Denmark, consort to Queen Anne, for he had been given his £50,000! Baron Stockmar, who was watching the situation carefully, made sure he saw certain extracts from the English papers. 'You must take a deep interest in politics,' had ever been his injunction, 'and that means a study of the country's press.'

It was not very comforting reading. The press reminded its readers that the Prince who was to be the Queen's husband was the second son of a German Duke and had an income of £2,500 a year. £30,000 would be riches to such a comparatively poor man. The Chartists were on the move; there was a great deal of poverty in the country which was in no mood to shower a fortune on an impecunious Prince even if he was going to marry the Queen. They doubted whether he was in danger of imminent starvation, which was more than could be said for many of Her Majesty's subjects. He would have been happy enough with the £30,000 if those who had previously been in similar positions had not been unquestionably awarded £50,000.

At least Victoria was loving. She deplored that he should have been so humiliated. She raged against those dreadful Tories; she was as devoted as ever and when she did not hear from him for a week she was alarmed. She wrote and told him that she watched for his letters and when they did not come she was afraid she was very bad-tempered with her dearest Lehzen.

That was not such a bad thing. Her dearest Lehzen had far too much influence. He had noted that she was not very efficient; and he believed that she was largely responsible for the relationship between Victoria and her mother, of which he disapproved. Victoria should have more respect for the family tie. Besides, the Duchess had been so charming to him and he was sure that he and she were going to be friends. He would most certainly insist on bringing about a reconciliation between Victoria and the Duchess and perhaps then he and his mother-in-law would endeavour to wean Victoria from this rather foolishly sentimental attachment she had for the Baroness.

Dear little Victoria! She needed to be guided and who better to guide a wife than her husband? There had been scandals in the Queen's household. He had heard and read accounts of the disastrous Flora Hastings affair. The Queen had behaved very impulsively and quite wrongly in that, and he was convinced that her actions had been urged on by the Baroness Lehzen. Oh, yes, he must save the Queen from an affair like that occurring again. The fact was that Victoria was too lenient. She was good herself and could not see the evil in others.

The first thing he would have to do was to introduce a moral note into the Court, which he feared might be lacking. This struck him forcibly when he saw the list of bridesmaids.

One of these was the daughter of Lady Jersey, a woman whom the Prince called notorious. She had been the mistress of George IV when he was Prince Regent. How was it possible to allow the daughter of such a woman to act as bridesmaid to the Queen? When he queried the matter the Queen wrote that it was the *daughter* who was the bridesmaid, not Lady Jersey; but Albert thought that no daughter of a notoriously immoral mother should be allowed to act as bridesmaid at the Queen's wedding.

Victoria stressed her point in referring to a certain Lady A at her Court. She liked this woman very much, she wrote:

*...only she is a little* strict and particular *and too severe towards others which is not right; for in my opinion one should be indulgent towards other people, for I always think that if we had not been well brought up and well taken care of, we might also have gone astray... It is very dangerous to be too severe...*

He was astonished. Clearly her moral attitude was at fault. It was *she* who had been unwisely brought up; and the reason was that she had taken far more account of her governess than of her mother. He could see that life was not going to be very easy as the Queen's husband – unless he took a very firm line. So much would depend on Victoria herself, and although she had been so loving when they had been together, he detected a faintly autocratic note in her letters.

This was more than ever apparent when he was considering the honeymoon. This was going to be a very important period. He pictured their being alone together for a few weeks, far from the influence of Lord Melbourne and the Baroness Lehzen. In that time he would be able to make himself so important to her that she would be quite willing to accept his advice, which was what a German husband expected of his wife. He feared that there would be a great deal in England of which he disapproved. He must have those weeks alone with her at Windsor.

Perhaps her reaction to this suggestion was more significant than any of the others in which her attitude might have been dictated by her ministers or the Tory opposition, for this was her own decision – and given somewhat imperiously. And was he wrong in thinking it a little patronising?

Dear Albert had not understood the matter at all.

*You forget, my dearest love, that I am the Sovereign, and that business can wait for nothing. Parliament is sitting and something occurs almost every day for which I may be required and it is quite impossible for me to be absent from London; therefore two or three days is already a long time to be absent...*

She might have fallen headlong in love with him when she had seen him, but during his absence she was quickly remembering that she was the Queen.

He pictured it. The two or three days – at most – at Windsor where in the fresh clean air he would be at his best. He hated London; he felt unwell and so tired in London. He did not like Buckingham Palace, where there were too many Ministers at hand, too much ceremony. At Windsor they could have ridden in the forest; they could have taken long walks in the clean fresh air; they could have retired early and risen at six. But in London she would be planning those interminable balls.

He could almost begin to ask himself whether his great good fortune was so wonderful after all.

What could he do? How could he protest already that he was not treated as an equal. Who knew, she might fall out of love as easily as she had fallen in.

He foresaw all kinds of difficulties ahead. He wrote to Uncle Leopold, implying that he felt melancholy and was gloomy about the future. Everything that had happened since he had left England made him feel that his new country was not ready to welcome him. He did not say that he felt there were two Victorias – the humble, tender, affectionate girl in love and the imperious young woman who, although she could forget temporarily that she was a queen, was inclined to remember it whenever any decision was to be made.

It was February – the marriage month. He must take a last farewell of the forests and mountains of his homeland. Ernest had come home because naturally he and their father must be at the wedding; so for the last time he and Ernest could roam the woods together, hunting, shooting, looking for rare relics such as had delighted them in their childhood and formed their 'museum'.

'What is the use now?' asked Albert. 'I shall never be able to see our collection again.'

'What nonsense. You will surely bring Victoria to Coburg on a visit.'

'She would find the time it takes too long to be away from her business.'

'You would have to put your foot down like a stern husband.'

'Not with the Queen of England,' said Albert wryly.

Ernest looked at his brother in a startled way. Ernest did not know of the correspondence which had taken place between Albert and his affianced bride.

'But let us talk of the old days,' said Albert quickly.

There were some necessary celebrations before he left the land of his birth. The people expected it. Their Prince Albert was going away to marry the Queen of England and everyone knew that would be a very good thing because the Prince would be King of that powerful country and he would never forget his duty to his native land.

There must be a ball, but balls in the ducal palace were very different from those in Windsor and London. They would be over at a respectable hour and although Albert would have preferred to do without them at all, he could submit to these with a fairly good grace. He must listen to the bands and the speeches of congratulation. Little did they know what an imperious young woman he was going to marry.

The time came to leave accompanied by Ernest and their father. His grandmother wept openly when she said goodbye; she had watched over him from his childhood days and he knew that she was thinking she would never see him again. As the carriage drove away he saw her attendants catch her as she fainted, and it was almost as though he were going to his own funeral.

There was another of those dreadful crossings when the sea was as rough as the last time. The boat was tossed on those malicious waves and Albert again knew what it was to be indifferent to death – in fact to consider whether it might not be preferable to the torments inflicted by the sea.

Eventually the white cliffs appeared and he staggered to his feet, knowing that a crowd would be waiting to see the Queen's prospective husband.

There was a faint cheer as he stepped ashore. He smiled. No one must know that he could scarcely stand up, that he was feeling wretchedly sick. He was at least on dry land and he must give them no opportunity of jeering at the Queen's husband.

He stepped into the waiting carriage; the people

cheered and he was driven off on the road to Canterbury where he would spend the night before going on to London and Buckingham Palace.

The people of Canterbury did not seem to dislike him; there were only a few murmurings of 'German', and as after a good night's sleep the effects of the sea crossing wore off he felt able to face what lay before him.

At the palace Victoria was waiting impatiently. There was no ceremonial greeting. The Queen had been replaced by the young girl in love.

She flew at him in her impetuous way.

'Dear, *dearest* Albert.'

She was looking up at him, her lips slightly parted to show those prominent teeth and the hint of pink gum; the blue eyes were adoring.

'It has seemed *so* long.' She had flung herself into his arms. 'I have been watching for *hours* from the equerries' room.'

She blushed, suddenly turning to Uncle Ernest and Cousin Ernest. She had forgotten everything but Albert.

Uncle Ernest smiled and murmured 'Charming! Charming!' and Cousin Ernest smiled and looked enviously at Albert.

'I am *so* happy to see you ... all,' she cried eagerly, gazing adoringly at Albert.

He could certainly not complain of her welcome.

During the afternoon and the next day which preceded his wedding he could complain of nothing in the Queen's attitude towards him. She chattered in a rather hysterical manner of her joy at their reunion; the days had been so long without him; she had been *desolate* when his letters had failed to arrive; these wicked Tories were *monsters* and she would *never* forgive them for the manner in which they had treated him. What she would have done without *dear* Lord Melbourne beside her, she did not know. It was angelic of dear Albert to accept Mr Anson as his secretary.

'But I have no choice,' he replied.

'You are so philosophical, dearest Albert. That is just another of your *dear* qualities which I love.'

He could not fail to be charmed by her; there was no sign of the arrogant Queen; nor had there been, he remembered, when they had been together. She just appeared in those letters – dictated no doubt by her ministers. And not once did she mention the Baroness Lehzen. In fact he did not see the woman. He had exaggerated her importance; he had nothing to fear; as long as Victoria acknowledged her duties to him as his wife, he would overcome all the opposition to him which obviously existed in some sections of the Parliament and the country.

Darling Eos had arrived safely in advance of his master, she told him; and wasn't it a blessing that he got on so well with Dashy?

'Darling Albert, I am so glad you will be staying at the palace. Mama thought that it was wrong for a bridegroom to spend the night before his wedding under the same roof as his bride. I told her it was nonsense.'

'Not very daughterly behaviour,' he commented, which made her laugh loudly. She did laugh too loudly. Later he would point out that it was rather unseemly. And a good daughter should honour her father and mother. Was it not one of the commandments? But it would have been awkward to have stayed somewhere else; and knowing these people they would probably have given him some inferior lodging which would have been humiliating and undignified. He smiled with her.

'Albert, you are so *beautiful* when you smile.'

There was no doubt that she was affectionate and he liked her frankness. There was a very engaging lack of guile.

The night before the wedding they read through the marriage service, even to his putting the ring on her finger.

They retired early – to Albert's satisfaction.

In the morning there was a letter from her asking her 'most dearly beloved bridegroom' whether he had slept well.

He had nothing to fear.

He looked out of his window and saw that the rain was teeming down. Not a very auspicious beginning to their life together, he thought, with a return of the gloomy feeling; then he re-read the note from his 'ever faithful Victoria'. Of what importance was the weather? She loved him; she doted on him; he would guide her in the way she should go and together they would bring great good to their marriage and the country.

He drove to the Chapel Royal amid the cheers of people who had lined the streets. They could not help admiring his looks for he was undoubtedly handsome in his uniform. (She had recently created him a Field Marshal.) He looked very different from the pale-faced, sick young man who had stepped ashore at Dover.

When he entered the chapel he felt ill at ease because he had not been properly informed of what was expected of him. He was unsure whether he should bow to the Archbishop of Canterbury or to the altar; he carried gloves in one hand and a prayer book in the other; and wondered whether he carried them in the appropriate hands. He was very uneasy; but his father and brother were close to him and they smiled reassuringly at him. His father was proud of him, Ernest envious in the best possible way, and suddenly he felt desolate. What should he do when they went away and left him here in this strange land?

And then Victoria arrived in white satin and flounces of lace surmounted by the ribbon of the Garter and her dazzling diamond necklace. He did notice that she prominently wore the sapphire brooch which he had given her; the face beneath the wreath of orange blossom was ecstatic, and he felt reassured at the sight of her. Her adoring eyes took in his magnificence – Field Marshal's uniform, the Order of the Garter, which she had also recently bestowed on him, his tasselled sash, his white knee breeches, the diamond star on his breast, and her eyes told him that she thought him beautiful.

She was trembling a little but as always very conscious of what was expected of her. Her presence calmed him and she whispered to him telling him what they were expected to do. She was both the nervous bride and the autocratic Queen. She trembled visibly – that was with emotion – but her voice when she made her responses was firm and clear.

Albert put the ring on her finger a little awkwardly perhaps and she had to help him along, but she loved him for his lack of poise. Dear, dear Albert! She would cherish him for ever more.

The ceremony was over. Victoria and Albert were married.

They drove back to the palace where the wedding breakfast and the guests awaited them, but before going to them they were alone together for a brief while, during which time she gave Albert a ring. He must wear it all his life, she told him, and they must never, *never* have any secrets from each other.

How tiresome, she added, that they must mingle with the guests.

'But, dearest Albert, that will soon be over. Then we shall be on our way to Windsor.'

Windsor! he thought. Fresh air! The trees and the fields! He would feel well there; it was an ideal place in which to start their married life. He would show her, with the utmost tenderness, that although she was the Queen, she was his wife and a husband must be master in his own house.

'Darling Albert, I know you love Windsor. So do I. It will be wonderful to spend a few days there before returning to my dear London. I never like to be away too long from my capital city. Other places seem a little *dead* when compared with it. And everyone of course is in London. They have to *come* to Windsor.'

A pained look crossed his face. What different

tastes they had!

'And when we get back to London there will be lots of celebrations. Everyone will expect it. Banquets and balls, I daresay.' Her eyes sparkled at the thought.

He feared his dear little Victoria was very frivolous. But this was not the time perhaps to attempt to improve her.

'Look,' she cried, 'there is the castle.'

'Magnificent,' said Albert with deep feeling.

'Dear Albert, I am so glad you like it. It will be one of your homes now.'

'It will be my favourite home,' he said.

'Because we shall spend our honeymoon there? Oh, Albert, what a delightful thought.'

'That and because it is in such a beautiful setting. I hope we shall come here often.'

'It is difficult of course when Parliament is sitting. You see, dear Albert, the Prime Minister cannot keep coming back and forth, nor can he stay at the Castle when there is so much business going on in the House.'

A gentle reminder that she was the Queen.

'I hope I shall be of use to you,' he said. 'I should want you to consult me now and then.'

'Dear Albert, you can be sure that if the need arose I should certainly do so.'

If the need arose! What did she mean by that? But he must not show irritation on his honeymoon.

They alighted from the carriage and Albert stood gazing in wonder. What splendid Gothic architecture!

'The terraces were made for Queen Elizabeth,' chattered Victoria.

'Beautiful,' murmured Albert. 'Grand. Imposing!' And he thought: How different from Rosenau, and he could not suppress a longing to be there.

'Those are the private apartments looking east,' explained Victoria. 'The state apartments to the north and the visitors' apartments to the south. But let us go in.'

The past seemed to envelop him as he went inside those thick stone walls, and as he did so he wondered what part he would play in the future. If he were King of this country, if this stately and glorious castle were his and he was introducing his bride to it, how proud and happy he would have been.

But he was the outsider; hers was the hand from which all blessings flowed. 'Come, Albert,' she was saying, 'I will show you *my* castle.'

In the great banqueting hall Kings of the past had feasted. Here Henry VIII had knighted a sirloin of beef and sported with Anne Boleyn. He pictured them all, the long line of English sovereigns ... mostly men but some female ... Elizabeth who would allow no man to share her throne and Anne whose husband, stupid Prince George of Denmark, had been given £50,000 a year when he, Albert, had been considered worthy of only £30,000.

'What are you thinking, Albert?'

'Of all the Kings and Queens who have lived here.'

'So you know our history.'

'But of course.'

'My clever Albert! But now the castle is mine.'

Mine! he noticed. *Ours* would have been so much more gracious.

They went to look at the suite which had been prepared for them.

'The royal bedroom,' she said with a blush and downcast eyes.

He went through to another room: 'And this?'

'My dressing-room.'

'There is a door leading to another room.' He opened it. It was a bedroom.

She was beside him. 'Oh that,' she said, 'is dear Lehzen's room. Hers is always next to mine.'

A cold fear touched him. Why should he be so apprehensive of that woman? She was only a governess.

'That will be changed now,' he said, trying to sound authoritative.

'Oh, no,' she replied lightly. 'I could never permit that. Poor darling Lehzen would be broken-hearted. You see, dearest, her room was *always* next to mine. One could not change that sort of thing. It would be *too* unkind. Besides, I should not wish it.'

Her loving gaze belied the arrogance of her tone; but he knew the Queen was very close at that moment.

He left her and went down to the drawing-room. She was ecstatically happy. How adorable he was, and how beautiful! Lehzen had not yet arrived. She would be coming later in the evening, so it was not possible to pop in for a chat with her, which was a pity. She had asked dear Lord Melbourne to come down to Windsor the day after tomorrow. She never felt completely happy unless she knew that he was close.

In the meantime there was dear Albert.

How pale she looked. She was really exhausted; and she had not got over the feverish cold which to her – and everyone else's – consternation had attacked her a week ago. She must be well for her wedding night. She threw off her tiredness and went down to the drawing-room.

Albert was seated at the piano, playing divinely and looking even more divine.

He stopped playing when she entered and rose to embrace her. What bliss, she thought. How I *love* dear Albert.

'But, dearest Albert, I interrupted your playing and it was *so* wonderful.'

He continued to play.

Afterwards he came and sat on a footstool at her feet and they talked of the future. She told him how happy she was to have such a wonderful husband and that she had never spent such a happy evening in the whole of her life in spite of the fact that she could still feel the effects of her recent fever and had had such an exhausting time.

She must retire early, said Albert, and submissively she agreed.

They rose early next morning and before breakfast they took a walk in what Albert called the wonderful fresh air.

February air was indeed fresh, commented

Victoria, but it did not matter because she glowed from the warmth of Albert's love; and she told him that there was nowhere she would rather be than walking in the gardens at Windsor on a cold February morning with her dearest husband at her side.

She was so hungry, she told him; she was ready for a good breakfast.

Albert smiled indulgently and said she was like a child.

'Don't forget, Albert,' she laughed. 'I am three months older than you.'

'No one would believe it,' he said.

'They know it.' She was solemn suddenly. 'That is one of the drawbacks of being royal. People know *everything* about one.'

'Everything?' he queried. 'Isn't my dearest Victoria inclined to exaggerate?'

'I was not aware of it.'

'Well your remark was not exactly *truthful*.'

She looked concerned. 'And one *must* be truthful. I will remember in future. Thank you, Albert, for pointing it out. I see that you are going to be *good* for me.'

He loved her in that moment. All was going to be well. She was enchanting, his dear little wife. He had been overawed because of the manner in which those around her behaved to the Queen.

'Come, my precious angel,' she said, 'let us go in to breakfast.'

Hand in hand they entered the castle, where an unpleasant surprise was awaiting Albert.

The Baroness Lehzen was seated at the breakfast table. She scarcely looked at the Prince; her

111

eyes went at once to Victoria.

'Good morning, dearest Daisy,' said Victoria. Daisy! Her name was not Daisy. He had discovered all he could about this Lutheran pastor's daughter and he knew that her name was Louise.

'My precious love, how are you this morning?'

'Oh, so happy, my dear.'

The Baroness gave a nod of approval. Then she said good morning to the Prince as though she had just become aware of him.

She poured Victoria's coffee.

'Just as you like it, my love.'

'Oh, thank you, dear Lehzen.'

Lehzen handed Albert his coffee.

He was mortified and angry, but he could not show it. Their first breakfast the morning after their wedding day and the Baroness Lehzen had to share it with them!

## Chapter VI

## THE HONEYMOON IS OVER

On the third day after the wedding, the honeymoon was over and the Duchess of Kent arrived at Windsor accompanied by Albert's brother and father.

Albert was delighted to see them; he felt that his father and brother would give him support; as for the Duchess, she made a special point of being gracious to him, telling him that she felt already that she had another son. Being indiscreet she hinted that Victoria was not the most grateful of daughters but that she had been led astray by a certain person – not very far from them at this moment, and indeed never very far from the Queen – and this was a matter of great grief to her.

Albert knew that the Duchess's enemy was the Baroness Lehzen and he was beginning to regard that tiresome woman as his also, which made a bond between him and his mother-in-law.

The Duchess put her finger to her lips in a conspiratorial gesture when she told him this; and as they could talk in German, which came easier to the Duchess than English in spite of the years she had lived in England, they understood each other very well.

They were allies from the very beginning.

It seemed that the entire Court was soon invading the privacy of Windsor. Lord Melbourne arrived and the effect this had on Victoria was startling. If he had been her own father she could not have treated him with greater respect and affection. She called him her dear Prime Minister and affectionately Lord M; they were always talking together; and often she would be alone in one of the closets with him, or they would walk together in the gardens.

The Duchess told Albert confidentially that Victoria was rather impulsive and had become attached to Lord Melbourne as she was inclined to do with certain people. Perhaps Albert might suggest to her at some time that there was no need to be quite so friendly with any of her ministers.

In less than a week after the wedding Victoria and Albert were back in London. There were levees and receptions and Albert was beginning to feel more and more wretched every day.

Now that the glamour of the wedding was over the press was looking critically at Albert and unpleasant cartoons and lampoons were appearing each day. Some said that Albert had come over to help himself to English gold; others said the Queen was master in the house and the Prince merely there for one purpose.

There were even unpleasant and rather coarse sketches on the stage concerning the royal pair. One comment was that they were seen walking early in the morning following the bridal night, and this was not the way to provide the country with a Prince of Wales. But money was the main theme of these comments. The Coburgs had a reputation for easing themselves into the best positions in Europe. Albert was accused of being greedy, of trying to snatch the crown from Victoria's head, of selling himself to the Queen of England for £30,000 a year which was a fortune to a man who had only £2,500.

It was humiliating. In his father's kingdom it would not have been allowed.

'We cannot interfere with the liberty of the press,' Victoria told him. 'Lord Melbourne is constantly saying this.'

'So we have to accept these coarse libels?'

'They have always been, Albert. We must forget them.'

'That,' he said coolly, 'is very difficult.'

'My dearest Albert, I assure you when these

things are said of you it hurts me far more than when they are said of me.'

He embraced her. 'You are a good wife,' he told her.

'That is what I want to be. I shall strive all my life to please you, Albert.'

How could he help feeling hopeful when she said such things, for she was so frank and she always meant what she said.

The cynical new version of the National Anthem did not exactly displease him. They were singing it in the streets now; and often he heard the words whispered below those of the original ones.

*God save sweet Vic, mine Queen*
*Long live mine little Queen,*
*God save de Queen.*
*Albert is victorious*
*De Coburgs now are glorious*
*All so notorious*
*God save the Queen.*

*Ah, Melbourne, soon arise*
*To get me de supplies*
*My means are small.*
*Confound Peel's politics*
*Frustrate de Tory tricks*
*At dem now go like bricks*
*God damn dem all.*

*The greatest gifts in store*
*On me be pleased to pour,*
*And let me reign.*

*Mine Vic has vowed today*
*To honour and obey*
*And I will have de sway*
*Albert de King.*

He was not sure whether he would rather be
thought of as a man scheming for a kingdom or
as a helpless boy who must obey his wife.

They were back in Buckingham Palace. Victoria
was happy and did not understand that Albert was
not entirely so. Her days were fully occupied.
There were always state papers awaiting her signature; there were interviews with Lord Melbourne;
there were secret conferences with Baroness
Lehzen and there was Albert. She told him that
the happiest part of the day was when they walked
together in the garden, arm in arm, and the dogs
gambolled around. She feared darling Dash was
getting rather old. He didn't play quite as madly as
he used to; but perhaps she was comparing him
with dearest Albert's lovely Eos.

There was always music. How she loved this
shared interest! She would listen enraptured
while Albert played something from Haydn – one
of his favourite composers; and when they sang a
duet together that was perfect bliss.

'Our voices are in complete harmony, dear Albert, as everything else about us.'

But he had his doubts. He was horrified that
she scarcely knew the names of any trees or
plants. 'Oh, is it?' she would say happily when he
told her. The birds were unknown to her. She
could not tell the difference between a blackbird

116

and a thrush.

'How have you been educated?' he demanded in tender exasperation.

'Oh, dear Daisy and I were never very interested in that sort of thing.'

'Daisy! You mean Baroness Lehzen. That is surely not her name.'

'It is *my* name for her. I christened her. I think it is a dear delightful name and suits her. I used to call her Mother once, for that was how I thought of her, but somehow that did not seem quite right.'

'It certainly does not,' said Albert severely.

'Oh, dear Albert, you are so easily shocked. Which is right, of course,' she added hastily. 'I fear you are very good.'

'Goodness is nothing to fear, dear angel.'

'It is something to strive for, I know, Albert. But you are so *very* good.'

'I am a little grieved that you and your mother seem to be on bad terms.'

'Oh, Mama can be very trying.'

'My dearest Victoria, I am pained to hear you talk thus of your mother.'

'*Dear* Albert, if you could know what it was like at Kensington before I became Queen. I was more or less a prisoner. And Mama was constantly quarrelling with my uncle King William and his wife. And you know Aunt Adelaide is the sweetest woman. She would never quarrel with anyone unless they forced her to it; and believe me, Mama did. There have been occasions when I have been really ashamed.'

'My love, we both wish to obey the commandments I believe, and there is one which begins – "Honour thy father and thy mother".'

'My dear love, you are so good yourself that you cannot conceive how tiresome some people can be. Now we will talk of something else because I am weary of the subject.'

There spoke the Queen. Not, Albert, please let us talk of something else, but we will.

He would have to explain that he must have some authority in his own home. He was not here just as a means of giving her an heir to the throne. He was a man; he was a husband; and although she might be Queen, she was also his wife.

But she was rattling on now about dear Lord Melbourne. He was looking older, she thought, and she feared he tired himself out. She was going to speak to him *very* severely because he obviously did not take enough care of himself.

Albert thought she saw a little too much of Lord Melbourne. Was it necessary?

'My dear Albert, it is *absolutely* necessary for me to be continually in touch with my Prime Minister. I am the Queen.'

'We cannot forget that,' said Albert with some irony which was lost on her.

She must return to her work, she told him; there were state papers to be looked through and signed.

'Albert, my love, you have no idea of the amount of papers I have to read.'

'No,' said Albert, 'but I should if you would show me and perhaps let me help you.'

'Why, Albert, how very kind of you!'

He was elated. He only had to ask and she

would allow him to read state documents, to discuss them with her. He would be admitted to those conferences which took place in the closet between her and Lord Melbourne.

But how different it was! She was seated at her table. 'Dear Albert, draw up a chair and sit beside me. There. That is very *cosy*. Here is the blotting paper. When I sign you can blot them for me and make a neat little pile.'

'But you must read the papers, surely?'

She laughed delightedly. 'Oh, I have already discussed all these matters with my Prime Minister. All that has to be done now is sign the papers. And it is *such* a help to have you there with the blotting paper.'

So that was what sharing meant. He had become a sort of clerk to blot what his employer wrote. That was his sole duty; the contents of the documents to which she put her name were a mystery to him.

He was constantly on the point of explaining to her; in his room he rehearsed what he would say. He would speak out; he would tell her that he felt wretchedly inadequate and he would go on feeling so if he were to be useless.

He discussed the matter with his father and brother. He was safely married now, was their advice; it was for him to tell his wife that he wished to be taken into her confidence.

'Why,' said Ernest, 'she adores you. You only have to ask for what you want.'

But they had only seen his loving little wife; they did not know Victoria the Queen.

Was he afraid of her? That seemed absurd ... she was so tiny; and she was so appealing in her devotion. How strange that he could not tell her exactly what was in his mind. He always thought he could; it was only when he was face to face with her that he could not bring himself to explain that he was far from happy.

He felt quite angry when on one occasion he went into his room to find the Baroness leaning against the table while the Queen sat at her desk. The Baroness held some papers in her hands and she had obviously been discussing them with the Queen.

So ... the Baroness knew what was in those state papers which were to be kept secret from him!

He turned away and walked out of the room.

'Was that Albert?' said Victoria.

Lehzen nodded.

'But why did he go away?' demanded Victoria.

'I daresay he wished to see you alone.'

'But I was really alone. *You* don't count, dear Daisy. By which I mean that you count so much ... if you understand what I mean.'

Lehzen said she understood exactly what her precious love meant and was happy because of it.

'I heard you last evening at dinner,' said Victoria with a laugh, 'telling your neighbour how perfect I am.'

'I told nothing but the truth,' declared Lehzen stoutly.

'Albert thinks me a little frivolous,' said the Queen.

Lehzen flushed angrily. 'Indeed.'

'Darling Daisy, you must not be angry with my dear Albert. He only criticises for my good.'

'There is nothing ... absolutely nothing to criticise.'

'Oh, come, Lehzen, you do sometimes yourself a bit you know.'

'I will not allow anyone else to.'

Victoria laughed and threw her arms about the Baroness's neck.

'Dear, *dear* Daisy, how lucky I am to have both you *and* Albert to love me so much.'

'Nobody on earth loves you as I do,' said Lehzen.

Victoria felt it was a faint criticism of Albert which she must not allow – but of course it was only said out of dearest Lehzen's excessive loyalty.

A few days later Albert said that he wondered about the manner in which her household was managed. There seemed to be a certain amount of overlapping.

'Overlapping, dear Albert what *do* you mean?'

'Several people doing the same job.'

'Oh, that is Lehzen's affair. She sees to everything.'

'Well, it doesn't appear that she *sees* with any great efficiency.'

'She prides herself on the way she looks after me and won't let anyone worry me.'

'Well, I will make doubly sure that no one does.'

'My dearest Albert, how *very* good you are. I was only saying today to dear Lehzen how fortunate I am. But you must not interfere with Lehzen's affairs. She would he most put out.'

'But, my dear Victoria, I should enjoy looking into some of the domestic arrangements at the palace. It would give me something to do.'

'My dear energetic Albert, please do anything you wish, but you must not interfere with Lehzen's domain. She would be so hurt. I forbid that.'

She spoke jokingly, but the edge was there.

He must mind his own business. He was rapidly learning that his duty was to be available whenever the Queen wished, to play at being the ideal husband, to provide an heir to the throne.

He left her and shut himself in his room to write letters to those friends, like Uncle Leopold, who might understand his feelings.

'I am the husband,' he wrote sadly, 'but not the master of the house.'

In less than a fortnight after the wedding Albert's father prepared to leave for Coburg.

'You are settled here now, my son,' he said, 'and I have my dominions to govern. Cheer up, everything will work out for the best if you are careful. Your brother need not leave yet. He can stay for another month or perhaps two. After that, this will seem like home to you.'

'I fear it never will,' said Albert sadly.

'Oh, come, the countryside is beautiful, the climate very much like our own. And think of your position here.'

'I think of it a great deal,' said Albert with melancholy.

'You will have Stockmar to help you. You know

you can trust him.'

Oh, yes, he trusted Stockmar; but he was a foreigner too, and what chance had they against the Queen and Lord Melbourne who seemed determined to keep him out.

He did not feel he could open his heart completely to his father. He admired him and respected him. He knew, of course, that there had been many romantic entanglements in his life but Albert believed this was due to the unhappy marriage. The most easy temptation to fall into was sexual. He was sure of it; and he could not blame his father for past excesses. Women had tempted him. One thing Albert was certain of he was going to avoid all such temptation. He would avoid all women but his wife. These alien English considered him gauche. Let them. He was certainly not going to get entangled with any woman.

And now another link with Rosenau was about to be broken. His father was going.

The carriage was at the door. He had said his final farewell. He stood watching it ride away with the tears in his eyes.

Then he turned and went slowly into the palace.

Victoria was waiting for him at the top of the staircase.

'My poor dear Albert...'

She barred his way, her own blue eyes filled with tears. 'I understand how you are feeling...'

He cried: 'You don't ... you don't...' and dashed past her into his sitting-room. He could not bear to talk to her then. He feared that if he did he would tell her that he wanted to go home, burst into tears and cry like any baby. He could hear her calling his name as she had run after him; swiftly he turned the key in the lock.

'Albert,' she cried. 'Albert, I am here.'

'I ... I wish to be alone.'

'You *can't* ... not from me.'

'Victoria, please go away. I am too upset.'

'No, no,' she said. 'I am going to comfort you. Open the door. Open it at once.'

He obeyed and she was ready to throw herself into his arms but he stood silent, unresponsive.

'Albert,' she cried, aghast, 'I want to comfort you. I know how you feel. Your father has gone away.'

'How can you know?' he cried. 'You have never known a father.'

'No, but I understand.'

'And you don't love your mother, so you can't understand.'

He turned away from her coldly, but she put her arms round him and held him tightly against her; she began to cry.

'Albert, my dearest, but I can't bear to see you unhappy. I love you, Albert.'

He turned to her then and they wept together.

He had been unkind, he said.

No, no, not unkind. It was all so natural. He must *share* his troubles. She must make him understand that.

They kissed and she was immediately wildly happy.

'God knows how great my wish is to make you happy and contented. I would do anything ... anything...'

How could he help but be touched and moved by such devotion?

But later he thought: Yes, she would do anything for me ... except let me share her throne.

Albert was deeply shocked. He would not have believed it of Ernest, although his brother had always laughed at him and called him a prude. But that Ernest should have had adventures which could produce such a result was a terrible blow and indeed a great lesson. Ernest had been looking unwell for some weeks.

'It is this strange country,' said Albert. 'You'll feel better when you leave.'

Ernest had let that rest for a while; but later – so he told Albert – he had become alarmed and seen a doctor.

'It was a woman in Berlin,' he said.

'A woman!' cried Albert. 'Good God, Ernest! You can't be serious.'

'Albert, for Heaven's sake do be a little more worldly. These things happen now and then, you know.'

'And those to whom they happen have to abide by the consequences,' said Albert severely.

'You're right there, my dear brother. I hope you never get into this sort of mess.' Albert was even more horrified which at least made Ernest laugh. 'As if you would.'

'Should one joke about such a serious matter? Ernest, I am glad our father doesn't know about this.'

'He knows, Albert. He understood. He is not immune from the temptations of the flesh as you are.'

125

'Should we say that I have taught myself to overcome them.'

'Well, I make a guess that dear little Vic keeps you busy.'

Albert was horrified. 'Ernest, what has happened to you?'

'A fate, alas, that catches up with many of us – except the virtuous like you, Albert. That is if there are any more like you ... which I very much doubt.'

Albert's affection for this brother overcame his shock. 'You must get the best possible treatment.'

'That's what I am doing.'

'And then, Ernest, marry. But not until you are completely well. You must not risk getting a sick heir.'

'You may trust me.'

'I shall tell Victoria. We have said we shall not have secrets from each other.'

'I understand,' said Ernest.

'I shall hate telling her but I think it is an unpleasant duty.'

'Don't worry. It'll only make her realise all the more that in taking you she got the better bargain.'

In hushed and solemn tones he explained the situation to Victoria, who flushed scarlet with embarrassment and horror when she heard.

'My dear Albert, but this is so *terrible*.'

'It's the reward of sin,' said Albert.

'Of course Ernest is very *gay*.'

'Too gay.'

'But he is your brother and therefore very dear to us both. Everything must be done to cure him.

126

Can he be cured, Albert?'

'Oh, yes. I gather he is only lightly infected. I have been talking to him of the benefits of married life.'

Victoria smiled radiantly. 'Oh, but we are so fortunate. Everyone cannot be as happy as we are.'

Albert pressed her hand in agreement and added: 'Ernest is a man who needs marriage if he is to lead a decent and honourable life.'

Victoria nodded gravely and then with one of her impulsive gestures she threw her arms about his neck and said: 'Oh, Albert, how very fortunate we are. I knew as soon as I saw you that you would be pure and faithful.' She looked at him in horror. 'Suppose I had chosen Ernest.'

'Then one person would have been most unhappy,' said Albert. 'Myself.'

'And I too, Albert. Oh, how wise I was! But then as soon as I set eyes on you, I *knew.*'

They were very content in each other for the rest of that day and night.


Victoria herself began to be worried. She had been married for about six weeks. It really could not be, she assured herself. It was far too early.

The only person she could talk to about it was the Baroness. 'Dear Daisy, can it be ... so soon?'

'Well, it certainly could,' said the Baroness.

Victoria began to shiver. 'I must confess, Daisy, that it makes me a little uneasy.'

'My darling, I'd be there all the time to look after you.'

'I know. Old Louie was there to look after my Cousin Charlotte but she died.'

'You mustn't compare yourself with the Princess Charlotte.'

'Why not? According to Uncle Leopold she was a healthy girl. That she should die having her baby was most unexpected.'

'Look, this is not the way to talk or think. My opinion is it's a little soon and you may be mistaken.'

'I hope so.'

'But you want a baby.'

'Not yet. I want to wait a while. Besides...' She shivered. 'Ever since Lady John Russell died having hers.

'Oh, that was different. She was old compared with you.'

'I am perhaps too small to bear children.'

'It makes no difference. Think of all the fun we'll have getting ready. All the lovely things. You must let me make some myself. Will you?'

'Darling Daisy, you shall do exactly as you want.'

'It'll be like dressing the dolls.'

'Oh, my darling dolls! What fun we had with them! I believe you're already planning the baby's layette.'

'Well, of course,' said Lehzen. 'We shall have to furnish the nursery afresh.'

'You make me feel almost excited.'

'You'll be excited, my love. You see.'

'I shall have my moments of fear. Do you know how many women die in childbed, Lehzen?'

'They are poor. It's different for a queen. You'll have all the best doctors. This will be the heir to the throne, remember. And I'll be there.'

'I've already started to think about names.'

'If it's a girl it must be Victoria.'

'How will you know which of us is which?'

'I will know,' said Lehzen. 'Never fear, I shall be in no danger of confusing the Queen and the Princess Royal.'

'But it should be a boy.'

'Then it will have a king's name.'

'Whatever you say, Lehzen, it is a terrible ordeal. It frightens me. I just cannot get Lady John out of my mind. She was so well just before and then...'

Tears began to fall down the Queen's cheeks; she had been very fond of Lady John and her dear children. She always invited them to come when their stepmother visited her; and she and they used to race up and down the corridors of Buckingham Palace with Dash, Islay or one of the other dogs at their heels.

Albert came in. He had been riding with Ernest and looked very handsome in his habit. Lehzen gave him a rather perfunctory curtsey which angered him because there was, he fancied, a trace of insolence in it. She did not retire as of course she should; and what was more irritating was that Victoria did not command her to.

'You have enjoyed the ride, Albert?' asked the Queen.

'Very much.'

'And Ernest is looking better, I think.'

'He is much better.'

'I am so glad of that.'

Lehzen was putting the Queen's wrap away with elaborate care, a task for one of her ladies of the bedchamber. What position in the household did Lehzen hold? he wondered in irritation. She behaved as though she were a member of the family.

Albert implied that he wished to speak to Victoria alone and she with perfect ease said: 'I will see you at six, Daisy.'

Lehzen, who had been so insolent with him, showed her respect for the Queen by her immediate acknowledgement of the order.

When they were alone Albert said: 'I see you have been crying. What has happened to upset you?'

She hesitated. Then: 'Well, Albert, I am not quite sure ... but I have fears ... I mean hopes ... that...'

Albert's face was illuminated by his joy.

'My dear little wife! But this is wonderful news.'

A momentary irritation crossed her face. It was all very well for him. *He* did not have to face the terrifying ordeal; he did not have to risk *his* life.

'Of course,' she said, 'it is too soon to be absolutely sure yet.'

'If it is ... oh, Victoria, if it is...'

'I confess I shall be a little frightened.'

'The first time is a little frightening I believe.'

'I am glad to hear that as a man you are aware of that.'

'But it will be a great blessing ... so soon. It is a good sign that we may have many children.'

She shivered.

'There will be great rejoicing ... everywhere,' he went on.

'I wish I were not so small. That might make difficulties.'

'I have never heard this is so.'

'Nor has Lehzen. But I believe it may have some effect and it is I who have to endure it, you know.'

'Lehzen! So you have already discussed this with her.'

'We were talking of it as you came in.'

He was silent. Now was the time to tell her that he resented the Baroness. The fact that this important matter – *their* secret – could be discussed with Lehzen was hurtful enough, but that she should have spoken of it to the woman before she did to him appalled him.

'I am sure,' he said, with sarcasm, 'that the Baroness, being an unmarried woman, knows a great deal about such matters.'

'Lehzen always makes it her affair to know all she can about anything that might happen to me.' Even her voice softened when she spoke of the woman.

He determined in that moment that he was going to be rid of her because he could never really hope to be master in his house while she was there.

Albert decided to confide in Baron Stockmar. To him he could speak in German and he knew that as a confidant of Uncle Leopold it was in his interest to help the marriage to succeed and that it was Uncle Leopold's wish – and therefore Stockmar's – that Albert should have a hand in the government of the country.

'I find my position becoming more and more intolerable,' he told the Baron. 'I am never allowed to know the smallest thing about the politics of this country. The Queen treats me as a pet to be fondled and to receive extravagant compliments; Lord Melbourne behaves towards me as though I am a child. They are both determined to exclude me.'

Stockmar nodded gravely. He, the expert observer, was fully aware of the situation.

'It is quite intolerable,' went on Albert, 'particularly as the Queen confides fully in the Baroness Lehzen. I have seen her reading state papers in the presence of the Queen. She has complete charge of the household. I am allowed no say in anything. I am occasionally permitted to blot her signature when she signs the papers. That is the limit of my usefulness. I sometimes wish that I had never come here. I might have had a small house of my own but at least I should have been master of it.'

The Baron said: 'You are too impatient. This matter needs very thoughtful action. In time you will succeed. I have no doubt whatsoever of the Queen's devotion to you personally. You have succeeded in your most important duty and that is to charm the Queen. She is as deeply in love with you as any young woman could be. That is your strength. Indeed if this state of affairs can be retained, you will be invincible. But what you have most need of at this time is patience.'

'I certainly need a great deal of that,' said Albert grimly.

'You are not sufficiently interested in politics.'

'How can I be when I am not allowed to know what is going on?'

'An unworthy observation for a man of Your

Highness's intelligence,' said the Baron. 'You are excluded from secret documents of state, but there is no reason why you should not make yourself fully conversant with the press. A cross-section of Whig and Tory writers will give you an insight into current opinions. You do not read the papers as you should. It is of equal importance that you should know the mood of the country, the position of the two parties and how public opinion stands. This will be a great compensation for the lack of access to private papers.'

The Prince was thoughtful; he knew this was sound advice.

'I will do this,' he said. 'But I can never discuss affairs of state with the Queen. Whenever I attempt to, she changes the subject and talks of something quite frivolous. Yet she can be closeted for an hour at a time with Lord Melbourne. There seems to be a conspiracy between them to keep me out.'

'The Queen's relationship with Lord Melbourne is an unusual one. Her Majesty came to the throne at the age of eighteen – a young impressionable girl with a determination to be a good queen. Her Prime Minister was Lord Melbourne – a man of social grace and great charm – worldly in the extreme. The Queen was immediately impressed by him. In her eyes he could do no wrong. Indeed, at one time some people thought she might *marry* Lord Melbourne.'

The Prince was startled and looked alarmed.

'Ah,' went on Stockmar. 'I see I am right and you have not made yourself cognizant of affairs in this country. You should not feel jealous of Lord

Melbourne. He has a subtle mind and he understands the position perfectly. He knew there was never any question of marriage between them and so did the Queen. She never knew her father, and consequently looked for a father in other men. Her relationship with your Uncle Leopold was one of the most passionate devotion on both sides and adoration as well on hers. When your Uncle Leopold was no longer there she turned to Lord Melbourne. But these were the father figures. You are the husband. All that passionate devotion will be yours in due course providing you know how to divert it in your direction. At the moment the Queen loves you devotedly. Everyone realises that she is madly in love with her husband. But in the same way as Lord Melbourne weaned her from Leopold so you will wean her from Melbourne. Everything is on your side and if you behave in the right manner you will be more wholeheartedly loved than ever Leopold or Melbourne were.'

'I know she has a loving nature.'

'She is overflowing with affection. She is good. You have in fact a wonderful wife but she is also a queen. She has been brought up with this knowledge and she has a sacred dedication to her duty. You are the most fortunate of young men to have such a wife and to be the husband of such a queen. But there are difficulties ahead which you will overcome. Your appearance is in your favour. It enchants the Queen, who is susceptible to good-looking people. Your calm and cautious character will stand you in good stead. You are her perfect complement. Your calm will always win against her violent temper. It is her chief fault and her great disadvantage. She loses her temper; you keep yours. Calm always wins over tempest. Remember that.'

'I am sure your advice is sound and I am greatly cheered by it.'

'Well, now a plan of action. You are going to make yourself knowledgeable politically. Lord Melbourne is difficult to approach because he is so much the Queen's man. But what of Sir Robert Peel?'

'The Queen hates him.'

Stockmar laughed. 'Peel is a brilliant statesman. He has been a little piqued by the affair of the Bedchamber a year or so ago. Who would not be? The Queen behaved in a very unconstitutional manner. You must read accounts of this. I will see that they come to your hands. But for the chivalry of Melbourne and the dignity of Peel the Queen could have been in a difficult position over that affair. And following so closely on the Flora Hastings scandal it made Her Majesty very unpopular. These are matters which you must study. The Queen, like most young monarchs, does not yet understand the importance of pleasing the people. Her very crown depends on it. That is something you will be able to teach her. In the meantime cultivate the men who, though they may not be governing the Country now, will be doing so in a very short time. Are you aware that the fall of the Melbourne Ministry is imminent? When it falls there will be a Tory Government. There must be no repetition of the Bedchamber affair. You will have to save the Queen from that folly. And when the new government comes in you may well be on friendly terms with the new Prime Minister, Sir Robert Peel.'

'Why, it sounds like treachery towards Victoria.'

'My dear Albert, you and I have no thought in our heads but to serve the Queen. This is the very best we can do for her. She will have to accept Sir Robert in due course; and she will do so because you will have taught her her duty towards her government and her country. You will even – in due course – help her to overcome this ridiculous – and between ourselves childish – dislike of one of the greatest statesmen of all time.'

'Baron, I begin to see that there is hope for me.'

'No one's future was ever more bright or hopeful,' said the Baron.

Albert did not find it difficult to strike up a friendship with Sir Robert Peel and to his great pleasure he discovered that the Leader of the Opposition was a man whom he could understand. There was a similarity in their characters. Peel was quite unlike Lord Melbourne, the handsome social success, being scarcely handsome and without social grace. His speech was direct and to the point; he was an idealist, the last description which could be applied to Lord Melbourne.

Albert's study of politics had taught him that Peel was a reformer. He had brought in the Bill for Catholic Emancipation and revised the Laws of Offences against Persons; also the forgery laws. He had created the Metropolitan Police Force. Clearly a man of ideas and courage, Sir Robert Peel was incorruptible; his sense of duty came before personal glory; he was a man whom Albert could not only understand but admire. Moreover, and this was a factor which had begun to have considerable weight with Albert, his private life was exemplary. Lord Melbourne's had been far from that. Although everyone seemed to have forgotten it, Melbourne's married life with Lady Caroline Lamb had been most unsavoury (although it was long since over, for she had died some years ago) and he had later been involved in two divorce cases. To have been concerned in one would have been quite shocking in Albert's eyes, but two! It seemed hardly possible that Lord Melbourne could be guiltless. Albert did not believe that people became concerned in such affairs by chance. And this was the man whom Victoria trusted as she trusted no other.

Now Sir Robert Peel was devoted to his wife, who shared his secrets and ambitions as all wives and husbands should; they had five sons and two daughters – a pleasant family.

Moreover, Sir Robert was pleased to talk to the Prince. There was none of that slightly patronising manner which he fancied he had detected with Lord Melbourne. Stockmar's advice was good. Politics were interesting; moreover they gave him something to do.

He could never mention Sir Robert to the Queen, though she was constantly talking of Lord Melbourne to him, holding him up as a sort of oracle.

Albert thought a great deal about the political situation. Peel had told him that an election would be inevitable very soon. The Whigs were holding on by the skin of their teeth and in fact it was only the Queen's favour which kept them in. Peel was, Albert realised in the light of his newly acquired knowledge, referring to the Bed-chamber Affair, but the Leader of the Opposition could not talk of this in detail to the Prince because it put the Queen in such a bad light.

An election before long and Peel the new Prime Minister seemed an excellent prospect to the Prince. It saddened him, though, to realise that what seemed so desirable to him was the last thing the Queen wanted.

He believed that he should try to influence her a little, subtly attempt to make her realise that her dislike of Peel was unworthy of her; and he decided to make the attempt as they sat at tea together. Victoria enjoyed presiding over the tea pot 'like an ordinary housewife', she said. She liked to pour out the tea 'just as you like it, dear-est Albert'. It was wonderful, she told him, how he had taken to the English tea-drinking custom. It was *so* civilised.

He smiled at her from across the table and said to her: 'You look tired, my dearest. You must not have so many late nights.'

She was pleased by his concern but hated to hear that she looked tired, which reminded her of that other affair: 'Was she or was she not pregnant?' She was not entirely sure yet but she rather believed she was. But she did not wish to be re-minded; moreover he was referring obliquely to her love of dancing which she insisted should take place whenever possible and she had danced until two that morning. Albert always fidgeted and

138

looked as though he would fall asleep at any moment. She *did* wish he did not feel so sleepy in the evenings. He really danced very well but she felt he did so reluctantly, which spoilt her pleasure.

So she felt a little irritated on the whole.

She said that she thought that Lord Melbourne was a little worried. That dreadful Peel man was a great thorn in his flesh.

'Well, my dearest, he is the Leader of the Opposition. One would expect them to have a few differences of opinion.'

'The Leader of the Opposition indeed, and that's where I hope he'll remain, although he would dearly love to be Prime Minister. He almost thought he was once but I put a stop to that. *My* government resigned because Lord Melbourne said he was powerless to pass laws with such a small majority and that dreadful Peel man thought he could take over. He came to see me. He is most unattractive and he prances about when he speaks like a dancing master.'

'He has a wonderful record.'

'Record! What do you mean, Albert, a wonderful record!'

'He has done so much good for the country.'

'Who has been telling you this nonsense, Albert?'

'Nonsense, my dear love? Can you seriously think that? What of the Police Force, which is the envy of the world. Whose idea was it? And who formed it?'

'Oh, that.'

'Come my love, be fair. Answer me.'

'It was just a law that was brought in.'

'And a good one, eh?'

'The Police Force has been greatly improved since it was formed.'

'Should you not give credit where credit is due?'

'Of course I would always give credit when it is deserved.'

'Well then...'

'But nothing is going to make me like your precious dancing master.'

These were the danger signals but Albert ignored them. She was a little frightened of the future. She hated this talk of politics. She wanted to laugh and talk of light matters and love with Albert.

'And now, dear Albert,' she went on, 'I am going to ask you to help me choose the material for a new gown.'

'Which I shall do with pleasure,' said Albert, 'but I do want you to look clearly at what is happening.'

'Look clearly at what is happening? What *do* you mean? *I* know what's happening in this country, Albert, far more than you do. You forget my Prime Minister visits me every day. I have conferences with him. I happen to be the Queen of this country.'

'As a statesman Lord Melbourne does not match up to Sir Robert Peel.'

She stared at him. She could not believe she had heard correctly. He had deliberately defied her. He had talked of politics when she did not wish to; he had decried her beloved Lord Melbourne; and he had applauded the man she hated as much as she had ever hated anyone.

She was trembling with rage. Her fingers closed about the handle of the full cup of tea before her which she had been about to drink when he had begun this distressing conversation.

She picked it up and threw it into his face.

Albert's reaction was astonishing.

He rose from the table and said to the astonished servant who had come forward, 'What do you think of that?' He bowed to his wife. 'I shall now go to change my clothes.'

He left her furious but wretched at the table.

Oh, dear, what *had* she done! It was that violent temper of hers. But really Albert should not have goaded her by praising that dreadful man. How could he admire Sir Robert Peel when she disliked him so? But to throw a cup of tea into her beloved Albert's face! The thought of him sitting there so beautiful with the tea on his face and trickling down his coat was terrible. And he had been so wonderfully calm. He had had every right to be angry; but all he had done was go to change his coat.

She could not be happy until Albert and she were friendly again.

She ran up to his room. The door was shut.

'Albert,' she cried, rapping on it.

'Is that you, Victoria?' His voice sounded just the same, so beautifully calm, just as though nothing had happened.

'Albert I want to talk to you. May I come in?' Her voice was humble. She felt humble. She was so ashamed of her outburst. Even Lehzen and

141

Lord Melbourne said she had a quick temper. Lord Melbourne called it 'choleric'.

Albert had changed his coat; he was standing at the window looking out.

'Albert.' She ran to him and threw herself into his arms.

He smiled tenderly. 'There now, it is over,' he said calmly.

'But it is *not* over. I did that to *you*.'

'The tea was tepid,' said Albert with a smile, 'and it was a very small cup.'

'Oh, my precious angel! How kind, how forgiving you are!'

'Shall we forget it?'

'Oh, yes, Albert. But I fear I never shall. It was unforgivable of me. It was so *ill-bred*.'

'Well, my dear, you would never listen to your mother and you only had your governess to tell you how to behave and I fear she flattered you because she was so eager to keep in your good graces.'

He held his breath. How would she take direct criticism of her idol?

She hesitated, about to defend her beloved Baroness, but so overcome with remorse was she that she let it pass.

'I should not have lost my temper, Albert.'

'No, my love, it is always a mistake to lose one's temper.'

'But you were very provoking.'

'Should one be provoked simply because an opinion adverse to one's own is expressed? However much one disagrees one should not, for instance ... throw a cup of tea.'

She laughed. 'Albert, I shall not throw another cup of tea at you.'

'Do so if you wish – providing of course it is not too hot and too large.'

She laughed; and he laughed with her. She clung to him, kissing him fervently. 'Oh my beloved angel, you are far too good for me,' she cried.

Albert's smile as he laid his face against her hair was a little complacent. This was progress, he felt.

## Chapter VII

## SHOTS ON CONSTITUTION HILL

The air was full of rumours. Almost every day there were cartoons in which the central figures were Victoria and Albert. Stories of their differences seeped out of the Palace. 'Victoria wears the breeches,' said the people gleefully. A certain amount of pleasure was expressed at this state of affairs. After all, was the comment, who was this Coburg Prince? More or less a pauper as Royalty went. Some might call him handsome – so he was in a pretty sort of way. But the ideal Englishman did not look like Albert, who was more like a pretty girl dressed up as a man. The way he sat his horse was foreign. And what of his brother? Ernest lingered on at the Court, didn't he? Was he hoping that some of the spoils would come his way? Ernest began to figure in cartoons holding out his hand, feeling in Albert's pocket. 'Don't forget me, brother,' was the caption. 'Spare a little for me.'

It was very unpleasant.

Worse still, news leaked out about the nature of Ernest's indisposition. There were shocked chortles. These Coburgs! They liked a good time ... at other people's expense if possible. That in itself was bad enough, but some people remembered that Albert's mother had been divorced, and the old scandal was revived. She had had a Jewish lover. Was it before Albert was born? People were sure it must have been. In which case their Coburg Prince was scarcely a prince at all, being a bastard.

This last rumour did not appear in print. That would have been too dangerous. But it did exist. Lord Melbourne did everything in his power to see that it did not reach the ears of the Queen.

Meanwhile Albert, remembering the success of the cup of tea incident, was eager to consolidate his new position and follow it up with a fresh advance. He was certain that the main reason why the Queen would not take him into her confidence as far as state matters were concerned was due to the influence of Lehzen; and his great desire was to discredit the woman in his wife's eyes.

The press liked the Baroness no better than it did the Prince. Her name constantly appeared and she was often invested with an almost sinister power. Albert, who was now reading the newspapers avidly, was continually discovering items of news about her. He read in the papers that no appointments were made without her consent; and this did not apply only to the domestic side of the Queen's life. He could not believe this to be

144

true, but, since the Queen did not confide in him, how could he be sure?

Of one thing he was certain. The domestic side of the household was mismanaged. With a true Teutonic talent for organization this had quickly become clear to him. He would have liked to make a clean sweep of many anomalies and he was determined to do so.

Often he was on the point of discussing the matter with the Queen, but, although he had come out victorious from the tea-cup upset, he was a little afraid of Victoria. There was great strength beneath her fluttering femininity and he had learned how stubborn she could be. At the moment when she had actually thrown the tea-cup there had been no love for him in those blazing blue eyes. What if she became so incensed with what she might call his interference that she ceased to love him? Stockmar had hinted that his trump card was her affection for him and that affection must not weaken. In fact it had to grow so strong that eventually she would give way to his wishes. That that could come about, he was certain; at the same time he knew that it could go the other way.

Perhaps the best way was to do it through his secretary, George Anson, who could impart his desire to Lord Melbourne and so it would reach the Queen. What a roundabout way for a man to ask a favour – no, his rights – from his wife! But of course she was no ordinary wife.

He was discovering George Anson to be a very capable young man. He had fought against having him in the first instance, but now he was realising that it was not such a bad bargain after all. Mr Anson was sympathetic and completely loyal and the fact that he was also secretary to the Prime Minister was not a drawback as he had feared. In fact he believed Mr Anson had represented him very sympathetically to Lord Melbourne, for that gentleman's attitude towards him had changed in the last weeks. He fancied that a little more respect was paid to him.

He told George Anson of his feelings and that he wished him to put the matter to Lord Melbourne not too forcefully – casually rather – as a suggestion rather than as a request.

Mr Anson understood perfectly; and so did Lord Melbourne, who told the Queen in that light and easy manner of which he was a master that perhaps the Prince might like to have – figuratively speaking – the keys of the household.

'But that the Baroness Lehzen always has had,' said the Queen.

Lord Melbourne smiled his quizzical smile which the Queen had always so admired. 'That was in the past. On the tenth of February a somewhat important change took place in Your Majesty's household.'

Victoria giggled – as she often did when alone with her dear Lord M. No one else made her laugh in quite the same way – not even Albert.

'Why don't you think about it?' suggested Lord Melbourne.

'I don't much care for that sort of change.'

'Not like that other of course,' said the incorrigible Lord M. 'I believe you cared for that one very much indeed.'

'Albert is an angel,' said Victoria.

'Even angels seek some occupation. That is why they are always depicted playing harps.'

She laughed aloud. 'Really you are most irreverent, Lord M.'

'I fear so,' he agreed. 'And I fear also that you may put this matter from your mind but do consider it.'

Considering things usually meant discussing them with the Baroness.

'Daisy dear,' said Victoria, when they were alone, 'I'm afraid my dearest Albert is getting a little restive.'

The Baroness's eyes had hardened a little. 'Surely not. He must be a very happy man.'

'Oh, he is happy in his marriage, Daisy, but he feels he doesn't make use of his talents.'

'He will want to use his talents to make himself a good husband to the best wife in the world.'

'Oh, darling Daisy, I am sure he feels that. But he wants to *do* something.'

'I doubt whether Lord Melbourne will want him *interfering* in politics.'

'I didn't mean politics. But I think he would like the keys of the household for instance.'

'The keys of the household?' This was her province. Once the Prince got his foot in he would attempt to oust her altogether; she had sensed the antagonism he felt for her. She had run the household ever since the Queen's accession. She was easy-going and the servants, who liked her for it, would want no change. Besides, it gave her power over appointments and that was a very pleasant thing to have. So she was seriously alarmed when the keys of the household were mentioned.

'It might take a burden off your shoulders, Daisy.'

'Burden. It is not a burden. Nothing I could do for my precious child could be a burden. And what would be said if the Prince concerned himself with the household? It is a woman's job. Imagine how the press would deal with that. There would be pictures of him in *skirts*.'

'Albert would hate that.'

'And what is more important, my love, so would you. What we all have to remember is that it is our duty and pleasure to serve the Queen ... in whatever capacity we are called upon to do so. What are titles? Do you remember on your accession you talked about a post for me, and I said, No, let there be no post. And you replied that I should be here as *your friend*. How well that has worked! Let the Prince be content to be your husband. I am sure that will be the best in the end.'

And Victoria was sure that her dear Baroness was right.

At the end of April Ernest left England, and Albert was very sad to say goodbye. Victoria came into the room where they were singing the song they had sung at the University *Abschied*, the student's farewell.

Victoria sat down quietly and listened, the tears in her eyes. 'You won't be so very far away, dear Ernest,' she said. 'You must visit us ... often.'

Albert said little; he was too moved for words.

'You see,' Ernest explained, 'we have spent so

148

much of our lives together.'

Victoria could always understand affection and she nodded; but Albert turned abruptly away and looked out of the window.

When Ernest left, Albert stood at the window watching his carriage until it could no longer be seen. She came and stood beside him, slipping her arm through his, but he took no notice of her. She believed he did not even know that she was there.

Her compassion changed to a slight irritation. After all she was his wife and surely a wife came before a brother.

After Ernest's departure Albert felt very lonely. He reviewed the situation as calmly as he could. Victoria was in love with him – more so than he was with her, although he had an affection for her. Perhaps she was more capable of affection than he was – but what sort of affection was it? Demonstrative certainly, but how deep did it go, when she would not give him an opportunity of sharing her state duties although she knew how passionately he wished it? Following Baron Stockmar's advice he was studying politics and this only made him the more bitter because he was discovering what a fascinating study it was and he would have delighted in sharing it with Victoria.

He felt alone in a strange land, now that his father and brother had left. He had Baron Stockmar of course and his friendship with Sir Robert Peel was growing. He and the Queen had not discussed Sir Robert since the tea-cup incident and he knew very well that she would disapprove of the connection. It was a very unhappy state of affairs.

And there was now no denying that the English disliked him. He was a German; he spoke English with an unmistakable accent; his manners were formal; he was solemn; he had no social graces; he found it difficult to be at ease in company and particularly the company of women. Even his looks were not those admired in England because, as the English said, they were not manly enough.

It was not only the people who disliked him. The royal family over whom he had been given precedence on Victoria's royal decree were angry over this. Why, asked the royal Dukes and their wives, should this upstart German princeling come before they did on all state occasions?

The Cambridges were particularly incensed because they had hoped that Victoria would marry their son George. George had spent a great deal of his childhood at Windsor with King William and Queen Adelaide because his parents were abroad and both the King and Queen would have liked to see a match between George and Victoria. This had given the Cambridges great hope but the Duchess of Kent and King Leopold had thought otherwise and Victoria's preference had certainly been for her Coburg cousin. Albert was beautiful; George Cambridge was an odious boy with a shocking complexion. That was her description of him; so the Cambridges sought to make life difficult for Albert.

When Victoria heard that the Duchess of Cambridge had remained seated while Albert's health was drunk she was furious.

'How dare she!' she cried to Lehzen. 'It is an insult to the Crown.'

'I suppose she feels that the Prince – apart from his connection with Your Majesty – is below her in precedence.'

'But the Prince is *my* husband.' Angry lights flashed in Victoria's eyes and Lehzen was quick to realise that she must be very careful when discussing the Prince, for determined as Victoria was to suffer no interference as the Queen, she was at the same time in love with her husband.

'Of course,' soothed the Baroness, 'the Duchess behaved very badly.'

'I should think so,' retorted Victoria, 'and I shall show my displeasure by not asking them to my next ball so that everyone will know how annoyed I am.'

Albert was very much aware of the slights and insults, but if Victoria would let him share her duties people would begin to respect him.

If only people would not be so tiresome, thought Victoria, everything could be wonderful. She had a husband whom she adored; she had a Prime Minister who was her very dearest friend and whom she trusted absolutely; she had darling Daisy who was as a mother to her; and she was the Queen. But Albert wanted to share her throne – and that was something she could not allow, for after all she was the Queen and he was only a prince from a small German dukedom; that horrid Sir Robert Peel was trying to oust Lord Melbourne who was really very lackadaisical about it and seemed to accept the fact that a Tory

Ministry was inevitable; and now dear Lehzen had taken a dislike to Albert and he to her.

How very irritating – and so foolish of them! No wonder she lost her temper with them now and then. And there were the newspapers who were always thinking up unpleasant things to say about her and Albert – and what was worse and so shocked Albert – *coarse* things. And the people didn't like him; they were always referring to him as 'the German'. All these irritations – not to mention the family who didn't like him, all except Mama of course, who doted on him and whom Albert was constantly visiting. Why did Albert have to be so contrary by forming a friendship with the Duchess and showing animosity to the Baroness, when she would have so much preferred it to be the other way round?

The uncles had hated Albert from the start when there had been all that fuss about precedence. Uncle Cumberland fortunately was safe in Hanover but he made his presence felt and was always thundering forth about his rights and what belonged to him. He was furious really because he had not become King of England, which he would have done of course if the English law had been like that of some countries which precluded women from mounting the throne.

And now Uncle Cambridge – probably annoyed because she had not invited him and his Duchess to her last ball, had made a really *coarse* remark about her and Albert at a banquet.

Albert hated banquets and she was always afraid that he would go to sleep over them. Often she had found it necessary to prod him during some entertainment. On this occasion Albert had seized an opportunity to leave a banquet early, not realising she supposed that the speeches had not been made. And when Uncle Cambridge made his speech he said that the Prince had left because he was so anxious to get home to spend the night with a very fine girl.

Albert was horrified when he heard this because the report said that the guests had all roared with laughter at the Duke's comment – coarse laughter.

'This sort of remark is obscene,' said Albert.

Previously Victoria would have been rather pleased that her uncle should have said that Albert was so anxious to return to her that he had left the banquet early, but Albert's disgust made her see it through his eyes.

'It cheapens us,' said Albert. 'It creates obscene images in the minds of the people.'

Of course, thought Victoria, it needed someone as *pure* as Albert to show how *disgusting* people could be.

She was furious with her Uncle Cambridge and the whole family.

'It is all because he wanted me to marry George Cambridge,' she said.

'They will always chatter in this way about us,' said Albert sadly, 'and the more so I think because I am only permitted to share the emotional side of your life.'

So they were back with the old controversy.

It seemed to Victoria that only with Lord Melbourne could she settle down to a cosy companionship.

She often thought of the old days when she and Lord Melbourne had been so important to each other. In fact if a day passed without her seeing her Prime Minister she had felt really miserable; and she used to hate it when he dined at Lady Holland's house for instance. She had several times told him that she could not understand what he saw in the woman and that she had a really vulgar mouth. Lord Melbourne always laughed at what he called her 'choleric outbursts and displays of the royal temper'; and very soon had her laughing with him.

He was now very happy that she was contented with her marriage (but perhaps she was not entirely contented, though she would be if Albert could be induced not to attempt to interfere) and he often told her so. But it did mean that her relationship with Lord Melbourne had changed a little. He was not quite so important to her, and perhaps she did stress a little too often that he would always be one of her dearest friends.

But in spite of the fact that things had changed and Lord Melbourne was showing his age a little he could still amuse her more easily than anyone else. Lord Melbourne loved to gossip and he knew so many interesting things about people. Albert, on the other hand, thought gossip demeaning. Albert was right of course. Oh, dear Albert was so good that he did dislike quite a lot of the things that had once seemed good fun – dancing, staying up late, gossiping about people. Compared with Albert, Lord Melbourne was really a little wicked ... or would have seemed so if she did not know that he was such a *good kind* man. Albert would say she was not being logical; but the fact remained that she did enjoy those sessions alone with Lord Melbourne in the blue closet when he would discuss China or Canada – which diversely situated countries were giving cause for concern at this time – and then switch to something quite frivolous in a way which in the past she had found so diverting and delightful – and still did.

It was Lord Melbourne who first brought her the news about Lord William Russell who had been found murdered in his house where he lived alone – apart from numerous servants of course.

'It is very mysterious,' said Lord Melbourne, settling comfortably in his chair for a cosy chat. 'Lord William was found in his bed, cold and stiff, so he had been dead some time. The bed was deluged with blood. His throat was cut so that his head was almost severed from his body.'

'How very shocking.'

'The details are too horrible for me to impart to Your Majesty,' said Lord Melbourne. 'Such affairs are best forgotten.'

'Oh, no,' said the Queen, 'I want to hear all. Poor Lord William, and what a sad shock for poor Lord John. How very tragic! It only seems a short time since poor Lady John died and left all those dear little children.'

Victoria was apprehensive thinking of Lady John, who had died in childbirth. It was certain now that she herself was pregnant and she was beginning to feel the effects. This in itself was endurable but when she thought of the actual event and what happened to poor Lady John she could be really frightened.

Lord Melbourne, who understood so much in what direction her thoughts were running, went back to the murder – a safer subject than child-bearing.

'They think that thieves entered by the back door and that when they were in Lord William's bedroom he awakened and disturbed them. Hence they cut his throat. The maid discovered Lord William's body in the morning. No one heard anything during the night.'

'I do hope they catch these wicked people. Poor, poor Lord John.'

'Oh, don't feel too sorry for him. I believe he is very interested in Lady Fanny Elliot.'

'What, Lord Minto's daughter?'

'His second daughter. The fact that Minto is First Lord of the Admiralty has meant that little Johnny has been frequently visiting Minto's house. It's clear that he is becoming very interested in Lady Fanny.'

'How old is she?'

'About twenty-five.'

'Little Johnny must be twice her age.'

'Yes, but it would be an excellent arrangement. Everyone cannot have a handsome young Prince for a husband, you know.'

'Of course they can't, and Johnny will be able to look after her and she will be able to look after all the children.'

'Exactly!'

'I feel a little protective towards Albert, being three months older than he is.'

'And his sovereign. A sovereign should always feel protective towards her subjects.'

'Is a husband a subject?'

'We are all Your Majesty's subjects.'

'It is difficult to regard husbands in that light.'

With his usual understanding Lord Melbourne agreed that it was.

'I shall be very pleased to hear that Little Johnny is happy again.'

'Oh, so far it is only a conjecture.'

The Queen burst into that loud laughter which in the old days Lord Melbourne had provoked so often.

'So,' she said with mock severity, 'this is just a piece of Lord M gossip.'

'It might well be that,' agreed Lord Melbourne.

'Well, I shall hope it is more for Johnny's sake. When do you guess the wedding will be?'

'He has yet to persuade the lady, don't forget. It is rather an undertaking, a widower with six children. Not every young woman wants a ready-made family.'

Victoria laughed and then was serious suddenly.

'Lord Melbourne, you know there will in due course be an addition to our family.'

Lord Melbourne bowed his head.

'Albert thinks we should make an announcement. He is so delighted, you see.'

'We are all delighted,' said Lord Melbourne, 'but I believe Your Majesty would think it more dignified to allow this good news to come out gradually.'

'I do. I shall tell Albert that that is how it shall be.'

Oh, yes, there was no doubt that she enjoyed her sessions in the blue closet with Lord Melbourne. If Albert were present – as she really believed he hoped he might be – it would not be quite the same. She did not want change and these delightful encounters could be spoilt by the fall of Lord Melbourne's government, his replacement by Sir Robert Peel, and the intrusion of Albert.

'Albert,' said the Queen, 'we shall make no announcement. The news will be known soon enough.'

'I think this is not good,' said Albert seriously.

'Oh, my dear love, Lord Melbourne and I have decided that it would be most undignified to mention the matter yet.'

Albert was silent.

'Albert, you are not sulking?'

'Sulking? Why should you think that?'

'Well, clearly because you wish an announcement to be made.'

'Oh, I understand by now that my wishes are of no account.'

'How can you say such a thing?'

'Because it is true.'

'But you know, Albert, I *always* wish to please you.'

Albert raised his eyebrows. 'No, I did not know this. In fact I thought the opposite. So much that I wish is ignored.'

'Now you are being difficult.' The royal temper was beginning to rise.

'If being difficult is stating the truth then that is so.'

'Albert, where are you going?'

'I am going out.'

'But we are in the middle of a conversation.'

'This conversation is over.'

'*I* do not consider it so.'

'But you must realise that it is. I wish an announcement to be made. The Queen and her Prime Minister do not. Therefore the matter is settled.'

Albert clicked his heels, bowed and went into his dressing-room.

'Albert!' she called; but he did not look back. 'Come here. Come here at once.'

He did not answer. So he thought he could go out when she wished to speak to him. She strode to his door. The key was in the lock on the outside. Triumphantly she turned it. Now he would not be able to go out. That would teach him to ignore her.

She waited. Soon he would try the door and come out. She saw the handle turn slowly. Now he knew that he was locked in. She expected him to hammer on the door, to demand to be released, to *beg* to be released perhaps. But there was silence from the other side of the door.

She waited; she put her ear to it. She could hear nothing, but she promised herself she soon would.

She sat down on the settee in the adjoining room where the quarrel had taken place. Very soon he would begin to agitate and then she would tell him that she would let him out if he promised to be good.

Good! It seemed a strange thing to ask Albert to promise. He *was* good. In fact his only fault was that at times he seemed to forget that she was the Queen. As she and Lord Melbourne had agreed it was certainly very difficult to uphold one's royalty in the family.

What a long time he was! She was growing impatient. She went again to the door, and listened. There was not a sound, so she retired and sat down again. Still nothing happened. Furiously she turned the key and opened the door. She gave a gasp of surprise for Albert was seated at the window, sketching the view.

'Albert!' she cried. 'What are you doing?'

He turned to smile at her. 'It is such a pleasant view from this window.'

She felt uncertain how to act. 'I thought you were going out,' she said.

'The Queen commanded otherwise.'

She turned away angrily but a few minutes later she was back.

She looked at the sketch and said: 'It's very good.'

'I will present it to you when it is finished,' said Albert with a smile. 'It will be a memento of the day you locked me in my room.'

'Oh, Albert!' she cried, full of contrition, 'that is something I don't think I shall *want* to be reminded of.'

'Why not?' he asked; and she noticed how beautifully blue his eyes were and she loved him dearly and she wished that there did not have to be these upsets.

She threw herself into his arms.

'Why,' she said, 'do there have to be these storms?'

160

Albert held her tenderly and replied, 'Well, at least it is not long before the sun comes out.'

She thought that was such a clever remark and that it was wonderful of Albert to be so calm although it did exasperate her now and then.

But the announcement was not made and it was as the Queen and Lord Melbourne had decided.

On her twenty-first birthday one of Albert's gifts to her was a very fine bronze inkstand.

'At least,' he said, 'I hope *this* will be of some use in your work.'

'Oh, Albert,' she cried, wilfully ignoring the implication, 'it is beautiful, and I shall think of you every time I use my pen.'

She was more affectionate on that day towards her mother than she had been for some time because Albert wished it. And since Sir John Conroy, who had been her mother's Comptroller of the Household in the old days and whose name had been linked with that of the Duchess rather scandalously, had now gone away, it did seem easier. Although of course the Baroness and the Duchess would never like each other. There were too many old scores to be settled.

'Twenty-one,' she declared. 'I feel very aged.'

The incorrigible Lord Melbourne said he quite understood that and he was sure she would feel much younger when she reached the age of forty.

There was of course a ball.

'No birthday could seem like one without that,' said the Queen. And how happy she was waltzing with Albert.

'I don't understand why you don't enjoy

dancing, Albert,' she said severely, 'because you dance perfectly.'

She noticed with pleasure that he did not want to dance with anyone else. How adorable he was, so single-minded in his devotion! And when one considered the manner in which some men behaved, she was very fortunate.

How she wished though that he enjoyed balls more. All through the evening he was glancing at the clock and he had hinted that in the next few months she would have to give up dancing. The thought depressed her, but she refused to consider it ... yet.

The day after her birthday Albert decided that he would have to take some action and he spoke to his secretary, George Anson, about his feelings. His position, he explained, was such an invidious one. He was completely shut out of the Queen's confidence. The nearest he had been to sharing that confidence was by being allowed to use the blotting paper on her signature. It made him very unhappy. He felt that the marriage would be a failure if the Queen would not allow him to share her confidence.

Mr Anson thought that the best thing that he could do would be to have a word with Lord Melbourne.

'That will be no good,' said Albert. 'I believe it is on Lord Melbourne's advice that there is this barrier between the Queen and myself.'

'I believe Lord Melbourne to be very eager for the Queen's happiness and this can only be if she remains happy in her marriage. If Your Highness will allow me to give him a hint of your feelings I am sure some good will come of it.'

With some reluctance the Prince agreed and as a result Lord Melbourne decided to approach the Queen.

When they were next in the blue closet he told her that he had something to say which was of a personal nature and he trusted she would forgive the meddling of an old man whose greatest concern in life was her happiness.

Those tears, which had always deeply moved her, were in his eyes and she cried: 'My dearest Lord M, but of course I know that you are the best and most faithful friend I ever had!'

'It is about the Prince.'

'Albert!'

Lord Melbourne nodded. 'He is not entirely happy, you know.'

'Not happy! Why, Albert is *perfectly* happy. He loves me as I love him. What more does he ask?'

'He asks a little more.'

'But what?'

'He feels shut out of your confidence.'

'But that is *quite* wrong.'

'Perhaps not entirely so. He complains that he knows nothing of what is going on in the country.'

'But that is state business.'

'Well, he is the Queen's husband. He is hurt because you talk of nothing but trivialities with him.'

'Nothing!' cried the Queen hotly. 'He says *nothing.*'

'Well, in a manner of speaking,' said Lord Melbourne soothingly. 'You know, there is no reason why you should not discuss affairs with him.'

The Queen was silent for a few moments, then she said: 'He might disagree and want things done differently from the way I ... we ... have decided they should be done.'

'There is no harm in the Queen's husband expressing an opinion.'

'I am afraid that if he did not agree there would be quarrels.'

Lord Melbourne looked at her quizzically. 'The *Prince* has a very mild temper.'

'But *I* have not.'

'Then it would be in Your Majesty's hands to preserve the harmony of married life.'

'So you think that I should discuss state affairs with Albert?'

'I think you might very well discuss anything with him.'

'Perhaps I have been a little indolent,' said Victoria. 'There are so many things I would rather talk of with Albert than state affairs.'

'A little sprinkling of state affairs will be the salt that adds the savour to the domestic potage.'

Within a very short time Albert discovered that he had won the first skirmish, and, although Victoria preferred to talk of love and cosy domestic affairs rather than politics, he was no longer completely shut out.

There was further disagreement with Albert over Mrs Caroline Norton, whom the Queen decided to receive at Court.

Mrs Norton's presence revived an old scandal which had concerned Lord Melbourne. A year before Victoria's accession the Hon. George Norton decided to sue for a separation from his wife Caroline and bring an action for damages against the man he accused of seducing her. That man was Lord Melbourne.

Fortunately for the Prime Minister the case of the Hon. George Norton v. the Lord Viscount Melbourne for 'criminal conversation' had produced a verdict for the defendant and Lord Melbourne had surprisingly emerged to continue as Prime Minister – something which it seemed few men could have accomplished.

The Queen, who was aware of the details of the case, wished to show her absolute trust in Lord Melbourne. Thus when Lady Seymour asked to be allowed to bring her sister, Mrs Norton, to Court, Victoria was willing to receive her.

'Not to have done so,' explained the Queen to her husband, 'would have been a condemnation of dear Lord Melbourne, and that I would never tolerate.'

'It seems a strange thing that Lord Melbourne should have been involved in *two* unsavoury affairs,' commented Albert.

'Lord Melbourne is a *brilliant* man and such men have many enemies ... wicked enemies. I know Lord Melbourne *very* well, perhaps better than anyone else, for he has been my constant companion since I mounted the throne and I say he is quite incapable of a dishonest act.'

'That may be,' said Albert, 'but the Queen must be beyond reproach and if she receives people to whom scandal has been attached this could arouse comment.'

'Then there must be comment,' cried Victoria, her eyes flashing. 'I would never condemn the innocent.'

Albert explained patiently that it was not a matter of condemning the innocent, but that no breath of scandal should attach to the Queen.

'There will always be scandal where there are wicked people to make it; and since to refuse audience to Mrs Norton would be construed as meaning that I suspected Lord Melbourne, I shall certainly receive her.'

And that was the end of the matter. She slipped her arm through Albert's. 'Dear, dearest Albert, you are so good yourself that you are inclined to be just a little severe with other people. Leave this to me. You need have no part in it.'

'As in so many things,' said Albert sadly. But he was hopeful. There was a change; and Lord Melbourne, on whom the Queen set such store, was not his enemy after all. He was even being very helpful.

He could believe sometimes that he was moving – though very slowly – in the right direction.

Lord Melbourne thanked the Queen for receiving Mrs Norton.

'Your Majesty's overflowing kindness is an example to all,' he said, with the inevitable tears in his eyes.

'Dear Lord Melbourne, it was the least I could do for a lady who has been so wronged. Albert was against it, but then Albert is so *good* that he does not always understand how easy it is for some people – who are less conventional in their behaviour – to find themselves in awkward situations. To tell the truth, Lord M, I sometimes wonder how I can live up to Albert's goodness.'

'Your Majesty has the kindest heart in the world,' said Lord Melbourne. 'And kindness is a much higher quality than moral rectitude.'

'Oh, Lord M, do you really think so?'

'I am sure of it. And I am sure the recording angel will agree with me.'

'Lord M, you say the most shocking things.'

'If they bring a smile to Your Majesty's lips I am satisfied.'

It was such good fun to be with Lord Melbourne, though the Opposition was giving them a great deal of trouble over the China policy, he said, and then there was the bill for the union of the two Canadas. He could see that trouble was looming in Afghanistan and he was not sure what would come out of that.

'That dreadful Sir Robert Peel, I suppose.'

Lord Melbourne raised his beautifully arched eyebrows, which she used to admire so much, and still did, of course. Lord Melbourne was a *very* handsome man but no one had *quite* the same breathtaking beauty as Albert.

'Oh, he's a good fellow, you know.'

'He's a *monster.*'

'All men, in a manner of speaking, are monsters who don't agree with the Queen and her Prime Minister – but apart from that they can be damned good fellows...Your Majesty will forgive my language.'

She bowed her head with a smile; but even then she thought: Albert would be shocked if he had heard the Prime Minister say damned in the presence of the Queen.

Yet how she had always loved Lord M's racy conversation! And if Albert ever joined them in the blue closet there would have to be a stop to it.

Lord Melbourne then went on to tell her that Lord William Russell's Swiss valet, Benjamin Courvoisier, had confessed to murdering his master. It was an intriguing story because the valet had come into his master's bedroom in Norfolk Place, Park Lane, stark naked so that there would be no blood on his clothes. He had borrowed from the Duke of Bedford's valet a copy of *Jack Shepherd* by the author Harrison Ainsworth and this had apparently inspired him. His motive was robbery as he wanted to get back to Switzerland.

Lord William always slept with a light by his bedside and someone from the opposite window saw the naked figure in the bedroom from across the road. He didn't come forward to give evidence because he was a well-known General and was spending the night there with a lady in society.

'How very shocking!' said Victoria.

'Well, that is the way of the world,' replied Lord Melbourne. 'Courvoisier has confessed. I doubt you will hear the story of the General and his lady friend, but it is being well circulated and the considered opinion seems to be that there is some substance in it.'

How very, very shocking! she thought. But she was glad to hear of it. Lord Melbourne did bring her all the little titbits of gossip which were *so* enlivening.

But she could not talk to Albert of them. He certainly would not approve.

They were going to Claremont. It would be good for her, said Albert, to get out into the fresh air more; he was going to be very strict with her, he told her playfully. They were going to rise early and retire to bed early; they would walk in the beautiful gardens; he would teach her something about the plants and birds – of which she was abysmally ignorant; they would sketch together; he would read aloud to her and they would discuss the book afterwards; they would sing duets together and play the piano. It seemed a delightful existence.

'Dear Albert,' she said, 'how careful you are of me.'

'But of course, my love, it is my duty.'

'Oh, Albert, is that all?'

'And my pleasure,' he added gently.

So to Claremont, but there were too many memories and even Albert could not disperse them.

She told him about dear Louie whom she had met there in her childhood. 'She had her own special curtsy and she was very much on her dignity until we were in her room alone … just the two of us, and then I was no longer the Princess Victoria, but her visitor. She used to make tea and we would sit drinking it while she talked of the old days, mostly of Princess Charlotte.'

'Yes. Uncle Leopold has told me so much about Claremont. It is an enchanting place.'

So more walking, playing music, retiring early

169

and rising early; it was all as Albert wished, and Victoria was not sorry for the change. But the place seemed haunted by Charlotte. Here Charlotte had given birth to the still-born child who should have been ruler of England; and Charlotte herself who was first to have been Queen, died also.

Louie was also dead. Sometimes when she went into her old room Victoria would imagine her coming out of the shadows to give that special curtsy to Victoria, the girl who had taken the place of Charlotte in her heart.

This had been Uncle Leopold's home and he wrote to her telling her how pleased he was that she was staying for a while at Claremont where she must, whether she wished it or not, be reminded of him. There, he reminded *her*, she had spent many happy days in her childhood. It had been a kind of refuge for her. He knew that she had been a little *plagued* at Kensington and how she had benefited from that respite she had enjoyed at Claremont.

It was true, of course. How she had adored meeting Uncle Leopold there! He had been the most important person in her life then, until she had become on such friendly terms with Lord Melbourne who, she now saw, had taken her uncle's place. And now there was Albert, dear beautiful Albert, whom she loved as she could never love anyone else in the world. There was a warning in Uncle Leopold's letter. He had heard that she was being just a little dictatorial with Albert. Oh, people did not understand how difficult it was to be the Queen and a wife as well.

She may have been given an impression, wrote Uncle Leopold, that Charlotte had been imperious and rude. This was not so. She had been quick and sometimes violent in her temper, but she had been open to conviction and always ready to admit she was in the wrong when this was proved to be the case. Generous people, when they saw that they were wrong, and that reasons and arguments submitted to them were true, frankly admitted this to be so. He knew that she had been told that Charlotte had ordered everything in the house and liked to show that she was mistress. That was untrue. Quite the contrary. She had always tried to make her husband appear to his best advantage and to display respect and obedience to him. In fact sometimes she exaggerated this to show that she considered the husband to be the lord and master.

He must tell her an amusing little incident. Charlotte was a little jealous. There had been a certain Lady Maryborough whom she fancied he had a liking for. This was absolutely untrue. The lady was some twelve or perhaps fifteen years older than he was but Charlotte thought he had paid too much attention to her. Poor Charlotte! At such times she was a little uncontrolled, which if she had become Queen would never have done. Her manners had been a little brusque, he confessed, and this at times often pained the Regent – 'your Uncle George'. This had its roots in shyness for she was very unsure of herself – probably due to her extraordinary upbringing – and was constantly trying to exert herself.

*I had – I may say so without seeming to boast – the manners of the best society in Europe, having early mixed in it and been rather what is called in French de la fleur des pots. A good judge, I therefore was, but Charlotte found it rather hard to be so scrutinised and grumbled occasionally how I could so often find fault with her.*

She understood the meaning between the lines of Uncle Leopold's long letter. How very similar her position was to that of Charlotte! Charlotte, of course, was never the Queen, but everyone thought she would be. The only daughter of King George IV – and married to Uncle Leopold. Uncle Leopold *was* a little like dear Albert. He was extremely handsome, clever and liked to take a part in affairs. Of course he was Albert's uncle as well as hers.

She thought a great deal about Charlotte. She had heard so much of the happy days her cousin had spent here, first under the adoring eyes of dear Louie and later under the tenderly corrective ones of Uncle Leopold.

It was so easy to substitute herself for Charlotte. They were of an age; one had a crown and for the other it must have seemed almost a certainty that the crown would have been hers. During the months when she awaited her baby she must have walked in these gardens of Claremont. Her husband Leopold was here, just as Victoria's husband Albert was. The husbands would even have looked alike for there was a strong family resemblance.

She could almost identify herself with Charlotte.

They were of an age, both just married, both in love, both pregnant and both aware of the burden of the crown.

She went to the rooms which had been Charlotte's. There the young girl had had her confinement. Her child had been born dead ... and she poor girl had followed after.

It was all so similar. How often during her life had Charlotte wondered whether there would be a brother to supplant her and block her way to the throne? How often had Victoria wondered whether Uncle William and Aunt Adelaide would have a child? Victoria could see those lovers Charlotte and Leopold and it was as though they were in truth Victoria and Albert.

She had made a habit of going to the room in which Charlotte had died, and thinking of what her cousin must have suffered. It was like poor Lady John Russell.

'I am afraid,' she whispered, 'that it will happen to me.'

One day when she went to the room and stood there looking at the bed and imagining that last scene which Uncle Leopold had described in detail – how he had knelt by the bed and wept for his beloved Charlotte and how her last thoughts had been for him – she was filled with terror because it seemed like a recurring pattern. The child within her would be as that other child; she would be as the poor princess who had died in her ordeal, and dear Albert would be collapsing by the bed in his grief as Uncle Leopold had. Yes, a tragic pattern.

The door handle turned silently. She gave a

gasp. She thought it was the ghost of Charlotte come back from the grave to warn her that her end was near.

It was Albert.

'Victoria, what are you doing in this room?' he asked.

'I come here often.'

'I know, and I ask why.'

'In this room my cousin Charlotte died having her baby. Had she lived she would have been Queen of England.'

'You should not come here, Victoria.'

'I feel impelled to do so.'

Then Albert spoke with the authority of a husband. 'We are leaving Claremont tomorrow,' he said.

She just lay against him, comforted. For once he was to have his way.

They were back in London and, although Albert disliked the capital and was never in it without planning his next visit to the country where he might breathe the fresh air which made him feel so much more alive and healthy, he was excited and certainly apprehensive because he had been asked to preside at a meeting. This was to promote the abolition of the slave trade and he was to make his first speech in England.

He was very nervous, he told Victoria. 'I have to convince the people of my serious interest in affairs,' he told her. 'I do not wish them to think me frivolous.'

'They could never think you that, Albert,' she told him fondly.

She had been very happy since he had drawn her away from her brooding at Claremont. 'How very silly I was,' she had said. 'And you, dearest Albert, showed me so in the nicest possible way.'

Yes, his attempt at playing the masterful husband had succeeded; and now, due to the joint efforts of Stockmar and Lord Melbourne, he was allowed to develop his interest in what was going on and this public appearance was the result.

'It is very difficult to speak in English,' said Albert.

'You will manage admirably,' the Queen told him. 'Let me hear your speech.'

It was short and, she said, excellent. She corrected his pronunciation and suggested he rehearse it again. She was delighted because she quickly knew it off by heart and could listen and correct without having to have the written version before her.

'It is well to be a little nervous,' the Queen assured him. 'I do believe that all the best speakers are. Lord Melbourne says that when he is completely at ease he never really speaks well.'

'Then I am comforted,' said Albert, 'because I am very nervous.'

'Dearest Albert, I shall be thinking of you all the time.'

'Which will give me the best of all comforts,' he told her. When he returned to her he was elated. There had been loud applause, he said, and everyone had seemed so kind as though they liked him.

'But of course they liked you,' she told him indulgently. 'How could they possibly do anything else unless they were *monsters*.'

So he was happier. He was really beginning to have some importance. His interest in music was talked of and he was offered a directorship of one musical society.

Lord Melbourne and Baron Stockmar looked on with benign pleasure.

Soon he will have a big say in affairs, thought Stockmar.

That will keep him out of mischief, was Lord Melbourne's opinion.

It was ten days after Albert had made his speech, a lovely warm June day, ideal, said Albert, for a drive. Why should they not take one in the droshky?

Victoria said that it would be delightful. 'There is nothing I really like so much as riding out with you, Albert, especially when the people cheer us. I think they like to see us together.'

Albert said that he found their drives in the country more delightful.

'Dear Albert, I must make you try to like my capital city a little.'

'There are too many people and the air is not as fresh as it is in the country.'

'But it is more exciting. I have always *loved* London more than any other place.'

'Then I must try to make you enjoy the pleasures of the country.'

She smiled at him fondly. 'Though I must confess, dear Albert, that the place I love best is where you are.'

'Then let us be in the country more often and

you will be happy.'

'But I am just a little happier in London with you than I am in the country with you.' She laughed loudly. 'Oh, I shall have to make *you* love London. Think, there is the opera; there are concerts; there is the play; there are the streets and the people and everything is so lively.'

Albert did not answer; but he was determined that they should escape to the country whenever possible.

The droshky was at the door. They got in and drove away from the palace towards Constitution Hill, their escort following. There were plenty of people in the streets and they recognised their little sovereign at once. She looked very pretty seated beside her handsome husband; the youth of the pair was very appealing.

As she sat there smiling she suddenly heard the sound of a shot close by. Albert had flung his arms about her as though to shield her.

'My God!' he cried. 'Don't be frightened.'

'Frightened...' she stammered; and then she saw the man stepping out into the road. He held a pistol in either hand. In that moment he fired straight at her. She bent forward just in time and the bullet went over her head.

The crowd was shouting: 'Get him. Kill him.'

There was pandemonium on the footpath; she saw the man start to run but someone had seized him.

'They've caught him,' said Albert. The horses were whipped up and the droshky drove back towards the palace.

She was weeping in Albert's arms.

'Oh, Albert, it is so terrible. That man tried to kill me. Imagine. He hated me so much that he wanted me dead.'

Albert stroked her hair.

'He was a madman,' he said.

'But he hated me. He wanted me dead. He must have done. He had risked his own life to try to take mine.'

'He did not hate *you* for yourself, my dearest. He wanted to kill the Queen. You'll see, it will turn out that he was mad.'

'To think, Albert ... every time I go out ... someone could *kill* me.'

'My love, how do any of us know what will happen to us from one day to the next? You must not take this personally. This is a shot at the Crown ... not at Victoria. Your Uncle George was shot at many times and so was your grandfather. People do these things; it is because of a madness.'

'You would have protected me with your life, Albert. I shall never forget the first thing that entered your mind was to shield me.'

'It is what I wish to do for the rest of our lives.'

'Oh, Albert, how wonderful you are. I don't deserve such a good kind husband.'

Albert said that they would try to be worthy of each other.

Then she said: 'I must not cry, must I? I must remember that am the Queen. I must learn to be calm and to take no notice when these things happen. I know my grandfather was very calm.'

'So were you, my love. You drove on back to the

palace. Many women would have fainted. Didn't you hear the people cheering?'

'I found the courage, dearest Albert, because you were beside me.'

Lord Melbourne called at the palace. The Queen was resting. The Prince had insisted that she should. He himself saw Lord Melbourne.

The Prime Minister expressed his deep concern for the Queen's health.

'My great anxiety,' said the Prince, 'was that the shock might have been injurious to her condition.'

'I trust not,' said Lord Melbourne.

'I feel that had it been so there would by now have been some sign. She appears to be well – just a little shaken, of course.'

'Very natural,' said Lord Melbourne, 'and wise of Your Highness to insist on her resting.'

'She will be gratified that you have called. I will acquaint her with the fact at the earliest possible moment.'

Lord Melbourne studied the young man gravely. A good fellow, he thought; a little too solemn to make a very gay companion for Victoria. He doubted there was as much laughter between them as there was when the Queen and her Prime Minister were together. But perhaps a little seriousness would not come amiss. She was devoted to him. That was obvious. He hoped she would be as happy as she deserved to be, which was very happy indeed. She was so affectionate, so eager to be good, although fond of pleasure – and why not? Perhaps she would teach this solemn young gentleman to be a little more gay, which would not be a bad thing.

But her happiness was bound up in the Prince. The marriage had already had its difficulties, which was understandable, considering the position and that rather imperious nature and choleric temper of Her Majesty.

Lord Melbourne loved her. She had changed his life three years ago when she had become the Queen. He had been responsible to some extent for making her what she was, and her fresh youth, her exuberant warm-hearted nature, seemed to him quite charming. He had to concede his place in her affections, he knew, for once he had been the most important man in her life. Being Lord Melbourne he would graciously step aside and try to make life as easy as possible for the young married pair.

'This terrible affair raises a problem,' he said now. 'It is a difficult subject to raise but however unpleasant – and of course unlikely – in view of Her Majesty's position, it must be arranged.'

Albert nodded. He guessed to what Lord Melbourne was referring.

'The Queen's life might have ended this afternoon.'

Albert turned pale. He does love her, thought Lord Melbourne; not with the same intense emotion that she has for him, but he loves her in his quiet, restrained way. Who could help it?

'It is distressing even to think of such a likelihood,' went on Lord Melbourne. 'But we must do so. There is another facet. In a short time the Queen will become a mother. She has an ordeal to face which has, on occasions, resulted in death.

Forgive me, but these possibilities – though I hasten to add that in this case they are im-probabilities – must be discussed.'

'I realise that,' said Albert.

'A Regent should be appointed and as you know it is always necessary to prepare these matters in advance of the improbability.'

'Whom would you suggest as Regent?'

'I feel, and I am sure that the Queen would agree with me, that the best man for the post would be the Queen's husband.'

'I can only trust that such an eventuality will never arise.'

'Amen,' said Lord Melbourne.

Lord Melbourne wrote to the Queen that he was anxious about Her Majesty and was pleased to learn that she was well on the morning following that unfortunate incident.

'It is impossible not to shudder at the thought of it,' wrote Lord Melbourne.

Viscount Palmerston wrote congratulating the Queen on her escape and begged to be allowed to express the horror with which he had heard of the diabolical attempt.

Uncle Leopold's letter said that he could not find words strong enough to express his horror at what had happened and his happiness and delight to hear of her escape from a danger which was very great indeed.

When Lord Melbourne arrived he kissed both her hands and the tears started to his eyes.

'It was terrible ... terrible...' he said.

'But I escaped and all is well.'

'For which I can never be sufficiently grateful.'

'And what of the man who tried to kill me?'

'They have captured him. He is a barman named Edward Oxford. He is mad and will spend the rest of his days in a lunatic asylum.'

'Poor man! How dreadful for him. But I am glad he was not in his right mind when he tried to kill me.'

'He will have no opportunity to make more attempts.'

'Dear Lord Melbourne,' said the Queen, 'I believe you are more shaken by this affair than I am.'

Lord Melbourne said he thought that was very likely.

## Chapter VIII

## THE PRINCESS ROYAL

The Baroness was disturbed. It was becoming increasingly clear that the Prince was establishing himself more firmly in the household and the closer he came to the Queen, must inevitably, as the Baroness saw it, drive a wedge between herself and Her Majesty.

Victoria was as devoted and loyal as ever; Louise Lehzen held her sway by a mixture of complete devotion, overwhelming affection and a touch of the old governess authority which she had used to good effect when Victoria was a child. With the arrival of Lord Melbourne in the Queen's life, Lehzen's position had not been affected. She was still in command of the household. A husband, however, was a different proposition and the antagonism between her and Albert grew every day.

She was terrified that one day he would ask for her dismissal. Victoria would never agree to that and for all her femininity and her demonstrations of affection, Lehzen knew better than anyone that behind this was a will of iron. She had to keep her hold on Victoria's affections and this she could have done until the end of her life, but since Albert had come and shown so clearly that he was her enemy she was beginning to feel afraid. The fact that Lord Melbourne had now become his ally added to her perturbation.

It had been very different when the Prime Minister had treated the Prince as of not much account, merely brought to the country to be a handsome husband for Her Majesty and of course to provide the heir. But if Lord Melbourne was going to treat him seriously and he was to have more say in affairs – and that meant affairs of the household as well as those of state – then the Baroness Lehzen could see trouble.

'For,' she told herself, as she sat disconsolately chewing her caraway seeds, 'we were against each other from the first.'

They understood each other too well. Two Germans living in a foreign land; in their way they were recognizable types. Albert's precise discipline, his love of order, his seriousness, his lack of humour, were characteristics which the Baroness had seen so many times in her fellow country-men. Her determination to keep what she had, her unswerving devotion, that sublimation of herself to an ideal – Albert would understand this.

The trouble was that each felt that their only way to succeed was to be rid of the other.

At first the Baroness had been delighted to see Albert relegated to blotting the Queen's signature; she was the one who was in the Queen's confidence; she had now and then read state papers and given her opinion; and the dear sweet Queen had listened as attentively as she used to in the old days when Lehzen told her stories as she did her hair.

But between them, Anson the secretary, Baron Stockmar and Lord Melbourne were changing that.

And now to make him Regent was the last straw.

Victoria noticed her preoccupation.

'Dearest Daisy, what is the matter?' she asked. 'You really are rather absent-minded, you know.'

'Well, I may as well say it. You notice everything. I always did declare that it was impossible to hide anything from you. I feel put out.'

'But why?'

'It is this Regency. The idea! I just can't bear to think of it.'

'Oh, *that*,' said the Queen, 'it's just a precaution, you know, in case…'

Lehzen turned away. 'How could they *think* of such a thing.'

Victoria put her arms about Lehzen and hugged her. 'You dear stupid old Lehzen,' she said, 'it doesn't mean I'm going to *die* because they have arranged for a Regency.'

'I don't like it.'

'Oh, dearest Daisy, nor do I. When I think of what lies before me ... and poor dear Lady John Russell...'

'My dearest love, I shall be at hand. I fear I may be rather brusque with *some people* if they try to keep me from you.'

'You need have no fear of being kept from me. *I* should never allow that.'

'I feel happier now.'

'Silly Daisy! You should never have thought of such a thing.'

'I can't help it. I don't like this idea of a Regency.'

'It's not so much the baby as the fact that that man shot at me. It could happen again and if it did ... well there would be no sovereign, so a Regent would be necessary for a time.'

'I can't bear to think of it. If I could get my hands on that fellow who tried to hurt you...'

'He was mad, Daisy. Lord Melbourne says he will be sent to an asylum.'

'It *terrifies* me. I want to be at hand *always* to make sure.'

'And so you shall. But don't be alarmed, Daisy. Remember I have always been in some sort of danger. Do you remember how terrified you all used to be that my Uncle Cumberland was going to try to do away with me?'

'And not without reason.'

'Oh, Uncle Cumberland is a very wicked man. I've no doubt of that. And even now he's the

King of Hanover he probably still dreams of taking the crown of England. He must be gnashing his teeth now that he knows that I'm going to have a baby. Oh, Lehzen, do you think that *he*... I mean do you think that this man Oxford was paid by my uncle...'

'He was a madman,' said Lehzen.

'Of course. Uncle Cumberland wouldn't dare. I wonder why uncles are always cast as villains. I suppose it was since the Princes were murdered in the Tower and their uncle Richard III was suspected of the deed.'

'Uncles are sometimes in a position to benefit from the death of their nephews and nieces. Like Richard III and the King of Hanover. But you are going to be safe. I shall see to that.'

'When I was little I had a vague notion that I was in danger, and it was easy to see why. I was never allowed to be in a room alone and someone always had to accompany me even down the stairs.'

'That was your mother's orders.' Lehzen was silent suddenly. There was a change in that direction. Victoria was seeing her mother far more than she did before her marriage and this was due of course to the Prince who was on very good terms with her.

'Why, Daisy,' said the Queen, 'there are tears in your eyes.'

'Oh, I was thinking of those old days. I can see you now studying, riding, playing with the dolls. I shall never forget the time when you saved up six shillings to buy a doll you wanted and then gave the money to a beggar. You were such a dear

186

good little girl.'

'Not always, Daisy. Remember the storms.'

'Oh, that temper of yours.'

The Baroness sniffed and went to a drawer, 'I have a handkerchief here,' she murmured, and brought out a sheet of newspaper. She thrust it back into the drawer so hastily that Victoria's curiosity was aroused.

'What is it you're trying to hide, Daisy?' she asked.

The Baroness looked confused. 'Oh, it's nothing...'

But Victoria had taken it from her hands.

It was a picture of Albert – easily recognizable – posing before a mirror while he tried on the Crown. *The Regent* was the caption beneath.

Victoria laughed, 'How they seize on everything! As if he would be smiling like that when he could only be Regent if I were very ill. Ah, what's that? Is it another?'

It was. This was a picture of Albert holding a pistol. His target was the Crown. 'Ah, mein dear,' was the caption on this one. 'I shall see if I can't hit you.'

Victoria was angry suddenly. 'Oh, how dare they! They are suggesting that Albert would like to see me dead. And what nonsense, because he wouldn't have the Crown if I were. Oh Daisy, how horrid people can be! But one thing, no reasonable person would believe that of Albert.'

'People know how ambition can make people do all sorts of things.'

'Men like Uncle Cumberland, not men like Albert. Albert is so good, Lehzen. No one but

187

myself knows how good.' She tore the cartoons in half. 'They are only fit to be burned,' she said.

But the Baroness wondered whether she had begun to ask herself how ambitious Albert was. After all he had been excessively hurt because he was not allowed to share her state duties.

'They are ridiculous,' agreed the Baroness. 'We all know that the Prince is not energetic enough for ambition. He would never wish to work as Your Majesty does. Why, he would fall asleep during the lengthy discussions on matters of state.'

'Oh, I think he would be interested. He has a very good brain. It is dancing that makes him tired, and light conversation and things like that.'

'He will have to change,' said Lehzen, trying to speak lightly. 'It will never do for him to go against the wishes of the Queen. What a glutton you always were for your dancing. You could dance all night without being fatigued.'

Victoria sighed. 'Yes, I wish Albert did enjoy dancing more. But then to him it would seem a little frivolous.'

'Nobody could take their duties more seriously than you do,' said Lehzen hastily.

Victoria burst out laughing. 'I heard you the other night once more telling your neighbour at dinner how wonderful I was.'

'I said nothing but the truth and I think it only right that people should do all in their power to please Your Majesty.'

Victoria sighed. She was thinking what fun it would be if Albert loved to dance as much as she did.

In August it was the Queen's duty to prorogue Parliament. It was one which she would rather have avoided, particularly in her condition. If only Albert could be beside her she would have welcomed his support. In the last months she had begun to rely on him far more than she had believed possible.

She talked it over with Lord Melbourne in the blue closet.

'Well,' said the Prime Minister, 'he can attend of course but not in your carriage. There would be an outcry. Your uncles would be pointing out that he had stepped out of place.'

'How I wish that I could have made him a king.'

'No Parliament should make a king. If they did they would soon be trying to unmake them, as I pointed out when this matter of the Prince's rank was discussed. Parliament did once. You remember what happened to your ancestor, Charles I?'

Victoria nodded. 'Poor Charles. He tried to be a good king.'

'But he believed in the Divine Right of Kings which in a monarch is asking to get one's head lopped off.'

'But the people were very anxious to welcome his son Charles II back to England. I think that one of the passages in history I like best is the return of Charles with all the bells ringing and the people singing in the street, all so happy because they had a king once more.'

'Old Noll Cromwell was too serious. He didn't make them laugh.'

'It astonishes me how people prefer sinners to saints.'

'Begging Your Majesty's pardon, but the gay are not necessarily sinners, nor are the humourless saints ... except often in their own opinion, which is not always the truth.'

'Perhaps our own opinions of ourselves are rarely the truth.'

'They are often a little prejudiced in our favour,' agreed Lord Melbourne.

'Well,' replied the Queen, 'we know our own motives, which other people don't. Oh, I do wish people would be a little *kinder* to Albert.'

'They will be in due course. He has to prove himself first. Already he is making strides in the right direction.' She looked pleased. 'And the people are very happy,' went on Lord Melbourne, 'to see their sovereign contented in her marriage. You should show yourselves often together; and when the child is born they will be delighted.'

'Which brings us back to what we were discussing originally. I do wish Albert could ride in *my* carriage for the prorogation.'

'I am sure that would give him a great deal of pleasure.'

'Myself also,' said the Queen.


She was at luncheon when a message came from Lord Melbourne. It must be important, she felt, for him to send it at such a time.

With trembling fingers she opened it.

Lord Melbourne, it seemed, had made a discovery. Queen Anne's husband, Prince George of Denmark, whose position had been similar to that of Albert in almost every detail, had very often behaved unceremoniously and by so doing established a precedent. There had been an occasion when on the prorogation of Parliament he had ridden to Parliament in the Queen's carriage.

A precedent had been established, therefore it was perfectly in order for Albert to ride in Victoria's carriage.

'You have good news?' asked Albert.

Beaming with happiness she handed him the letter.

They had ridden together to Parliament; she had read her speech and Albert had been beside her all the time.

'Dearest Albert,' she said, when they had returned to the Palace, 'I felt so comforted to have you there.'

'It is my place to be always beside you,' said Albert.

And he was pleased.

She thought how wonderful it was to be married and deeply in love with one's husband. The only trouble was that in just over three months' time she had to face her ordeal. She was feeling well and taking exercise and had completely recovered from the discomforts of the first months. When she could forget the horrors of childbirth – and surely royal childbirth was worse than other people's because it was such a public affair – she was perfectly happy.

She told the Baroness what a success the prorogation had been.

'It was always something I wanted to avoid,' she said. 'That and the opening. But it seemed so different this time because Albert was there, looking so proud and so *beautiful* that I am sure I read my speech better than I ever did before.'

'You have always read your speech *perfectly*,' said Lehzen rather sourly.

The time for her confinement was drawing near. The child should be born at the beginning of December. Lehzen was busy making layettes; she was anxious that no one else should do this. She would have liked to shut the Queen away and allow no one to come near her. That was out of the question and Victoria even became a little irritated by what she called Lehzen's fussiness. She preferred to forget the coming ordeal.

There was plenty in the political situation to help her do this.

'Trouble, trouble, trouble,' said Lord Melbourne. 'And far more intense in Your Majesty's far-flung dominions than ever it was at home.'

'I'm thankful that the Union of the Canadas Bill was passed without alarm, but a majority of nine was not very much on your policy in China.'

'That's true, but you must always be prepared for our defeat. I believe Your Majesty is aware of this.'

The Queen's face hardened. 'It is something I pray will never happen.'

'It is not easy to pass rules with only a slender majority, you know.'

'But you have managed to for some time.'

Lord Melbourne grimaced. 'With Your Majesty's help. But for your refusal to change your bed-chamber ladies, it would be Sir Robert Peel who would be sitting here today.'

'It would most certainly not. *He* shall *never* be invited into the blue closet.'

Lord Melbourne laughed. 'But seriously,' he told her, 'you should prepare yourself for a change of government. Talk it over with the Prince.'

'Albert is inclined to admire Sir Robert Peel. I never want to talk about that man with Albert because it makes my temper rise.'

'You will overcome that dislike. It is not good for a queen to bear personal animus towards a great statesman.'

'I shall never like Sir Robert Peel,' said the Queen shortly.

Aunt Augusta had become very ill and the family knew that she was dying. The Queen, who had an enduring affection for her family, was deeply affected. She had always been a pet of the aunts and was in constant touch with them. They looked forward to her visits and she had been determined from the time of her accession that they should know that the Queen never forgot the duties and affections of the niece.

There was poor Aunt Sophia, about whom scandal still lingered, although it was long ago when she had borne her illegitimate son. Sophia's eyesight was fading fast, for she suffered from cataracts, and this was a great sadness for she had loved tatting and embroidering and many a bag fashioned by Sophia's hands had come into Victoria's possession. Now one of her great pleasures were the visits from her dear little niece who had become the most important lady in the land. There was dear old Aunt Gloucester whom Victoria had always thought of as a sort of grandmother. And poor Augusta who now needed special attention.

Victoria was always 'her darling' and she referred to her as such.

'Is that my darling come to see me?' she would say; or, 'I hear my darling was such a success at this or that function.'

It was very touching, said Victoria.

She would sing to Aunt Augusta when she visited her – very often some of Aunt Augusta's own compositions, for in her youth this aunt had been quite talented. Had she not been a princess she might have been a musician or an artist. 'But I was not encouraged,' she once told Victoria. 'My mother, your Grandmama, Queen Charlotte, believed I did my duty by walking the dog and making sure that her snuff box was filled. She was a great snuff taker. And your grandfather, King George III, thought that there was only one musician worthy of the name and that was Handel.'

Poor dear Aunt Augusta who had never really done what she wanted to!

Victoria was always interested to hear stories of her aunts' early life with her grandparents. It was pleasant to feel that one belonged to a family, and because it happened to be the royal family that did not mean that it was in all fundamental details different from any other. One of Lord Melbourne's great charms was that he had lived such a long time and could enchant her with stories of the past – many concerning the eccentric members of her family.

It was so sad, therefore, to contemplate the breaking with yet another of these links with the past.

Aunt Adelaide, the Dowager Queen, nursed Aunt Augusta. Adelaide could always be relied on at such times. There was something very unroyal about Adelaide, and Victoria had loved her from the time when she had presented her with the Big Doll and tried so hard to bring her to the parties of which Victoria's Mama did not approve.

Albert said: 'You must not wear yourself out, my love, with these visits to your aunt's sick room.'

'But she loves to see me, Albert. I could not fail her.'

Albert always understood the need to do one's duty.

It was rather a relief when on the 22nd of September Aunt Augusta died. All the family were gathered together in the death chamber, but it was the Dowager Queen Adelaide who had nursed her through her illness, to whose hand she clung at the end.

Albert took his wife back to the palace where he masterfully insisted that she rest. As soon as the funeral was over he was going to take her down to Claremont to get her right away.

Lehzen said that surely Claremont was not a good choice; but the Queen, since Albert had suggested it, decided that she would go there.

Once in the old mansion she realised that it had been rather a mistake to go there. Lehzen was right. It would have been much better to have gone to Windsor.

She found herself hurrying past the room in which Charlotte had died and she began to brood on her own ordeal which was very close now.

Lehzen at last insisted on their return. A very unpleasant rumour was being circulated that the Queen had had a premonition that like her cousin Charlotte she was going to die in attempting to give the nation its heir. It was for this reason that she had gone to Claremont. One story was that she was having the lying-in chamber decorated in exactly the same way it had been done at the time of Charlotte's death.

'My precious love,' said Lehzen, 'it is quite morbid to be here. You should be in London. That will be much better for you. It was a foolish idea to come here.'

Victoria was silent, knowing whose idea it was. But she was glad to return to London.

The government was involved in such political trouble, and so great was Victoria's fear that it would fall, that she forgot her personal discomfort.

The oriental situation was very grave. Afghanistan was in a state of uproar; fighting had broken out in China and Lord John Russell and Lord Palmerston were disagreeing with each other within the party.

'A split in one's own ranks is more dangerous than any attack from the Opposition,' said Lord Melbourne. 'It could bring the government down.'

In concern the Queen wrote to her Prime Minister:

*For God's sake do not bring on a crisis; the Queen really could not go through that* now, *and it might make her* seriously ill *if she were to be kept in a state of agitation and excitement if a crisis were to come on; she has already had so much lately in the distressing illness of her poor aunt to harass her.*

Albert, who had had a desk brought into her study and placed beside hers, had been reading the documents which had been arriving at the palace and she found how comforting it was to discuss these affairs with him. 'Now,' he said, 'I can be of real use to you.'

'Dear Albert,' she murmured, 'that will be a great comfort.' It was amazing how dependent pregnancy made her feel and what pleasure she took in seeing that handsome face so near her own. She could tell him of her fears of the government's collapse and he could soothe her by replying that if the government did fall it was her duty to be just towards any new government which the country might desire.

'I could never accept that dreadful Peel man,' she said.

'But my dear love is a queen and would never forget that, and, however difficult you found it, remember I should be there to help you.'

'Yes, Albert,' she said meekly.

It was very comforting to talk to Albert about that wicked man Mehemet Ali who was causing all the trouble. But the French were being their usual difficult selves and once again Uncle Leopold was deploring the English attitude towards that country.

England with Russia, Prussia and Austria had delivered an ultimatum to Mehemet Ali insisting that he leave North Syria or be ejected by force. France, although deeply involved, and committed to help, stood aloof, which made the situation a very dangerous one, and conflict in Europe must of course give greater cause for alarm than what was happening in the East.

Uncle Leopold wrote that while he did not think France had acted wisely he could not help adding that England had behaved harshly and insultingly towards France. Victoria was able to reply that no one but France was to blame for her unfortunate position, for that country was committed to join the allies and had refused.

*Still,* she wrote, *though France is in the wrong, and* quite *in the wrong, still I am most anxious, as I am sure my Government also are, that France should be pacified and should again take her place among the five great powers...*

*Albert, who sends his love, is much occupied with Eastern affairs and is quite of my opinion...*

It was comforting to be able to write that. Uncle Leopold had always been anxious that Albert should have the opportunity to advise her. Well now he had, and he was on her side. Not that Albert's opinion could weigh against that of Lords Melbourne and Palmerston; but there was no doubt that Albert could offer his opinions, which Lord Melbourne said were balanced and reasonable.

As the weeks passed there were continually dispatches from the Prime Minister and the Foreign Secretary; and they and other Ministers were calling frequently at the palace. The oriental controversy aggravated by the intransigent attitude of the French was the matter of the moment.

'When the baby is born it ought to be called Turko-Egypto,' said the Queen with grim jocularity.

It was November and, although the baby was not expected before the beginning of December, three doctors – Sir James Clark, Dr Locock and Dr Blagden – together with the nurse, Mrs Lilly, were all installed in the palace. As Dr Stockmar was also at Court Albert had asked him to be ready to assist if his services should be needed.

Three weeks before the expected time the Queen's pains began. In spite of previous apprehension she was quite calm. Albert remained in the room with the doctors and Mrs Lilly and Victoria's greatest concern was that the pain would be so great that she might be unable to restrain her cries. That, she feared, would be most undignified, for waiting in the next room were the Archbishop of Canterbury, the Prime Minister, Lord Palmerston and other important Ministers and gentlemen of rank. Close by, but in a separate room, were members of her household. It was the public nature of the proceedings which was so undignified, but this did make her determined to exert the utmost control.

Albert was a comfort. She sensed his anxiety. Dear Albert, everything must go well for his sake.

How wonderful it would be if she could produce a dear little boy exactly like his father – and what was more important was that he should be as *good*.

After twelve hours of labour the baby was born. The Queen lay back exhausted but triumphant. Albert came to the bed to hold her hand.

'The child?' she asked.

'Is perfect,' answered Albert.

'A boy?'

The doctor answered. 'It is a Princess, Your Majesty.'

There was a moment of disappointment. Albert pressed her hand warmly.

'Never mind,' she said. 'The next one will be a Prince.'

'My dearest,' said Albert, 'we should not be sad because we have a little girl. It is a poor compliment to you. Why, this child could become a queen as good as her mother.'

'Dear Albert. Then you are not displeased?'

'If you get well quickly then I am content,' said Albert.

Mrs Lilly had washed the little Princess and placed her naked on a velvet cushion. Then she walked with her into the room where the members of the government had been waiting.

'Here is Her Highness the Princess Royal,' she announced.

The old Duke of Wellington came forward to peer at the child.

'Oh,' he said in a tone of mild contempt, 'a girl.'

Mrs Lilly glared at him. 'A Princess, Your Grace,' she said sharply, for she would have the old gentleman remember that although the precious child was a girl she was as royal as any boy could be.

## Chapter IX

## IN-I-GO JONES

The baby was to be named Victoria after her mother, and the names Adelaide Mary Louise were added. The Dowager Queen was delighted that the child was called after her; she was so happy, she told the Queen, that she had experienced the blessing of motherhood. Poor Adelaide, how she had always longed for a child of her own; but being of the sweetest of temperaments she would not grudge anyone else the happiness which she had missed.

'Aunt Adelaide will be ready to spoil the child,' said Victoria to Albert.

'That must not be allowed,' replied Albert. He was determined to be a good father and that did not include spoiling his offspring.

It was rather awkward that she had the same name as her mother, but Albert had wished it. 'Such a *delightful* compliment,' said the Queen – and she herself had thought it appropriate, so the child was Victoria.

'She is like a little kitten,' said the Queen and from then on the child was called Pussy and sometimes, to vary it, Pussette.

Victoria discovered that although she had enjoyed racing up and down the corridors of Buckingham Palace with the Conyngham children or those of the John Russells, she was not so fond of little babies. She was delighted, of course, to be a mother and so quickly to have produced a child (it was only nine months since her marriage) but that did not mean that she wanted to spend all her time in the nursery. She was no Aunt Adelaide.

A wet nurse was procured with other nurses and the Baroness Lehzen decided that the nursery was a place in which she should reign supreme. Victoria was delighted that dear Daisy should superintend the baby's domain and returned to her everyday life.

The oriental situation had taken a turn for the better. Mehemet Ali had given up his claims to Syria on the intervention of the allied fleet and stated that he would relinquish the Ottoman fleet if the allies would give him possession of the Pashalik of Egypt.

'A very happy end to the year,' commented Victoria to Albert. 'The crisis over and a baby in the nursery.'

Uncle Leopold was delighted that she had proved herself able to bear healthy children. It was always a fear in the royal family that this might not be the case. George III had had far too many but his sons, George and William, had not followed his example; and now at the age of twenty-one, after less than a year of marriage, the Queen had produced a child. There would of course be more, as Leopold implied in his letter.

*I flatter myself,* he wrote, *that you will be a delighted and delightful* Maman au milieu d'une belle et nombreuse famille.

Indeed! thought Victoria when she read it. The idea of going through all *that* again to produce a large family did not please her. Of one thing she had made very sure. If she had another child – and she did not intend to for some little time – she would arrange that the child was born before any of the dignitaries were summoned to the palace.

'For I will not have a public birth again,' she confided to Lehzen.

'I should think not,' said the Baroness. 'I had thought that the Prince might have realised your wish for privacy when Pussy was born.'

'It's the old tradition, Lehzen. Remember the baby in the warming-pan rumour? They think someone might smuggle in a spurious child.'

'What nonsense! But I shall insist that my dearest love does not suffer *that* again. And I hope that the next occasion will be postponed for at least two years. I know you look blooming, but you do need time to recover from having the child.'

Victoria wrote a little tersely to Uncle Leopold. He did like to interfere just a little too much. He had tried to tell Lord Melbourne and Lord Palmerston how to conduct the Turko-Egyptian matter and he was constantly criticising Lord Palmerston.

*I think, dearest Uncle, you cannot wish me to be the*
'Maman d'une nombreuse famille' *for I think you will see with me the great inconvenience a* large *family would be to us all, and particularly to the country, independent of the hardship and inconvenience to myself; men never think, at least seldom think, what a hard task it is for us women to go through this* very often.

No, she would certainly wait a few years. Lehzen was quite right about this.

Poor Dash was showing his age. He no longer leaped up barking and wagging his tail when a walk was mentioned. Instead he was rather inclined to hide himself so that he didn't have to go out. He slept in a basket by the royal bed; he used to be very fierce and at the least sound would waken everyone near by.

But on that early December morning Dash slept on while the door handle of the Queen's dressing-room was slowly turned and silently opened.

Mrs Lilly awoke and looked about her.

'Is anyone there?' she whispered.

There was no answer so she sat up, listening.

Another sound. There was no doubt about it. Someone was prowling about the Queen's dressing-room.

She went to the door, listening. An unmistakable sound. Yes, someone *was* in there. She locked the door and called one of the pages.

He came rubbing the sleep out of his eyes.

'What is it?' he asked.

'When I unlock this door,' said Mrs Lilly, 'you will go in and bring out whoever is in there.'

The man stared at her. 'Someone...'

'Do as I say.'

'Me! Why? Suppose he's got a gun?'

A figure with a candle had appeared in the corridor. It was the Baroness Lehzen.

'What is happening here?' she demanded. 'You will awaken the Queen.'

'Oh, Baroness,' said Mrs Lilly, 'I'm sure I heard someone in the Queen's dressing-room.'

'*Mein Gott!*' cried the Baroness. 'And you stand here. The Queen may be murdered.'

She pushed them aside, unlocked the door and strode into the dressing-room like an avenging angel. Her precious darling in danger and these fools standing about doing nothing. She was thinking of the madman who had taken a shot at Victoria on Constitution Hill. So were the others, but this had the opposite effect on the devoted Lehzen.

She looked round the room. She could see no one. The only place where anyone could be hidden was under the sofa. Thrusting the candlestick into the hands of Mrs Lilly she pushed the sofa to one side.

There was a gasp. Cowering under the sofa was a small boy, his clothes ragged, his face dirty, his eyes wide with astonishment.

Who was the boy? He had been some days in the palace, he told them. He had hidden under the sofa on which the Queen and Prince Albert had sat and had lain there listening to them talking together; he had been to the throne room and sat on the throne; he had been in the nursery and heard the new baby Princess cry.

He loved Buckingham Palace. He confessed to having been there before. Last time had been in 1838 when he had spent a week there and he could not resist paying another visit.

People remembered the excitement of two years earlier. Of course he was the Boy Jones. Someone had waggishly christened him In-I-go Jones.

It was considered to be an amusing incident. The boy had done little harm. He had merely been curious.

The Queen laughed when she heard of it, but Albert took a different view.

'My dear love,' he said, 'it alarms me that people could so easily get into the palace.'

'It was only a boy,' said Victoria.

'Only a boy this time. But if a boy can get in so easily how much more easily could someone enter who might wish to do harm.'

'He came before,' said Victoria; 'fancy that.'

Albert was thoughtful.

Albert had been making an investigation of the manner in which the household was managed. He was determined to find out how it was possible for a boy to get into the palace and spend several days there unobserved.

In one of the kitchens he found a broken pane of glass. 'How long has that been broken?' he asked.

The kitchen hand to whom he addressed the

question scratched his head. 'Well, Your Highness, it were done last Saturday week. I know for sure.'

Another kitchen hand came up and said the window had been like that for a month.

'Whose duty would it be to see that it was repaired?' the Prince wanted to know.

They didn't know, but they would call the chief cook.

'It's like this, Your Highness,' said the chief cook, 'I'd write and sign a request to have the glass put back, but the Clerk of the Kitchen would have to sign it too.'

'And did you?'

'I did, Your Highness, two months ago.'

'Send me the Clerk of the Kitchen,' said Albert.

The Clerk of the Kitchen remembered signing the request but then it had to go to the Master of the Household.

The Master of the Household had signed so many requests that he did not remember the pane of glass in particular, but his duty was to take it to the Lord Chamberlain's office and there it would await attention.

'And what happens there?' asked the Prince.

'The Lord Chamberlain would sign and then it would go to the Clerk of the Works, Your Highness.'

'*Mein Gott!*' cried the Prince breaking into German, as he did when seriously disturbed. 'All this for a pane of glass! And meanwhile people can break into the palace and, if they have a mind to, murder the Queen.'

His orderly Teutonic soul was outraged. He was certain that this was not the only anomaly. The servants' domain was a little kingdom on its own. He could see that there was no discipline whatsoever. Servants absented themselves when they thought fit, or brought in their friends and entertained them at the Queen's expense.

He was horrified.

His questions quickly aroused suspicions which were deeply resented. The Baroness Lehzen, who was in charge of the keys, although she had no special title, never bothered them. She had other matters with which to concern herself than what went on in the kitchens. As long as she had her caraway seeds served with every meal, and when there was a state banquet or a dinner party food appeared on the table, that was all that mattered.

The servants grumbled together that they wanted no meddling German coming to their quarters to spy on them.

The Prince's investigations were reported to the Baroness, so she was ready for him.

He came to her room one day and told her about the pane of glass which had been missing for months because the inefficiency of the system had made it impossible for the request to reach the right person.

'I did not know Your Highness would concern himself with such a little thing.'

'It is of great concern. That boy got into the palace. How?'

'Not through that broken window surely?'

'He was in the palace because there is a lack of security.'

Lehzen said: 'As soon as I heard a commotion near the Queen I was out of bed. I have looked after her for years. The slightest sound ... and I am there.'

'That is not the point,' said the Prince patiently.

The Baroness broke into German. He followed. It was easier for them both. The Baroness was trying hard to control her anger; she had to remember that he was the Queen's husband. He found it easier to remain calm. He must not quarrel with her. She would distort what he said and carry tales to the Queen.

But in those moments there was one fact which was clear to them.

There was not room for them both in the palace.

Albert said: 'My love, I want to talk to you about palace security.'

'Oh, Albert, are you worrying about the Boy Jones?'

'It has started me thinking, and I have been looking into these matters. Really, there are some strange things going on in your household.'

'What do you mean, Albert?'

'Well, for one thing it takes months to get a pane of glass repaired.'

'Does it?'

'All because of stupid mismanagement. I want to go into all the details of the household management. I think we could dismiss several of the servants who are of no use at all.'

'Dismiss them! Oh, but Albert, where would they go?'

'To some households which could find work for them. There is not enough here for so many.'

'It has been going on for years, Albert.'

'All the more reason why it should go on no longer. I want the keys of the household.'

'Lehzen has them.'

'Well, they must be taken away from her.'

'*Must*, Albert?'

'Yes, since she mismanages everything in this way.'

'Albert! I couldn't possibly take the keys away from Lehzen. She would be so *hurt*.'

'Then hurt she must be. You should tell her that I am not satisfied with the way in which she allows the household to be run.'

'But I am satisfied, Albert.'

'How can you be?'

'Because it has been running for years and I never heard any complaint before. Besides, it is not for you to run the household.'

'I disagree.'

She was tired and the baby was always crying and not such fun as she had thought a baby would be. She was worried about Dash, who wouldn't eat anything and looked at her with sad mournful eyes. And Albert plagued her about the household!

'I shall certainly not speak to Lehzen,' she said. 'And Albert, I must beg of you not to interfere when I do not wish you to.'

Albert clicked his heels and bowed. Now he was going to be tiresome. He was going to retire to his room and be very calm and behave as though nothing had happened. How maddening calm people could be! Every minute she was getting nearer to an outburst of anger.

It was coming.

'You forget that this is *my* household. If I am satisfied that is all that matters. You are not the ruler of this country though sometimes I think you imagine you are.'

Albert was at the door.

'I wish I had never married,' she shouted. 'I wish I had never allowed myself to be persuaded.'

Albert had gone.

She stared at the door.

Oh, dear, dear Albert, she thought. Whatever had made her say such a silly thing!

Albert was gently forgiving but when he showed signs of raising the matter of the household he saw the danger signals in her eyes. He decided to wait. He had made some advance and his position had greatly improved in the last months; he was sure that if he were patient eventually he would bring Victoria to a logical point of view, and then she would be able to see that Baroness Lehzen was doing a great deal of harm.

So Albert began planning for Christmas, which should be spent at Windsor; and the Queen, who loved festivities and was only too delighted to have Albert friendly and appearing to have forgotten their differences, listened excitedly.

She was happy sitting beside Albert as the carriage rolled along, the nurses following behind with Lehzen and dear Pussy.

Albert was telling her about Christmases at Rosenau and how he and his brother had gone into the forest and brought home the yule logs. All the presents had been arranged on tables under the Christmas trees and each member of the household had his or her own table.

It had been very similar in Kensington Palace, said Victoria. After all Mama had come to England from Leiningen and had brought the same family customs to Kensington.

'I want this to be a *very* happy Christmas,' said Victoria, feeling contrite about the terrible thing she had said to Albert. She took his hand, and laughing added: 'I shall try to control my terrible temper and then I shan't say things I don't mean and for which I am so sorry afterwards.'

Albert pressed her hand and said he loved her generous heart.

So she was very happy driving along the frosty roads and she shared Albert's pleasure at the sight of the stately castle and could scarcely wait to step within its ancient walls.

It was a wonderful Christmas. Albert threw himself wholeheartedly into the task of decorating the apartments. He ordered many trees to be cut and between them he and the Queen adorned them with candles and little gifts which could be tied on. Beneath them were the surprise parcels and Victoria could scarcely wait for Christmas Day when the packages should be unwrapped amid cries of pleasure and delighted amazement.

It was all rather as it had been when she was a little girl and she remembered how different Mama had been on such occasions. In fact Mama, who was with them at Windsor, had changed a great deal since the departure of her Comptroller of the Household, Sir John Conroy, and the arrival of Albert, who always referred to her as Dearest Mama. As for the Duchess, she was very fond of

Albert and this had meant that relations between Victoria and her mother had changed.

Again the trouble was the Baroness, who had thought the Duchess had treated Victoria harshly when they were all at Kensington and they would never really get on.

So there were the Duchess and Albert ranged against the Baroness. Victoria frowned. Whatever happened, she had told herself, no one – simply *no one* – was going to turn her against her dearest Lehzen.

But Christmas was not a time for conflict. They must all be happy together and because she was sorry for her outburst Victoria had agreed to a *quiet* Christmas. There would be no grand ball, just an evening when they might dance a little or play games and Albert would leave his beloved double chess and play a round game in which everyone could join. Mama could have her whist which would keep her awake and satisfy her; and even Lehzen fell in with the general view because she said she did not want Victoria to be exhausted. It was too soon after her confinement and she must take care.

She and Albert rode out in the morning and what fun it was galloping down the long avenue to Snow Hill where the statue of her grandfather George III had been erected.

'He was always quarrelling with Uncle George,' she said, 'but at least Uncle George had that statue put there to his memory.'

'It would have been better to have tried to please him while he was alive than to erect a statue to him when he was dead.'

'You are right, Albert,' she said solemnly.

They galloped through the Great Park and she told Albert the legend of Herne the Hunter, one of the keepers who was said to have hanged himself on an oak tree and now haunted the forest. If he appeared to anyone it meant they would die.

Albert was reminded of the legends of the Black Forest and recounted some of them.

She listened avidly. How beautifully Albert told his stories; how handsome he looked on horseback; and how happy she was to have such a husband! There should never really be any differences between them. If only she had not such a violent temper; if only Albert were not so maddeningly calm; if only he and Lehzen could get on together; if only he would realise that after all she was the Queen and, although he was her dearly beloved husband, he was not a king and only a consort and she must have the final say in everything...

But why disturb such a lovely frosty morning with such thoughts.

Albert drew up his horse to admire the perpendicular Gothic architecture of St George's chapel. Albert knew a great deal about architecture and was able to make her see buildings as she never had before. But then Albert knew a great deal about so many things – music, literature, art.

He said on that Christmas morning: 'The Court could be more interesting if you invited intellectual people to dinner now and then and perhaps to pay visits.'

'Intellectual people?'

'I meant writers, artists, scientists ... people like that.'

The Queen was pensive. 'There would be a lot of clever talk, I daresay, which I shouldn't understand.'

'You would in time.'

She was silent. She was certainly not going to have people talking over her head at her dinner parties. But she did not wish to spoil this morning by saying so.

She started to gallop and Albert followed; they rode side by side for a few minutes in silence.

Then she cried: 'Oh, Albert, what a pleasant ride. How I am enjoying it!'

They sang duets; they played the piano; they sketched the view from the windows because it was too cold to sketch out of doors. 'My hands get so red,' said the Queen.

What a happy Christmas that was.

But sadness followed. Going to Dash's basket one morning she found him dead.

She wept bitterly. Lehzen said: 'He was old, my love, and he didn't enjoy the last months. It was rather sad to see him.'

She threw her arms about the Baroness. 'Do you remember when he came? That odious Sir John Conroy gave him to Mama but he was my dog from the first.'

'He took one look at you and loved you.'

'Darling, darling Dashy. He was always *so* faithful. He used to come to the blue closet when I was with my Prime Minister. Lord M was fond of him and he liked Lord M. All dogs like Lord M and one understands why. But Dashy *loved* him. He was always licking his boots.'

Lehzen said it was no use grieving as it was all for the best. She must think of poor Dash whose legs were getting stiff with rheumatism and was now out of his pain.

She agreed and felt much better. Then Albert suggested that Dash be buried at Adelaide Cottage, which he had particularly loved, and designed an effigy. Beneath it the beloved body was laid and a plaque was put up to extol his virtues, his selflessness and fidelity.

Victoria knew that every time she visited his grave she would remember the dear companion of her childhood.

The sojourn at Windsor was marred only by the death of Dash and that had been imminent for some time now. She was finding that she enjoyed the country life far more than she had thought possible.

She told Albert that she was changing her mind about the country and when she saw how this pleased him she enlarged on the subject.

'In the past I could not wait to get back to London,' she said, 'and I was always quite wretched to leave it. But now I am married I am quite unhappy to leave the country.'

Albert was delighted. She was coming his way; he had every hope of success; he would wean her from her pleasure-loving ways; he would make her the serious docile companion he longed for.

He pressed her hand.

'No regrets of your marriage?'

'Dear Albert, how could I have been so *wicked!*'

'You wicked, my love? Never. It is just that ungovernable temper of yours. It is like an old troll of the mountains who puts words into your mouth which your loving heart could never have conjured up.'

'That is true, Albert. How clever of you. I often think how happy I am, and what a poor sort of existence mine was before I was married.'

'Go on thinking so, my love, I beg of you.'

'You are so good and so patient.'

'Together we will fight that old troll of a temper, eh?'

She laughed delightedly. 'Then if you will fight it with me, Albert, we shall surely conquer it.'

'I am so happy that you are growing to love the country more.'

'Well I am beginning to *see* things differently. You know I couldn't tell the difference between a blackbird and a thrush and I didn't know wheat from barley or gorse from hawthorn. It makes such a lot of difference when you *know*.'

'Of course it does. That is why I think you would enjoy having interesting people at the palace.'

Her lips tightened a little. 'I shouldn't want a banquet to become a sort of lesson, I fear.'

The danger signals. He must remember that too much haste would impede progress.

She went on: 'And although I do enjoy the country that does not mean that I dislike London and the amusements we have there.'

'Of course not,' said Albert calmly. He changed the subject. 'Have you decided on the date for Pussy's christening?'

'An idea came to me. What do you think of the

217

tenth of February?'

'That,' said Albert, 'is a very important date to me.'

'It is the most important date in my life,' replied the Queen fervently. 'So, dearest Albert, Pussy's christening day shall be on the anniversary of our wedding.'

Harmony continued at Windsor.

Mr George Anson called on Lord Melbourne to discuss the progress of the royal couple.

Lord Melbourne listened intently to Mr Anson's account of the Prince's dissatisfaction with the company which the Queen kept around her.

'The Prince,' said Mr Anson, 'would like more literary and scientifically minded people to be entertained.'

'Understandable,' said Lord Melbourne.

'But Her Majesty does not wish this. She fears that she would be at a loss with such people.'

Lord Melbourne nodded. 'She would want to take her fair share in the conversation and would not care for it to go over her head. A pity something wasn't done about her education. Oh, I know she speaks German, Italian and French – not only speaks them well but writes them. She has a smattering of Latin. If she were not a queen she would be an accomplished young lady, but there has been lack of more cultured tuition. She has a naturally shrewd mind and is quick to pick up information. She is musical, but she has read very little I fear and has hardly any knowledge of the classics. It is a great lack.'

'The Prince naturally finds the evenings dull,'

said Mr Anson. 'He is bored with his double chess every evening and now of course he is drawn into the round games which seem positively childish to him.'

'It is to be hoped that he doesn't look for excitement in dangerous places,' said Lord Melbourne.

Mr Anson looked surprised.

'Well, my dear fellow, there are some very beautiful ladies at Court. I have often felt the Queen was ill advised to choose her ladies for their beauty, which she appears to have done. She loves beauty particularly in the human form.'

'The Queen is delighted with the Prince's utter indifference to other ladies.'

'It's early days yet,' said the Prime Minister. 'I told her this and she was very indignant. But, if he is going to be bored in the evenings, she should take care. The Prince has been very successful so far. Oh, I know there have been some stormy scenes. I know well that royal temper. But his success has been remarkable. It may well be that very soon you will be seeing the company at the palace becoming literary and scientific and far more intellectual, but the Prince must be wary.'

'He knows that very well, Lord Melbourne.'

'And the Daisy lady?'

'Still reigns.'

'A battle royal will take place there one day. And until it is won our Prince should walk very carefully. I have no doubt of the outcome. Albert is a very good chess player. He'll know the strategy. His danger is impatience.'

'He is a very patient man, Prime Minister.'

'He needs to be. Let him remember that and

he'll be the victor. I'll prophesy that if he is clever enough he'll clear the palace of his enemies and be master in his house.'

Lord Melbourne was a little sad, thinking of the days when he was the most important one in the Queen's life. What a happy time that had been! He had lost his cynicism and had felt like a young man in love. But he had not been a young man and the object of his devotion was a young girl – a queen – to whom he could never speak of love.

But there was love between them – on his side an enduring love. That was why he wanted above all things to see her happy.

And she would be of course, and he would know that she was when Albert became master in the house. A long battle lay before the Prince. He, the Prime Minister, hoped that he would live long enough to see that battle won, for only if the Prince was the victor could Victoria be happy.


## Chapter X

### LORD MELBOURNE DEPARTS

The Christmas holidays were coming to an end. Lord Melbourne wrote to the Queen condoling with her because, against her will, she must return to London for the opening of Parliament. It was an ordeal which the Queen would have happily missed.

The Queen had reproved Lord Melbourne for

not coming to Windsor. It was a long time since she had seen him and he knew that she did not like to be away from him for too long.

He could not, wrote the Prime Minister, leave London because of the uncertain state of politics and when she did arrive in London he would have a few words with her about the speech from the throne, which would have to be more carefully worded than usual because of the country's rather uneasy relations with France.

He was very happy though, he wrote, to hear that she was reluctant to leave the country, which he construed as meaning that the simple pleasures shared with her husband were more enjoyable to her than the unavoidably public life in London. He believed that this meant she was very happy and there was nothing on earth that Lord Melbourne desired more than her happiness.

'Dearest Lord M,' murmured the Queen when she read that letter. At least one thing would make her happy to return to London; she would see her Prime Minister.

Uncle Leopold wrote that although discretion had prevented his being present at Victoria's coronation and wedding, he would come to the baptism of the Princess Royal.

Albert was delighted. It would be a wonderful reunion and they would have so much to talk about. He must not of course mention their differences. Uncle Leopold would make a big issue of that and could well give all sorts of advice not only to Albert but to Victoria which might prove fatal to Albert's hopes.

On the 23rd of January Victoria opened Parliament and when that was over all her thoughts were directed to the christening. At the beginning of February the weather turned very cold and there was ice on the lake in Buckingham Palace gardens. The Prince's eyes sparkled. It reminded him of the skating he and Ernest had so much enjoyed in Coburg.

Day after day the frost continued and a few days before that fixed for the christening Albert declared that the lake was hard enough for skating.

Victoria wanted to join him but he begged her not to. 'I should be overcome by anxiety. It is too soon after Pussy's birth,' said Albert.

Because he begged and did not command, Victoria was happy to fall in with his wishes and touched, she said, by his care of her. So each day she and her ladies would go out into the grounds of Buckingham Palace to watch the skaters, and the Queen was delighted with the figure Albert cut on the ice. He was an expert.

The palace garden with its forty acres was a consolation to Albert for having to live in London. The lake was delightful and there was a pleasant summer-house situated on a mound for which he had plans. He was one day going to have it decorated and made into a refuge from the great palace which, though so close, was invisible during summer when the trees were thick with leaves.

On the day before the christening it seemed a little warmer. The Queen commented on it to the

Duchess of Sutherland and some of the other ladies as they made their way to the lake where the Prince was already skating. He liked her to watch him.

As she came near to the lake she saw Albert. He waved to her. She waved back.

'How beautifully he moves!' she murmured.

As Albert skated towards her there was a sudden sound of cracking ice and the Prince, throwing up his hands, disappeared. Where he had been was a big hole of dark water.

The ladies started to scream. One of them ran to the palace to get help. But Victoria could only think that Albert had disappeared beneath the ice.

She ran to the lake. 'Albert!' she cried desperately.

His head appeared.

'Albert, I'm coming,' she said, though she was not quite sure what she could do.

'Go back!' called Albert. 'It's dangerous.'

But she took no notice. Cautiously she ventured on to the ice, testing it with her foot before taking a step forward. She held out her hands to him.

Albert by this time was scrambling out. 'My dearest,' he panted, 'keep away.'

But she had seized his arm and was pulling him out of the water.

The ice seemed firm where Victoria stood and later she heard that it had been broken just where Albert had fallen in and had lightly frozen over again, which was why it was so weak at that particular spot.

Clinging together they reached the bank.

'My brave love!' said Albert. 'You might have joined me beneath the ice.'

'You are shivering,' said Victoria sternly. 'I must get you into the palace at once.'

The christening was a great success. Pussy behaved very well and did not cry as the Queen had feared she might. She appeared to be fascinated by the lights and the uniforms and everyone commented on her intelligence.

The old Duke of Wellington stood proxy for the Duke of Saxe-Coburg and Gotha as one of the sponsors; Leopold was another. Queen Adelaide with the Duke of Sussex and the Duchesses of Kent and Gloucester made up the rest.

After the ceremony, which took place in Buckingham Palace, at six p.m. there was a dinner-party over which the Queen presided.

Beside her was her dear Lord Melbourne and she told him that she was reminded of the old days when he dined almost every evening at the palace and indeed had an apartment there.

She noticed that tears filled his eyes and she was deeply touched.

'You will always be my dear friend,' she said warmly, 'and none of your other friends will be as fond of you as I am.'

'Your Majesty once told me that before. I have never forgotten, nor shall I ever.'

'Dear Lord M.' She touched his hand briefly and then, because it was such an emotional moment, she changed the subject by asking what he had thought of the ceremony.

'It went off perfectly,' said Lord Melbourne, 'and I could not help but be impressed by the chief performer.'

'You mean?'

'The Princess Royal. She looked about her, conscious that all the stir was for her. This is the time that character is formed.'

The Queen laughed aloud and repeated Lord Melbourne's remark to the rest of the company.

She remembered how in the old days a dinner-party was always gay and amusing when Lord Melbourne was present, and rather dull when he wasn't. It was different now of course that there was Albert.

Albert was sneezing violently.

'Oh, dear,' said the Queen, 'I hope your ducking is not going to make you ill.'

'It's only a cold,' replied the Prince. He looked at her fondly. 'I shall never forget how promptly you saved me.'

'I didn't save you. You saved yourself.'

'You showed great presence of mind. Different from your attendants. I was proud of you.'

'Oh, Albert, I can't describe my terror when I saw you disappear.'

'My love, there was no real danger. The lake is not deep and in fact the ice was quite firm except at that one small spot.'

'I thought of so many things in the space of those few moments,' she said. 'I thought of them carrying you into the palace ... dead, and I knew then that if that had been so I should want to die too.'

Albert kissed her tenderly.

'My dear love, we are happy are we not?'

'Completely, Albert.'

'We must try always to keep it as it was during that moment when I disappeared and you came out on the ice to rescue me.'

'We will, Albert,' she cried fervently. 'We *will.*'

All Albert suffered from the skating incident was a severe cold. Victoria insisted on making sure that he did everything to rid himself of it. Having suffered that moment of intense fear when she had thought of losing him she realised how much she loved him.

She was blissfully happy for a few weeks. Then she made a discovery.

She was once more pregnant.

'It can't be,' she moaned. 'It is much too soon.'

Albert was delighted, but inwardly she was resentful. As she had remarked to Uncle Leopold, men seldom understood what child-bearing meant, that terrible ordeal being quite beyond their com-prehension.

Lehzen grumbled that it was far too soon. Victoria should have had a year in which to recover from Pussy's birth, she said, implying that Albert had been inconsiderate in forcing this new pregnancy upon her. Even the Duchess of Kent expressed the desire that there should have been a longer interval, although there was not a hint of criticism of Albert from her.

Victoria was even more difficult than she had been during the first months of Pussy's gestation.

She began finding fault with everyone and her ladies were beginning to dread approaching her. The famous temper flared up at the slightest provocation, and the atmosphere was quite different from that which had prevailed at Windsor during Christmas.

She was anxious too about the government. Trade was bad and the finances of the country were weak. When Lord Melbourne came to see her he was quite clearly uneasy and she felt that he tried to keep this from her. She could guess what it meant. The Opposition was being difficult again and the idea of losing her Prime Minister with the ordeal of childbirth looming ahead of her angered her.

Her pretty pink and white complexion faded during those months; she looked pale, even sallow. Her nose looked longer, her eyes less blue and her mouth sullen. I'm quite plain, she thought, and Albert is beautiful.

She noticed then how pretty some of her ladies were. How foolish she had been to choose them because she liked the look of them. If she did, other people might – people like Albert, for instance.

Albert had always disliked the society of women and she had at times been a little critical of his awkwardness with them, but she fancied that this was changing.

She had heard him chattering away with Miss Spring-Rice in German. That very pretty young lady spoke the language quite well and gave herself airs because the Prince naturally liked to talk in his native tongue.

'I trust you enjoyed your conversations with the young lady,' said the Queen after she had listened to them as she said 'going on and on'.

'It was very interesting,' replied the Prince. 'Her accent is not at all bad. She has an amusing way with her verbs which I have to correct.'

'And there is something I have to correct. I don't care to hear you giggling with that silly frivolous creature.'

'We talked in German,' said the Prince. 'I do not think that could be described as giggling.'

'*I* describe what you were doing as such,' said the Queen haughtily and left him. In her room she looked into her mirror.

'I was never pretty,' she said, 'but being pregnant has certainly *not* improved my looks.'

Lehzen said that when a woman was going to have a child nature did something to her, put an aura around her, gave her special attractions.

'Don't talk nonsense,' snapped the Queen. 'Where is this aura? Show it to me.'

'It is something you can't point to.'

'No, it is something to pacify me. It doesn't exist. Sometimes, Lehzen, I think you imagine I am a child in the nursery. This is no longer so, and please remember it. I will not be treated as though I'm a querulous child.'

Lehzen looked so sad that Victoria cried: 'Oh, Lehzen, I'm sorry. I've become terrible lately. And what's worse I quarrel all the time with Albert.'

'Well, as he's responsible for your condition, he must understand.'

'He does. He is an *angel*.'

She must try to be reasonable; she must make

Albert see that it was this violent temper of hers and the fact that she was so soon to have another baby which was affecting her.

She was charming to Albert for a few days and he, the dear good angel, behaved as though nothing unusual had happened, and then she began to be jealous because he seemed to enjoy the company of Miss Devereux who was really very beautiful and dignified and rather like Albert in temperament.

'It's the first few months that are the worst in a pregnancy,' comforted Lehzen. 'After that you'll settle down and become quite serene as you did last time.'

'*You* can all take it very calmly,' retorted Victoria. 'You don't have to go through it all. You're like Uncle Leopold.'

'My precious love!' cried Lehzen aghast. 'You must know that I suffer all the time ... with you.'

Victoria threw her arms about the Baroness and said she was a beast. She did not deserve her dearest Daisy nor that dearest and kindest of husbands. And she felt better comforting Lehzen.

But she was soon irritable again.

She came upon Albert talking to Miss Pitt, one of the prettiest of her maids of honour – a rather reserved young lady with whom Albert had often had a friendly word.

Miss Pitt was carrying a very beautiful bouquet of flowers and the Prince, who was passionately interested in horticulture, had paused to admire it.

'The spring flowers are perhaps the most beautiful,' he was saying, and Miss Pitt was agreeing with him. Miss Pitt was holding the flowers out to him to smell when the Queen came in.

Victoria's expression was stormy, and Albert, noticing this, tried to soothe her.

'Look at these beautiful flowers, my love,' he said, smiling. 'I think we should grow more flowers in the gardens.'

The Queen took the flowers and looked at them distastefully.

'They are yours, Miss Pitt?' she enquired.

'Yes, Your Majesty. I was passing through when His Highness stopped to admire them.'

To admire *them*, thought the Queen looking at Miss Pitt, whose prettiness was enhanced by her blushing.

'Well, leave them with me,' said the Queen with a nod, and Miss Pitt, interpreting this correctly as dismissal, curtsied and retired.

The Queen's angry eyes met those of Albert over the flowers. Then deliberately she tore the bouquet to pieces, scattering the flowers all over the floor, and went to the door.

At it she paused. 'There. Now you may gather them up and take them to Miss Pitt. It will give you a chance to see her again and tell her how much you admire her flowers ... and her.'

Albert merely looked at her sadly and she ran to her room, threw herself on to her bed and burst into tears.

Albert asked Lord Melbourne to call on him and when the Prime Minister arrived, he told him that the Queen was unaware of this meeting.

'I am seriously concerned,' said the Prince,

'and I feel that owing to your friendship with the Queen and your affection for her, you are the one best to advise me how to act.'

Lord Melbourne, who had grown to respect the Prince, replied immediately that he was at his service. He understood. Baron Stockmar, the Prince's chief adviser, was out of England at the time, and it pleased the Prime Minister that the Prince should turn to him.

'I am very anxious about the Queen,' went on Albert.

Lord Melbourne nodded gravely.

'Her present mood will pass, I know,' said the Prince. 'It is entirely due to her condition and, although this year it is more exaggerated than last, it springs from the same source.'

'I know Your Highness is capable of exercising great patience and realises the absolute necessity to do so.'

'That is true,' replied Albert gravely. 'I am thinking of the inevitable change of government.'

Lord Melbourne nodded gravely. 'It can't be delayed much longer. In fact, but for the Queen's action, we should have been out two years ago.'

'That is my point,' said Albert. 'There must not be another bedchamber incident. I believe that if the Queen were to behave once more as she did on that occasion the Crown would be in danger.'

Lord Melbourne looked grave. 'It should certainly be prevented.'

'It must be prevented.'

'You have surely not spoken to the Queen of this matter?'

'It is impossible to speak to the Queen. She flies

into a temper it often seems without reason. To mention such a matter to her now would have disastrous consequences, I fear.'

'Then what do you propose?'

'That this must be settled without the Queen.'

'You cannot mean that her bedchamber ladies can be dismissed without her knowledge.'

'Sir Robert Peel will find himself in a similar position to that which confronted him two years ago. What if there is an election and your Ministry is defeated?'

'It is almost a foregone conclusion that it will be,' Lord Melbourne said wryly. 'The Queen would, of course, be obliged to accept a government which had been elected by the people.'

'And if she refused to change her household and if Sir Robert Peel refused to take office until she did?'

'The Queen would be obliged to obey the Constitution. She would have to give way.'

'What a humiliation for her! I want to spare her that.'

'I would wish that, too.'

It was true, thought Albert, that Lord Melbourne saw the danger and wished to spare the Queen; but Lord Melbourne's way was always to let things go and hope that they would work out all right. That was not Albert's way.

'Lord Melbourne,' said Albert earnestly, 'how long can your Ministry continue in office?'

'We shall certainly be out before the end of this year. Long before the end of it, I think.'

'And there will be an election?'

'It seems inevitable.'

'And Peel's party will be returned?'

'I fear so.'

The Prince believed so too, though he did not fear it. He believed Sir Robert Peel would make a better Prime Minister than Lord Melbourne.

'My plan is,' said Albert, 'that before there is a Tory Government the chief Whig ladies of the Queen's bedchamber shall already have tendered their resignations. Then the Queen will be spared the humiliation of having to bow to Sir Robert's wishes.'

'But how will you bring about these resignations?'

'Would you have any objection to my consulting Sir Robert Peel on this matter?'

'I would have none and indeed am entitled to have none. I believe Sir Robert will welcome your suggestions.'

'Then I will see what can be done.'

'All this is to be secret from Her Majesty?'

'Absolutely. It would be quite impossible while she is in her present mood to discuss it with her. You think I am foolish to attempt this.'

'I think you are very brave,' replied Lord Melbourne.

The Prince discussed the matter with his secretary Mr Anson, who, discreet and astute, grasped the situation immediately and agreed with the Prince that there was only one way of dealing with it and that was as the Prince proposed.

If Peel came into power the bedchamber ladies would have to be changed, and as the Queen would have to bow to this it would be a humiliation for her and a triumph for Sir Robert.

'We must remember,' said Mr Anson, 'that Sir Robert was deeply humiliated by the Queen two years ago and if he were a ruthless and vindictive man he might insist on retaliation.'

'I do not believe Sir Robert Peel to be that kind of man,' said the Prince, 'and I want to do everything in my power to save the Queen from humiliation.'

'And Your Highness would wish me to approach Sir Robert on your behalf, and sound him as to his course of action should he become Prime Minister.'

'That is what I wish,' said the Prince.

'Then shall we decide exactly what I shall say to Sir Robert?'

The Prince bowed his head. There was no doubt that like Lord Melbourne, Mr Anson considered the Prince to be a very brave man to risk rousing the Queen's anger which, over such a matter which she would consider an interference with her personal concerns, could be more fierce than it had ever been before.

Sir Robert Peel was very interested when George Anson told him that it was the wish of a 'common friend' that he should put a certain matter before him, particularly so when he discovered that that friend was the Prince Consort.

Sir Robert Peel, a man of great courage and high ideals, knew that it was almost certain that before the year was out he would be Prime Minister; although he believed this would be the best thing possible for the country he was not looking forward to being sent for by the Queen and having to face a humiliating situation such as that which had confronted him two years ago when the Queen had refused to give up the ladies of her bedchamber who were all related to prominent Whigs. These Whig ladies were still in their positions but the situation would be different now. On that other occasion Lord Melbourne had resigned although the government had not actually been defeated, but in view of Lord Melbourne's small majority he had decided it was impossible to carry on. Therefore in taking over from Melbourne, Sir Robert would not have had a majority in the House – until there was an election of course – and in those circumstances he had not felt it possible to form a government which would incur the hostility of the Queen. It was different now. The Melbourne Ministry would soon be defeated in the house; a general election would be called; the Tories would get a big majority and it would then not be possible for the Queen to defy them. If then Peel insisted on her changing her bedchamber ladies she would have to do so. It was an unpleasant situation which Sir Robert Peel would have given a great deal to avoid.

Dedicated, as Melbourne never could be, responsible for so many reforms, Sir Robert was completely lacking in those social graces which made Lord Melbourne so popular in many of the great houses and chiefly in Buckingham Palace and Windsor. He could be witty and amusing in his home; he could be dynamic in the House of Commons; he was cool and courageous, a great leader and reformer; but in the presence of the young girl who was Queen he was at a great disadvantage, being aware that she disliked him intensely – and illogically – largely because his rise must mean the fall of Lord Melbourne.

Having met the Prince Consort and found him a man of temperament similar to his own he had been hopeful. It seemed possible that Albert might be able to guide the Queen, to teach her the value of logic, to make her understand that government is not necessarily in good hands because those hands happen to be owned by a gentleman of great personal charm. He was eager to hear what Anson had to tell him.

Sir Robert said: 'You may speak absolutely frankly to me and every word you say shall be between us two. I shall not, without permission, mention what we discuss to any of my colleagues, not even the Duke of Wellington.'

George Anson said that it seemed almost certain that there would soon be an election and there was little doubt of the result. He reminded Sir Robert of a contretemps which had put him in a very embarrassing position two years ago when the Queen had sent for him and asked him to form a government. The Prince was anxious that there should be no such recurrence of such an embarrassment.

'The last thing I wish to do is humiliate the Queen,' declared Sir Robert sincerely. 'I would waive every pretension to office rather than do so.'

'But if you did, Sir Robert, someone would take your place and the situation would be the same. The Prince wishes to know whether, if certain offices in the Queen's Bedchamber were vacant at the time you took office, you would be prepared to consult with Her Majesty as to who should fill them.'

Sir Robert waited for George Anson to go on.

'The three principal posts are held by the Duchess of Sutherland, the Duchess of Bedford and Lady Normanby. Now, suppose these ladies voluntarily resigned before you came into power, no unpleasant situation would arise.'

'That is so,' said Sir Robert.

'Voluntary resignations,' went on Anson, 'and the posts vacant when the new government comes in. This is what the Prince feels will settle the matter satisfactorily.'

Sir Robert agreed that if this could be brought about a great deal of embarrassment would be saved on both sides.

Lord Melbourne was very grave when he called on the Queen.

'I know what you have come to tell me,' she said. 'I have seen it coming for some time now.'

'The main struggle will take place over the sugar duties,' said Lord Melbourne. 'And the Tories have threatened to bring up the matter of corn.'

She nodded.

'And this time it will be the end.'

'Well, we have been teetering on the edge for a long time,' said Lord Melbourne. 'We cannot teeter forever.'

'Oh, my dear Lord Melbourne, what am I going to do without you?'

'Your Majesty is in a different position now

from that which you occupied on that other occasion. Now you have the Prince to stand with you.'

'He is so good,' said the Queen, 'and I fear that I am very hasty and say things which I don't really mean.'

'Your Majesty is going through a very difficult time.'

'There is no excuse for me. Women are having babies all the time.'

'But they don't have the additional burden of governing a country.'

'Lord Melbourne, you are trying to make me sorry for myself.'

'Indeed not, Ma'am. Any one of your subjects would envy you for having such a good and patient husband.'

The Queen was almost in tears. 'How right you are. But that only makes me the more angry with myself for being so unkind to him and when I get angry with myself I am angry with him for making me so.'

'It is what is known as a vicious circle,' said Lord Melbourne.

'If only he were not so *good*.'

'A very trying quality,' said Lord Melbourne with a touch of his humour.

'We should admire it.'

'As we do.'

'But it is so hard to live up to. And you are right, it is trying when one is fretful and peevish and bad-tempered to be confronted by someone always wearing a Sunday face.'

Lord Melbourne was amused at the term. 'Sunday faces,' he suggested, 'should perhaps be kept for the day when they are intended to be worn. To wear a Sunday face on a Wednesday would be like wearing Court dress to go marketing.'

Trust Lord Melbourne to make her laugh! It occurred to her fleetingly that it was partly his flippant worldliness which had made her so devoted to him in the past. Although a good kind *feeling* man, Lord M was never pious. He would never have a Sunday face to put on even on a Sunday.

Perhaps one of the reasons for her irritability was Albert's unswerving goodness, which made her feel and act as though she were far from good.

But she was being disloyal to Albert, and that was the last thing she wanted to be. She was miserable when she quarrelled with him. She was devoted to her dear Prime Minister but she passionately loved her husband.

'We are forgetting the seriousness of all this,' she said. 'Oh, dear Lord Melbourne, I cannot bear it if you leave me ... now.'

'We shall meet ... often, I hope.'

'And you will continue to write to me.'

'I shall be entirely at your service.'

'But it won't be the same. You won't come every day. I can imagine that Peel person objecting!'

'He would only object if I discussed politics – a very reasonable objection. Give Peel a chance. You'll recognise his virtues.'

'It could never be the same.'

'But you will remember that you have the Prince beside you. You can trust him completely. I respect his intelligence. You are very fortunate to have such a good husband.'

'I know.'

'Let *him* know how you appreciate him. Don't shut him out.'

'How I wish I did not lose my temper.'

'You'll learn to control it.'

'When I think of some of the things I have done and said to Albert I shudder.'

'Albert will forgive you.'

'He is the most forgiving, kindest man in the world.'

On that note the Prime Minister took his leave, promising to report any new development in the situation to the Queen.

Before leaving the palace, Lord Melbourne saw George Anson. He told him that he had just left the Queen and that her mood was one of deep contrition because of recent scenes with Prince Albert. In Lord Melbourne's opinion the Queen was coming out of one of her difficult phases; this seemed to Lord Melbourne a good moment for Albert to speak to her about the new proposals to deal with the bedchamber affair in the event of the government's being defeated.

Consequently Albert went to the Queen. He looked very handsome and she thought as she always did when she saw him that there was not another man in the world to equal him in appearance. His gaze was tender. Lord Melbourne was right. She was indeed fortunate.

'Albert,' she cried tearfully. 'You do love me, Albert?'

'With all my heart,' said Albert fervently in German, which he always used in his most tender moments.

'I am *so* difficult.'

'My dear love, I understand. No sooner is Pussy born than you are to have another child. You are very young and it has been a little too much. But you are better, I can see that.'

'You are so good, so patient, and even younger than I.'

'By three months. It is nothing. And it is my duty to be patient. Besides, I love you.'

'I will try to deserve your love. But I wonder whether I could ever be as *good* as you, Albert. And there are trials ahead. I have just seen the Prime Minister. A crisis is looming. Trade is bad. The finances are low. There is trouble about sugar and corn. And Sir Robert Peel is trying to oust Lord Melbourne.'

'If the government is defeated on the budget, they will have to resign.'

'It is exactly as it was before.'

'Not exactly,' said Albert. 'Then the government had a small majority on the Jamaica Bill and resigned. Peel was not strong enough because had he formed a government he would have had a minority in the House. The position is changed. If the government was defeated on the budget, Peel would go to the country and there would almost certainly be a big Tory victory.'

'That is what Lord Melbourne says. I dread that man Peel's becoming Prime Minister. I dislike the man and he dislikes me too.'

'I do not believe that to be true.'

'Dear Albert, you think everyone is as kind and forgiving as you are.'

'I don't think Sir Robert is a vindictive man. He

was very humiliated at the time of the bed-chamber affair two years ago and would naturally not wish to be placed in such a position again.'

'And when he comes to me and *demands* that I change my bedchamber women?'

'Victoria, I have something very serious to say to you.'

'Yes, Albert?'

'You know, don't you, that everything I do is for your benefit. My great concern is to spare you pain.'

'*Dearest* Albert, I know it.'

'I spend my days wondering how I can be of use to you.'

'And I repay you by outbreaks of my horrid temper.'

'Yet I know the tenderness of your heart and that you love me.'

'Oh I do, Albert, *I do*.'

'Then you will understand my motive, whatever you think of my action. We have to face facts, Victoria. The government is going to fall and the Tories are going to be victorious. Sir Robert Peel will come to you and you will be obliged to ask him to form a new government.'

'I dread it. He will prance on the carpet like a dancing master and he will domineer and humiliate me and tell me that I shall have to have the ladies he chooses for me.'

'He will not, Victoria, because I have been in communication with him on this matter.'

'*You* ... in communication with Sir Robert Peel!'

'I thought it best ... in fact I thought it the only

way to save you from a humiliating situation. You are the Queen and expect subservience. But you are my wife and I was determined to protect you from humiliation, inconvenience, and if need be from yourself.'

She looked at him in astonishment. He looked stern and masterful and she felt a thrill of delight in this new strong Albert.

'Please tell me, Albert,' she said.

'I have arranged – and Sir Robert has agreed to this – that the distressing matter of your household ladies shall be avoided. It is not possible for your household to be composed of ladies from such prominent Whig families as it is now, when your government is Tory. It would be a point of immediate controversy when the new government came in. So ... some of your ladies ... the leading ones like the Duchess of Bedford and Lady Normanby and the Duchess of Sutherland, are going to resign of their own accord *before* the new government comes in. Thus when there is a new ministry those posts will be vacant and it will be a matter for you and your new Prime Minister to decide who shall fill them.'

'Albert ... *you* have arranged this?'

He nodded, his heart beating wildly, as he waited for her anger to show itself. But it did not. A look of immense relief came over her face.

'I have been so dreading it,' she said. 'Oh, Albert, *thank* you.'

Albert seized her in his arms; he kissed her in a manner which for Albert was quite abandoned.

'Oh, Albert,' she said meekly, 'I was dreading it all ... but I see now how different everything is. I have *you*.'

Albert was exultant. This was more than a temporary triumph. The way was clear ahead. He believed that he could now take the place beside the Queen which he had always known he must have if his marriage was to be happy.

There were great obstacles ahead, he knew, but this success had shown him that he could succeed.

When Lord Melbourne came to see the Queen, delightedly she told him what Albert had done.

'You can rely on the Prince to stand beside you,' said Lord Melbourne with tears in his eyes. 'I shall now not feel so badly about ceasing to be your Prime Minister.'

'I shall never be completely consoled,' she replied, noting the tears and feeling her own well up. 'But it is true that Albert has been a great comfort to me over this matter.'

'And so it shall be through the years ahead.'

'I believe it will. You know he arranged this without consulting me.'

'Which was the only way it could have been done. He was determined to have no opposition.'

'I was delighted. It had been worrying me a great deal. And to think that Albert saw it all and knew exactly what to do.'

'Very commendable,' said Lord Melbourne. 'And Your Majesty must also applaud the part Sir Robert has played in this.'

'Albert says he could have been vindictive.'

'He could, but he is a noble and gallant gentleman.'

'My dear Lord Melbourne,' she cried, 'and so are you. I am most impressed by the manner in which you have always spoken of your enemy.'

'We are only enemies in the House of Commons; outside it we are quite good friends.'

'Nevertheless he and his policies are the reason I am going to lose you. I shall find it hard to forgive him for that.'

'Your Majesty must not allow your kindness to me to affect your feelings for Sir Robert.'

'If you should be defeated at the polls you will still be my friend, Lord Melbourne. I shall insist upon it. You will visit me *often*; you will write to me. We must never forget that we are friends.'

Lord Melbourne was too moved to speak for a few moments and then said brightly, as though to cover up his emotion, 'I have some news for Your Majesty.'

'What news?' she cried, trying to catch his mood.

'News which will please and interest you. Lord John Russell really is going to marry Fanny Elliot.'

'Really? He certainly needs a wife with all those children. How many of them are there?'

'Six.'

'Oh, yes, four of them were dear Adelaide's before she married him and the youngest little girl was Lord John's. Then there's little Victoria named after me, whose coming was responsible for Adelaide's death. I wish them every happiness. I have always been so fond of Johnny.'

But Lord Melbourne had left her the thought of the first Lady John Russell who had died giving birth to a child and she was reminded unpleasantly of her own ordeal which was coming closer.

Then the sense of well-being which Albert's care for her had brought her began to wane; and she trembled at the thought of facing the hazardous business of once more bringing a child into the world.

Lord Melbourne soon had an opportunity of speaking to Prince Albert when he congratulated him on the successful outcome of his little manoeuvre.

'It could not have been achieved without the cooperation of Sir Robert,' said the Prince.

'It's to be hoped that Her Majesty realises this.'

'She still dislikes him.'

Lord Melbourne smiled tenderly; then he was serious and said regretfully: 'It will be Your Highness's place, not mine, to correct her in this.'

'I hope I shall be successful,' said Albert.

'Your Highness *must* be successful.'

'I want to thank you for your help, Lord Melbourne.'

'My duty, Your Highness. My greatest desire is for Her Majesty's happiness.'

'Then we share a goal.'

'Your Highness, I should like to offer a word of advice.'

'Please do.'

'Get rid of the governess.'

Albert's calm manner belied his inner excitement. 'If only I could,' he whispered.

'She will always work against you. It may well be that many of your differences with the Queen have had their roots in her behaviour.'

'I have long believed this to be so. She is in-efficient. I blame the Queen's lack of education on her.'

'Her mother should not have segregated her from the Court and should have given her better teachers. The Baroness has done what she believes best and her devotion is without question. The Queen overflows with affection; she is completely loyal. But if you are going to have a happy married life, and that will contribute to a successful reign, you must get rid of the governess.'

'Lord Melbourne, I am in absolute agreement with you.'

'Her Majesty is at this moment grateful to you. She is ready to lean on you. Perhaps this is the moment to tell her that the governess should go.'

Albert was thoughtful. Then he shook his head.

'She would never agree. She would become excited and when she does so her temper is vio-lent. To attempt to win her consent to the Baroness's dismissal now would be dangerous. I confess I am alarmed – considering her condition – when she flies into these tempers. I shall wait.'

'But it will be your ultimate object?' asked the Prime Minister.

'You can be assured of that, Lord Melbourne.'

The political crisis reached its head. The govern-ment had been defeated on the budget and as it did not resign a vote of confidence was taken, the result of which was 312 in favour of the Oppo-sition, 311 for the government. Lord Melbourne's Ministry was defeated by one vote, and there would now be an election.

The Queen was distressed but at least Albert had arranged matters so that she could not be humiliated over her bedchamber ladies.

Albert was delighted because he had been offered an honorary degree and must go to Oxford to accept it.

'You will of course accompany me?' he asked.

'But of course, Albert, I am so proud of you and nothing pleases me more than when other people realise your worth. I see it is to be on the fourteenth. That is very soon. I will tell Lehzen to make preparations for our departure immediately.'

'Victoria.'

'Yes, Albert?'

He hesitated. 'Do we need Lehzen?'

'Need Lehzen? Why, Albert, Lehzen and I have *never* been separated.'

'This would be a very short separation.'

'Nevertheless we should be apart and that hasn't happened before.'

'It is different now you are married.'

'In a way, Albert, yes, but being married is no reason why I should change towards my dear friend.'

Albert said: 'I thought she was invaluable in looking after little Vicky.'

'But of course she is.'

'You did not propose taking a baby of a few months on a trip to Oxford?'

'But of course not, Albert.'

'The Baroness is in charge of the nurseries, is she not?'

'She is, you know, Albert.'

(Yes, I know it, thought Albert, and regret it, and it will not be for long.)

'Then she must be there to take charge of the baby. Vicky cannot be trusted to the nurses.'

Victoria saw the point of this. Lehzen would have to stay behind.

It was only a half victory. He hated the thought of Lehzen's being in charge of his children. Judged by his meticulous standards the woman was quite incompetent – but at least on this occasion he had arranged it so that they could escape from the Baroness for the while.

The Oxford journey was quite a success although Victoria did miss Lehzen.

'Do you realise, Albert,' she said, 'that I have never before been parted from the Baroness since I was five years old.'

'It is a very long time,' said Albert, thinking, far too long.

When they returned to Buckingham Palace Lehzen greeted her as though their separation had lasted years.

'I have been so anxious,' she said. 'I thought that you might be feeling a bit low and I shouldn't be there to look after you.'

'My lowness was only due to being parted from you, dearest Daisy,' said the Queen.

The Duchess of Kent, who was taking a tour of the Continent, wrote from Amorbach where she was staying in the house of her son and Victoria's half brother, the Prince of Leiningen:

*It is like a dream writing to you from this place. My heart is full. I am so occupied with you and Albert and the precious little creature...*

She showed the letter to Albert, who was moved by it. Mama would not have been writing like that a year ago. This change in their relationship was largely due to Albert and she must realise that it was far better to be on affectionate terms with one's own mother than to harbour animosity.

'Mama has changed so,' she said to Albert.

'Perhaps you have too a little, my love,' he said.

She did not think so. She had *always* been ready to be on friendly terms. It was Mama and that dreadful John Conroy who made it impossible.

Lehzen sniffed over the Duchess's letter when Victoria showed it to her.

'It remains to be seen how long this mood will last,' she commented.

'Albert is delighted and in fact has really done everything to bring this change about.'

Lehzen was silent, but after a while she said that she was glad the Queen was not of a temper to be led by people who might not have a real understanding of the true state of affairs.

The elections would soon be taking place and there was an air of excitement in London. The Queen thought that it might be rather pleasant to go into the country for a while, paying a round of visits. There were several Whig houses who would be honoured at the prospect. Secretly she thought it was a good way of showing her people which side she supported – as if they did not know this! There had been enough talk about her and Lord Melbourne.

The trip to Oxford had been interesting and she would enjoy taking Albert into some of her subjects' stately homes.

'Let us travel as we did before,' said Albert. 'It was most enjoyable... It gave us an opportunity of being together more often.'

She was delighted at the prospect until she realised he meant that the Baroness should stay behind.

'Travel without Lehzen! Impossible!' she cried.

'It was not impossible before.'

'Oh, but that was such a short time.'

The Prince was in despair. He feared he would never rid the household of the woman and he was coming more and more to the conclusion that she was a mischief maker, at the heart of the trouble, and that life would never run smoothly for him and Victoria while she was there.

The Princess Royal was refusing to eat; she lay whimpering in her cot and the Queen was quite anxious.

'She is such a cross child,' she said to Lehzen. 'She never seems to smile nowadays.'

'It's her teeth,' comforted Lehzen. 'She's bound to be fretful.'

Albert was continually in the nursery questioning the nurses as to what the baby had to eat. Lehzen would stand, lips pursed, listening, and the looks she gave him were venomous.

I must get rid of her, he thought.

He approached Lord Melbourne again.

'That woman must go,' he said. 'She is constantly interfering between me and Victoria. Could you not advise the Queen that we should be better without her?'

Lord Melbourne appeared to consider this. He knew full well how devoted the Queen was to the Baroness, and while he believed the royal household would be better without the latter, he did not intend to jeopardise his friendship with the Queen by showing open animosity to the Baroness. No, that was for Albert. All the time the Queen and Lord Melbourne had been friends Lehzen had not been a menace to their relationship. She was, therefore, the Prince's affair; he must be the one to get rid of her.

Albert went on: 'If you could bring about her removal before you leave office that would be a good thing. It would be easier coming from you. She will never accept it from Peel.'

'Your Highness, Her Majesty would tell me that the Baroness's position in the household is not a state matter and therefore no concern of the Prime Minister. And rightly so. This is a domestic matter. The Queen would therefore resent my interference. It is for Your Highness to remove this woman and now is perhaps the time.'

'I couldn't do it – not with the new baby so soon to arrive.'

Lord Melbourne advised his usual policy: Put it off.

'After the child is born is the time,' he said. 'Particularly if it is a boy. There will be great rejoicing and the Queen will be very happy. Yes, put it off until then.'

Albert sighed; he longed to tell the Queen exactly what he felt, but he dared not. He feared storms, which could be so bad for her in her condition.

But Lehzen did not accompany them on their tour.

The excuse was that Pussy was not as well as they would have hoped and therefore Lehzen must remain behind to superintend the nursery.

It was a delightful tour. They visited Panshanger, the home of Earl Cowper, Woburn Abbey, the Duke of Bedford's place, and finally – and most happily as far as the Queen was concerned – they were entertained by Lord Melbourne at his country house, Brocket Hall.

'There!' said Albert. 'Did you not enjoy your round of visits?'

'Completely,' replied the Queen. 'And I'll tell you what pleases me most. It is to see how people are beginning to appreciate *you*, Albert.'

'You make me so happy,' said the Prince.

'Dearest Albert. Everything would have been perfect if we had had dear Pussy and Lehzen here.'

The Prince felt a little deflated; but the fact was she had enjoyed the visit, separated from Lehzen as she had been and with the prospect of Lord Melbourne's imminent departure from the premiership. He was becoming the most important one in her life.

Very soon after their return the results of the election were known. It was, as had been expected, a decisive victory for the Tories; Sir Robert Peel's representatives in the house would number 368,

Lord Melbourne's 292.

The Queen shut herself into the blue closet to brood alone for a short while, thinking what this meant.

There could be no way out of this. Sir Robert Peel would be her new Prime Minister – and she must say goodbye to her beloved Lord Melbourne, but only she assured herself as Prime Minister. He would remain her dear friend.

On that hot August day she waited in the blue closet, the scene of so many happy meetings. She had thought of it as their particular sanctum and had always refused if possible to see anyone else there. And now he was coming for the last time as her Prime Minister and she felt very sad.

He came and stood before her; she looked for the tears in his eyes and was certain that she would find them.

She held out her hands; he took them both and kissed them. 'So it has come,' she said.

'It was inevitable. Only Your Majesty has kept it at bay for these last two years.'

'At least I did that.'

He smiled tenderly. 'And now, there is the Prince to stand beside you. It will be easier now than then. That is something I remind myself of continually.'

'I shall never forget,' she said.

'Nor I. But this is not the end, you know.'

'I am determined that it shall not be.'

'May I give Your Majesty one piece of advice?'

'You must go on giving me advice for years to come.'

'Since Your Majesty is so kind I will not hesitate to do so now. I beg of you send for Peel without delay. If you did not it might be construed as a slight. It is my earnest desire to see you on good terms with your new government.'

'I shall never like Peel. He fidgets. He is nervous and that makes me uneasy.'

'You will put him at his ease. There is already an understanding between him and the Prince.'

'Oh, yes, Albert is quite fond of the fellow.'

'As you will be ... in time.'

She shook her head. 'I shall never forgive him for taking you from me.'

'I am here still. Perhaps Your Majesty will continue to write to me. I think the loss of those letters would be something I could not bear.'

'I shall write to you as before and you shall advise me, and I shall always think of you as my dear ... dear friend.'

'And you will lean on the Prince. You will find him strong and shrewd.'

'I have the best husband in the world, I know.'

'He will be a great comfort to you and may I say it is a comfort to me to leave you in such good hands.'

She was too emotional to speak and he went on to say that he should not stay. She had not yet sent for Peel. People would know how long he had been with her. They must not be unwise.

She clung to his hands for a moment; then he bowed and left her.

She went to her room and blinded by tears she collected some of her drawings together – her favourite ones. Some of them he had seen before and admired. They should be his – her last gift to him as Prime Minister. He would understand that by giving him her own work she meant him to have the best that she could offer.

As soon as he received the drawings he wrote to thank her for them.

*Lord Melbourne will ever treasure them as remembrances of Your Majesty's kindness and regard, which he prizes beyond measure.*

*They will, as Your Majesty says, certainly recall to recollection a melancholy day, but still Lord Melbourne hopes and trusts that with the divine blessing it will hereafter be looked back upon with less grief and bitterness of feeling, than it must be regarded at the present.*

She wept over the letter. She remembered so much from the past: the first day when she had become Queen and he came to cheer and comfort her with his dear presence; she remembered their conversations, his witty, often inconsequential remarks which had amused her so much; she remembered her jealousy when he had spent too much time at Holland House. Then she had been a young girl – a queen it was true – but carefree, as far as a queen could be. She remembered the first summer of her reign. She had never really spent such a joyous summer. Then she had not realised that cares and anxieties went with the pomp, ceremonies, gaiety and the freedom of being Queen.

But that was past; now she was a wife, the mother of one child and soon to have another;

and she knew that she had to be wise and strong; and now that she had lost her dear Prime Minister she must try to come to terms with the one she was sure she was going to dislike.

Almost immediately it was necessary to see Sir Robert Peel. The interview was brief, lasting only twenty minutes but Sir Robert was less ill at ease than he had been on that disastrous occasion two years ago; and very anxious for the Queen to know that he wanted their relationship to be smooth and easy. He was as respectful as she could wish. He said he would give her a list of the members of his cabinet for her approval. There was no hurry over this matter, said the Queen, and she would prefer to study the list at her leisure. Sir Robert left and the Queen sighed with relief.

Victoria immediately sat down to write to Lord Melbourne and tell him exactly what had happened. She ended by writing:

*What the Queen felt when she parted from her dear kind friend Lord Melbourne is better imagined than described; she was dreadfully affected for some time after, but is calm now. It is very, very sad and she cannot quite believe it yet. The Prince felt it very much too, and really the Queen cannot say how kind and affectionate he is to her, and how anxious to do everything to lighten this heavy trial; he was quite affected at this sad parting. We do, and shall, miss you so dreadfully; Lord Melbourne will easily understand what a change it is, after these four years when she has had the happiness of having Lord Melbourne always*

*about her. But it will not be so long till we meet again.*
*Happier and brighter times will come again. We*
*anxiously hope Lord Melbourne is well and safe. The*
*Queen trusts he will take care of his valuable health,*
*now more than ever.*

She was weeping over the letter when Albert
came in. 'Read it,' she said. 'Oh, Albert, I shall
have to learn to be without him now.'

Albert took her hands and looked steadily into
her face.

'You will have to put your trust in me now,
Victoria.'

'I do, Albert.'

'All your trust,' he answered.

She nodded; but he was thinking of the Baroness
who still remained as the shadow between them.

The Queen was now getting so heavy that her
thoughts were largely taken up with her approaching confinement. Lord Melbourne wrote almost
as frequently as he had in the past; he called often
and so she did not miss him as she had feared she
would. Albert admired the new Prime Minister
and it was wonderful how he was able to ease the
situation between Peel and the Queen. ('Although,' she often said, 'I shall *never* like him; and
as for his ever taking the place of dear Lord Melbourne that is quite impossible.') Lehzen fussed a
good deal and was always insisting that she rest
and should not be disturbed. She even tried to get
Albert out of the bedroom, but Albert would not
accept this.

Victoria was less irritable and not nearly so

nervous as she had been before the birth of the Princess Royal. That young lady was however giving them cause for anxiety. Pussy would not eat; and she was always crying. Sir James Clark had said she could not take rich foods and put her on ass's milk and chicken broth. Albert said he thought this was not enough for the child and Lehzen insisted that if these were the doctor's orders they must be followed.

'Certainly they must,' said the Queen. It was, as Lehzen had said, Pussy's teeth which were coming through which made her peevish. It was the same with all children.

And on the 9th of November the Queen's labour began; she had arranged with Albert that ministers and dignitaries should not be told until the birth was imminent. She was not going through what she did last time with people gathered in the next room listening to her cries of agony.

The child was born. She lay back exhausted and triumphant.

Albert, beside her, beaming with pride and joy, had given her the good news.

'My dear love, we have a Prince of Wales.'

# Chapter XI

## NOT THE QUEEN,
## BUT ALBERT'S WIFE

There was great rejoicing throughout the country. All the dreary prognostications of the Queen's going the same way as her cousin Charlotte were forgotten. Only two years married and she had two children and the second was a healthy boy.

The press could not forgo its lampoons but they were good-natured. Sir Robert Peel and Lord Melbourne were depicted as the palace nurses – Melbourne holding the Princess Royal and Peel holding the Prince of Wales.

'My baby's better than yours,' was the inscription in the balloon coming from Melbourne's mouth.

'But I have the boy,' was that from Peel's.

The bells rang; the cannons fired; and the Queen recovered quickly from her confinement.

There was great discussion about the boy's name.

'I want him to be called Albert after his father,' said Victoria; 'and I fervently hope that he grows up *exactly* like him.'

Albert was, she realised, not a name that had been used for English kings and she must remember that this lusty child who screamed a good deal to show what a fine pair of lungs he had, was the future King of England. Edward was a name which had been used by kings many times. There had been six already, so it would have to be Edward she supposed.

Lord Melbourne, who was writing as frequently as ever and on as diverse subjects as he did before, attempted to imply that the name of Edward would be more suitable for the future King of England. It was a good English appellation, wrote Lord Melbourne, and has a certain degree of popularity attached to it from ancient recollections. Albert? Yes, that was an excellent name, went on the tactful Lord Melbourne. It was Anglo-Saxon like Ethelred, but it had not been so much in use since the Conquest.

The Queen laughed. Since Lord Melbourne had ceased to be her Prime Minister she was relying so much on her husband; she was, if that were possible, more in love with him since the birth of the Prince of Wales than before.

'I shall insist that the boy's name is Albert,' she said. 'I know dear Lord Melbourne thinks Edward more suitable; but as I want him to be like his father in *every* respect, I shall name him Albert – though Edward could come next.'

She sat down to write to Uncle Leopold.

*Our little boy is a wonderfully strong and large child with very dark blue eyes but somewhat large nose and a pretty little mouth. I hope and pray he may be like his dearest Papa. He is to be called* Albert *and* Edward *is to be his second name.*

Baron Stockmar, who considered it his duty to know what went on at Court, was disturbed because of the Queen's feelings for Lord Melbourne.

He had never approved of the Queen's almost fanatical devotion towards her Prime Minister, but there had been some excuse because of Melbourne's position. Now he no longer held that position yet the Queen and he continued to behave as though he did.

People were talking, Stockmar told himself, and this would never do.

He had been visiting a friend's house when the subject had been brought up and someone had said that there was no doubt that the Queen and her one-time Prime Minister corresponded daily because Mrs Norton, who was known to be a great friend of Lord Melbourne's (hadn't he once been cited as co-respondent when George Norton had tried to divorce her), had said so.

Stockmar brooded on this conversation and shortly afterwards found occasion to visit Sir Robert Peel.

He congratulated the new Prime Minister on the ease with which he had slipped into office.

'I am pleased to see that the Queen is contented,' said Sir Robert – and added with a wry smile, 'at least far more contented than I had dared hope in the circumstances.'

Stockmar, who prided himself on his Teutonic frankness, said: 'The friendship with Lord Melbourne never pleased me. The Queen's emotions were too much involved.'

'She was so young at the time of her accession

and Melbourne has all the necessary airs and graces to please a young girl. So many of us lack them.'

'Countries are not ruled by airs and graces,' replied Stockmar.

'True,' agreed Peel, 'and I hope now that the Queen will find all her happiness in the circle of her family.'

'The friendship with Lord Melbourne persists,' said Stockmar.

'It is my sincere endeavour to please Her Majesty and her personal friendships are not the concern of her government.' His tone became suddenly serious. 'But if I were to discover that the Queen were taking advice on public matters in another place, I should without hesitation resign and would not remain in office another hour.'

Stockmar agreed that this was the only proper course of action, and as the guardian of palace morals, believed it was his place to act.

He immediately wrote to Lord Melbourne.

When Lord Melbourne received Stockmar's letter he was very angry.

'God eternally damn it,' he cried. 'Flesh and blood cannot stand this. Who is this interfering old German? Germans! I always disliked them. And the Queen has married one!'

Then he laughed at himself. Of course it was wrong to continue to write to the Queen. Of course it was not ethical. But what could he do? For four years she had been his life. He had thought of little else but how to guide her, how to amuse her. And she had cared for him too. He knew she had cried bitterly when they had had to say good-bye.

He was a fool. He was past sixty and in a strange way he was in love with a girl of twenty-two, a queen who was married to a young German Prince and was madly in love with her husband at that.

He wanted them to be happy. He had helped them to be happy and like a fool he was clinging to this correspondence because it was all he had left.

He waited for her letters each day. He treasured her affectionate remarks. He looked often at the little charm she had given him to attach to his keys. 'It will bring you luck,' she had said. 'I worry about your health you know.' Then there were the etchings which she herself had made. She had given them to him because she knew he would treasure something that had meant a good deal to her.

But he was gradually losing his hold. If the letters stopped that would be the end. She would always remember him with tenderness but he would no longer have a part in her life. But it had to be. That had been clear right from the beginning.

When Stockmar came to see him he was his suave self.

'Well, Baron,' he said, 'so you and Sir Robert are uneasy about my correspondence with the Queen?'

'It must stop,' said Stockmar. 'It is highly dangerous.'

'I don't know what Her Majesty will say. I am

often upbraided for not being prompt enough in my replies.'

'The Queen must be made to understand. She must be told.'

'My dear Stockmar, that is not the way to deal with the Queen; the correspondence should gradually discontinue. You may leave it to me.'

Stockmar nodded. He had made his point and he knew Lord Melbourne was a man of honour.

This German is a power at Court, thought Lord Melbourne. He is right, of course, he is shrewd; but there is no wit in him, no humour. What will they do to my sweet Victoria between them – these Germans, Stockmar and Albert?

Christmas had almost arrived and the royal party travelled down to Windsor to spend it at that favoured spot.

The Queen was excited and happy. Pussy seemed to have recovered from her teething troubles and really was fast becoming very bright and amusing. 'The Boy' as they called him was clearly very healthy and need give his parents no concern. It was a very happy party. The weather was bright and frosty and the Queen and Albert could enjoy rides and walks in the park and the forest.

There was the excitement of presents. Albert wanted Christmas at Windsor to be exactly as the festival was celebrated in Coburg and it was fun decorating the trees for Christmas. How Pussy loved the flickering candles and even The Boy stared at them in wonderment. Present-giving ceremonies were always a delight to the Queen and it gave her great pleasure to see Pussy with her parcels – although the dear little thing didn't really understand what it was all about.

The Boy was too young to be of much interest to her, for she had never liked little babies very much. He bawled a good deal and at times – in spite of having his father's eyes – looked rather like a little frog. Pussy however looked so pretty and often in the mornings Lehzen would bring her in and sit her on the bed. Lehzen liked to sit on the bed too and demonstrate new phases of Pussy's cleverness; but often when she came Albert would be there and would take the child from Lehzen and turn his back on the Baroness which she could not ignore, so she had to leave them, although she did not like it one little bit.

Victoria was aware of the dislike these two had for each other and sometimes she felt irritated by one of them and sometimes by the other.

But Christmas was a happy time and she very much enjoyed the ball on New Year's Eve, when at midnight as the clocks were striking twelve, all the music stopped and there was a fanfare of trumpets to usher in the New Year.

She was standing with Albert who pressed her hand fervently. She saw the tears in his eyes, and she knew he was thinking of all the New Years' Eves he had spent in his own country.

She told him that night that she understood his feelings and knew that he must often think of his native land which he had left for her sake.

'Don't think I don't appreciate that, my dearest Albert,' she said. 'I often think of it and I know then that you mean more to me than anything on earth ... even more than the darling babies.'

He was deeply moved, but he was asking himself: more than Lehzen?

It must be so, for the time was coming when she would have to choose between them.

Baron Stockmar was watching the situation between Victoria and Albert with deep attention. His goal was to see Albert in the role of supreme guide and counsellor of the Queen. It was the very reason why he was in England; he had a wife and family in Coburg with whom he spent only a few months of the year; but he had long come to the conclusion that his mission in life was not to follow the medical profession which was what he had set out to do but to take a hand in governing Europe. He had soon discovered his bent when he had won the confidence of King Leopold and now that of Albert. Albert relied on him; he had been responsible in educating Albert to take his role; he had stimulated Albert's interest in politics; and he was certainly not going to stand by and see Albert pushed aside by a woman who had been the Queen's governess for years and so wormed her way into that loyal heart.

Not only had Stockmar Albert's confidence but that of the Queen also. She had been fond of him since the days when Uncle Leopold had been living in England; it was almost a command of Leopold's that she should be and in those days she had obeyed Leopold without question. Stockmar's attitude was unusual; he ignored court etiquette; he would suddenly leave a gathering without asking the Queen's permission; he would even pack up suddenly and leave for Coburg when the mood took him. This eccentric and completely independent attitude added to his prestige, and even the Queen would not have wished to offend him.

Stockmar had told Albert that the Baroness must leave the Court, and it was his task to see that this took place.

Albert, who was in full agreement with this point of view, continued to hesitate. The Queen's uncertain temper, his dislike of scenes, his fears of his own inadequacy overwhelmed him; and he delayed taking action.

The baptism of the Prince of Wales was to take place on the 25th January.

Soon after the New Year the Queen and her family had returned to Buckingham Palace. Victoria had lost the exuberance which she had felt at Christmas and was moody and depressed.

'It's after the birth,' said Lehzen. 'It often happens to women.'

Lehzen herself became ill and the doctor diagnosed jaundice which turned her yellow and made her look even less attractive than usual. Pussy was losing weight and cried a great deal. She was jealous of the new baby and screamed every time she saw him.

Albert said that a few days at Claremont away from it all would do Victoria good and he was going to insist on their going – just the two of them. To his surprise Victoria agreed and they spent a few happy days there. Victoria told him she so much enjoyed Claremont now; she had lost her silly fancies because at the house just before Pussy was born she really had believed that she too might die. It was a morbid silly fancy, she knew; but all that had gone now that she had Pussy and The Boy.

But the thought of Pussy, whom she was beginning to love dearly, made her anxious. The little girl was now a delightful toy, very pretty to look at and the sight of her in her little white merino dress trimmed with blue (a present from the Duchess of Kent who would have to be watched because she was *spoiling* her) and the little lace cap on her head, she really was a darling – especially when she talked, which Lehzen said was quite remarkable for one of her age. Pussy really was an unusual child. Albert did not call her Pussy; for him she was Vicky to distinguish her, as Albert said, from that very important Victoria, her Mama.

So now that she was at Claremont she wanted to get back to see how Pussy was.

It was a bitterly cold day when they returned; they hurried up to the nursery and were disturbed to discover that Pussy's health had not improved while they were away.

Albert picked up the child and exclaimed in horror. 'She has lost more weight, I am sure,' he said. He turned and saw the Baroness's eyes on him. With her yellowish face and the hatred in her eyes she looked really malevolent.

Albert went on, 'The child is being *starved*.'

One of the nurses, who took her cue from the Baroness and understood from her that the Prince was of small account, replied almost rudely: 'We follow the *doctor's* instructions here, Your Highness.'

269

Albert walked out of the nursery, followed by the Queen.

'This is a conspiracy,' he said. 'Everyone – yes, everyone – is conspiring to keep me out of the nursery.'

Victoria, who was as worried as Albert by their daughter's health, cried out in anger: 'You mean that for me, I suppose.'

'I mean that I am worried by the manner in which my child is treated.'

'You would like to drive me out of the nursery, I suppose,' cried the Queen, her temper taking possession of her so that she was scarcely aware of what she said. 'Yes, that is what you would like to do so that you would then be at liberty to let our child die.'

The Prince could not believe he had heard correctly. To let his beloved child die! The Queen had gone mad. Oh, that violent temper. How could he deal with it? When it seized her she lost all logic, all sense of proportion. But to accuse him of wanting to see his little Vicky dead! It was too much. He was about to offer a protest as vehement as hers when he remembered the warnings of Melbourne and Stockmar.

'I must have patience,' he said; and turning abruptly left her.

Alone he reasoned with himself. If he exercised control, which he was quite capable of doing, Victoria would get the better of the argument. She lost her temper and made unforgivable statements; he remained calm and later forgave her; it was a recurring pattern; then it all started again.

If he wished to live in peace he would be obliged to stifle his opinions for fear of upsetting her. No, it was not the way.

He was going to say what he felt; if Victoria could lose her temper so must he; if she was going to fling abusive statements at him he was going to retaliate.

As he guessed it was not long before she came to him; she stormed in, her eyes blazing.

'So you have been trying to avoid me?'

'That is not so, although I can understand why you should think it considering the manner in which you behave.'

'I! It was *you*, Albert, who criticised the nursery. They are doing *everything* for Pussy and you came in and upset them all.'

'It was time they were upset.'

'How can you say such a thing!'

'Because it's true and I am not going to stand by and watch my daughter neglected.'

'Neglected! When we are all worried so much about the child that we are ill ourselves. Nobody could care more for her than Daisy...'

The mention of that ridiculous name gave Albert the spurt he needed. He really did lose his temper.

'It is your *Daisy* who is at the root of the trouble. She is unfitted to have the care of the child just as she was unfitted to have charge of you. It is for this reason that we have these displays of ungovernable rage which should have been checked in your infancy.'

'Albert, I don't think you realise what you are saying.'

271

'I realise fully, and I shall no longer be treated as though I am of no importance in this house.'

'You forget I'm the Queen.'

'That would be impossible. You constantly remind me of the fact.'

'How ... *dare* you...'

'Listen to the truth for once.'

'Albert! Have you gone mad?'

'Is it mad to dare speak the truth to the Queen? No doubt you think so. But let me tell you this, I am going to do it.'

'I wish,' said the Queen, 'that I had never married.'

'At least,' retorted Albert, 'that could be one point on which we are in agreement.'

She stared at him in amazement. This was unlike the Albert she knew.

He decided that there was no turning back. He went on: 'Your Doctor Clark has not looked after the child in a proper manner. He has poisoned her with his calomel and you have starved her. I am of no account here. *You* are the Queen. I was merely brought in to provide you with heirs to the throne. I shall have nothing more to do with this matter. Take the child away, do as you like, and if she dies you will have her death on your conscience.'

Victoria stared at him; but he had left.

She began to sob wildly.


'There,' soothed the Baroness, 'try to lie still. I will give you something warm and soothing. Your poor head must be aching. As if you haven't enough with all you have to do without *people*

272

behaving in such a way as to distress you.'

The Queen was scarcely aware of the ministering Lehzen; words kept going round and round in her head. What he had said. What she had said. What *had* she said? She wished she had never married! She had actually said that to *Albert!*

Who would have believed it possible to be so unhappy after the bliss of Christmas!

'You must cheer up,' said Lehzen. 'You must try to hold yourself aloof from this ... this ... wickedness. You must remember that you are the Queen. It used to be so different when you could take all your troubles to Lord Melbourne. Of course it is Stockmar who interferes so. He is trying to deprive you of Lord Melbourne. Oh, to think that the Queen could be so treated!'

But she was still not listening with all her attention. She kept going over that perfectly dreadful scene. There had never been such a scene. Always before Albert had been so calm. To see Albert in a temper was a terrible thing. It simply was not Albert.

Lehzen was saying: 'Lie down, my precious. You are so overwrought ... and when I think of all your anxiety...'

'Oh, leave me alone, Lehzen,' she snapped.

Lehzen merely smiled tolerantly. Lehzen implied that *she* understood. The Queen's temper was short and naturally so, considering all she had to contend with.

Alone, lying on her bed, pressing her hands to flushed damp cheeks, she thought of life with Albert and all it meant to her. There *must* be an

273

end to this terrible state of affairs. They must explain to each other, that they did not mean those terrible things they had said.

She waited for him to come to her, his usual calm self, to tell her that he was sorry; then she would say she was sorry too and they would agree that there just must never be a scene like that again.

She could endure it no longer. She wrote a note to him. She forgave him for what he had said yesterday. He attached too much importance to unimportant matters; he listened to rumours about certain people and believed them; if he would come to her and discuss his grievances she could explain so much to him and there would not be these distressing disagreements.

When he received this note Albert decided that this was a crisis in his marital affairs which could affect the whole future and he went to Baron Stockmar to ask his advice.

He told him in detail what had happened. He was worried about his children, for he believed the nursery was mismanaged; the household was in chaos. Witness the fact that the Boy Jones had been able to enter the palace and remain in it unobserved for several days. The Queen was completely under the spell of an intriguing old woman who hated him and was determined to wreck his marriage; the Queen's education had been so neglected that she felt inferior in the company of intellectual people and therefore avoided that company; and what was more her hasty passionate nature made it quite impossible to reason with her.

The Baron listened attentively.

'Everything you say is true,' he answered, 'and it is a state of affairs which must not continue. The Baroness Lehzen must go.'

Albert was relieved. He had been right to come to Stockmar; even Victoria would have to listen to him.

'I fear I spoke out too strongly,' said Albert, 'but I felt it was necessary. I know you advised patience and calm and rightly so; but I was discovering that because she relied on my patience and calm she made no attempt to hold her temper in check. She made me feel like a child. It is more than I can endure.'

'This is the moment when firm action must be taken. The Queen is being ill advised and subversively supported. That advice and support must be withdrawn ... and soon.'

The Prince nodded eagerly.

'We shall have to deliver an ultimatum. You cannot ask the Queen to choose between you and Lehzen for obviously you cannot leave her.'

'Leave Victoria!' Albert turned pale at the thought, and Stockmar smiled.

'An impossibility of course, but if it were not so and you threatened it, I have no doubt that her regard for you would make her ready to dismiss Lehzen. But no, we cannot do that, but if *I* threatened to leave, if I offer her my conditions, I think that might be effective. It will be a matter of her choosing between Lehzen and myself.'

Albert was relieved and yet at the same time a little apprehensive. Lehzen whom she loved so devotedly, or Stockmar who was a sort of god in the household. Stockmar who could criticise even Lord Melbourne? Albert wondered what would happen if she agreed to let Stockmar go. He pictured himself attempting to stand against Victoria with Lehzen behind her.

However, some action must be taken; and if anyone could solve their difficulties it was Stockmar.

When Victoria read Stockmar's note she was horrified. Stockmar was always candid and to the point. He stated quite clearly that he was displeased by the recent conduct of the Queen towards her husband and if such violent and undignified scenes occurred again he would not stay at Court. He would retire to Coburg and settle down with his family, which he had wanted to do for a long time.

Impulsively she replied to Stockmar that she hated these scenes, but Albert must not provoke them. He should not believe the foolish things she said when she was in a temper. Of course she did not mean them, and she only said them in the heat of the moment when she was not feeling well.

She could not ignore the implications that Lehzen must go. This last scene had made the animosity between the Baroness and the Prince so obvious. She remembered the happy time she and Albert had had when they made their tour of the Whig Houses just before the election; she thought of Christmas and how wonderful Albert had been with the Christmas trees and how he had danced Pussy on his knee and explained to her about Christmas in Coburg.

How could she *live* without Albert? He meant more to her than anyone else on earth – Pussy, The Boy and Lehzen. She was happiest alone with Albert. Dear Lord Melbourne had told her that Albert would be a great comfort and Lord Melbourne was as usual right. But this was not a matter of being wise; this was a deep need.

She *loved* Albert; she would always love Albert. She could never be happy away from Albert and she knew that nothing in her life could ever be as important to her as her love for Albert.

The Baron looked sternly at the Queen.

'I can assure you,' she said, 'that quarrels with Albert are far more distressing to me than to him.'

'Then they must no longer be provoked,' said the Baron. 'And there is one reason why they start. Let us be frank. The Baroness Lehzen and the Prince are not good friends, never will be good friends and there will always be trouble while the Baroness remains in your household.'

The Queen was very pale and agitated. It was true of course. Lehzen and Albert – although of the same nationality – were sworn enemies and they could never be anything else. Strange that the two people she should love so dearly should be so very different. Albert was so meticulous, such a good organiser; Lehzen was always in a muddle; and she had to admit that the nurseries were not properly run. What if Pussy was suffering because of that?

She said: 'There is a mistaken idea that Baroness Lehzen is a sort of power behind the throne. That is not so. Lord Melbourne understood perfectly. She was good to me when I was a child; she was like a mother to me; I only want her to have a home with me. That's all. There is too much speculation and imagination.'

'I think she should go away,' said Baron Stockmar. 'Indeed she must go away.'

'You mean for a holiday?'

'A long holiday,' said Stockmar. 'You would see then how differently your household could be managed.'

Victoria now knew that all she really wanted was to be back on good terms with Albert. Suppose Lehzen went back to her home in Coburg for a long holiday. Then they could see how they managed without her. 'Dear Daisy,' she would say, 'it is so long since you saw your home. You have worked far too much. You know that you are not well. There was that attack of jaundice. Have a long rest.'

Poor Daisy! She would understand of course. Perhaps in her heart she would know that there was no room at the palace for her while the Prince was there; and the plain fact was that Victoria could not be happy without Albert.

Stockmar smiled benignly.

'I can see that Your Majesty has made up your mind.'

He went back to Albert. 'I have made her see reason.'

'You cannot mean that the Baroness is going!'

'In due course. I'm certain that before the year is out she will have said goodbye to the palace.'

'But the Queen has consented to this?'

'Not in so many words. But she realises that I shall not stay here if Lehzen remains and even more important she knows that you and Lehzen cannot continue amicably under the same roof. She has to choose between her old governess and a happy life with her husband. I had no doubt that when she saw exactly how matters stood she would have no hesitation in making her choice.'

Albert seized Stockmar's hand and wrung it warmly.

'There is still need for caution,' said the Baron. 'We have won the first skirmish only. The main battle is to be won. You will act with care. Your task, even when the Baroness is gone, will be to show the Queen that, although in public she is the Queen and you are only her consort, in the home you are the master.'

'You think it is possible to show Victoria that?'

'Not only possible but a necessity. Her nature demands that you should do this. You must be very careful indeed until Lehzen departs and even after that you will tread warily. Make no concessions. Be your calm self; that disconcerts her. But I think you were wise on this one occasion to match your temper with hers. But not again. From now on you will be the calm, judicious husband.'

Stockmar laughed – something he rarely did.

'I think I see victory,' he added.

The Queen waited for Albert to come to her. Why did he not? She had made concessions. She was going to agree to the Baroness's going on a long holiday. Now she expected him to come and tell her how pleased he was and how much he appreciated the sacrifice she was making for him.

She went to his sitting-room and found him there reading. How dared he be so calm.

'Albert,' she said, 'I had thought that you would have come to see me.'

He raised his eyebrows and smiled at her. 'You were not in a very pleasant mood when we last met.'

'Nor were you,' she reminded him.

'It was most regrettable.'

'Put your book down, Albert. I have to talk to you.'

Albert said coolly: 'Is that an order?'

'When I come in I expect you to put aside what you are doing.'

She frowned. She was longing for him to embrace her and tell her how noble she was to agree to do without Lehzen and to tell her he adored her for her self-sacrifice; and there he was serenely sitting there, looking as though he found his wretched book more interesting than she was.

Oh, he was clever, of course. And she was not. And he wanted to have clever people to dine with them so that they could all talk over her head and he could show how much more clever he was than the Queen.

'If it was a request instead of a command I might be prepared to concede,' said Albert with a grave smile.

'A request. Must I then *request* the privilege of speaking to you?'

'It might be considered courteous to do so.'

'Courteous!' she cried. 'Am I expected to curtsy every time see you as well as ask permission to speak?'

Albert rose, went through to his bedroom and shut the door.

She hurried after him and when she tried to open the door found that he had turned the key in the lock.

'Open this door at once!' she cried.

There was no answer. Furiously she hammered with her fists on the panels.

'Open this door!' she commanded.

Albert was standing on the other side of it. 'Who is that?' he asked.

'Who is that?' she cried in passion. 'You know who it is. It is the Queen.'

She waited. The door remained locked.

She took the handle and shook it.

'*Who* is there?' asked Albert.

'The Queen is here,' she said. 'Open this door at once.'

She waited for the sound of a key in the lock. It did not come. She was very near to tears. She felt wretchedly unhappy. She had agreed to Lehzen's taking a holiday and now Albert was being unkind to her.

She would not endure it. Again she hammered on the door.

That maddeningly calm voice answered: 'Who is that?'

'As though you don't know!' she cried, her voice rising to a hysterical note. 'Open this door I say.'

'*Who* is there?' he repeated maddeningly.

'The Queen!' she answered regally. Silence. He would not open the door. Oh, how dared he?

She was so miserable. She wanted Albert to be kind and loving again; she could not endure these differences. Albert was right in a way. She *was* imperious. She *did* have a violent temper, and when it was roused she said things that would have been so much better left unsaid.

She wanted to lean on Albert's chest and sob out her miseries. She wanted to tell him that only if they were together, as they had been on those blissful occasions which were all too short, could she be entirely happy. No matter who went away, she would still be happy if only Albert continued to love her.

She went back to the door and this time rapped on it somewhat gently.

Albert's voice came again, more gentle this time. 'Who is there?'

'This is your wife, Albert,' she answered tearfully.

The door was unlocked. Albert stood there, his arms outstretched.

She ran into them and clung to him.

'Oh, Albert, never, never, *never* let us quarrel again.'

# Chapter XII

## A LONG HOLIDAY FOR THE BARONESS

The baptism of the new baby was an important occasion because the child was the heir to the throne.

The chief sponsor was to be the King of Prussia who had travelled to England to fulfil his role. Albert met the King at Greenwich and travelled with him to Windsor where the Queen was waiting to receive him. Victoria had always been delighted to entertain guests particularly when the entertainment was a grand ball; and a grand ball it must be to be worthy of Frederick of Prussia.

The King turned out to be charming. Although as tall as Albert he was very fat; he was going bald and his whiskers were very sparse, the Queen noticed; but his charming manners and obvious desire to please made up for that.

He was very interested in everything he saw and was delighted with the children, particularly Pussy, whose health had improved a little and when she was well she was so very lively. The Queen insisted on his dancing a quadrille with her and although he told her that it was a long time since he had danced and he feared he cut rather a poor figure, he danced with the Queen and it was a very pleasant ball.

The real purpose of the visit though was the baptism, and as little Albert Edward was the heir to the throne it was decided that he should be baptised in a consecrated building. Hence instead of the palace baptism which had been the lot of the Princess Royal, this more important ceremony was to take place in St George's Chapel, Windsor.

Albert Edward, the Queen was delighted to note, behaved perfectly, although he did not show Pussy's intelligent interest in everything. (She would never forget Lord Melbourne's amusing remark that the little Princess Royal was perfectly aware that everything was for her benefit); but of course the chapel was a beautiful setting and this was a far more grand occasion.

Albert, who was so musical, decided that there should be no anthem, although one had been specially composed for the occasion.

'No,' he explained to Victoria, 'if we have a new composition everyone will be paying attention to that and discussing the merits of it. They are not here to criticise music but to rejoice in the birth of the heir to the throne. So there will be no anthem. We should leave the chapel on a note of triumph. I suggest the Hallelujah Chorus.'

'But that is wonderful,' cried the Queen. 'We all know it and it is certainly triumphant music. Poor Mr Elvey is going to be very disappointed that his anthem is not sung, though.'

'There will be plenty of occasions for us to hear Mr Elvey's anthem,' said the Prince. 'There can only be one christening of the Prince of Wales.'

'You are absolutely right, Albert,' said the

Queen; and she said afterwards how imposing the ceremony was. The music was particularly beautiful.

The absorption with the baptism meant that it was possible to put off telling Lehzen that it had been decided she should have a long holiday. The more she thought of it, the more Victoria wondered how she could ever do it. She kept postponing it, which meant that she found herself avoiding Lehzen's company. Albert was aware of this and decided, as he had over the affair of the bedchamber ladies, that he must take action.

He found Lehzen alone one day and asked her how she was feeling. She was clearly not looking well, he told her, and he believed it was due to that attack of jaundice from which she had never fully recovered.

She replied that she was recovering and that she had so much with which to occupy herself that she did not notice her own slight indisposition.

'The Queen is concerned about you,' said Albert. 'She is saying that you have never had a real holiday.'

The Baroness's face softened at the mention of the Queen. 'Her Majesty's heart is very tender for those she loves. I am well enough. A spell at Windsor will make me completely well again.'

'The Queen thinks you need a *complete* change. It must be years since you were in Coburg.'

'Coburg! Is the Queen thinking of paying a visit? She has not mentioned this to me.'

'The Queen could not of course leave the country. She was thinking of you.'

The Baroness gave a short sharp laugh. 'Her Majesty knows that my place is by her side.'

'Not if you are unwell and need to regain your strength,' replied the Prince and left her.

The Baroness was alarmed. What did that mean? No, Victoria would never agree to banish her. Banish her? But he had said a holiday. Oh, but she knew his devious ways. Once let him get her away and he would try to keep her away.

She was not going.

She went to the Queen in the unceremonious way which their relationship had made possible.

'I believe there is a plot afoot,' she said.

The Queen rose to her feet. She raised her eyebrows. Really, it was true that Lehzen did take advantage of their affection. She knew of course what this meant and feeling very unhappy about it was immediately irritated with Lehzen who made her feel so.

'Plot, Lehzen. What are you talking about?'

'The Prince is trying to separate us.'

'He – and I – are concerned for your health. *We* think a good long holiday is what you need.'

'A holiday. What do I want with a holiday? My pleasure is serving you.'

'That is the point. You have never had a change. That is why the Prince and I have decided you shall have a nice long holiday in Germany.'

'In Germany!'

'It is your home, remember.'

'This is my home.'

'Now, Daisy dear, *do* be sensible. You have often talked of your sister and brother in Bückeburg and said how you long to see them. There are your brother's children too. You will be so happy to see them all again.'

'And you are quite happy to do without me.'

'My dear Daisy, I want you to be well and happy. Albert and I have talked it over. Everything will be settled for you. There will be no shortage of money. We want you to be happy, for I shall never forget all you have done for me.'

The Baroness was speechless. It was all arranged. She had thought she was winning this battle against the Prince, but this was his silent victory.

Victoria was happy. There was a new understanding between herself and Albert; she took a pride in her newly acquired humility; it pleased her – and Albert – that she should defer to him in almost everything. Albert was often in the nursery; Pussy's diet was changed and she began to thrive. Albert was right, of course. The only sadness was poor Lehzen, who was subdued and unlike her old self. She did really treat me as though I were a child in the schoolroom, thought Victoria. It had to stop; and this is the best way of doing it.

Albert had exciting news just after little Albert Edward's christening.

'My brother is to be married,' he said. 'Dear Ernest!'

'That is wonderful, Albert. Who is to be his bride?'

'Princess Alexandrine of Baden.'

'I do hope they will be as happy as we are because no one could have a *more* perfect marriage,' said the Queen, cheerfully ignoring the storm which had only just subsided.

'That would be asking a great deal,' replied Albert fondly. 'My stepmother wishes me to be present. She knows of course that you can't.'

'Oh, Albert, you will want to see your brother married, but I shall *hate* us to be separated.'

'I shall not go,' said Albert.

'Dear Albert, but he is your brother and I know what ties there are between you.'

Leave Court, thought Albert, with Lehzen still there. Who knew what would happen in his absence? This was one of the most significant periods of his life, he was well aware; what happened now could affect the whole future. He would be a fool to go away and leave Victoria with Lehzen. It would be to retire from the battlefield on the point of victory. Besides, what of that terrible sea crossing which he loathed? That he would have endured; but he was certainly not going to leave Victoria until Lehzen had set out on her 'long holiday'.

'I shall *not* go,' said Albert. 'I am not going to leave you.'

'My dear Albert, we must explain to Ernest. He will understand, I'm sure. I have a plan. Let us ask them to spend their honeymoon here. Ernest was here when we were married. He saw our happiness. Now we will suggest that he allows us to see his.'

'That is a wonderful idea and worthy of my dearest love,' said Albert; and the Queen glowed with pleasure.

'When is the wedding to be?' she asked.

'The third of May at Carlsruhe.'

'Then they must come here immediately afterwards.'

Albert said they should invite Ernest without delay. 'I do hope that Ernest is quite well and er ... fit for the marriage,' he added gravely.

The Queen flushed. She knew Albert was referring to that most unpleasant indisposition Ernest had suffered from at the time of their marriage. It was the result of his brother's 'excesses' Albert had told her. He feared that Ernest could be a little frivolous.

'Now he is to be married he will be different,' said the Queen. She looked adoringly at Albert. 'My dear love,' she cried fervently, 'how glad I am that I chose you. Not that I had the smallest doubt in my mind once I had seen you.'

Albert said solemnly that they should be thankful to God for their good fortune ... *both* of them.

The Baroness had been stunned by the manner in which she was being dismissed. A few months before she would not have thought it possible. She had been foolish; she had been deceived by the violence of the recent quarrels. She had not realised that in spite of these Victoria's love for her husband had been growing deeper every day. She knew her beloved child. When she loved she did so whole-heartedly. The adored one became perfect in her eyes. Lehzen had once been so. But she should have been warned by the Queen's relationship with Lord Melbourne, whom Victoria had openly adored. At one time everything Lord Melbourne did and said was right. How much more affection and devotion would she have for a husband. Lehzen had miscalculated. She had tried to oust Albert from his position and the inevitable outcome was that she was being ousted from hers.

She tried to visualise life without Victoria. It was impossible, she thought at first. Victoria was her child. Every day since she was five and had been put in her care every thought had been for her. How foolish she had been! If she had been prepared to accept Albert, if she had tried to make their life more smooth, she would not have been banished now. For banishment it was. Lehzen was no fool. A long holiday meant for ever. Her home would be over there not here. Perhaps she would pay a visit to the Queen. A visit ... to her *home!* For her home was where her beloved child was.

But she must be realistic. She must not antagonise the Queen. If she accepted her fate stoically she would be asked back. They would write to each other. It would be so easy to lose everything now. She must hold on to something.

So she smiled sadly and made her preparations.

'I have written to my sister,' she told the Queen. 'She wants me to stay with her. We shall be company for each other. My brother's family will be pleased to see me, they say.'

The Queen smiled radiantly. 'Oh, dearest Daisy, I am so happy. And your brother has children. You will love helping with them, I know. You are so good with children.'

'Yes, I shall be very interested in them.'

'And there is no need to worry about money, Daisy. The Prince says we must make quite sure that you never have to do that. The Prince is so good at arranging everything.'

Yes, thought Lehzen, he is very good at arranging to be rid of me.

'I shall always love you,' said the Queen emotionally.

'There,' said Lehzen, 'we mustn't cry, must we?'

The Queen was ready to laugh; it was the laughter of relief.

'Always the governess, Daisy,' she cried and kissed the Baroness fervently. 'Always remember, Daisy dear, that I will do anything...'

Anything, thought Lehzen, but oppose the Prince's wishes and allow me to stay.

Albert was teaching Victoria a great deal and one thing was what a good Prime Minister they had.

'Peel is a dedicated statesman,' he told her, 'and we need such a man at the head of affairs.'

'I shall always regret my dear Lord Melbourne,' replied the Queen.

'A charming fellow, of course, but not the calibre of Peel. To tell the truth, my love, Melbourne – whom I admire and respect in so many ways – excels more socially than politically. We need an adept politician at the moment.'

Victoria felt she should protest out of loyalty to her old Prime Minister but she was beginning to see that Albert was right. Albert, in his serious way, studied politics and knew what he was talking about. It was no use merely being charming and witty when some serious action was needed.

Albert had always liked Sir Robert Peel and because she was beginning to believe that Albert was almost always right, she looked differently at the new Prime Minister. It was amazing how he responded. Although he lacked Lord Melbourne's *grace* he was quite charming, always so respectful and there was no doubt that he was a good man.

'I never thought I could like Sir Robert,' she told Albert. 'But that is changed, thanks to you.'

Albert was very gratified and they seemed closer than ever.

The country was in great difficulties. Engaged in war in China, it had to contend with trouble in Afghanistan and the West Indies. America was indignant with England because of the practice of searching ships to discover whether they were carrying on the slave trade. This was merely to make sure that they were not British ships masquerading under the American flag, but the British were dangerously unpopular because of the practice. But of even greater concern was the trouble at home. Unemployment was great and growing; the price of food had risen and wages were pitiably low. People had left the country to flock to the towns and there was no work for them there, or the wages were such that they could only live at starvation level. Revolt was in the air. People were no longer in the mood to accept glaring inequalities. Rioting was breaking out in the coal mines of Wales and Staffordshire; the pottery district followed and there was trouble brewing in Lancashire. A strong force had to be kept in Ireland where a potato famine was threatened. The high taxes imposed there were causing dangerous dissatisfaction.

Unlike his predecessor, Sir Robert Peel with-held none of these facts from the Queen for the sake of her comfort.

He was a man of ideas and he was pleased to discuss them with the Queen – the Prince being present.

'All these troubles are jeopardising the coun-try,' he said, 'and we shall have to take drastic action. I have come to the conclusion that we can no longer expect the poor to bear the country's burdens. We have to look to those in better finan-cial circumstances. I am going to propose an Income Tax not to exceed sevenpence in the pound on all incomes over £150 a year.'

Albert nodded gravely and the Queen said: 'That is an excellent measure. There must be no exemptions. I shall expect to pay as everyone else.'

Sir Robert smiled and said that knowing Her Majesty's shrewd assessment of facts and her right-mindedness he had been certain of her support and that of the Prince on his measure.

Yes, the Queen was beginning to appreciate her Prime Minister.

Lord Melbourne was continuing to write to her in spite of Baron Stockmar's disapproval; but the letters came less frequently and she was afraid that she often left his unanswered for days. It seemed that she was continually excusing herself on account of pressure of business or the arrival of visitors. How different from those days when she had upbraided him if she did not see him every day.

Now he wrote to her about the proposed income tax and told her that she should exert her royal prerogative and refuse to subscribe to such a scheme.

How different he was from Sir Robert, who was *so* realistic. Of course she wanted her subjects to know that if there were going to be unpleasant measures she wanted to share in them.

Lord Melbourne had kept her distressingly ignorant of social evils; he did it, she knew, because he hated to distress her, which was very kind, and she knew he was the most *feeling* of men but Sir Robert and Albert treated her as though she was a *serious* person, and naturally the Queen must know everything that is going on. She smiled tenderly over Lord Melbourne's letter, 'Dear Lord M,' she said to herself. 'He has become such an *old* man lately.'

It seemed an excellent idea to give a charity ball. What could be better, said the Queen, than to enjoy oneself and do good at the same time?

Even Albert – who disliked balls so much – agreed that this was an excellent idea. It was to help trade and as it was a *bal costumé*, Albert was to go as Edward III and she as Queen Philippa; the members of the Court would be dressed in the costume of that time. The Duchess of Cambridge had arranged to bring a party from her household which would be dressed as royal people and their courts from Spain, Italy and France. It was a grand occasion, thoroughly enjoyed by Victoria; and because of its success another ball was arranged to be given at Covent Garden in aid of the Spitalfields workers.

'What an excellent – and delightful – way of helping trade,' cried the Queen.

Albert said that it had been effective on this occasion but a habit should not be made of that kind of entertainment because the magnificent costumes and the gaiety did in a way draw attention to the different lives led by the rich and the poor.

Albert was absolutely right of course; but she did enjoy the dancing.

Albert thought it would be an excellent idea if her birthday was spent at Claremont where they could be quiet and enjoy the country. The country no longer bored her as it used to. There was so much of interest to be learnt and Albert was teaching her to enjoy the scenery and the wildlife. She feared she had been very ignorant of these things in the past.

'Oh, it was the way you were brought up,' said Albert, smiling tolerantly. 'Not your fault in the least. But that will be remedied now. It is such fun to teach you these things and I must say, my love, that you are an apt pupil.'

Poor Lehzen, all the Queen's faults were laid at her door; all her virtues had been inherited. Victoria was so comforted by the implication that she did not examine it very closely. Even the violent temper, so to be deplored and even now feared lest it should break out, was attributed to a lack of control during her formative years.

At Claremont there was a ball for her birthday. Even Albert realised that she could not be denied that, though in time he was sure she would realise the futility of such a pastime, and they danced in the gallery.

It was such a happy birthday, shadowed a little by the memories of other birthdays when Lehzen had been so happy arranging treats. And Lord Melbourne was not present either. Times changed. She was very kind to Lehzen, but not too familiar lest she thought there was to be a return to the old ways and her hopes should be raised, which would be cruel, for more and more Victoria was seeing how right Albert was and how really there was no place for Lehzen at Buckingham Palace.

She wrote to Lord Melbourne telling him about the birthday.

'The Queen was grieved,' she added, 'that Lord Melbourne could not be there.'

It was a beautiful Sunday in June and the Queen and Albert were returning to Buckingham Palace from the Chapel Royal at St James's. Crowds lined the Mall to see them pass; the Queen was quite popular now. The people were delighted with the babies and although they would never really like Albert who was still called 'the German', most people agreed that the devotion of the royal couple was an example to all. There was no longer slander about the Queen and Lord Melbourne; the Flora Hastings scandal had been forgotten.

Albert, looking very handsome in uniform, sat beside her nodding to the cheers.

'The people seem very pleased with us today,'

he said.

'They do,' replied Victoria, turning slightly to bow to the crowd on her right.

Albert said suddenly: 'Victoria, did you hear that?'

She turned to him. 'What was that?'

'I may have been mistaken,' went on Albert, 'but I am sure I saw someone take aim at us and heard a trigger snap.'

'Albert!'

'I may have been mistaken. No one seems to have noticed anything.'

She reached for his hand and gripped it firmly. 'Can you see anything now, Albert?' she asked.

'Nothing unusual. It must have been a mistake.'

'If it was someone planning to take aim he may still be lurking in the crowds.'

'Behave as though nothing has happened. I shall be watchful.'

They were relieved when they reached the palace.

'It must have been a mistake,' said the Prince.

In the afternoon Sir Robert Peel, accompanied by the head of the police, called at the palace.

'We have some disturbing news,' said Sir Robert to Victoria and the Prince. 'A boy named Pearse has told the police that while he was in the crowd in the Mall he saw a man who was standing close to him lift a pistol and point it at the carriage. He did not apparently fire. The boy heard him murmur to himself that he had been a fool not to do so.'

Turning pale Victoria looked at Albert, who said: 'I must tell you, Sir Robert, I saw this man.

I mentioned it to the Queen at the time. I thought that I might have been mistaken.'

'This is no mistake,' replied Sir Robert, 'and I think every precaution will have to be taken, for this man may make the attempt again.'

A long discussion followed. Victoria was very alarmed. It was not the first time she had been shot at. It was a terrifying experience even when one escaped, but at least it was unexpected and all over before one realised that it was happening. The man might decide not to act again for months. They couldn't stay in all that time.

At length it was agreed that Victoria and Albert should take their drives as usual. The equerries, Colonel Arbuthnot and Colonel Wylde, were called in and told what had happened; they were to ride very close to the carriage and one would watch the right-hand side of the road and the other the left; the drives would be taken at a faster pace than usual.

The Queen spent a sleepless night. She was frightened, she said. 'For Albert what if *you* were to be killed.'

Albert said that would be better than that she should, but he trusted Sir Robert's thorough precautions; the police would be out in force and at the first sign of trouble he would put himself between the Queen and the gun.

'But that is exactly what I fear, Albert,' she cried.

It was a very uneasy pair who drove out the next day. The Queen carried a parasol which was lined with chain mail and the carriage was surrounded by guards; the colonels rode very close to the carriage and the pace was brisk.

The sun shone hotly as they drove towards Hampstead; there were crowds of people about but that did not add to their peace of mind. The drive was almost over and Victoria, relieved to see the trees of Green Park, said to Albert: 'But imagine, it could go on like this for months before he decides to make his second attempt.'

They were approaching the palace – on one side of them the park, on the other the garden wall – when Albert saw the man again but not before he had fired. The shot went under the carriage; they heard the shouts of 'Get him! Catch him!' as the horses were whipped up and the carriages rumbled through the gates of Buckingham Palace.

Albert took the Queen's trembling hand and with his arm about her led her inside.

Sir Robert Peel reported to the palace immediately. The man had been arrested. He was a certain John Francis, a joiner by trade and twenty-two years old. When arrested he was truculent but this attitude soon changed when he was sentenced to death.

Victoria was distressed.

'You see, Albert,' she explained, 'I cannot bear that people should hate me so much that they want to kill me.'

'He was a madman.'

'Perhaps, but he did it and sometimes I wonder whether there will always be these people who want me dead. It makes me very uneasy. All the same I do not like to think that he is going to die because of this.'

'He deserves it.'

'I am going to ask that his life be spared in any case.'

'I know well your tender heart,' said Albert, 'but examples have to be made.'

'That's true. All the same I am going to ask Sir Robert what can be done about sparing his life.'

Sir Robert pointed out that the royal prerogative of mercy could not be exercised except under the direction of government but since the Queen felt so strongly on the matter, he would have the case considered.

The result was that John Francis's death sentence was commuted to transportation for life.

Albert said that had John Francis been hanged as he so richly deserved it would not have entered the head of John William Bean to follow his example. Bean was four feet tall, a hunchback and therefore easily identified.

Since Francis had attempted to kill her, the Queen had become very popular and whenever she drove out crowds congregated to see her pass by.

She and Albert were driving to the chapel in St James's Palace, when the hunchback pointed the pistol at them. A boy of sixteen named Dassett, with the help of his brother, seized the hunchback and shouted to the police. Thinking the deformed Bean to be only a child and his captors not much more, the police believed the affair to be a game and told the brothers to let the little fellow go. But the Dassett boys kept Bean's pistol and showed it to another policeman. There could be no doubt that it was a dangerous weapon and, thinking the Dassetts had been seen to fire it and were pretending to be innocent, he was about to arrest them when their uncle – who had brought them to see the Queen ride by – hurried over and by this time others said that they had seen what had happened. When powder was found to be in the pistol the Dassett boys were commended and it did not take long to identify the hunchback, who was an assistant in a chemist shop, and he was promptly arrested.

Sir Robert, who was in Cambridge, came hurrying back to London on hearing the news and presented himself at Buckingham Palace.

When the Queen entered the room his emotion was so great at the sight of her that tears came into his eyes and he could not control his voice.

So deeply affected was the Queen that the somewhat frigid and formal Sir Robert could feel so deeply about her safety, that from that moment every vestige of the dislike which she had fought so hard to overcome disappeared. It was the constant tears in Lord Melbourne's eyes which had made her so devoted to him and now she had discovered without a doubt that Sir Robert was just as kind and *feeling* a man and none the less sincere because he was not always proclaiming his devotion.

'My *dear* Sir Robert,' she cried, 'we are once more safe.'

'Ma'am,' replied Sir Robert brokenly, 'I must ask you to excuse me. For the moment...'

'Albert and I understand,' said the Queen warmly.

Although Sir Robert recovered his habitual demeanour he could not altogether hide his emotion. The law must be tightened up, he said, or these attacks might continue. It so often happened that an offence was committed and accompanied by a great deal of publicity and then someone else would attempt it.

Sir Robert never prevaricated as Lord Melbourne had, the Queen noticed. A Bill was immediately introduced into Parliament which set out that any attempts on the life of the Sovereign would be punishable by seven years transportation or imprisonment of three years, the miscreant to be publicly or privately whipped.

Bean was sentenced to eighteen months imprisonment.

This, said Sir Robert, would deter people from thinking it was an afternoon's amusement to take a shot at the Queen, for, he was convinced, this was not a serious attempt on her life. There was unrest throughout the country over the appalling social conditions but no one could blame the charming young Queen for this.

That was an eventful summer, with two attempts on her life, the imminent departure of Lehzen and so many visitors to be entertained. The Queen's uncle Mensdorff had come over in June and had in fact been in the carriage behind the Queen's and Albert's at the time of the Francis affair; Uncle Leopold and Aunt Louise had paid a fleeting visit to be followed by Albert's brother Ernest and his bride in July.

In addition to all was the change in so many

relationships. Lehzen was preparing to depart. 'After so many years,' she said sadly, 'one collects so many belongings.' The Queen's presents to her – so numerous over the years – would all be taken and treasured until she died. There was a subtle understanding between them that this was good-bye. Lehzen knew that on the day she departed the palace would cease to be her home.

There was also the Queen's changed relation-ship with her Prime Minister and her growing dependence upon Albert. She was now discussing everything with him and there had been scarcely any flaring up of temper, and then only over trivial things which she could very quickly laugh at with Albert.

Albert made a clean sweep in the nurseries and dismissed several of the nurses whom he said were incompetent or disrespectful. Lady Sarah Spencer Lyttleton, a lady of charm and efficiency, took charge and the Prince was pleased with her. Later he would examine the household management, but he would wait until Lehzen had left for now that he had gained his point he did not wish to be too hard on her. All he asked was that she slip quietly away and then he would begin introducing his reforms in earnest.

Albert was very happy to be with his brother. He and Victoria took the pair to Claremont but Victoria secretly believed that Ernest preferred the gaieties of London. It was an excuse to have a few balls to entertain them, but Albert was never really happy on these occasions and she supposed really they were rather superficial entertainments.

She was a little hurt by Albert's grief when his

brother departed and would have been so happy if he had not cared *quite* so much, but of course it did show what an affectionate nature he had and she could not expect Albert to forget his devotion to his brother – the companion of his childhood and early youth – because he had entered into the most perfect marriage with Victoria.

The Cambridges had always been antagonistic to Albert and Victoria had turned against them for this reason. Relations could be so tiresome. There was Uncle Cumberland who could not be content to be King of Hanover and was always making some criticism of his niece, simply because he thought she had what should be his, which was nonsense. There was no law in England against a woman ascending the throne and as Uncle William had said the people often preferred it. 'Sailors will be more ready to fight for a bonny lass.' Those were some of the last words Uncle William had spoken. But Uncle Cumberland thought differently. In fact until it had been proved that Francis and Bean were almost witless she had thought they might be agents of Uncle Cumberland, because in her youth there had been genuine scares that he was plotting against her.

It was not that she expected the Cambridges to *plot* against her. They would not dare do that. But they had wanted her to marry George Cambridge and they had thought they had had a good chance of bringing this about because in the old days George Cambridge (while his parents were in Germany) had lived with Aunt Adelaide and Uncle William and they had tried to make a match between George and Victoria. Being the King and Queen it might have seemed that they had a good chance of bringing this about. But, thought the Queen fondly, I had seen Albert.

They were most provoking, these Cambridges, always doing something to irritate her, mostly slighting Albert, so when she heard the scandal about George she could not help feeling a *little* pleased, which was very wrong of course. But they did give themselves airs.

It was whispered that the Duke of Beaufort's daughter, Lady Augusta Somerset, was pregnant and that recently she had been very friendly with George Cambridge. As Lady Augusta was the Duchess of Cambridge's lady-in-waiting George would see a great deal of her, and it was very likely that he was the father.

Albert, disclosing that he deplored any form of impurity, was horrified that it should exist within the family circle.

'Your Court, my love, has been rather lax,' he said, affectionately chiding. 'I think that is something we shall be obliged to alter.'

'Of course, Albert,' she agreed.

'You must invite the Duchess and express definite instructions that Lady Augusta is not included in the party.'

'And what of George?'

Albert considered that it was difficult to exclude her cousin but in the circumstances necessary.

The Cambridges were furious. The Duchess demanded of the Queen why her son and lady-in-waiting should be treated in this way.

'It is always those most concerned who are the

last to hear of what is going on around them,' the Queen told her.

'I am completely ignorant of what Your Majesty suggests.'

'Then I should ask your son ... and lady-in-waiting. The Prince and I will not tolerate immorality at Court. There has been too much of it in the past. We have decided to take strong measures against it and these will be used even against members of our own family.'

'This is a cruel mistake,' said the Duchess, but the Queen lifted her shoulders and fluttered her fan.

The Duchess was not going to allow the matter to pass, particularly when both her son George and Lady Augusta assured her that the accusation was false.

'The Queen is behaving as she did over Flora Hastings,' said the Duchess. 'When the honour of people has to be vindicated this sort of thing must be brought out into the open.'

The news leaked out to the press. The Cambridges saw to that. The Queen's German husband was so pure, was the comment, that he could see evil where it did not exist.

Lord Melbourne was disturbed. Being an inveterate gossip himself he could see the implications of this affair far better than Peel could. It was an echo of Flora Hastings and they all knew what harm that had done. The Queen certainly did, for she had been taunted by the wronged woman for months afterwards. There had been two attempts at assassination; some parts of the country were in revolt against social conditions; people were hungry and dissatisfied; there was rioting in the Midlands. The Queen could not afford another Flora Hastings scandal and the best thing that could happen would be that Albert, who was accused of being the instigator of the gossip, should without delay apologise to the Cambridges and Lady Augusta.

This was very difficult and degrading, said Albert; but as it became clear that the rumour was without foundation he realised it must be done.

He did it rather brusquely and he and the Queen hoped that the matter would end there. But the Queen's nights were disturbed by dreams of Flora Hastings rising from the grave to stand at the foot of her bed reproaching her.

She told Albert about it and recalled the pamphlets which were put into circulation at the time by malicious people. The one which haunted her most was that which was titled: 'A case of Murder against Buckingham Palace.'

'It was horrible, horrible,' she shuddered. 'I want no repetition of that.'

'There will be none,' soothed the Prince. 'These rumours were without foundation but we are right to keep a close watch on the morals of the Court and, my dear love, we must continue to do so.'

Victoria agreed that they must. And the Cambridges continued to slight Albert whenever the opportunity arose.

It was September, the month when Lehzen was due to depart. Albert, with, as Victoria told herself, *perfect* understanding, realised the strain those last weeks would bring so he decided that he and the Queen should take a little holiday. The babies could be left behind and Lehzen was still in charge of the nursery. The change would do the queen good.

'Shall it be Claremont?' asked the Queen.

'Oh, no,' said Albert, 'much farther afield. I have heard that Scotland is very beautiful.'

Scotland! The Queen had never thought of going so far but the idea was as she said *very* appealing and since Albert wished it they set off.

The tour was a great success. Her Majesty's loyal subjects of the North were very pleased that she should visit their country. Edinburgh was a delight.

'A unique city,' cried the Queen.

The glens and the heather-covered hills delighted the Prince. They reminded him of home, he said, which was the greatest compliment he could pay them.

The Queen found them truly magnificent and determined to see more of this beautiful part of her realm.

It was such a joy to be with Albert who was the *perfect* companion. He was not always serious and did like an occasional joke. For instance when Lord Kinnoul received them at his country mansion and was so eager to show them the beauties of his estate he fell backwards in his enthusiasm and rolled head over heels down a grassy bank. Having got up he almost fell down another and would have done if Albert had not seized him in time. The Queen caught Albert's eye and they could not help smiling and as Lord Kinnoul was none the worse for his fall it seemed a great joke. They talked about it when they were alone and as the Queen said in her account of this in a letter to Uncle Leopold they nearly 'died of laughing'.

From Dalkeith they went to Perth, 'most beautifully situated on the Tay,' wrote the Queen; and on to Scone Palace, 'fine but rather gloomy'. Then to Dunkeld and the Highlands.

Oh, the beautiful *beautiful* Highlands! She would always remember her first view of them and she would love them for ever. And what was most effective were the encampments of the Highlanders who were there, of course for the express purpose of paying homage to her. *Dear* people, in their kilts and their shields and swords. *So* romantic. What an excellent idea it had been to come to Scotland. She could never thank Albert enough for bringing her here. At Dunkeld Lord Breadalbane had brought out his Highlanders with a battalion of the 92nd Highland Regiment in honour of the royal visit.

How enchanting! She was delighted, and when she did not think of poor Lehzen back at the palace getting her things ready to leave she could be completely happy.

What a wonderful night that was, for as far as she could see from her bedroom window the bonfires blazed; the Highlanders danced their own dances by torchlight and the bagpipes played their strange and exciting music.

'I have fallen in love with Scotland,' said the Queen fervently.

She was delighted to have discovered this beautiful realm, but another discovery pleased her less.

She was once more pregnant.

Lehzen sat silently in her room. So this was the end. Tomorrow she was leaving the palace and that meant that she would in fact go out of Victoria's life for ever.

A year ago this would have seemed an impossibility. How quickly life could change!

She could see clearly now where she had been wrong. She should never have attempted to make trouble between a husband and wife. She should have known that the Queen would be the most loyal of wives. But it was too late. She had to make a new life. There were young people where she was going – her brother's children. Perhaps she could take them to her heart as she had taken Victoria. But there would never be anyone who could mean to her what Victoria had meant. She was philosophical now. She was getting old. She had had her day.

Her devotion to her dearest child was selfless and she could say with absolute sincerity that what she wanted more than anything was Victoria's happiness.

She could never like Albert. He was stern, serious and prudish; he could never really enjoy life because he was so eager to do his duty, and one sensed that he felt there was something sinful in enjoying the good things of life. He would mould her to his way. She would change. She would always be sincere, deeply affectionate, loving to dance and gossip, the adorably human Victoria of the past, but he would change her.

It is time I went, said Lehzen.

She would see the Queen for the last time today. She would be calm; there must be no stormy parting and tomorrow very early she would slip quietly away. She did not want Victoria to be harassed by painful goodbyes.

Lehzen had gone.

The Queen was deeply affected. After all those years they had parted. She could not remember a time in her life when Lehzen had not been there.

In a way she was relieved. The last months had been a strain. And Albert would be so delighted. It was what he had always wanted; he blamed Lehzen for everything that had gone wrong; and it was true he had made her see the Baroness differently from the way she had before.

It was better that she went and the last thing Lehzen wanted her to be was unhappy – just as she herself longed for Lehzen to find peace and happiness with her family.

The end of a phase was always a solemn time. She wanted to recapture the spirit of those old days absolutely as they were then, not as she saw them now, and the best way of doing this was to read through some of her old journals.

She blushed a little as she read. Had she really felt like that about Lord Melbourne? She wrote of him as though they were lovers. She had been thoughtless then. It was all rather artificial really. That was not true happiness.

But reading the journals made her realise how contented she was with life.

'Thank God,' she said aloud, 'that Albert has taught me what real happiness means.'

311

# Chapter XIII

## A VISIT TO THE CONTINENT

With Lehzen out of the way Albert decided to investigate the management of the household which he was well aware was in need of urgent reform. He quickly discovered that offices were still in existence which had been inaugurated two hundred years before although some of them were nothing but sinecures. There was no discipline; the servants were terrified lest they should do work which was not in their province and the most ridiculous anomalies prevailed. There was a Lord Steward who in the reign of Victoria's grandfather George III, had control of the entire household except the royal apartments; but recently the office of Lord Chamberlain had been inaugurated and no one was quite sure what duties he was supposed to take over from the Lord Steward. There could be a dispute over the cleaning of windows for instance and although the Lord Chamberlain might order the insides to be done there was a difference of opinion as to who was responsible for the outsides which meant that the outsides went uncleaned for months. None of the servants was sure to whom he or she was responsible, which from a certain point of view was an advantage because it gave quite a number of them liberty to do all sorts of things which, under proper authority, would have been forbidden.

It was one person's duty to lay a fire, another's to light it; which meant that very often there was no fire at all.

At the time of the visit of the Boy Jones Albert had discovered that a broken window could remain so for months at a time because no one knew whose duty it was to replace it; he had even discovered brown paper pasted over broken windows because the servants could not as they said 'abide the cold wind coming through'. And this in one of the most magnificent of palaces in the world!

Something had to be done and with characteristic efficiency Albert set about doing it.

He studied accounts; he found that the Queen was being cheated. He looked into the amount of food and drink which came into the palace and discovered that some of the grooms were drunk every night.

'My love,' he said, 'you are paying very heavily for inefficiency and a badly run household.'

Victoria, who was beginning to think that everything he did was wonderful, declared that she could not imagine how she had ever lived without Albert to look after her. He must do everything he wished.

There was fury among the servants. Who was the Prince coming over from Germany to interfere with their pleasant lives? It used to be so good in the old days with the old Baroness liking a joke and shutting her eyes to anything that might, as she said, upset the Queen. As long as her caraway seeds were scattered over everything she ate she didn't care what went on in the servants' quarters.

Albert was indifferent to his unpopularity; he was used to it in any case. He was going to make sure that Victoria had a well-run home.

On one occasion he went quietly into the nursery and found one of the under-nurses bouncing the Prince of Wales up and down on her knee.

'Now what's popsy-wopsy laughing at?' the nurse was demanding. 'Popsy-wopsy's laughing 'cos his liddle toes are tickled.'

'I do not understand,' said Albert. 'By what absurd name were you addressing the Prince of Wales?'

'Oh, it's just baby talk, sir.'

'Please do not use such baby talk to His Royal Highness.' He went at once to Victoria.

'There is a most unsuitable person in the nursery,' he said. 'She was moving The Boy up and down on her knee and talking *nonsense* to him. No wonder he is so backward.'

'How stupid of her!' said Victoria who a few months before would have laughed at popsy-wopsy's liddle toes being tickled. 'I will send for Lady Lyttleton at once.'

Lady Lyttleton was sent for and the result was that the under-nurse was dismissed on account of her unsuitability.

There was no doubt that the royal household was more efficiently run and the Queen was delightedly impressed. The rooms were warmer (at no greater cost, Albert told her) and the palace was not only a much more comfortable residence but a safer one.

Albert was wonderful.

She was growing more and more to appreciate the quiet of the country because there she and Albert could live a more intimate life. They could take walks; they could ride; they could come home and play music or sing duets. Albert – in a laughing way – had undertaken her education. 'Rather neglected, my love, in some respects.' Another slight to Lehzen whom she had begun to think of as poor Lehzen. It had been a very dull childhood, she supposed; in fact any part of her life which had not included Albert seemed dull. 'To think I ever thought that I was happy before my marriage. I did not know what happiness meant then.'

In the evenings Albert read to her from Hallam's History. 'You cannot rule a country well without knowing how your predecessors did it,' said Albert. Previously she would have thought it such a dull book. How different it was, read by Albert.

Lord Melbourne, with whom she corresponded now and then, was delighted that she was so happy. 'An example to all her subjects,' he wrote, and she could imagine the tears in his dear eyes as his pen moved over the paper. He was pleased too that she and Albert were reading Hallam together. It was a wonderful education.

Sometimes Albert would go to the nursery and bring Pussy into the bedroom and the dear child would sit on the bed; she looked like a little doll, she was so pretty. 'Remarkably like her dear Mama,' said Albert. The Boy, she feared, was not

315

going to be as bright as his sister.

'Pussy was speaking when she was his age,' said the Queen.

'He is not going to be as intelligent as our little Vicky,' said Albert.

There had been none of the irritable moods at the beginning of the present pregnancy.

'This little one is behaving well,' said the Queen.

It was a very happy year apart from the social unrest throughout the country which was making some of her ministers very anxious. As if it wasn't bad enough to have trouble abroad the people at home had to be difficult. Menacing, Lord Melbourne called them. Wales had joined the bands of troublemakers and there rioters were dressing up in women's clothes and calling themselves 'Rebecca and her daughters'; they were smashing toll gates and causing a great deal of uneasiness. The Irish – always troublesome – were agitating; even in dear Scotland there was trouble about private patronage of the Established Kirk; and at home Mr Cobden was quarrelling with Sir Robert over the Corn Laws. It would all have been very distressing if Albert had not been there beside her. Albert was passionately interested in these matters; he was present at her meetings with her ministers; he read all the state papers with her. Her constant cry was: What should I do without Albert?

On April 25th they were delighted when a daughter was born. Three healthy children in four years of marriage. 'How very lucky we are,' said the Queen.

She was to be called Alice. 'A good old English

name,' the Queen declared, 'and perhaps Maud, and as she was born on Aunt Gloucester's birthday, Mary after her.

There was all the preparation of the christening.

'We had better ask Uncle Ernest this time. He was so annoyed because he wasn't invited to The Boy's. Perhaps he won't come all the way from Hanover. I hope not. I never feel very comfortable when he's around. But I shall insist on darling Feodora's coming. It will be a lovely excuse to see her again.'

The christening was a great success, although the King of Hanover having rather ungraciously accepted the invitation, arrived late, and the service was over before he put in an appearance.

Alice behaved beautifully and did not cry during the ceremony. In fact, as the Queen remarked to Albert, she reminded her of Pussy. Did he remember how bright Pussy was at her christening, just as though she knew what it was all about?

There was a *déjeuner* afterwards and the tables were beautifully decorated with gay June flowers. The Queen was happy to see her half-sister and they looked forward to some exciting talks about their respective nurseries. There was so much the Queen wanted to ask darling Feddy because she was so much more experienced a Mama than she was.

The King of Hanover as usual caused a little uneasiness. He had always been extremely ugly, having lost an eye which gave him a most sinister aspect and this may have been due in some measure to the stories which circulated about him, but of course he had been involved in a murder case and he was very unscrupulous and he would have been King of England if Victoria had not lived to claim the throne.

He wanted to see the nursery and when Victoria saw him pick up The Boy in his arms and study him with his one penetrating eye she felt a shiver of alarm run through her. Oddly enough the child was not in the least perturbed and seemed to find this strange great-uncle interesting. Pussy, with her usual intelligence, regarded him curiously, but she showed no fear either. But Victoria could guess what Uncle Ernest was thinking when he held The Boy. This child would one day be King of England and everyone knew that this was a role Ernest had coveted beyond everything.

Soon the guests were departing. Victoria wept to see darling Feodora go and she remarked to Albert how sad it was that royal people had so often to leave their homes. Albert could agree wholeheartedly with that. She knew he often thought of his brother and father with the utmost affection.

Victoria would never say it to Albert but she did think that Albert's family were not so worthy of his affection as they might be. His brother had led a rather wild life; they had been aware when he was staying with them of very unpleasant evidence of this. As for his father, he too had not been exactly moral and now he was worrying them to give him an allowance. They were so rich, he said, and he was poor. He did not understand what expenses the British Monarchy had to face.

Considering all this it seemed more wonderful than ever that Albert had turned out to be such a good man.

How fortunate she was in her husband.

Uncle Ernest's visit triggered off a series of rather alarming incidents. People wrote anonymous letters threatening to kidnap the children. Others wrote warning that plots were afoot to do so. Most of them, said Sir Robert, were written by mad people, but one could never be sure.

The Duchess of Kent, to whom Victoria had now become reconciled (Albert wished it), now seemed to have changed her character. She adored the children and Victoria was constantly warning her about spoiling them, but it was gratifying to see the change in her since the departure of Sir John Conroy. She was very happy and always listened attentively to what Albert said, and no longer tried to manage her daughter.

The Duchess was now very concerned about the children's safety and she was certain that her wicked brother-in-law, the King of Hanover, was a menace.

'He would do anything to get the throne. He would not stop at murder.'

Albert thought that, while every precaution should be taken, it was unwise to make accusations without firm foundation.

'Oh, you have no idea, dear Albert,' said the Duchess. 'You who are so good cannot conceive the wickedness of some people. When Victoria was a child he set about rumours that she was weak and sickly to prepare the people for her death. I

319

knew that it was his idea to get some of his spies into Kensington and have her poisoned. I would not allow her to be alone for one moment.' She looked ruefully at her daughter. 'Oh, I know she didn't always like it, but everything I did was for her good.'

'I am sure of it, dear Mama,' said Albert, so Victoria was becoming sure of it. 'And don't worry about the children,' he went on. 'I shall see that every precaution is taken.'

And he did so with his usual efficiency. The last thing he did before retiring was to examine all the locks in the nursery. Lady Lyttleton, whom he trusted, always accompanied him on this tour; and when everything was locked the keys were in his possession and no one could have them without asking for them.

It seemed hardly likely that the King of Hanover would be able to murder the Queen and her children all at one time, and if he had, it was a certainty that the people of England would never have accepted him; but the Prince was taking no risks with his family. Uncle Ernest was the bogy Napoleon had been to an earlier generation. At least it was true that he was staking a claim for Princess Charlotte's jewellery which was in Victoria's possession. It seemed dreadful, thought the Queen, to quarrel over jewellery, but if she passed over the gems to him she was going to find herself with hardly any ornaments to wear and so many of the ladies at Court could outshine her in that respect even now.

Not that jewels affected her very deeply. She did not greatly care for dressing up. The home life, the quiet pleasant evenings, the visits to the nursery and the company of dear Albert were so much more rewarding.

Alice was a good child, placid and fat, so she was playfully nicknamed Fatima. Pussy was still the favourite because she was undoubtedly going to be the clever one. She could already chatter amusingly and beside her, her brother seemed a dull, heavy child. He was no longer called The Boy, but Bertie. He was really rather naughty and quite backward. Pussy had ceased to be jealous of him. She had no need. She was constantly laughing at him for being such a silly.

As the months began to pass and as the unrest in the country had subsided somewhat Albert suggested that they take a trip in the new yacht, the *Victoria and Albert*.

'You have always wanted to meet the King of France, and I am sure Louis Philippe would be delighted to see us,' said Albert. 'There is nothing like personal contact to bring about peaceful relations. If Sir Robert thinks it is a good idea we might make a little trip after the prorogation of Parliament.'

'You mean go to France?'

'The French family are at the Château d'Eu and we could be there in a few hours after leaving Southampton.'

Victoria thought this, like most of Albert's ideas, wonderful.

Albert then began to work out the journey in detail, and what a great pleasure it was to see how he thought of everything!

They boarded the yacht as arranged, cruised about the Isle of Wight and the coast of Devonshire for a few days and then crossed to Tréport. On their arrival the King of France and the Prince de Joinville came out to the yacht by the royal barge to welcome them and they were rowed ashore in this. Crowds were there to welcome them and shout *Vive La Reine*.

Victoria was so happy to meet members of the French royal family. Among them was Aunt Louise – Uncle Leopold's wife – who was the daughter of Louis Philippe and had come to Tréport so that she should be there during Victoria's visit.

The King and Queen were charming, and the only sad note was the memory of the recent death of the Duke of Chartres, which had occurred when he was thrown from his carriage. The deep mourning of his widow, Helene, was a constant reminder.

It was interesting to be shown the château like a dream castle, said the Queen. The family portraits were impressive and the Galerie des Guises very grand indeed.

As for the chapel it was beautiful with its statues of saints and stained-glass windows.

The King was determined to make the visit a success. It was very important that it should be, Albert had told the Queen, and Lord Aberdeen, the English foreign secretary, agreed with him. For so long there had been bickering between the English and French.

'It was their fault,' said Victoria.

'Oh, there are faults on both sides,' answered Albert.

'Uncle Leopold is inclined to blame us. But then as Lord Melbourne said he leans towards France. It's on account of having a French wife, I suppose. Dear Louise, she is my favourite aunt.'

She did agree with Albert that it was an excellent way of bettering relations between the two countries. No one could be more charming than Louis Philippe, she was sure; and it was going to be very difficult after this visit to think of them as enemies.

Everywhere they went the people lined the roads to gaze at them and cry *Vive La Reine d'Angleterre*. It was most affecting, said the Queen, and how charming the women looked in their national costume. Such pretty caps and coloured aprons.

The visit was all too short, not more than five days and on the fourth the King arranged a pastoral entertainment. Char-a-bancs were waiting for them and Albert and Victoria went off in the first, sitting in the front with the French King and Queen. The Princesses sat behind and the rest of the party followed in other vehicles. Their destination was one of the King's hunting lodges in the forest where a delicious *déjeuner* was eaten alfresco fashion. Albert was delighted to be in the country and the Queen was proud to notice how he astonished everyone with his knowledge of botanical subjects.

It was such a pleasant drive back to the château where in the Galerie des Guises a little theatre had been set up. The last evening was to be spent in watching two plays.

'What a delightful finale,' cried the Queen. 'We

must entertain our guests in this manner at Windsor.' The first of the plays was serious and beautifully acted; the other was a comedy which, as the Queen said, sent her as well as the rest of the company into fits of laughter enough to kill one.

The next day they left and taking the Prince de Joinville with them, returned to England although they did not intend to stay more than a night or so before going on to Belgium to see Uncle Leopold.

They stayed at the Pavilion, which the Prince de Joinville thought was the strangest palace he had ever seen.

What joy it was to be under the same roof as Uncle Leopold, particularly as Aunt Louise had by this time rejoined her husband and was waiting to play the hostess in her husband's palace as she had in her father's. It was wonderful to see their children, of whom she had heard so much. She was particularly impressed by the little Princess Charlotte who was much the same age as Pussy, but, said the Queen, not so naughty.

Uncle Leopold was most affectionate and told them how he had planned their marriage when they were babies in their cradles and it was one of the great joys of his life to see how happy they were together.

'I look upon you both as my children,' he said; and they both solemnly assured him that he had been a father to them.

What a delightful trip that was! Uncle Leopold accompanied them on a tour of his most important cities – Brussels, Antwerp, Ghent and Bruges.

There were wonderful art treasures to be seen in these fine old towns. The time passed so quickly when one was with loved ones, and all too soon they were at sea on the way home. Victoria wrote to her uncle from Windsor:

*We were so happy to be with you, and the stay was so delightful but so painfully short. It was such a joy for me to be once again under the roof of one who has been a father to me...*

'Such a happy visit,' said the Queen when they reached Windsor, 'but I am most contented to *be home* with my dear, dear family.'

## Chapter XIV

### *POOR* LORD MELBOURNE

Victoria sat fanning herself while Albert crawled round the nursery floor with Pussy on his back. How he doted on that child! Not that he spoilt her. Albert was far too wise for that, but Victoria had noticed how as soon as he stepped into the nursery his eyes went to his little Vicky. She was becoming quite imperious, knowing the effect she had on them both; but she really was the prettiest, liveliest child of three they had ever seen.

How different was The Boy. He was healthy enough, but at the age of two he could scarcely speak at all, let alone chatter away *intelligently* as Pussy had at that age.

'What is the name of my big ship?' demanded Pussy. 'Tell me, Mama.'

'If it is the yacht on which Papa and I have been sailing it is the *Victoria and Albert*. It was named after Papa and myself.'

'I'm Victoria, not Pussy really,' said the amazing child, 'so perhaps it was named after me.'

Was there ever such intelligence? Albert's eyes shone with pride as, still on all fours, he carried his shrieking daughter over to her mother.

'Gee up,' said Pussy.

'Oh, I have become a horse have I?' inquired Albert.

Pussy considered this. 'No, a ship is best.'

She took Albert's hair and began to pull it.

'You will hurt your dear good kind Papa,' chided the Queen. 'Your cousin Charlotte would never do that.'

Pussy was all eagerness to hear about Cousin Charlotte. She clambered down from Albert's back and came to sit on her mother's lap.

'Cousin Charlotte is my Uncle Leopold's little girl. She is Aunt Louise's too.'

'Why?' asked Pussy.

'Because they are her mother and father.'

'Is she big?'

'Oh, yes. She is big and pretty and not nearly so naughty as some people I know.'

'Pussy?' asked the Princess Royal delightedly.

Bertie wanted to hear about this, so he toddled over and clutched his mother's skirts.

'Well, Bertie,' she said, 'you have come to hear

326

too, have you?'

'M'm, m'm, m'm!' said Bertie. Really it was distressing that he could only mumble. When one considered Pussy at his age! After all he was only a year behind her.

She picked up Pussy and sat her on her knee.

Albert stood up, his eyes adoring Pussy, while the Queen told her daughter about the wonderful trip they had had visiting the King of France and then dearest Uncle Leopold and Aunt Louise who had this wonderful daughter Charlotte.

Pussy listened attentively and then suddenly said triumphantly: 'If Charlotte is so good why didn't you have her instead of me?'

At which tears came into the Queen's eyes and she held her daughter tightly. 'Papa and I wouldn't take *anyone* in place of you, my darling,' she said.

'M'm, m'm, m'm!' said Bertie, but neither of them noticed him.

Later the Queen said that she had been so impressed by the excursion to the hunting-lodge of the King of France that she had thought it would be exciting if they had a small place they could go to. They both loved Windsor but it was a castle. What she meant was a small house where they could forget affairs of state and live like an ordinary family, where they would be more close, more intimate – just like any mother and father in the heart of their family.

Albert was enthusiastic and they decided to discuss the affair with Sir Robert Peel.

She was so happy to be back with the family. She

was often in the nursery and the only child who really gave her cause for anxiety was Bertie. He seemed unable to learn, she remarked to Albert, not because he was exactly stupid, although Pussy's extraordinary intelligence often made him seem so, but because he had no inclination to learn. He was lazy; and it made it all the more difficult because the nurses made such a fuss of him, and when he was taken out people would look at him in his carriage or wherever he happened to be and admire him. One woman in the park had actually put her head into the baby carriage and given him a great smacking kiss.

Bertie seemed to relish this, as though he already knew that he was the Prince of Wales and if he couldn't compete in the nursery he would in the streets.

Pussy was as bright and as naughty as ever. Even Albert who, while being devoted to the children, was always ready to be stern with them for their own good, could not resist Pussy. Ever since they had returned from the trip to Belgium she talked of Cousin Charlotte and sometimes when she was planning some especially naughty act she would put her head on one side – like a judge, Albert said – and murmur: 'Now I wonder what Charlotte would do.'

Victoria and Albert went into fits of laughter over Pussy's slyness – when they were alone of course. It would have been quite wrong to have let her know how her piquant naughtiness amused them.

They were so anxious that the children should have the right upbringing. 'You remember, my dearest love, what the Baroness Lehzen did to you.'

Victoria was almost ready to agree that Lehzen had been very wrong in so many things.

'You can't start too early,' said Albert; and Victoria was worried about the manner in which they should say their prayers. It was a point she had meant to raise with Feodora when they had last been together. So she wrote asking how her children performed this necessary duty.

Feodora replied that they said them in their beds, not kneeling. 'How absurd to find that necessary, as it could have nothing to do with making our prayers more acceptable to the Almighty or more holy.'

She went on:

*Dear Pussy learning her letters I should love to see and hear. Has Bertie not learned some more words and sentences?*

The answer to the last was No.

The Queen feared that Bertie was going to be something of a problem, and Albert said that it *might* be necessary to introduce a very stern discipline where the boy was concerned.

Alice, dear Fatima, seemed to increase in size every day; she rarely cried and her placid smile was a joy to behold.

Victoria did wish she could spend more time in the nursery, and more and more her thoughts turned to that little country house where they could live *en famille*. They had visited the Isle of Wight several times and both she and Albert thought it very beautiful, so when Sir Robert suggested that Osborne might prove a suitable residence, they agreed at once and plans were set in motion to purchase it.

The savour had gone from life for Lord Melbourne. Each week he realised that the Queen was becoming more remote. She was always gracious, always kind, but the lapses between the receiving and answering his letters was growing greater and he had realised that he must no longer write to her of politics. Gone were the days when she would not act without his advice; he heard, too, that she was becoming more and more attached to Peel. This was a good augury, he admitted, but it hurt him. He thought often of that occasion when she had refused to let him go and how in the amazing Bedchamber Affair had routed Peel solely for the purpose of keeping Lord Melbourne in office. It had been quite a scandal and after it people had publicly called her 'Mrs Melbourne'; and even now he was still her dear good friend as she told him when they met or she wrote to him; she was loyal and affectionate; and of course he loved her, as she had once loved him. For she had. He had no doubt of that.

During his stormy married life he had found great comfort in literature; he turned once more to that solace. He spent many an evening at Brooks' where his conversation was still an entertainment. He slept little. His political career kept him busy; he read voraciously into the early hours of the morning but about a year after he had left office he began to feel vaguely unwell. His mind wandered a little; he talked a great deal to himself; a habit he had had for years but previously he had done it in private or was aware of it. Sometimes in the presence of his colleagues at the club he would address a remark to someone who was not present. 'One of Lord Melbourne's odd quirks,' it was said.

But it was an indication of what was to come. One morning he awakened to find that he could not move one arm. He had had a stroke.

The Queen was deeply concerned when she heard of this. She sent the kindest messages; as soon as he was well enough she would come to see him or he must come to see her. Every day there was word from her.

He recovered and was almost his normal self.

He called on the Queen and she was delighted to see him, though secretly finding him rather wan. She noticed that he dragged one foot a little and his arm hung rather awkwardly.

When she remembered the handsome, alert man who had called on her at the time of her accession she felt a little sad. Albert comforted her and so did the children.

Then she began to think of her former much loved Prime Minister Lord M as 'Poor Lord Melbourne'.

A new year had arrived and before January was out, Albert heard that his father was dead. Duke Ernest had been ailing for some time and Baron Stockmar had often warned the Prince that he must expect his father's death at any time; but this did not lessen the blow when it came. Albert's family feeling was strong and there was despondency throughout the palace. Albert sat with his head buried in his hands while the Queen knelt beside him and they talked of 'Dearest Father'. They had forgotten the fact that he had been continually importuning them, that his morals were questionable; in death they saw only his virtues.

'My dearest Albert,' said the Queen, 'I suffer with you. That helps. Your grief is shared you know.'

'You are *all* to me now,' replied Albert mournfully.

They both poured out their wretchedness to Doctor Stockmar who was in Coburg with his family. They wanted him to return to England. They needed him. Dr Stockmar promised that he would come, but in the meantime Albert should return to Coburg for his father's funeral.

The Queen was horrified.

'It will be the first time during our married life that we have been separated, Albert!' she exclaimed.

'I know, my love, but this is a necessity.'

Victoria wept silently. 'And at such a time, my darling, you need me.'

Albert admitted this, but it was his duty to leave her. He could not allow his father to go to his grave unattended by his son.

'Of course you must go, my dearest,' cried the Queen. 'Oh, if only I could come with you.'

'Alas, my love, you have your duties here.'

She was touched by Albert's thoughtfulness, for a few days later he told her that he had written to Uncle Leopold to ask if Aunt Louise might come to Windsor and spend the time of his absence with the Queen.

'I thought she was the one who could best compensate you for not having me here,' said Albert.

'No one could do that,' answered the Queen, 'but Aunt Louise would come nearest to it. Oh, Albert, how good of you to think of me in the midst of all your sorrow.'

'My dear love,' replied Albert, 'you are constantly in my thoughts.'

There was another cause for mild depression. She was once more pregnant. She loved her family but, as her mother said, a little longer rest between the children's arrival would be desirable. Of course she was strong and obviously made to bear children, but it seemed that no sooner was one delivered than another was conceived.

Besides, she did feel wretched at the beginning of her pregnancies and this, together with the knowledge that she was to part with Albert, made her desolate.

But for Albert's sake she tried not to show her feelings. He was delighted about the child. He longed for a boy this time and the thought of the new arrival, she knew, did a good deal to cheer him, so perhaps it was selfish of her to dread the coming ordeal so much.

Aunt Louise came to Windsor and it was wonderful to show her the children and confide to her about the one that would make its appearance some time during the month of August.

On a bleak March day Albert left for Coburg.

'Write to me, darling,' begged the Queen, and

Albert promised he would. True to his word he wrote as soon as he reached Dover and a few days later there was another letter from Cologne.

'Your picture has been hung everywhere so you look down on me from the walls... Every step takes me farther away from you – not a cheerful thought.'

He had met Uncle Leopold on his journey through Belgium and he understood this dear kind uncle was making his way to England to join his wife and comfort Victoria.

Victoria read the letters through again and again. Only this absence could make her realise the extent of her love for her husband. She was a little jealous of his devotion to his family, which was wrong of her, she admitted. Even the children could not compensate her. When she was in the nursery she was sad because Albert was not there to crawl round with Vicky on his back and bounce Fat Alice on his knee and shake his head over Bertie's shortcomings.

Albert has become *everything* to me, she thought.

His brother Ernest came to meet Albert when he arrived in Gotha. The two brothers embraced.

'It is good to see you, Ernest,' said Albert. 'Alas, that it should be in such sad circumstances.'

Ernest was always philosophical. 'We mustn't regret too much. He would have been an invalid if he'd lived. You can imagine how he would have felt about that. It was the best thing possible.'

Albert replied that if they could look upon it in that way, it would be an immense relief.

'But, my dear brother, it is the only way because it is the truth.'

Ernest was a little worldly and Albert wondered what sort of life he was leading. He took after their father in his interest in women. Albert stopped himself thinking ill of the dead.

'Ernest, you are the Duke now. You will have your responsibilities.'

'But I won't be nearly as important as you are, Albert. Uncle Leopold tells us that in all but name you are the King of England.'

'Victoria is a good loyal wife. We are very happy.'

'I knew you'd do it. She dotes on you. You are very good-looking, Albert. And that moral rectitude of yours ... well, I suppose it really works.'

'You are teasing, Ernest. I suppose it takes our minds off dear Papa.'

Albert's step-mother looked pathetic in the long black veil worn by German widows. She was staying at Albert's grandmother's house and they greeted each other affectionately for they had always been fond of each other. His grandmother almost swooned with joy at the sight of him.

'Oh, my little Alberinchen!' she cried and clung to him.

They all wanted to hear about his life in England and temporarily the purpose of his visit was forgotten while he talked to them of Victoria and the children and how devoted they all were to each other and how each day Victoria deferred more and more to him.

'It was not always so,' he explained. 'At the beginning she had evil advisers, but once I had cleared them off we became very very happy together.'

His grandmother and step-mother could not hear enough of the children. The cleverness of little Vicky was his main theme.

'Alberinchen with a daughter!' cried Grandmother Saxe-Coburg. 'And she nearly four years old! Why you will soon be finding a husband for her, Albert. Some handsome German Prince, eh?'

Albert agreed that the time would soon pass.

'And a son too! Tell us of little Bertie.'

'He is strong and quite handsome but not as sharp as his sister.'

'That'll come,' said Grandmama Saxe-Coburg wisely.

He gave them the presents Victoria had sent for them and as soon as he was alone he was writing to her:

*Could you have witnessed the happiness my return gave my family you would have been amply repaid for the sacrifice of our separation. We spoke much of you. So many questions are put to me that I am scarcely able to answer them...*

*Farewell, my darling, and fortify yourself with the thought of my speedy return. God's blessing rest upon you and the dear children.*

He felt a little complacent. He was greatly loved by his family and he returned to them as an important person. In England he might be thought to be merely the queen's husband, but they all believed – and there was a great deal of truth in this – that he was virtually the King. Moreover Victoria's loving letters were arriving constantly. She was never one to hide her feelings.

She was desolate, she wrote, longing for his return.

He could smile. He had achieved a great victory. Never again would he be shut out from her confidence. Never would the Queen forget that she was the wife.

He owed his success to following the advice of Stockmar and of course to his own calm God-fearing nature.

Stockmar must come back to England. He must consult him about Bertie. The boy who was to be King of England must be disciplined.

It gave him a certain feeling of chagrin that the child who could scarcely string a sentence together (and Vicky could chatter away at his age) and when he did stuttered, should one day be King of England, while he, Albert – handsome, clever, so beloved, could never be anything but the Prince. Even Victoria, for all her devotion, could not change that.

Perhaps that was why Bertie irritated him mildly.

He dismissed such a thought; it was unworthy of the man Albert believed himself to be. After all Bertie was his son. In bringing Stockmar to advise, in imposing a strong discipline, he was giving Bertie the best possible upbringing.

Soon he was on his way back to Windsor. Victoria was in a fever of excitement.

It was six o'clock in the evening when he

arrived and she was watching for him. She flew to meet him and flung herself into his arms.

'Albert! You are indeed back. What happiness to see you again.'

Albert kissed her, called her his dear little wife, told her how much he had missed her.

'Oh never, never, never let us be parted again!' cried the Queen.

The next morning Albert wrote in his diary:

'Crossed on the 11th. I arrived at six o'clock in the evening at Windsor. *Great joy.*'

Soon after his return it was Victoria's twenty-fifth birthday.

'What a truly great age!' she cried. Seven years since she had ascended the throne! More than four years a wife and three children in the nursery and another soon to be born. What a great deal had happened since she was eighteen! Birthdays made one think back over the past. She would write to poor Lord Melbourne to let him know that she had not forgotten him. Was it only six years ago that she had looked upon him as a god? What a foolish girl she had been! But then she had not had Albert to guide her.

Albert had given her as a birthday present a beautiful portrait of himself.

'There is nothing, *nothing* I could have liked better,' she cried. 'Oh, Albert, it is *just* like you. You look so serious and so manly. I shall always love it and remember the day you gave it to me.'

Her eyes full of tears, she studied the picture with the group of angels in the background holding a medallion on which were the words *Heil und Segan.*

'Health and blessing,' she murmured. 'Oh, Albert, my darling, may you always enjoy them both.'

Before the end of May the Emperor of Russia caused a great deal of consternation by announcing that he was paying a visit to England – and was on his way. 'But we have made no preparations,' cried the Queen.

'We will take care of him,' replied Albert calmly. 'I wonder what his motive is. You can be sure it is political.'

'I am grateful to have you and Sir Robert at my side at such a time,' said the Queen fervently.

'Good relations between this country and Russia can do nothing but good,' said Albert; so the Queen was sure this was so.

The Emperor was a little eccentric, as might be judged from his rather unceremonious arrival. First he went to the house of the Russian ambassador and there spent a night, but it was not long before he was installed in Windsor Castle. A magnificent edifice, he called it, and one of which the Queen must be justly proud. 'It is worthy of you, Madame,' he told her, for he was very gallant.

In spite of the fact that he was given one of the finest bedrooms in the castle he sent his valet down to the stables to procure hay and when this was brought a leather sack (which he had brought with him) was stuffed with it. He slept on this sack wherever he was and it always accompanied him on his travels.

He was very good-looking and in his youth had been reckoned to be one of the most handsome men in Europe. But there was something a little odd in his face.

Discussing this with her children's governess, Lady Lyttleton, the Queen decided that it was because he had light eyelashes and his eyes were so large and bright.

'They have no shade,' said Lady Lyttleton.

'Exactly,' agreed the Queen.

'And occasionally one can see the white above his eyeball which makes him look savage.'

'I believe he got that from his father, Emperor Paul. I have heard it mentioned.'

'He looks somewhat autocratic.'

'Yet sad, and he does not smile much. All the same he is most friendly and the Prince says that it is a good thing that he should come and visit us in this way.'

It was Albert who guessed at the Emperor's reasons.

'Of course,' he said, 'it is because we visited the King of France recently, and he does not wish us to be too friendly with the French.'

Sir Robert Peel, who had had many conversations with the Emperor, confirmed this. The latter had also wished to discuss the question of Turkey, which appeared to be on the verge of collapse.

He told Sir Robert: 'I don't want an inch of Turkish soil, but I won't allow anyone else to have one.'

Meanwhile the Emperor was fêted everywhere – at the opera, at the races, at reviews and banquets, all given in his honour. The Queen was enchanted when he said of Albert: 'Nowhere will you see a handsomer young man; he has such an air of nobility and goodness.'

That was enough to win her heart, so she forgave the Emperor for descending on them so suddenly and obliging her in her present state, which was beginning to become irksome, to appear so often at tiring ceremonies in public.

The children were waiting for the summons to the small drawing-room that they might say good-bye to the Emperor, and Lady Lyttleton was trying to impress upon them the importance of the occasion.

'He is the Emperor of Russia. You must be very polite to him. Do you hear that, Bertie?'

Bertie nodded.

'He doesn't know anything,' said Vicky, giving her brother a contemptuous push.

Bertie returned the push; and said 'Yes, yes, yes.'

'He played with my bricks today,' complained Vicky. 'They were Mama's bricks. She used to play with them in Kensington.'

Bertie laughed, delighted to have played with Mama's bricks, for although he spoke very little he could understand what was being said.

'You are not to do it, Bertie,' said Vicky severely.

'Will,' answered Bertie.

Lady Lyttleton said: 'Now, now. We don't want any quarrelling, do we, or Mama will not be pleased.'

They were both sober at the thought.

'Nor,' added Lady Lyttleton, 'will Papa.'

'Papa loves me,' said Vicky.

'Of course he loves you all,' said Lady Lyttleton. 'You, Bertie and Alice.'

'He loves me best,' announced Vicky. 'So does Mama.

'You're a conceited little girl,' said Lady Lyttleton.

'What's conceited?'

'What you are.'

'Then,' said Vicky, 'it must be nice.'

This was too much for Bertie, who kicked his sister.

'That was a very ungallant thing to do,' said Lady Lyttleton.

Bertie looked very pleased with himself and was sharply told: 'And that is not a nice thing to be.'

'Course it isn't,' retorted Vicky, 'if Bertie's it.'

'Now this is not the way to prepare yourself to meet the great Emperor, is it? Why can't you be like Alice? Look at her – smiling away so contented and happy.'

'We can't be babies all the time,' said clever Vicky.

It was time for them to make their way to the small drawing-room. There was the Emperor – a glittering figure, big and grand; Mama and Papa were standing together talking to him.

'And these are the little ones,' said the Emperor. 'Ah, the Prince of Wales.'

Vicky thought she should be seen first but the Emperor had picked up Bertie, who was smiling rather shyly and enjoying the attention. Mama and Papa were smiling kindly too.

'And the Princess Royal.' Now it was Vicky's

turn. He clearly thought her very charming, but even Vicky was too overcome to show off. She had planned to say the sentence in French, which she had learned off by heart, and which she had said to Mademoiselle Charier who taught her French. Mademoiselle Charier had told Mama, who had thought it was wonderful, and had written it in a letter to Uncle Leopold to tell him what a clever daughter she had – cleverer than his Charlotte. It was only pretence, of course, on Mama's part, that Uncle Leopold's Charlotte was more good and prettier than Vicky. She could see that in Mama's eyes and by the way Papa looked at her and the way Mama held her tightly when she said that in spite of Charlotte's being so wonderful she wouldn't change Vicky for her.

Now Baby Alice, crowing with pleasure, was clearly very interested in the rather strange-looking Emperor.

Then they were all sent back to the nursery and Lady Lyttleton said they could watch the Emperor leave.

He and Papa went off together to Woolwich and Mama came into the nursery to tell them that they had behaved very well for the Emperor and she was very proud of her little family.

She was a little sad, Vicky noticed, as she always was when Papa went away.

'Where is Woolwich?' asked Vicky.

'It is not far from London. Papa will say goodbye to the Emperor there and come back to us. You will like that, won't you, Pussy?'

'I am not Pussy,' said Vicky. 'I am the Princess Royal.'

The Queen exchanged glances with Lady Lyttleton. Really this daughter of hers was most astonishingly precocious and clever of course. If only her brother took after her!

No sooner was the Emperor's visit over than there was trouble and the Queen feared that she was going to lose Sir Robert Peel. It would have been ironic if she had paused to think back a few years when Lord Melbourne's Ministry had been in danger of being replaced by the Opposition with Sir Robert at its head. At that time this had seemed the greatest tragedy of her life. Now she was in despair lest Sir Robert's Tories should be defeated and a Whig government take their place. *Poor* Lord Melbourne could never return as Prime Minister of course, but she had to admit that if he could she would not have wanted him. Albert had taught her to realise that Sir Robert was a better Prime Minister than Melbourne had ever been, and how she relied on Sir Robert. It was most tiresome that with the Emperor's visit just over and her body becoming more and more cumbersome, this crisis had to arise.

Sir Robert was concerned about the high cost of living and the riots which occurred because of this and proposed to ease matters by reducing the tax on sugar. The motion was defeated because of the defection of some members of his own party.

The Queen was very angry. Albert told her that a Jewish member of the party had placed himself at the head of the rebels. His name was Benjamin Disraeli and he was clearly angry because Sir

344

Robert had not given him a post in the cabinet.

'A most undesirable person,' said Albert. 'He has married a woman years older than himself ... for her money of course.'

'How very shocking!' said the Queen.

'She was the widow of Wyndham Lewis,' explained Albert, 'the member for Maidstone – a forward person, she has written to Sir Robert asking him not to ignore her husband but to give him a post in the government.'

'What dreadful people! And now he is making this trouble.'

'He is, you might say, a ringleader.'

'Oh, if only people would be patriotic and think of the country rather than their own ambitions.'

Albert agreed. When Sir Robert called they would discuss the matter, and see if resignation could be avoided.

To the Queen's delight it was. The government asked for a vote of confidence and even people like that dreadful Mr Disraeli did not want to see the Whigs in power so the government had its vote of confidence.

'But it makes one realise,' she confided to Albert, 'how very insecure the government is.'

No sooner was this crisis over than another arose – this time with the French who, secretly angry because of the visit of the Emperor of Russia, seized the sovereignty of Tahiti and put the British ambassador there under restraint.

The French were prevailed upon to make reparations and Lord Aberdeen, the Foreign Minister, with Sir Robert and Albert, were attempting to bring about more friendly relations with France when she was brought to bed to give birth to her fourth child.

To Albert's great joy it was a boy.

He was christened Alfred.

## Chapter XV

## IN ALBERT'S NATIVE LAND

Life had become more simple. The Queen, once gay, fond of balls and banquets, had become eager to retire from the limelight. Certain members of the Court considered her old-fashioned, rather dowdy and above all, prim. Inspired by Albert, she was taking a very stern attitude towards moral lapses, forgetting that once she had admonished him for his puritanical views. Albert was right in this, she believed, as he was in everything else.

Albert would never be really accepted. He was the foreigner, the German; but the happy family life of the royal couple was an example to all and the majority of people applauded it. Albert's clearly defined lines of right and wrong embraced so whole-heartedly by the Queen became the law of the Court, and the country was affected by them. Respectability was all important. To sin was to be not respectable and therefore if anyone sinned, they could only expect to be received in society if they were never found out. The Queen who could in no circumstances violate her marriage vows considered that only those who deserved to be outcasts from society would do so, and no one who had been involved in scandal could be received by her. Everyone must lead an exemplary moral life. Marriage was sacrosanct. She and Albert set the pattern – which was of course Albert's – and everyone must conform to it. A subtle change was creeping over the country. The swaggering days of the Regency were far behind. The age of Victoria and Albert had begun.

The happiest times for the Queen were those when she could escape with Albert and the children to her 'dear little house' Osborne on the Isle of Wight. There it was such fun to live quietly without being surrounded by all the trappings of Court life. There the children could enjoy the sea and fresh air and she and Albert could temporarily forget the cares of state and live like an ordinary family.

Albert, however, had plans for rebuilding Osborne. He made sketches of what he would like the house to look like. She was well aware that he was just a little homesick for Germany, which of course was natural, in spite of their happy life together. She knew how she would feel if she had had to leave her home; but secretly she believed *she* could have been happy anywhere with Albert. He was with her, of course, and it was only rarely that she saw the nostalgia in his eyes. But when he was in the country he could imagine he was back in his Thuringian forests. Dear Albert, he had such a devoted family. And who could wonder at it? Anyone would adore Albert.

Baron Stockmar was in constant correspondence and advised them on almost everything they did. Albert said that later on when Bertie was a year or so older he was going to implore Stockmar to come to England because he did want his advice about the education of the boy. Of all the children he was most concerned about Bertie.

When Parliament was prorogued and it was suggested that she and Albert might visit his family in Germany the Queen was delighted. Sir Robert Peel thought it a good idea and plans were made for the journey.

The Queen told the children of the proposed trip and of course Vicky wanted to go with them. Bertie looked expectant. He was beginning to understand that he was the Prince of Wales and had a position of special importance. Albert had said that they must make sure that he did not become arrogant.

'How I should love to take darling Vicky with us,' said the Queen. 'But she is so young yet and I should not always be able to keep an eye on her.'

Albert was regretful too. He would have loved to show his darling to his family. He admitted to the Queen that he had never seen a child who was so bright for her age.

Vicky cried and pleaded and was a little astonished that her wishes were ignored. Bertie was not sure whether he wanted to go or not. He had an idea that life might be more tolerable for him in the nursery without his parents' super-vision. He was very fond of Lady Lyttleton and found that he did not stammer nearly so much in her presence as he did in that of his parents. So he could regard his parents' departure with equanimity, which was more than Vicky could. Bertie liked Fat Alice too, who laughed when he tickled her far more than anyone else did, and Baby Affie, as they called Alfred, seemed to like him too.

They were at Osborne where the children were to stay for the summer holiday when the day came for the departure. Vicky sat on the Queen's bed with Alice beside her while Victoria dressed. Vicky kept asking: 'Why can't I go, Mama? Oh, why can't *I* go to Germany?'

'One day you'll go, my pet. But not this time.'

'Why not?'

'Because Papa thinks it best.'

That settled it. Even Vicky knew that what Papa decided must be right. Therefore she must accept the sad fact.

All the children were at breakfast with them – even Baby Affie who, like Alice, was a good placid child.

Vicky sat next to her father, looking very sad; and they all talked in German, which they did often because Papa liked it. Vicky could speak it as fluently as she could English; and even Bertie could mumble his few sentences in German as well as he could English.

When they left, Vicky, Bertie and Alice were all in the doorway with Lady Lyttleton to wave them goodbye. Vicky was almost in tears. Poor brave little Vicky!

'She was heartbroken,' said the Queen to Albert. 'But the dear brave child held back her tears.'

They reached Buckingham Palace later that day, but how desolate it seemed there without the dear children. 'I shall be glad to start on our journey,' said the Queen. 'I miss them so dreadfully.'

Sir Robert called and assured them that they need have no qualms. The political situation was good; there were no troubles looming on the horizon; they could take a holiday without any fears that they might be neglecting their duties.

'Everything is in such good hands, Sir Robert,' said the Queen. 'We know that.'

It was a happy note to leave on and apart from the fact that the dear children had to be left behind the Queen could have been perfectly happy.

The crossing was rather rough, which did not suit dear Albert, but at least he had his wife to look after him this time and when it was over he quickly recovered. How enchanting to be in a foreign country where everything looked so different from how it did at home. The Queen was delighted with the peasant girls in caps and cloaks going to market with their brass jugs. To see these things for the first time was thrilling, but to observe them in the company of her dear Albert, who always saw everything so much more clearly than anyone else, was not only the greatest pleasure but a lesson in observation. Lehzen used to say that she missed nothing but, when they sketched together what they had seen, she was astonished at Albert's powers of observation.

They were both happy to be met by the King and the Queen of the Belgians at Malines. Uncle Leopold welcomed them warmly to his country and was clearly very happy to see them together. He always reminded them that he had arranged their marriage when they were both in their cradles, and was pleased when Victoria said that they owed their happiness to him, which was true.

After accompanying them to Verviers Uncle Leopold and Aunt Louise took a fond farewell. Victoria wept at the parting but soon they were crossing the Prussian frontier and Albert was in his beloved Germany.

The King of Prussia met them at Aix-la-Chapelle and from then on they were entertained royally. Albert was clearly very happy to be back in Germany and the Queen shared his enjoyment. For the first time he could show her all those beauties which previously he had described to her with his eloquence or his sketch book. There was an elusive fairy-tale quality about these mountains and forests, which delighted her. She was completely happy, and she realised that perfect happiness for her was having Albert to herself. She loved the children dearly; she was going to do her duty by them; but the one person who meant more to her than the rest of the world put together was Albert.

And how pleasant were these dear German relations. She felt so much more at home with them than with the French.

Albert whispered that his heart was set on a Prussian alliance for Vicky. He wanted to see her Queen of Prussia. She agreed that there was nothing she would like better. Their favourite child would grace any throne, and since she could not have Victoria's this would be the next best thing.

They visited museums and universities. The

King was very proud of his kingdom, and eager to show it off; Albert told the Queen that he had already hinted to him that the two houses might be linked in marriage in due course and the King was pleased with the idea.

Albert was deeply moved to visit the places where he had passed such happy times before coming to England. They went to Bonn and met some of Albert's old friends from his university days; a statue of Beethoven was to be unveiled and there were concerts in honour of the great musician; at the unveiling the Queen was secretly amused because when the statue was uncovered it had its back to her and Albert. Victoria caught Albert's eye and they exchanged looks of amusement; how they laughed at the incident when they were alone. Albert was not only good, Victoria reminded herself, but also ready to see a joke.

The King gave a great banquet for them and made a charming speech in which he asked everyone to fill their glasses. He recalled the days when the British and the Germans had stood together at Waterloo, brothers-in-arms, and he wanted them to drink the health of Her Majesty, the Queen of the United Kingdom of Great Britain and Ireland; he also wanted them to drink to her august consort.

When the Queen, overcome by emotion, rose and kissed the King on his cheek, there was loud applause.

What a wonderful experience to travel through Germany and see Albert's emotion and delight in his own homeland. How his eyes sparkled at the sight of those forests and mountains, at the charming little castles which were dotted over the countryside. Best of all was arriving at Coburg; and there was Albert's brother Ernest – now the Duke – waiting to greet them. Dear Ernest who looked so well and happy and whom she hoped was not straying from the paths of virtue as he had once. But this was not the time to think of such a thing. Here he was looking quite handsome – though not nearly so handsome as Albert – in full uniform, having travelled in an open carriage with six horses. Everywhere people lined the roads to cheer them – countrymen and buxom country girls in pointed caps and layers of petticoats. 'So charming,' whispered the Queen to Albert.

On the way they again met Uncle Leopold and Aunt Louise who got into the carriage and sat with them. Ernest alighted and a horse was brought for him. He rode along beside the carriage and, the procession following behind them, they came to the palace. As they approached, pretty girls in native costumes threw flowers into the carriage. How good of Ernest to arrange such a welcome!

And what a large family! The Duchess of Kent, who had been visiting her relations, was there to greet her daughter and there were more cousins and aunts than Victoria had ever known she possessed.

What a lot of chatter, embracing, exclamations of delight! The Queen's emotions were always ready to be aroused; her eyes filled with tears as she kissed the relations who were hers as well as dearest Albert's.

Ernest said that he had put Rosenau at their disposal because he knew that Albert's birthplace was his favourite residence.

'How wonderfully, *wonderfully* kind,' cried the Queen.

And she too loved Rosenau. How could she do anything else? It was here that blessed being first saw the light of day. She wrote sentimentally of it in her journal.

*How happy, how joyful we were on waking to find ourselves here at dear Rosenau, my Albert's birth-place, the place he most loves. He was so happy to be here with me. It is like a beautiful dream.*

And even as they awoke they were greeted by the voices of singers from the Coburg theatre whom Ernest had engaged to sing below their window.

Her eyes shining with joy, she insisted on Albert's showing her the little room where he and Ernest used to sleep with their tutor Florschütz of whom Albert had talked to her so often.

'Albert, what an enchanting view!'

'I have never seen a finer,' said Albert.

'Oh, I can picture you so well ... when you were no older than Bertie.' She frowned slightly. 'Oh, I do hope and pray Bertie grows up *exactly* like you.'

'He shows no sign of it at the moment,' said Albert grimly.

But they must not talk of unpleasant matters on such an occasion.

'What are these little holes in the wall paper?' she wanted to know.

'Ernest and I made them when we were fencing.'

'How interesting! And this is the table at which you used to sit. I can picture it all. How happy I am to be here! I was always a little jealous of everything that went before in your life. I wish that I had always been there.'

'My dear love is inclined to be a little jealous.'

'I should be terribly, Albert, if you ever gave me cause. Do you remember when I threw Miss Pitt's flowers all over the floor?'

Albert remembered perfectly well.

'And I never really have any cause to be jealous, have I?'

'My dear love, how can you suggest such a thing. Of course you have not. You are my wife so how could I possibly care for any other woman?'

'Of course not. I am stupid. You never do *look* at anyone else, but Lord Melbourne once said that men who were perfectly faithful in their youth often became quite flirtatious in middle age.'

'You did pay rather too much attention to Lord Melbourne at one time,' chided Albert.

She admitted. 'I have learned so much ... thanks to you, my dear Albert. *Poor* Lord Melbourne.'

Albert was able to celebrate his birthday at Rosenau.

'What a happy occasion!' cried the Queen. 'It is more than I could have hoped for. To celebrate your *dear* birthday here.'

Ernest arranged for the singers to begin the great day's celebrations by chanting below his window and on this occasion there was a band. How wonderful to hear the march and *O Isis and Osiris* from *The Magic Flute;* and it was a beautiful day with the sun shining brilliantly. The previous day Victoria with Ernest and his wife Alexandrine had dressed Albert's birthday table with flowers and laid all the presents on it.

What an enchanting way to begin a birthday with all the presents and the people from the surrounding country calling with flowers to greet Albert, whom they remembered as a boy.

There was one who came forward with a bouquet for Victoria and said when it was presented: 'I congratulate you on your husband's birthday and wish that he may live for many and many a year and that you may soon come back.'

With tears in her eyes the Queen said this was her fervent wish too.

What a perfectly happy day! 'I have never been happier in my life,' said the Queen earnestly. Then she remembered the children.

If they were here... But she knew in her heart, and she was too honest to pretend, no one *no one* could ever mean to her what Albert did.

He is my *all*, she said.

How sad to leave Rosenau! But it was time to begin the journey home. 'I feel I have shared your childhood with you in some measure,' she told Albert. 'It makes me closer to you.'

Albert was deeply touched and called her his 'dear little wife'.

If they could stay longer, if they need not go back to England and the squabbles between the

Tories and the Whigs and the fears that that dreadful Disraeli would behave so badly that he brought his own party down, how happy she would be! It was like living in a paradise.

She sighed. 'I must be thankful for such a perfect holiday.'

It was not quite at an end. She and Albert with Ernest and Alexandrine paid a visit to the Gräber Insel, an island on which were the family graves. They were taken to it by a boatman which made Victoria shiver a little because, she whispered to Albert, it was like Charon rowing them across the Styx. There were buried members of the House of Saxe-Coburg, and the flowers which grew on their graves were tended by a strange man, very old and gnarled, who lived there all alone.

Victoria gripped Albert's hand firmly.

'Are you cold?' he asked.

'No. As they would say at home: someone must be walking over my grave.'

'This makes you morbid,' said Albert. 'My dear love is very easily affected.'

'By death,' she agreed. 'I cannot bear to think of anyone I love being dead.'

Albert smiled at her tenderly, but she was glad when they left the Island of Graves.

And how fresh and beautiful the Thuringian forest looked after that sad island. The haymakers came running to wave to them as they passed and again Victoria was loud in her praise of the pretty costumes.

How poor Grandmama Saxe-Coburg wept when they said goodbye. She clung to Albert, calling him *Mein Engel's Kind*. Poor, poor Grandma, who must be thinking that it might well be that she would never see Albert again. She was old and it could not be long before she was lying under a flower-covered grave on the Gräber Insel.

Sir Robert had warned them that if they paid a visit to Germany they must on their way back call on the King of France, who was already put out by the Russian visit, and would be more so, if after spending so much time in Germany, they did not call on him too.

At Tréport Louis Philippe was waiting to greet them as before and Victoria was gratified to discover that he had named a gallery in the château in honour of her last visit. In this gallery Victoria saw, among others, Winterhalter portraits of herself and Albert.

'How very gracious,' said the Queen.

Because a contretemps had arisen between the French and British governments concerning the marriage of the Infanta of Spain, Lord Aberdeen and Lord Liverpool had joined them in order to have discussions with M. Guizot, the French Foreign Minister. It was all very amicable but not nearly so happy of course as being with the dear German relations.

After a day and a night with the French the royal yacht set sail for England and at noon had arrived at the Isle of Wight. They drove to Osborne and to the great joy of both the Queen and Albert, Lady Lyttleton was standing at the door, Affie in her arms, with Vicky, Bertie and Alice beside her.

The children shouted with joy when they saw their parents and ran forward to fling themselves into their arms.

It was too much to expect that the prosperity with which the year had opened should continue. That summer had been the wettest in Ireland in living memory with the result that the potato crop was mined. The terrible famine which followed was responsible for acute starvation and many deaths, and it was inevitable that the Corn Laws would have to be reviewed immediately. Lord John Russell announced that he was in favour of repealing the Corn Laws; but knowing that he had insufficient support to bring about the necessary reforms, Peel resigned.

When he called to see the Queen she received him with great sorrow, but even at such a time she remembered that similar occasion when she had feared to lose Lord Melbourne. How impulsive she had been then, how unconstitutional; and how differently she would act now. She did not want to lose Sir Robert and she made that very clear, but she was not childishly stubborn and emotional about it. It was a political issue and she must accept it as such.

Sir Robert suggested that she send for Lord John Russell, asking him to take on the Premiership.

This happened just before Christmas, when she would have been so much happier bringing in the yule logs and showing the children how Christmas was celebrated in dear Papa's country. She and Albert would do that of course; but there was this tiresome matter to be settled first.

'And if the government falls and we have the Whigs back we shall doubtless have that tiresome

Lord Palmerston back in the Foreign Office.'

Albert agreed with her on that point. Palmerston was a tiresome man who was inclined to patronise Albert and treat him as a boy. Very different from Lord Aberdeen!

It was with relief that she received the news that Lord John declined the offer.

That *impish* Disraeli had laughingly said (and this was widely reported) that Lord John being in 'no mood to accept the poisoned chalice handed it back to Sir Robert, who had no alternative but to take it back'.

So Christmas came with Sir Robert still in office. It *was* so like that other occasion, but how different she was. How much more dignified, how diplomatic and queenly.

There was one she had to thank for the change – that blessed being, Albert.

In the midst of this political upheaval the Queen became aware of the now familiar signs of pregnancy.

'Oh no, no!' she cried in irritation. 'It is far too soon!'

'It seems,' she complained to Albert, 'that I am no sooner delivered of one child than another is started.'

'It is life, my love,' said Albert calmly.

'It is all very well for *you* to feel so serene about it,' cried the Queen with a flash of temper. '*You* don't have to suffer all the inconveniences culminating in that painful ordeal.'

Albert patted her hand and she was immediately contrite.

'Oh, Albert,' she said, 'what a temper I have!'

Albert agreed gravely.

'But it is tiresome, you must agree.'

'It is married life,' said Albert.

Even so, she thought, a queen did have a strenuous life and although it was her duty to give the nation heirs she had already presented that exacting taskmaster with two sons and two daughters. Already the press was commenting on her growing family. There had been cartoons of an impoverished-looking John Bull, with patched coat eating a tiny bloater off a cracked plate shouting: 'Hurrah. Another royal birth. I can pay for it with my income tax.'

It would have been most desirable to have at least a lapse of a few years now. She was still very young. Besides a family of four was adequate for her satisfaction and the nation's purse.

She was feeling like this because during those months of pregnancy she was never well. Because she had discovered that she had the perfect husband did not mean that was the end of her violent temper. It still was ready to break out when she was provoked, and to rise in the morning feeling sick and depressed made it very ready to flare out, as her attendants had discovered. The Queen's pregnancies were almost as much disliked by those around her as by herself.

A few days after Lord John had been unable to form a government and Peel was back in office the Queen invited Lord Melbourne to dine at the palace. He had been much in her thoughts lately because of the similarity of the predicament confronting Peel's government and that of his own during the famous Bedchamber incident. She had neglected him lately, had not answered his letters for weeks at a time and was rather ashamed of herself.

Poor Lord Melbourne, she must not forget what a great friend he had been to her. Although she, being so impulsive and inexperienced, had attached more to the friendship than was really there, that was not his fault.

Lord Melbourne was delighted to receive an invitation. As he bent over her hand his eyes filled with tears, but somehow they did not move her as they had in the old days. She could only see the difference between this poor pathetic old man and the fine handsome witty Prime Minister who had called on her on the first day of her accession and for four years had seen her every day.

'Dear Lord Melbourne,' she said, 'you are to sit beside me at dinner. I have arranged it.'

It *was* pathetic to see his happiness. One thing which had not changed was his devotion to her.

As the meal progressed they talked of the past. Lord Melbourne recalled little incidents which she had forgotten and she could see that he was enjoying it immensely which pleased her. But it was inevitable that the conversation should turn to politics and the great issue of the moment was the repeal of the Corn Laws.

Lord Melbourne seemed to have forgotten that he was no longer Prime Minister; and it was very likely that if Lord John Russell had been able to form a government there would not have been a place for Lord Melbourne in it, for he was now far too sick a man for office. He talked of the Corn Laws and Peel's sudden change of opinion with regard to them.

'It's a damned dishonest act, Ma'am,' he declared vehemently.

The Queen laughed uncertainly and tried to change the subject, but Melbourne seemed to have forgotten that they were seated at a dinner table in the company of others; he appeared to have an illusion that they were alone in the blue closet when he was allowed the privilege of interrupting the Queen and repeated his assertion against Peel.

'Lord Melbourne,' said the Queen regally, 'I must beg you to say nothing more on this subject now.'

There was a silence. The old man was crestfallen. The glories of the past had slipped away and left him exposed to the indignities of the present. The Queen was overcome with pity. She *had* loved him and she was not of a nature to forget old friends.

She said gently: 'I shall be glad to discuss the matter with you at any other time.'

Melbourne looked at her gratefully. She had helped him salvage his dignity.

Tears shone in his eyes; and after that she thought of him as Poor, *poor* Lord Melbourne; and, remembering past glories, so did many others.

With the new year the political crisis worsened.

It was an unusual situation with Sir Robert standing out against the rest of his party deter-

363

mined to bring about the repeal of the Corn Laws – a very strange situation with a Prime Minister supported by his Opposition and his own party against him.

Albert took a great interest in these matters and insisted that the Queen did too, although with the irksome period to be lived through and all the discomforts which beset her, she found it difficult. A woman at such a time should be able to devote herself to domestic matters, she complained.

There was strong criticism of Albert because he was firmly behind Sir Robert and visited the House of Commons when the debate on Free Trade was in progress. The press raised a torrent of abuse. The House of Commons was no place for foreigners, said the press; nor was it proper for the Queen's husband to show his approval of a measure by putting in an appearance during a debate. Moreover it was something which would not be tolerated. Albert was made to realise that he must not set foot in the House again.

Sir Robert was abused daily in the press; he was a 'turncoat' and a 'traitor' to his party, said his enemies, and they were men of his own party. The most virulent attacks came from the rebel Disraeli who, it was perfectly clear, had an eye on the premiership and was never going to forgive Peel for not giving him a place in the Cabinet.

In early June the Queen's fifth child was born. It was a girl and she was christened Helena.

'Two boys and three girls,' she whispered to Albert when he came to sit beside her bed. 'We have quite a large family now, Albert.'

Albert said this made him very happy, in such a way that she felt it was all very well worth while.

'And what is going to happen about Sir Robert?' she asked.

'That, my love,' replied Albert, 'remains to be seen.'

Well, she thought, whatever happens, I have dear Albert and five children, and when one is so blessed in one's home life, providing the country is safe, politics must seem less important than the family.

Sir Robert remained firm in his endeavour; the bill was passed in all its stages through the Commons and was sent to the Lords where it sailed through. Peel had repealed the Corn Laws, but on the very day when the bill was finally passed, Peel was defeated on the Irish Coercion Bill; his government fell and on this occasion Lord John Russell was able to form a government.

The Whigs were back in power.

## Chapter XVI

### BERTIE IN TROUBLE

Bertie was once more in disgrace. Since the coming of Alfred, who was now of an age to take notice, he had begun to speak fluently and to take an interest in his brother. Alfred applauded most things Bertie did and quite clearly admired him, so Bertie began to have quite a good opinion of himself. He could not compete with clever Vicky of course but in the little boys' world he shared with Alfred he was supreme.

He would shout at Alfred, push him or pull his hair; but whatever he did Alfred bore stoically and gazed at him with admiration.

It was different during lessons because then he must sit with Vicky and hear her recite her French poetry or almost always come up with the right answers to sums. He felt it was no use trying to compete and so much more fun to think up some new game to play with Alfred and Alice too, who admired him. He might not be the favourite with his parents but he was with his younger brother and sister.

Miss Hildyard, one of the governesses, said that as he was not attending he had better stand in a corner.

He shook his head. 'I *won't* stand in the corner,' he said truculently. 'I am the Prince of Wales and Prince of Waleses don't stand in corners.'

'It's not Waleses,' said clever Vicky, 'Because there's only one Wales.'

'That is right, Vicky,' said Miss Hildyard, 'and Bertie will go and stand in the corner.'

'I *won't*,' declared Bertie.

And as Miss Hildyard tried to seize him he cried: 'Don't dare touch the Prince of Wales.'

Vicky burst out laughing and said he had a temper as bad as Mama's and wouldn't Mama be in a temper when she heard how naughty Bertie had been. 'Because you will tell her, won't you, Miss Hildyard?'

Miss Hildyard said she was sorry to have to

complain of Bertie's naughtiness and if he would be a good boy and go and stand in the corner until his fit of naughtiness had passed she would say nothing to His Royal Highness Bertie's father, nor to Her Majesty Bertie's mother.

Bertie considered this but Vicky was watching him so he picked up a book and threw it at the window. There was a cracking as the glass splintered. Vicky said: 'Oh!' Bertie stared at what he had done; and when they had all recovered from the shock Miss Hildyard said that now she would have no alternative but to report Bertie's wickedness (he noticed with alarm the different description of his conduct) to his father.

So there was Bertie standing before his father, and in the latter's hand was a long thin cane. Bertie knew from experience that this would soon be applied to him and he dreaded the ordeal, but he was not sure which was worse, the actual sting of the cane or the lecture which preceded it.

Bertie, said his father, was a great anxiety to his parents. He had no sense of responsibility. If he grew up into a good man (which his father feared was very unlikely) he might if his mother died be the King of England.

Bertie had heard this before but he listened to it every time awestruck. Somehow Papa managed to imply that if Mama died it would somehow be his fault because he would then be the King.

Because he was the Prince he owed it to God, his country and his parents to be more than ordinarily good, but alas, his wicked nature prevailed and he was more than ordinarily bad; and because this was so it was his father's painful duty – which hurt him far more than punishment could hurt Bertie – to administer a more than ordinarily severe beating. Bertie would now place himself across the chair which was waiting to receive him and suffer the full force of his father's blows.

Bertie had no recourse but to obey and as the blows descended his cries were loud and protesting.

At last the Prince seemed satisfied and Bertie was sent to his room, there to remain until he was in a sufficiently penitent mood to say he was sorry to Miss Hildyard, to Mama and to his father for the great grief he had made them suffer.

Bertie lay face downwards on his bed sobbing. It was too uncomfortable to lie the other way.

The door opened and he knew it was Mama. She sat by the bed.

'Bertie, I hear you have again been very wicked.'

Bertie did not answer.

'You have been rude to Miss Hildyard; you have broken a window; and worst of all you have grieved Papa.'

Bertie was moved to stutter: 'He ... he didn't have to...'

'What do you mean, Bertie? Do you think Papa would shirk his duty? You, by your wickedness, have forced him to beat you. You know how that must have hurt him.'

'He hurt me,' said Bertie fiercely.

'Then how much more do you think Papa has been hurt?'

'He wasn't beaten.'

'Oh, Bertie, will you *never* understand anything?

There are things that hurt more than canes. You have the best, kindest, dearest Papa in the world and you have made him unhappy by making it necessary for him to beat you.'

Bertie thought it wiser to sob.

'I am going to leave you to think about this. But you *must* be a better boy. Remember how you have grieved your Papa and me and I am sure that when you think of that and how you love him and me you will be very sorry for what you have done and turn over a new leaf.'

With that she left him.

He didn't believe Papa was more hurt than he was because nobody could be. He started to cry again. And he didn't love Papa. He didn't love Mama much either.

This was a startling discovery to make but at least it made him stop thinking of his smarting body.

The Queen was discussing the problem of Bertie with the Prince.

'Something will have to be done about him, Albert.'

'I have given him a caning which he will remember for some time.'

'Poor Albert. It was *courageous* of you. I know how you must have felt about that. But it had to be done and it was best that you should do it. I'm afraid a tutor's caning would have little effect on Bertie. Now he realises that you are angry with him he will understand that he must mend his ways.'

'I was not angry, my love. I was hurt that our

son could behave so badly.'

'I know, Albert.'

'Someone must take a firm hand with him. These tutors and governesses are aware that he is the Prince of Wales and can't forget it. Bertie knows this. He can be shrewd enough; it is only where his lessons are concerned that he is stupid. Something will have to be done.'

'If only you could teach him, Albert, that would be the best thing possible, but of course you are so fully occupied. My dear Albert, I fear you are overworked already.'

Albert said that his great desire was to help the Queen and this meant keeping up to date with everything that was going on. But he had an idea.

'I shall write to Stockmar and explain our predicament to him. I shall implore him as he loves us both – which I know he does – to come at once. After all the education of the heir to the throne is as important as anything can be.'

The Queen thought that an excellent idea.

'Trust you, Albert,' she smiled, 'to hit upon the right solution.'

Politics were soon claiming the Queen's attention. Some politicians, she remarked to Albert, seemed determined to plague her. There was for one, that dreadful man with the greasy dyed hair, Mr Disraeli, who had made everything so difficult for dear Sir Robert; another man whom she detested was a Mr Gladstone. He had recently resigned because he objected to the government's proposal to increase a grant to an Irish college where men were trained to become Roman Catholic priests.

'What a *dreadful* man to make such a fuss over such a matter,' declared the Queen. She had seen him once or twice and taken an immediate dislike to him, although he did have a charming wife. But perhaps the chief nuisance was Lord Palmerston.

In the days when Lord Melbourne had been Prime Minister she had enjoyed Lord Palmerston's company. She knew that he had led a rather shocking life and this, she regretted to think nowadays, had then attracted her. She had thought him interesting and had been amused when Lord Melbourne had told her that he was nicknamed Cupid, for reasons which were clear to all. Later she had heard that when visiting Windsor he had been seen making his way along the corridors to certain ladies' bedrooms during the night. Very, very shocking. Albert was aware of this side of Lord Palmerston's nature and had he been the best of Ministers could never have liked him because of it.

Within the last few years Lord Palmerston had settled down. After being a very gay bachelor for fifty-five years, he had suddenly married; and the lady he had chosen to be his wife was a widow three years younger than he was, who happened to be Lord Melbourne's sister. Emily Lamb had been married when she was very young to Lord Cowper and rumour had it that Lord Palmerston and she had been very great friends for some years. The friendship was perhaps too intimate for propriety; in any case when Lord Cowper died Palmerston married his widow.

Fanny, Lady Cowper's daughter by her first marriage, who was lady-in-waiting to the Queen, did not like the idea of her mother's marrying an old roué like Lord Palmerston; the Queen now heartily agreed with her; as she said to Albert, there was something very unpleasant about widows' remarrying... In the event of the direst possible tragedy of which she could not bear to think for one moment, *she* could *never* bring herself to act in such a way.

And now that Lord John Russell was the Prime Minister, Lord Palmerston was once again Foreign Secretary; poor, *poor* Lord Melbourne having no place in the Cabinet. He said, with that generosity which she remembered so well, that of course it was quite right that he should not be offered one, for he was too infirm to hold it, but it seemed so hard when one remembered the past.

Lord Palmerston seemed to respect no one. He managed whenever possible to devise a course of action for himself and then explain it after he had carried it out. It was wrong, but he could always shrug himself out of any difficult situation, pretending that it was of no great importance.

The Queen suspected him of withholding state papers from her. She resented his attitude towards Albert which was that the Prince was merely a pleasant young man who must not be allowed to think that his opinions carried any weight.

A matter which had for some time been considered one of international importance had become a crisis. The question was the marriage of the young Queen Isabella of Spain and her sister. Louis Philippe had long had an eye on Spain. Before he came to the throne it had been an ambition of the French that Spain and France should be one. This might be brought about by the marriage of the King's son to the young Queen of Spain. This was something which would never be permitted and Louis Philippe knew it. But he had a plan. As it would never be accepted by the rest of Europe that the son of the King of France should marry the Queen of Spain he would not press this. Instead his son, the Duc de Montpensier, should marry the young Queen's sister, the Infanta Fernanda, while the Queen married her cousin, the Duke of Cadiz.

Before any objection could be made to this, the marriages had taken place. It was then discovered why Louis Philippe and Guizot, that wily Foreign Minister of his, had made the arrangement. The Duke of Cadiz was impotent; therefore the Spanish throne would go to the heir of Fernanda and Montpensier and thus Louis Philippe would achieve the influence he had hoped for.

When the Queen realised what had happened she raged against Louis Philippe.

'What a sly old man! And when you think how he pretended to be such friends with us and gave the children those lovely presents.'

'We should be wary of people when they give us presents,' said Albert.

'But these were such lovely presents and Vicky loved her doll. It had eyes that opened and shut and had real eyelashes; and Bertie's soldiers were beautiful.'

'If our foreign service had been more efficient we should have seen this coming,' said Albert.

'I never did like that man Palmerston and why

Little Johnny wanted to give him the Foreign Office I can't imagine. Of course Johnny married a widow in the first place. Lord Melbourne told me that Johnny, on account of his size, used to be called the Widow's Mite.'

Albert did not smile; he did not appreciate such jokes. She supposed they were not really very funny but she did remember laughing immoderately at the time.

'Then of course there was that sad affair of his wife's death. It upset me so much and then he married again and they are very happy together ... *not* a widow the second time.'

'It is a pity,' said Albert, 'that he brought Palmerston into the Cabinet.'

It was not long before there was a big difference between the royal pair and the Foreign Minister. Lord Palmerston had such odd ideas. There was Civil War in Portugal and one would have thought that in such a conflict he would have been on the side of the royalists. Not so; his sympathies were with the people.

'I consider Lord Palmerston to be a most dangerous man,' said Albert.

So of course the Queen agreed.

Stockmar, in answer to the entreaties of the Queen and Albert, arrived in England. He was warmly greeted and carried off to Windsor for conferences with the anxious parents of the Prince of Wales.

'We are very worried about Bertie,' announced the Queen. 'He refuses to learn and is so high-spirited that it is sometimes difficult for his tutors and governesses to control him.'

'I have forced myself to cane him many times,' said the Prince. 'It was distressing but necessary.'

'It may well be that he is being pampered by people in the nurseries and schoolroom,' said the Baron. 'That could be responsible. And if he says he won't learn he must simply be made to learn.' Stockmar's dry old face twisted into a reluctant smile. 'I think you may well have been a little soft with the child.'

'My parental feelings had to be overcome,' said Albert.

'Albert was wonderful,' murmured the Queen. 'I have been deeply impressed by the way he has handled the difficult matter.'

'Yes,' said Stockmar. 'But leave this to me. I will go to the schoolroom and discover what is happening there; and perhaps a tutor should be appointed for the Prince of Wales – a man of learning who will not hesitate to use the rod.'

Stockmar was conducted to the schoolroom where Vicky was seated at the table writing out French verbs and Bertie was being coaxed to read by Miss Hildyard.

There was consternation. Miss Hildyard rose and curtsied as the children wriggled down from their seats.

What a *nasty* old man with Papa and Mama! thought Bertie; and then was aware that the old man in question was staring at him.

'Bertie, come and greet our dear good friend Baron Stockmar,' said Mama.

Bertie came forward and was peered at. There was a smudge of blue paint on his blouse. Vicky had pointed it out an hour ago and he could feel those nasty old eyes concentrated on it.

If all the grown-ups would turn their backs for a minute he would put out his tongue at that old man just to show Vicky what he thought of their Baron Stockmar.

'So this is the backward one,' said the Baron. 'Why's that, eh?'

'Because,' said Vicky, 'he is not the forward one.'

'Vicky will speak when she is addressed,' said Papa gently. 'It is for Bertie to answer.' But Bertie did not care about being backward and wasn't frightened of the old Baron.

'Sullen, it seems,' said the Baron. 'Well, we must remedy that.'

The Baron turned away and they all began talking to Miss Hildyard.

Baron Stockmar inspected the books and asked questions about the lessons. Some of the governesses, trying to show Bertie in the best possible light, said that he was a very sociable child; he was very good with the younger children, who adored him and he would play with them for hours; in fact the first person they looked for when coming into the nursery was Bertie.

'Sociability,' said the Baron, 'is a bad sign. It shows a frivolous nature.'

'He is rather inventive,' said Miss Hildyard.

'Inventive?'

'Yes, Baron. He has a lively imagination.'

'You mean he tells lies?'

'Oh no.'

'But yes,' said the Baron. 'What else?'

'He devises amusing games for the children.'

'Games. Lies! That child is on the road to

disaster. And no aptitude for lessons! That will have to be remedied.'

He went on to say that sometimes it was necessary to apply learning with the cane. The governesses were disturbed by this picture of Bertie as a desperate character when he was merely a normal little boy, but it was impossible to attempt to change the Baron's view, particularly when it was supported by Bertie's parents.

When he was alone with the Queen and the Prince, Stockmar said: 'I think we should appoint a tutor for the young villain and give him firm instructions that he must get results, which with such a child must mean meeting recalcitrance with severity.'

Stockmar found the man. He was Henry Birch, the rector of Prestwich, who having taught boys at Eton and being a Reverend gentleman, seemed highly suitable.

Bertie awaited his arrival with some trepidation.

It was September and the thought of escaping from London delighted both the Queen and Albert. The very name Osborne was, as the Queen said, like music in their ears and now that Albert had such plans for improving the place there was an added excitement in planning a trip to their dear island.

The children were happy there. There they could play on the beach and run about in the gardens of eight hundred acres, conscious, as their parents were, of a freedom they did not normally enjoy. Bertie had occasional uneasy twinges about the future but he was not one to worry about what might be coming to him. The present was his concern and how best to enjoy it. If he could escape from tutorial control he knew how to do that very well.

Even Papa seemed different in Osborne and would sometimes play games which made him seem like an ordinary person; and Mama would watch them playing and applaud everything Papa did. Still it was good fun and gave Bertie a pleasant, comfortable feeling to be on such terms with his parents.

When they arrived that September there was a great deal of talk about the foundation stone which had been laid for a new Osborne. The old one was on the point of collapse and a new Osborne was in the process of being built. There was an exciting smell of paint in the house. One part of it was completed and this was where they lived while the rest of it was being planned by the Prince.

The Queen declared her contentment to be at Osborne. 'Oh how I should love to live the simple life always,' she cried.

Albert agreed that it would have been far more comfortable for them both if they had been wealthy gentlefolk instead of royalty. Secretly Albert wondered whether Victoria was entirely sincere – although she would be aware of this of course; one of her greatest qualities was her honesty – because she was always very conscious of her dignity as Queen and sprang to defend it if it was assailed in the smallest way – sometimes by him. As for Albert, because he was conscientious and sometimes found his duties arduous, they were at least self imposed. It was difficult to understand all the truth, in any case there were so many facets of it that perhaps there was not a simple answer to any one of their problems.

But here they were at Osborne and this was a special occasion because for the first time they were occupying the new Osborne – and although there was so much to be done in the house, they were in a way entering it for the first time.

Such an occasion must be celebrated.

As they came into the house – the Queen going first – one of the maids threw an old shoe after her. For the moment the Queen thought that she was the victim of an attack and turned sharply, but there was Mary Kerr, one of her Scottish ladies-in-waiting, standing there unabashed and explaining to Her Majesty that she had to throw the shoe after the Queen otherwise there would have been no luck in the house.

Everyone – even the Prince – joined in the laughter and the Queen picked up the old shoe and thanked Mary for it.

Dinner was taken in the new dining-room and afterwards the company retired to the drawing-room where the curtains were drawn back and the lights shone forth over the sea. It was a wonderful evening and everyone present wanted to drink the health of the Queen and her husband as a house-warming.

This was done and the Prince said that there was a hymn they sang in Germany on such an occasion and he would like to sing it now.

The Queen's eyes filled with tears of love, devotion and happiness as she listened to her beloved husband's voice:

*God bless our going out, nor less*
*Our coming in...*

Victoria had rarely seen Albert so obsessed by anything as he was about Osborne. He always worked conscientiously. To see him going through the state papers was a lesson to anyone, she often declared. But one was conscious all the time that this was a duty. Osborne was a pleasure and he was almost childish in his enthusiasm.

'Come and look at this,' he would say and take her from what she was doing and explain how it would look when it was finished.

He was in constant consultation with workmen. If it were not somehow disrespectful one would say that Albert was *almost* like a child with a toy over Osborne. And what a wonderful job he was making of it!

'Sometimes, my love, I think you should have been an architect. I even go so far as to think that you would have enjoyed being a *builder.*'

Albert smiled indulgently.

He would slip away at all times to see how the work was progressing. One night at about ten o'clock he left the drawing-room and was making his way through a wooded part of the grounds when he was roughly seized.

A policeman had him by the arm.

'What are you doing here, eh?' demanded the policeman.

Albert, who never acted without due thought, was silent, and the policeman went on: 'Prowling about the place. Up to no good I'll be bound. You come along with me.'

The servants' quarters were close at hand and the young policeman, delighted that he had arrested, as he thought, a suspect, opened the door and pushed the Prince into the servants' kitchen, where they were seated round the table over the remains of supper.

'Caught this beauty on the prowl,' announced the policeman.

There was a second or two's silence after which all the servants rose to their feet. The policeman stared at his captive. One of the women said in a shrill voice: 'It's His Highness...'

But there was no need. The policeman knew. The Prince acted characteristically. He turned and walked out without a word. In fact he had said nothing during the entire episode.

As soon as the Prince had gone the babel broke forth. 'Now you've done it.'

'Fancy arresting his Royal Highness!'

'You'll hear more of this, young fellow. There's one thing we have to remember here. The important one is not so much Her Gracious Majesty but His Royal Highness ... and that's because it's the way Her Majesty wants it.'

The poor young man could scarcely bear his humiliation, especially as he feared it might end in dismissal, and the next morning when he was summoned to the Prince's study he felt this was indeed the end.

Trembling with mortification the policeman bowed. The Prince inclined his head. Then he said: 'I have called you here to commend you on your attention to duty. I have already mentioned to your superiors that you acted with promptitude last night and that you should be put in line for promotion.'

The young man began to stammer, but the Prince coldly waved him away.

The policeman couldn't resist looking in at the kitchens to tell them what had happened.

'Well, you could have knocked me down with a feather when you dragged him in last night,' said the cook. 'But you couldn't see from his face what he was thinking.'

'That's it,' said one of the kitchen hands, 'you never can. He's like one of them there masks.'

'Cold as a corpse,' said the cook. 'But *just* – you've got to give him that.'

One of the older women shook her head and said: 'He might have said it last night, that would have made his nibs here sleep better, eh? But that's him all over – *just*, I grant you. But he likes to torture you a bit.'

'Perhaps he tortures himself too,' said a pert kitchen maid. 'The good are like that sometimes.'

When the Queen heard of the incident she laughed uproariously. 'The idea of arresting *you*, Albert. And how *good* of you to speak up for the man. It is pleasant to know we are so well protected at dear Osborne.'

Bertie loved the sea and making sandcastles. He shrieked with laughter as the tide came in and flooded the moat. Affie toddled along beside him, shovelling sand into pails, Bertie's devoted henchman.

A boy – a little older than Bertie – carrying a basket of fish which his father had caught and which he was taking to a customer, strolled along the beach and watched the progress of the castle. Bertie, who always liked to show Alfred how clever he was, demanded to know what the boy was looking at.

'At the castle,' said the boy.

Bertie became very haughty. 'You must not look unless I say you may.'

'You can't stop me,' said the boy.

Bertie jerked the basket from the boy's hand and the fish were scattered all over the sand, at which the boy's face grew scarlet and he punched Bertie in the chest. Bertie was unprepared and went sprawling into the sandcastle. He jumped up and came at the fisher boy but he was no match for him. In less than five minutes Bertie was bleeding from the nose and had a bump on his forehead.

Affie began to scream and attendants were soon running up. The fisher boy thought it was wise to retire and Bertie was taken back to the house.

Such an incident could not be passed over unnoticed. The Queen would want to know what had happened to Bertie's face and the truth must be told.

There was nothing to be done but to consult the Prince, who immediately summoned Bertie.

'So you have been fighting?' he said sternly.

Bertie stammered: 'Y ... yes, Papa.'

'And for what reason, pray?'

'He ... he ... this boy...'

'*Which* boy? Pray try to be less incoherent.'

When Papa said 'pray' it usually meant one really was in trouble but Bertie felt confident that he was not in the wrong about this. It was that wicked boy who had beaten him; he had scarcely been able to touch his adversary; Bertie put a hand to the bump on his brow and said: 'Affie and I were building castles and the boy came along. He stared without asking if he could. I knocked his fish all over the sand.' Bertie wanted to giggle at the thought of the squirming fishes. He elaborated a little: 'Great big fishes ... a big whale and he was going to swallow Affie so I picked up a big stick.'

'You will go to your room, Bertie, and wait there until I send for you,' said his father.

Bertie went to his room but was not disturbed. The boy would be punished for fighting the Prince of Wales and he liked his story about the whale. He went on with it in his mind. It swallowed Affie and it was like the Jonah story. Bertie kept it and talked to Affie from inside and then he climbed into the whale and rescued Affie.

His father sent for him and when he went into the study the Prince said: 'We are going to see your fisher boy. I have discovered who he is.'

Bertie felt very proud. Now he would stand beside his father and that boy would know what a bad thing he had done.

The fisher boy came into the room where the Queen and the Prince received visitors. With him was a man who was clearly his father. They looked very shy and awkward as though they wondered what was going to happen to them – and well they might, thought Bertie.

The Prince had gripped Bertie's shoulder and pushed him forward.

'Ah,' he said, 'you are here. My son has an apology to make to yours. He is very sorry he behaved so churlishly. Now, Bertie, let me hear you say how much you regret your conduct and that you promise not to behave in such a way again.'

Bertie was astounded. Papa had got it wrong. It was the boy who must apologise to him.

'I am waiting,' said the Prince.

He really meant it. Somehow, Bertie was in the wrong again. He couldn't understand it but there was nothing to be done but obey so he said that he was sorry that he had upset the basket of fish. He had behaved badly and would never do it again.

'And now,' said Papa to the visitors, 'I will have you conducted to the kitchens where you will be amply compensated for the loss you suffered.'

The boy and his father, as confused as Bertie, bowed their way out. The Prince was still gripping Bertie's shoulder. He looked at him with an expression of mournful regret in his face but Bertie saw a gleam in his eye which he always associated with an imminent caning.

He was right.

'You will go to your room and prepare for a beating, which I shall administer myself. Lies I will not tolerate. First you disgrace us by indulging in a fight with a fisher boy and then you tell me monstrous lies.' He put his hand to his forehead. 'I have no alternative but to beat the wickedness out of you.'

Bertie went fearfully to his room.

They could not stay at Osborne for ever. With the opening of Parliament imminent it was necessary to return to London, but the whole family was sad to leave dear Osborne.

'Never mind,' said the Queen, 'we shall be back soon, and won't it be fun to see what dearest Papa's plans have added to the house. How fortunate we are to have such a clever Papa!'

Vicky said that Papa had told her what he was going to do about the new staircase. He had shown her the drawings.

Surely not, thought the Queen, before he has shown me! Really sometimes she thought Albert thought more of his daughter than of his wife.

Albert certainly doted on their eldest daughter. She supposed it was because Bertie was such a disappointment.

Down on the shore they went to embark on the royal yacht. One of the yachtsmen picked up Vicky and carried her on board, but Vicky hated to be carried. She thought it made her look like a child, and in front of Bertie too. 'There you are, my little lady,' said the yachtsman as he set her down.

Vicky said coldly: 'It would be well for you to remember that I am a Princess, not a little lady.'

The Queen, who had been standing by, said sharply: 'You had better tell the kind sailor that you are not a little lady *yet* although you hope to be some day.'

Vicky was startled. It was not often that she was reproved by her parents. She blushed scarlet with mortification. Bertie was sorry for her. He knew what it meant to be snubbed in public. He allowed himself to be lifted aboard without protest.

And back at Buckingham Palace was Mr Birch.

Bertie regarded him with some suspicion when he was brought to the schoolroom by his father and Baron Stockmar.

'You will find the Prince of Wales somewhat backward, I fear,' said the Baron. 'He is not exactly devoted to study. But I have worked out a curriculum for you to follow and I think if you will abide by this you cannot go far wrong. I have His Highness's approval of what I have mapped out. But you will see for yourself.'

Bertie was quaking inwardly, wondering what a curriculum was. Surely something horrible since the Baron had devised it.

'If he is disobedient,' the Prince was saying, 'you have my permission to beat him. It is a procedure I have often found myself forced to follow, even though it has invariably been very painful to me.'

Bertie listened to an account of his short-comings and when his father and the Baron had left him alone with Mr Birch he almost expected him to bring a cane and apply it right away. Instead of this Mr Birch smiled at him and said: 'Let us sit down and look at this plan of work, shall we?'

'Is it a ... cur...'

'Curriculum? A very long word for nothing very much. Just a plan of what we are going to do together.'

'Is it very hard?'

'I don't think you're going to find it so.'

'I'm not clever like Vicky.'

'How do we know?'

'They know.'

'Ah, but we might surprise them.'

'Might we?'

'We can never be sure, can we?' said the strange Mr Birch.

Bertie laughed suddenly, not because it was very funny but because he was relieved. Something told him that he and Mr Birch were going to be friends.

He was right. With Mr Birch lessons were not so difficult. He had a way of explaining things which made them amusing or interesting.

In the first place he had said that they would take lessons alone. He had not come to teach the Princess Royal. As soon as Vicky was no longer there to show how much cleverer she was, Bertie became less stupid. He found he could give a wrong answer to Mr Birch and not be laughed at.

He told him once how when they were in the gardens years and years ago and Mama had been telling them about flowers, he had asked if the pink was the female of the carnation. They had all laughed at him so much that he had been afraid to ask any more questions. This had come out when Mr Birch told him that he must always ask if he did not know.

Mr Birch listened gravely. Then he said: 'We all have to learn at some time. It is no disgrace not to know. You must always ask if you don't understand anything. Never be afraid that I would laugh.

There are so many things I myself don't know. And so it is with all of us.'

Yes, thought Bertie, Vicky did not know everything; nor did Mama; nor even Papa.

He began to look forward to lessons. He ceased to stammer. He no longer wanted to throw books at windows. He was happy.

Mr Birch had changed everything, and Bertie loved Mr Birch.

## Chapter XVII

## REVOLUTION

A new year had arrived and by February alarming news reached the palace. The Queen, once more pregnant and expecting to have her sixth child in April, was terribly shocked to hear that France was in a state of unrest.

Albert brought the news to her as she lay in bed resting because as usual pregnancy was irksome. Albert sat by the bed and said gloomily: 'The revolution has begun.'

'Albert. It can't be.'

'It is so, my dear. The mob is marching on the Tuileries.'

'Oh dear. The poor King and Queen! What will become of them?' She sat up in bed. 'It is terrible, Albert. I picture it. Advancing now as they did before on poor Louis XVI and Marie Antoinette. How dreadful! Poor dear Aunt Louise will be demented.'

'It is a terrible thing to have happened.'

'Perhaps it will pass. If the King is strong and has the Army with him...'

Albert shook his head. 'It is a sad thing to see a monarchy totter. All royal houses must deplore it.'

'And to think I was so angry with poor Louis Philippe only such a short while ago. I can't bear to think of what he may be suffering at this moment. Such terrible things can happen. A mob can be fearful. To think it was such a short while ago that he sent the doll and the soldiers to the children. Who would have thought this possible!'

'It is well for all of us to remember that this sort of thing could happen at any time.'

'Not here, Albert. Not in England.'

Albert did not answer and she remembered what the people had been like at the time of the Flora Hastings scandal, and the stone that had been thrown at her carriage at the time of Flora's funeral.

Fearfully she awaited news from France. There was nothing comforting when it came. It was a repetition of that terrible revolution at the end of last century. At midnight the tocsins had sounded throughout Paris, the sign for the people to rise. It was almost exact in detail. The royal family were in flight. Victoria could picture them hurrying across the Tuileries gardens and she was imagining it happening in Buckingham Palace.

'Louis Philippe must fight,' she had told Albert. 'He cannot run away.' But the French King had the terrible memory of the disaster which once before had overtaken his family. He had no wish to suffer as they had and when he was presented with an act of abdication he immediately signed it. He was so fearful that he said to everyone who came near him, *'J'abdique, j'abdique.'*

When the Queen heard she buried her head in her hands. She could not get out of her mind the picture of the mob's marching on Buckingham Palace.

The palace was alive with rumours. The French family had arrived, said some. They were smuggled into the palace. Others said they had been executed by the mob.

'There are always rumours,' said Albert.

Lord Palmerston called. The Queen swallowed her dislike and received him immediately. Albert remained with her.

Palmerston bowed to the Queen and gave Albert that benign smile which suggested he thought him a young man of no great importance, but since he was the Queen's husband he would indulgently allow him to be present while business was discussed.

'Your Majesty,' said the Foreign Minister, 'it seems certain that the King of France, if he escapes, will try to reach England. If Your Majesty wished to put a ship at his disposal the Foreign Office would have no objection, but I must warn you that if Your Majesty attempted to harbour royalists, the country might object.'

'I don't understand you, Lord Palmerston. Are you suggesting that I should turn my own family away?'

'I am suggesting, Ma'am, that taking into consideration the state of the country at the moment – Your Majesty will have been made aware that there has been a certain amount of unrest in various areas – it would not be wise to make too great a show of supporting the royalist cause.'

'Lord Palmerston, we *are* royal,' said the Queen imperiously.

Lord Palmerston bowed, smiling his superior smile as though he realised he must placate the children.

'Ma'am,' he said, 'it is my duty – and I am sure Your Majesty would always insist that I should not shirk that – to warn you that there is unrest throughout Europe. A revolution in one country could spark off one in others. Like fire revolution can easily spread.'

'Do you suggest that here in England...'

Lord Palmerston as usual had no compunction in interrupting the Queen. 'I suggest, Ma'am, that we should take every precaution that it should not happen here. Many of the small kingdoms of Europe are shaking at this moment, Ma'am. The success of the revolutionaries in France will inspire others throughout Europe.'

Albert spoke then. 'This is so,' he said, and Victoria could see by the expression on his face that he was thinking of Ernest and Alexandrine in Coburg.

The Queen was calmer.

'Very well,' she said. 'At least I may offer my relations the means of escape.'

Uncle Leopold was in a ferment of anxiety:

*I am unwell in consequence of the awful events in Paris. How will this end? Poor Louise is in a state of despair which is pitiful to behold. What will soon become of us God alone knows; great efforts will be made to revolutionise this country; as there are poor and wicked people in all countries, it may succeed.*

*Against France we, of course, have a right to claim protection from England and the other powers. I can write no more. God bless you.*

Poor Uncle Leopold. What anxiety must be his! He was so near to France, so close to the French royal family. And Aunt Louise, what was she thinking?

And from poor stricken Aunt Louise:

*My dearly beloved Victoria, I understand by an account arrived this morning, and which seems to be correct, that my unfortunate parents arrived in England before yesterday evening; but I don't know where they are.*

There was a letter enclosed which Louise begged Victoria, if she were able, to give to her mother.

Before sealing her letters Louise had heard that her parents were in London.

'I thank God from the bottom of my heart for their safety,' she wrote. 'In my agony I did not wish for anything else.'

What terrible times! Poor Albert was very depressed and unhappy. She knew his thoughts were with Ernest in Coburg. He was picturing the mob marching on the palace there; he would see them with their greedy hands on the treasures of Rosenau.

Lord Palmerston called on the Queen and in Albert's company she received him.

'Your Majesty will be pleased to hear that the King and Queen of France have arrived safely in England,' he told her.

The Queen said that the news was the best she had heard since this terrible revolution had begun.

'I have a communication from a Mr Featherstonhaugh, our consul at Le Havre. When the King and Queen came to Le Havre he had everything ready for their embarkation. It was not easy. You will see that Mr Featherstonhaugh arranged for the King and Queen to have passports in the name of Mr and Mrs Smith and the King was disguised. It was necessary for him to shave off his whiskers, wear a casquette – a sort of cap – on his head, a coarse overcoat and a pair of goggles.'

'The poor King!' cried Victoria. 'And the Queen ... how she must have suffered!'

'Mr Featherstonhaugh should be congratulated,' went on Lord Palmerston. 'By great ingenuity and at considerable risk to himself he smuggled the King and Queen on board. An hour after the steamer sailed gendarmes were at the quay waiting to arrest them.'

'So they are safe!' sighed the Queen. 'Where can they go?'

Albert said: 'I suppose there would be no objection to their going to Claremont. It is almost a private residence.'

Lord Palmerston bowed his head. 'I think,' he

said, 'that the royal French family might find refuge in Claremont.'

It was so worrying. There were riots all over the country although these were not quite of the same nature as those which had occurred in France and other European countries. People at home, comforted Lord John Russell, were not quite so excitable as they were abroad, which was well. Revolutions never brought gain to a country, least of all to the people who created them. The trouble in England was mainly the risings of the Chartists, who wanted more privileges for the working classes. They were not satisfied with the Reform Bill and wanted more than had been granted them.

'I never liked the Chartists,' said the Queen. 'And the thought of riots here after what has happened in France is very alarming.'

'The situation here is under control,' said Lord John.

Albert was not so sure. He was very worried. His thoughts, of course, were far away in Germany.

Then a fresh blow struck them. Albert came to the Queen holding the letter in his hand and he was in tears.

'Albert, what has happened?' cried the Queen.

Albert could only shake his head and Victoria took the letter from him.

'From Coburg,' she said in some dismay. 'Oh dear. Poor dear Grandmama ... *dead*. My poor, poor Albert, I know how you loved her, and so did I.'

'She was a mother to me,' said Albert brokenly.

'This is too much in addition to everything else.'

'She was an angel on earth,' said Albert. 'Always good and loving to us all.'

Victoria wept to think of that dear body lying under flower-covered earth in the Island of Graves which they had so recently visited.

The days were uneasy. On one bleak March day news was brought to the palace that the Chartists had assembled in Trafalgar Square and were planning to march on Buckingham Palace.

Very large, expecting her child to be born very soon, the Queen's great concern was for the children.

'Keep them happy in the schoolroom,' she ordered. 'They should not understand what this could mean.'

Going to the window she could see the mob marching up the Mall. They were coming closer and closer to the palace. This was what had happened in Paris.

She closed her eyes and thought: Is this the end then? Is this what I was brought up to, trained for? Albert was beside her. Dear Albert, still mourning for his grandmother, and anxious for his homeland!

She waited in trepidation for disaster but nothing happened and Lord John called at the palace to tell her that the rioters had dispersed.

'They had no real heart for it,' he said. 'They've too much sense.'

Such alarms were terrifying though.

She hoped they were not having any effect on the child.

She remembered that it was Lord Melbourne's birthday. She hardly ever saw him now because he spent most of the time down at Brocket. It was said that he had gone a little strange. She knew this was true because he imagined quite falsely that he was in financial difficulties. She herself had lent him money to help him over a difficult period, which did not in fact exist. She thought of him now and then, just a little guiltily, for in her domestic happiness she had been inclined to neglect him. But perhaps it was because she did not like to think of those extravagant entries in her diary when she was so devoted to him that she could not bear a day to pass without seeing him. She wrote to him:

*The Queen cannot let this day pass without offering Lord Melbourne her and the Prince's best wishes for many happy returns of it in health and strength.*

She went on to write of the terrible revolution which had swept France and was threatening Europe.

'Too gloomy a letter for a birthday,' she finished, 'and the Queen must apologise for it.'

It cheered her a little to picture Lord Melbourne's delight when he received it.

Three days later she gave birth to a daughter. This was her sixth child.

'We'll call her Louise,' she said. 'I hope she doesn't turn out peculiar, having been born at such a time. Aunt Louise will like the baby's being called after her. Perhaps it will cheer her a little.'

The confinement had passed off much better than the Queen had expected. The new baby was a placid, healthy child, rather like Alice. For two weeks Victoria did not leave her apartments in the palace and Albert carried her from the bed to her sofa. The march to Buckingham Palace which had petered out before anything violent happened seemed to have sobered up the trouble-makers. How she longed to be at Osborne with dear Albert and the children and forget all the unpleasant things that were happening in the world!

But how could one forget the poor French family and dear Aunt Louise who must be suffering torment?

Still she was feeling better and blustering March was over and April was here with a promise of the spring.

She and Albert were going through their etchings together and Albert was telling her where she had quite succeeded when Lord John Russell was announced. As soon as he entered the Queen could see by the gravity of his expression that something was wrong.

'I had better tell Your Majesty and Your Highness of my concern without delay. The Chartists are planning a big meeting to take place on the 10th and it is to be in London. The Cabinet fears they may mean trouble this time.'

'Oh, how can they! I have just got up from childbed and they dare to do this?'

'They consider only themselves, Ma'am,' said Little Johnny. 'We shall take every precaution at the palace, and we hope they can be halted before they reach it.'

'Have they ... threatened *me* ... *us*?'

'No, Your Majesty. They propose to march to the Houses of Parliament. But a mob can so easily get out of hand. I thought you should be warned. The Cabinet will discuss what measures can be taken.'

The Queen bowed her head.

When Lord John returned, Albert walked with him out of the palace while the Queen sat brooding.

Was it coming, she asked herself, all the terrible things that had happened in France? She and Lehzen had studied history together, and she knew what had happened in France during the big revolution. She had shivered when she had read of the fall of the Bastille and the flight of the King and Queen to Varennes, their capture, their bitter humiliation. She had felt so sorry for them because she had guessed what it must have meant for royalty to fall so low. But had she understood before? Now she could hear the shouts of the mob; she remembered them not so long ago when they had marched up the Mall. That was a rehearsal; the next would be the real thing.

Revolution, the abolition of monarchy – that was the plague which was spreading across Europe!

What of the new baby – but two weeks old? Dear little Louise! What sort of world had she been born into? What of Pussy, Bertie, Alice, Alfred and

Helena? What terrible fate had befallen the Dauphin of France? Who could say? It was a miserable end and the more terrible for being so. What if such a fate were waiting for Bertie?

She felt hysterical with terror and when Albert came back he found her weeping helplessly.

'Victoria, you must be calm. You must not give way.'

'It is very well for you,' cried the Queen, suddenly losing control. 'Have you just got up from bearing a child? Have you suffered nine months of discomfort? Oh, no, you have not. You are like every other man. It is a fine thing to have a family, you continually tell me. Very fine ... for you. You don't have to suffer.'

'Victoria, for Heaven's sake, don't get so excited.'

'Get excited, when the mob is coming to tear us all apart. They will attack me, not you. You do not count for much. I am the Queen.'

In vain did Albert try to soothe her; she could only weep, and suddenly her temper would flare up and she would accuse him of heartlessness.

It was like a return to those days when there had been quarrels between them. He knew that when she was in such a mood he should leave her to herself but then she upbraided him for his cynical indifference.

Later that day Lord John called again at the palace and saw Albert. He said that the Cabinet had decided that it would be advisable for the Queen, the Prince and the royal family to leave for Osborne two days before the Chartist gathering was to be held.

The Queen's relief was intense. As soon as she was alone with Albert she clung to him and asked forgiveness for her ill temper. At this sign of contrition Albert was as always ready to be kind and tolerant.

'You found it trying,' he said, 'because it is only two weeks since the baby's birth.'

'I don't mind anything, Albert,' she cried, 'as long as you and I are together.'

On the 8th of April they left for Osborne. What peace to be back in the dear house and lie in the drawing-room looking out towards the sea. Yet she was fearful of what was happening in London and she pictured them all flying from England in the royal yacht. To where? If all Europe was in a revolutionary ferment where could they go?

She almost wished that she were back in London. Perhaps to run away from a crisis was not the best way of handling it. She began to feel rather ashamed. It was of course due to the fact that she had had a child. She always felt depressed afterwards – not herself. It was trifles that upset her. She believed that in a big crisis she could be calm.

As it was she could not settle to anything.

The terrible 10th dawned. She walked in the grounds with Albert, discussing the possibilities. 'I ought to be there, Albert. I wish we had not run away.'

Albert pointed out that they were here on the advice of the Cabinet and they must take that advice. If the government and the police force were going to deal with a delicate situation it was as well not to complicate the matter by having the royal family to protect. So Albert soothed her and she declared that if they could only escape from state duties, and she could live quietly and comfortably with the best of husbands, she would be the happiest woman in the world.

Albert patted her hand and said that at least his dear love was back with him and that quick-tempered, rather unreasoning person who supplanted her usually at the beginning of pregnancies and immediately after childbirth had disappeared; he in his turn could be content with almost anything if only his dear love banished that other person for ever.

'Oh, Albert, I will try,' she promised. 'Indeed I will.'

There was exciting news from London. The Chartist march had misfired. Only a fraction of those expected to march arrived at Kensington Common which was to have been the gathering point. When the Police Commissioner told the ringleaders that the march was illegal and must be disbanded, this edict was accepted. The leaders were taken in cabs to the House of Commons where they presented petitions in which they protested about conditions in the country. After that they quietly went away. It was all very orderly.

What relief!

There was a scare later on when the rumour reached Osborne that the Chartists were coming to the Island. Many of them had been seen landing at Cowes – rough, unkempt fellows with the blood lust in their eyes.

Albert set about marshalling the help of everyone on the estate. The farm workers gathered, brandishing their sickles and the builders their shovels, ready to protect the Queen and her family.

Victoria gathered the children together in the schoolroom and told them that she was not quite sure what was going to happen but they must be prepared for anything.

They were almost hysterical when the news came that the party of bloodthirsty revolutionaries were a club of young men who had come over to the Island for their day's outing.

But that was an indication of the atmosphere during those spring and summer months of 1848. Revolution across the Channel and unrest throughout Europe had produced an atmosphere of tension which the Queen had never known before.

During that uneasy summer the Queen and Albert often discussed the state of the world. The Emperor of Austria had been forced to abdicate and throughout Germany there was a movement to abolish royalty; Italy was shaken by revolution. Uncle Leopold's Belgium stood firm, as did the Russian Empire; and in England of course the 'friends of the revolution' could get no firm footing. Uncle Leopold was regarded with great respect by the Belgians, who realised what he had done for their country; the Russians under the great Tsar were powerless to revolt; and the English temperament was not suited to revolution and the people could only make half-hearted attempts at it which came to nothing. The general opinion appeared to be the Queen's, that revolutions brought no good to anyone.

All the same if there was trouble, the Isle of Wight was easily accessible and therefore not a very safe refuge, and they had the children to think of.

'Albert,' said Victoria one day, 'do you remember how much we enjoyed Scotland? I don't think I ever saw a more beautiful place.'

'I remember it well,' replied Albert. 'I was reminded of home.'

'If we had a little home in Scotland rather like dear Osborne we could be sure of a little more privacy there. Let us take a trip there, Albert. Who knows, we might find a dear little house up there just as we have here.'

Inquiries were set in motion and it was decided to rent a little castle for six weeks. This belonged to the Duke of Fife and was called Balmoral.

As soon as they arrived both the Queen and Albert were impressed by the beauty of the countryside. Albert declared that it reminded him of home so much that he was sure he could be happy there. The Queen was delighted. Here she and the family could live the simple life. They could all go out together like any family party and they did. Albert was able to shoot the birds and stalk the deer just as he used to at home in Coburg; and the children could ride their ponies while the Queen sat and sketched. It was all very simple and pleasant; and the people of the neighbourhood were delightful, not treating them as royalty at all. In fact these good simple people would have no idea how to treat royalty.

It was all very refreshing.

'We must come again to Balmoral,' said the Queen.

Alone in Brocket Hall Lord Melbourne thought of the happenings of the year which would soon be over. Revolution in France and threatening all Europe – even England could be in danger. And the Queen – the sweet young Queen who had meant so much to him and had been so charmingly innocent – he hardly ever saw now.

She was not only a wife but a mother now – a mother of six and it seemed only yesterday that that wide-eyed girl had stood before him so touching, so affectionate, so eager to learn.

They had been as close and as intimate as people can be who are not lovers – yet they were lovers. It is possible to love not physically but with heart and mind. He was her ideal; she was his creation, and he was now nothing to her but poor Lord Melbourne; yet to him she had remained the meaning of existence. He could still see her now and then, receive a letter from her – congratulations on his birthday, perhaps, but it was only on such occasions that she ever thought of him.

Life was wearying. His books were there. Sometimes he would sit fingering them, for the very touch gave him pleasure; but he would read a page and not know what he had read and he would hear himself murmur: 'Oh, no, Ma'am, I couldn't agree with that.' In his mind he was seeing her, talking to her, thinking of her ... always her.

There was greatness in her. He hoped Albert would not suppress it. 'Damned morality,' he growled. 'Too much of it can strangle the mind. May she be preserved. Victoria the Queen...'

'He must not overpower you, Ma'am. Oh, you adore him. You were always too ready to adore those you had affection for. You saw only black and white, good and bad, and nobody is entirely bad, no one entirely good, not even Albert.'

He chuckled to himself, remembering how she had told him she had no wish to marry. And then Albert came and that was the end of her objections; and the end of her great friendship with her Prime Minister.

His servant came in and found him talking to someone whom he must have imagined to be sitting opposite him. It was nothing. Lord Melbourne had talked increasingly to himself in the last few years. But suddenly he fell to the floor in a fit and the servant knew that this was no ordinary day in Lord Melbourne's life. He was right. It was the last one.

The Queen was saddened by the news.

'He was my great friend,' she reiterated. 'He came to me on the day of my accession and I trusted him absolutely.'

'Perhaps too much,' said Albert.

'Perhaps. But he was such a dear good man. I remember how his eyes used to fill with tears almost every time he saw me, and he was not an emotional man at other times. He realised the great responsibility.'

'He was not a great statesman,' Albert reminded her.

'No, but he was a dear good man.'

The Queen wept silently. She owed him that; but very soon she was hardly thinking of him at all and when she did it was to find that she was inclining towards Albert's view of him.

'Poor, *poor* Lord Melbourne,' she said.

## Chapter XVIII

## LORD PALMERSTON OFFENDS THE QUEEN

The Queen was happy to see the dawn of another year. That of 1848 had not exactly been a comfortable one. The shadow of revolution seemed to have passed and although there were troubles enough, revolution, the greatest horror of all, seemed remote.

Lord Palmerston was a constant cause of irritation. The Queen had had to reprimand him for withholding state papers from her; his excuse was that during the difficult period when it was feared that the mob might march on Buckingham Palace and the Queen had gone first to the Isle of Wight and then to Scotland it had not been easy to have these papers brought to her. It was absolutely impossible to snub the man. He was impervious to royal darts and behaved as though they had been administered by some irresponsible child. His greatest fault was making a decision, acting on it and then presenting it as *fait accompli*.

'How I should like to be rid of that man Palmerston!' sighed the Queen.

But she must be thankful that life was comparatively peaceful and that she was not pregnant ... at the moment. She was nearly thirty. Really I am getting old, she thought; she had been Queen for twelve years, a wife for nine and was the mother of six. Looking back, she could say that life had been eventful.

The political situation was as always unsteady. How she wished that Sir Robert were back in office. It was a most extraordinary state of affairs for the House seemed to be divided between the free traders and the protectionists and Lord John's Ministry was kept in office by the support of Sir Robert and his supporters. The Leader of the House, Lord George Bentinck, had died suddenly and his place taken by that flamboyant man who seemed always to be calling attention to himself, Benjamin Disraeli.

Then ... the Queen was pregnant again. Was there to be no end of this child-bearing? Certainly this had been a slightly longer respite than usual. It was not that she did not want more children, but she did want a little rest.

Last summer had been such fun at Osborne. The children had enjoyed it so much and she was delighted that Bertie was so much better than he used to be. He had lost that frightful stammer and she had excellent reports from Mr Birch. It was true that when Albert asked questions, which he often did, Bertie sometimes stumbled or gave the most ridiculous answers, but she insisted that he had improved.

She herself gave the children reading lessons; and she was so happy when they sat together each reading a paragraph and passing the book round as they went along. Albert would sit there smiling at them, correcting them when they mispronounced a word, for they read a great deal in German. Then they would say the poem they had learned, and even little Helena had her piece to say.

Vicky usually scored. She was such a clever child and, as the Queen said to Albert, they mustn't be hard on poor Bertie because he couldn't compete with such a clever sister. Albert was not sure and inclined to be a little severe, and Victoria accused him, when they were alone, of favouring Vicky a little too obviously.

Albert always hotly denied this and one of their little storms might blow up but it would soon be over, and the Queen felt that it was a pleasant family quarrel – after all, Albert's fault was only in loving their darling daughter too much.

Albert was all for making the children do useful things, so they all had their patch of garden at Osborne, each with a spade and trowel, their own flowerpots and working aprons with their initials on them.

Osborne was growing more and more beautiful every year and there was great excitement about planning the gardens. Albert of course did everything so well.

There was sea bathing too, which was said to be so good for one. Victoria, clad in an all-enveloping bathing costume, would slip out of her bathing machine which had been drawn right down to the sea, and have a dip before climbing back.

It was a wonderful life at Osborne. She was so *snug* in the little rooms – so different from Windsor Castle or Buckingham Palace; she had had two writing tables placed side by side in her study so that she and Albert could do what work had to be done together.

Once she said to him: 'Albert, sometimes I wish we could leave the children behind so that we could be quite alone together.'

Albert was pleased but he did not think it very becoming in a parent to wish to be without her family. But he agreed they were too rarely quite alone.

'Perhaps,' said Albert, 'it is because it happens so rarely that it is so precious to you.'

She denied it. If she was with Albert alone every hour of the day those hours would still be as precious to her.

And then there was Balmoral.

The summer was for the Isle of Wight; the autumn, when the hills were purple with heather, was the time for Scotland.

She began to feel that Balmoral excited her even more than Osborne. The country was more wild and rugged; the people more strange. Albert was continually comparing it with the Thuringian forest which meant that he loved it – and so did she.

She ordered that the children be dressed in kilts; Albert wore one too. As for herself she had dresses made in soft satin or royal Stuart tartan. She found the Scottish accent charming; the gillies were such good people; they treated her with a rough sort of courtesy. They might refer to her as 'me dear' which was a most unseemly manner in which to address a queen, but she felt so safe with them and she knew that while they would not accord her the dignity of her rank they would give their lives to save her from danger.

Dear good people! she called them. She decided to learn their country dances and took lessons. They were very strenuous but this was before she was sure that she was pregnant again; and when the dancing master told her to try and dance 'like a lady, me dear', she took it all in good part and laughed hilariously with Albert about it afterwards.

They must all try to speak in Gaelic; it would help them to understand the people better. 'The dear Highlanders are such a dignified people,' she said. 'They are so strong and so faithful.'

Albert agreed with her. He would take them fishing with him and come back in a good mood if he had caught something big and quite silent if he had failed.

'No need to ask,' Victoria would cry gaily. 'We know by your face.'

Albert always seemed much better when he was in the Highlands. The climate suited him. She was sure he would not get those dreadful winter colds which he sometimes had during the winter if he could live all the time in the country.

'The winter would be rather severe up here,' she reminded him, but Albert was used to the icy winters of Germany and he said he would like to skate on the lake.

'I shall never forget the time of Pussy's christening when you were skating on the lake at Buckingham Palace. Do you remember?'

The Prince remembered it very well, how the ice had broken under him and he had gone down into the icy water. 'I had the fright of my life,' said the Queen.

'But you were very brave, my dear love,' said Albert. 'Very different from your attendants, who almost had hysterics.'

'I was so concerned for you. Do you know, Albert, I think that was the start of your colds. You seem to get several every winter.'

'I should be all right in the country.'

'Skating?' she asked laughing. 'I should feel content only if one of these dear Highlanders was with you. John Brown is a very fine young man. So trustworthy.'

Albert agreed that he was and he talked wistfully of life up in the Highlands and heartily wished, as she did, that they could spend more time there.

But it seemed there always had to be trouble. Ireland was giving great cause for concern. Conditions where the potato famine had brought ruin and starvation were terrible, and the stories of hardship made her weep; she thought it was most unchristian that people should be unable to afford coffins to be buried in and had to be thrown into pits and covered over with earth, so great was the mortality.

The Irish were in a state of revolt – like the rest of Europe, and although she pitied them she was horrified to hear of the murder of landlords.

One day in May she was driving down Constitution Hill when an Irishman named William Hamilton fired at her. When he was captured it was found that his pistol was not loaded, but he was transported for seven years.

The Queen was a little shaken but less so than she had been on previous occasions; and when later in the year it was suggested that she pay a visit to Ireland she did not flinch from it.

Strangely enough the visit was a great success. The Irish, who a short time before had been on the edge of revolution, found their sentimental hearts were touched by the sincere concern of the little Queen.

Soon after the return from Ireland there was good news from India. The Punjab had been taken into the British Empire and the Maharajah, to show his immense respect for the Queen whom he accepted as his ruler, presented her with the Kohinoor diamond.

'The finest I have ever seen,' said the Queen. She showed it to the children. 'But it is what it stands for which is the most important thing.'

The following May, a few weeks before her thirty-first birthday, the Queen gave birth to another child, a son. Albert was delighted and the Queen struggled out of the lethargy which always followed childbirth in her case to rejoice with him.

A few days later all the children were brought in to see the new baby, led by ten-year-old Vicky and nine-year-old Bertie. Alice, Alfred, Helena and Louise stared wide-eyed at the infant boy in

413

their mother's arms.

The Prince said they must all kneel and thank God for the blessing of another brother, which they did, and the Prince and the Queen looked on, finding it difficult, as the Queen said afterwards, to restrain their tears at such a touching scene.

Albert had become very excited at the prospect of a great Exhibition to be set up in Hyde Park. This, said Albert, would be a great boon to industry, it would provide work for many people and he could see nothing but good coming from it. There would be a great deal of work to be done and they would need a year to do it, but he believed that the whole of Europe would be talking of it and it would be remembered as the greatest spectacle as yet to have been staged.

The Queen caught his enthusiasm and listened to his talk of projects.

Dear Albert, he was as excited as a child. He had called in Paxton, the great planner of gardens, and between them they were considering an idea to build a big house of glass – a kind of conservatory – no, more than that. It should be the centre of the Exhibition. A glass palace, one might say.

The Queen caught his excitement. She was sure it would be a very good thing. How much better if the ministers could plan this kind of thing instead of always being at each other's throats on some issue or other.

But even about this project they had to argue and try to spoil it. Albert and his committee had decided that the great exhibition should be held in Hyde Park and several of the Members of

Parliament were arguing against this. Poor Albert was in despair when *The Times* too came down against it.

'It's such folly,' groaned Albert. 'If we are turned out of the park, the work is done for.'

But such a terrible tragedy occurred that all the thoughts of the Exhibition were driven temporarily not only from the Queen's mind but from Albert's too.

On the 28th of June Sir Robert Peel was riding in Constitution Hill when his horse suddenly shied and he was thrown to the ground. He was so badly injured that he could not move and lay on the ground until some people passing in a carriage saw him, pulled up and recognising him, took him home to his house in Whitehall Gardens.

He could not be taken to his room but was put on a sofa in one of the downstairs rooms and there he remained for four days until he died.

The Queen was very upset; so was Albert.

'He was a great man,' said Albert. 'I shall never forget what he did for me in the days when I was so bitterly misunderstood.'

The Queen thought with remorse of those meetings with Sir Robert when she had believed he was about to replace Lord Melbourne. She had been so beastly to him and had called him 'the dancing master'. But that was when she had been so *blind* and looked upon Lord Melbourne as a sort of god, so that anyone who dared to attempt to replace him must seem like a monster.

She wrote condolences to heart-broken Lady Peel. How sad! There was so much trouble. Poor

Aunt Sophia had died two years ago; Aunt Gloucester was behaving very oddly and was clearly feeble in the mind, for at Louise's christening she had forgotten where she was and, leaving her seat in the middle of the service, came to the Queen and knelt before her. It had all been very distressing and she had managed to coax Aunt Gloucester back to her seat but not before everyone present had noticed such odd behaviour. And now Uncle Cambridge was very ill and it seemed likely that he would not be long for this world. All the aunts and uncles were slowly going, dropping off the tree of life like over-ripe fruit. Then came the news from Belgium that dear Aunt Louise, who had suffered so terribly when her family were driven out of France, was herself ill and incurable, which hurt Victoria most of all, for Uncle Leopold's wife was dearer to her than any of the old aunts and uncles.

The Queen said that she and some of the children must go to visit Uncle Cambridge, who was very ill, and they must do their best to cheer him up. So with Bertie, Alfred and Alice and one lady-in-waiting, she set out. Uncle Cambridge was too ill for them to remain long and on their way back she was telling the children about the days when she lived in Kensington Palace. As they were turning in at the gates of Buckingham Palace the crowd came very close to the carriage. In view of those occasions when she had been shot at, the Queen felt a little nervous and was leaning forward to protect the children if necessary when suddenly a man stepped close to the Queen and lifting his heavy-handled cane brought it down with great force on her head. The fact that she was wearing a bonnet may well have saved her life. Before she lost consciousness she saw Bertie's face flush scarlet and a bewildered Alfred and Alice staring at her in dismay.

Almost immediately she recovered from the faint and heard her lady-in-waiting say: 'They've got him.'

People were crowding round the carriage. She cried: 'I'm all right. I'm not hurt.'

This was not true; she was badly bruised and it was clear that the padded bonnet had saved her from great injury.

She had arranged to go to the Opera that evening and declared that she would not be put off by a few bruises delivered by a madman. Her reception at the Opera was such that it almost made it all worth while. Her forehead yellow and blue, a black eye and a throbbing headache could be forgotten in the loyal demonstrations of the people.

Her assailant turned out to be a certain Robert Pate, a man of good family whose father had been High Sheriff of Cambridge, and who himself had held a commission in the Army for five years. He was sentenced to seven years transportation. It was rather an alarming incident because it seemed without motive and Pate had shown no sign of insanity on any other occasion. Many people had often seen him strolling in the park, a dandy who swaggered somewhat but otherwise was normal.

The Queen did not believe he was insane, and she thought it was horrid that defenceless women should be so exposed. An attempt to kill her because of some imagined grievance or antagonism to monarchy would have been understandable, but to strike a defenceless young woman on her head with a cane was brutal and inhuman.

She shrugged the incident aside and thought of that unhappy wife, Lady Peel, and when she contemplated what widowhood meant she could not grieve long because of a knock on the head.

Uncle Cambridge died as they had expected he would and that was sad. She wrote to tell Uncle Leopold of it and added:

*Poor dear Peel was buried today. The sorrow and grief at his death are so touching, and the country mourns over him as over a father. Everyone seems to have lost a personal friend... My poor dear Albert, who has been so fresh and well when we came back from Osborne, looks pale and fagged. He has felt, and feels, Sir Robert's loss dreadfully. He feels he has lost a second father.*

It was true. Albert was very depressed. He did get depressed rather easily. And what with this terrible attack on her, Uncle Cambridge's death, the people who were so dreadfully carping about the proposed Exhibition and now the loss of Sir Robert, he thought the outlook was very gloomy indeed.

'There were so many we could have spared more easily,' he said; and she knew he was thinking of all those short-sighted people who were trying to foil his plans – and of course Lord Palmerston.

There was no doubt about it, Lord Palmerston

418

was very trying.

For instance the affair of General Haynau was dreadfully mishandled by him. It was true that the General had come to England uninvited after being involved in the suppression of the Hungarian rising, during which he had become notorious for his excessive cruelty. There were rumours of his conduct which in the hands of the press were exaggerated no doubt, thought the Queen. In any case he was said to have hanged soldiers whom he captured, to have burned people alive in their houses and gone so far as to flog noblewomen. The cruelty practised by this man was an echo of mob behaviour during the French revolution.

Cartoons of him appeared in the press. Although these were caricatures the General had several distinguishing features (tall and thin, deep-set eyes and bushy brows) which were accentuated and he was immediately recognizable when one day he visited Barclay's Brewery which he wanted to inspect. Unfortunately he wrote his name in the visitors' book and this coupled with his rather striking appearance made it clear to the brewer's employees that he was the notorious General. They were incensed and decided to show their disapproval and one man threw a load of straw down on his head which sent him sprawling in the yard.

There was a cry of: 'Down with the Austrian butcher!' and the workmen seized him and rolled him in the dirt; they let him get up and as he ran they ran with him; he escaped into a public house and ran upstairs, but the mob caught him and chased him down to the river's edge and were about to throw him in when he was rescued by a police launch.

When the Queen heard what had happened she discussed it with Albert.

She was horrified, she declared. Whatever the man had done he was a visitor to these shores and he had been treated most inhospitably.

To ill-treat such a personage as the General was an insult to Austria and an apology must be sent without delay.

The Foreign Secretary was fully aware of this and when the Queen sent for him he took with him the draft of the apology. He arrived at the palace urbane and smiling, bowed to the Queen and gave that rather insolent greeting to the Prince which was almost a nod.

'A very regrettable incident,' said the Queen.

'Very, Ma'am,' agreed Palmerston. 'And lucky it was for the fellow that the police came along, otherwise...' Palmerston smiled almost with relish.

'You have prepared the apology?' She held out her hand, regal, as always, with this man whom she disliked.

He handed it to her.

It was worded to show that Palmerston had no sympathy with the General; it did express a certain mild regret that he had been mishandled but the final paragraph pointed out that he had been unwise to visit England in view of the reputation he had recently acquired.

When she came to the last paragraph the Queen was flushing hotly.

'That will be considered quite insolent,' she said. 'It must be removed at once before the apology is sent.'

Palmerston smiled. 'That cannot be,' he said.

How dared he tell the Queen what could and could not be!

'It has already gone, Your Majesty.'

She was speechless. So was Albert. How dared he send such a document without their approval.

'We must immediately send a further apology,' cried the Queen. Palmerston bowed his head, and said nothing.

'So,' went on the Queen, 'you will prepare a draft, Lord Palmerston, and bring it to me for my approval, which will explain to the Austrian Government that there has been a slight error.'

Palmerston smiled blandly and shook his head.

'No, Ma'am, it would not be possible for Your Majesty's Foreign Secretary to take such an action.'

'You mean you will not obey *my* wishes?'

'I mean, Ma'am, that were you to insist on your Foreign Secretary's taking such an action, I should no longer be Your Majesty's Foreign Secretary.'

He then asked leave to retire and it was readily given. When he had gone the Queen's wrath exploded. How dared he! She would accept his resignation. Master Palmerston should understand that he could not behave towards his Queen in such a manner.

It was Albert who had to soothe her, Albert who hated Palmerston as much as she did.

'You cannot dismiss your Foreign Secretary, my love. That is for Lord John Russell to do. He is the Prime Minister.'

'Then I shall make my wishes clear to him.'

'My love, this fellow Palmerston is the strongest man in the government, alas. Russell could not stand against him. This is not the way.'

Of course she knew that Albert was right. Palmerston could not be dismissed as easily as that.

They discussed the man frequently.

'If only Sir Robert were here,' wailed the Queen. 'He at least was a strong man.'

But Albert doubted whether even Sir Robert would have been able to stand up against Lord Palmerston.

There was tragic news from Uncle Leopold. Aunt Louise, who had been getting weaker for some time, had died.

Victoria, who had called her the best beloved of all her aunts, was desolate.

'Poor dear Uncle Leopold,' she cried. 'It is the second time in his life that he has been left alone.'

It was very tragic and the Queen could not help thinking of the dear children who were left motherless.

'How I wish we were nearer,' she sighed.

As it was, there was nothing to be done but write long and loving letters to Uncle Leopold, assure him that both she and Albert thought of him constantly, read through his dear letters and remember the happy times she had spent in the company of dear dead Louise.

# Chapter XIX

## NAUGHTY BERTIE

Baron Stockmar disliked the Prince of Wales. The boy was as unlike his father as it was possible for any child to be. All that the Baron had admired in his protégé, Albert, was missing in Bertie. Albert was reserved, Bertie was loquacious. Bertie already showed signs of being a social success; he was charming the female servants – a very bad sign, noted the Baron. Bertie was gay, sunny-natured and enjoyed amusing people and being amused. In other words Bertie was frivolous. Although he was now learning moderately well he could not exactly be called academically bright. His brothers and sisters – with the exception of Vicky – were inclined to bestow on him that sort of hero worship which was not good for his character. Alfred and Alice were his constant companions. He was very chivalrous towards Alice and shielded her when they were in trouble; as for Alfred he was prepared to take any inferior role in their games just for the joy of serving Bertie.

Bertie would soon be ten years old and in Baron Stockmar's view, he was proceeding at no small speed down the road to ruin.

Something must be done.

Once his mind had been made up, the Baron

423

lost no time in offering his opinion to the Prince.

'I am deeply concerned about the future of the Prince of Wales,' said the Baron.

The Prince was all attention.

'I am not very impressed by his character.'

'He has always been a source of anxiety to me,' agreed the Prince, 'as he is to Victoria.'

'We must think, my dear Prince,' said Stockmar, 'of that boy's future. When he is of age he will take precedence over *you*. When I contemplate that I am truly grieved.'

The Prince's emotions were such that he could not allow himself to examine them. They were at the root of his feelings for Bertie – and perhaps the Queen's. This boy who had few good qualities according to his standards – and they had become the Queen's – was already superior in rank to his father. Indeed he was second only to the Queen. There was in the Prince's mind – although he could not examine this either – a certain pleasure that Bertie's conduct should give them cause for criticism.

'I am grieved too,' said the Prince and added hastily: 'I continually ask myself what can be done for his *good*.'

'That is what we must consider. This man Birch for instance, is he the right tutor for the Prince of Wales?'

'Bertie has learned a little since he came.'

'A little! He should have learned a great deal.'

'Bertie has never been studious.'

'My dear Prince, if Bertie has decided he does not wish to study he must be made to change his mind.'

'There were plenty of canings in the past.'

'Perhaps there should have been more in the present.'

'Mr Birch has been given a free hand. He believes that his method with Bertie will bring results and to a certain extent it has.'

'To an infinitesimal extent,' said the Baron. 'And that is not good enough.'

The Prince agreed.

'So,' went on Stockmar, 'what I propose is that we supplant Mr Birch. And I have not been idle. I think I have the man.'

'My dear Baron, what should we do without you?'

Stockmar smiled complacently. 'You know how close your affairs are to my heart. I think of you constantly even when I am racked with pain.' The Baron whose illnesses were as important to him as his love of power digressed slightly to tell the Prince of his latest symptoms. Then he went on: 'It is Frederick Gibbs, a barrister, who I think will fill the post admirably. He is a very serious man. That is what the Prince of Wales needs. There is too much unbridled laughter wherever he is.'

Albert was in complete agreement with the Baron as always. So Mr Frederick Gibbs was summoned to the palace.

Bertie stood before his parents who were seated side by side on the sofa.

'Bertie,' said his mother, 'your Papa and I have something to tell you.'

Bertie waited.

'Your dear Papa and I are not satisfied with

your progress.' Bertie's attention wandered. Another of the lectures, which he received from time to time, was clearly about to begin. He believed he knew how it would go. You must work harder; you must be more serious; life is not all play, and so on. And Mr Birch had promised him that they would go on an imaginary journey around the world; they would have the atlas out on the table and they would imagine they were with Sir Francis Drake. Mr Birch would play the part of Sir Francis and afterwards Bertie would play it with Alfred and Alice and even Helena and Louise could be shipmates.

As his mind wandered on delights to come he heard his mother say: 'So Mr Gibbs will be taking the place of Mr Birch and papa and I are sure that then we shall see some improvement.'

Bertie started and began to stammer. 'Mr B ... B ... B...'

The Queen and the Prince exchanged glances. There you see, he stammers just as he used to!

His father was frowning at him. 'Good Baron Stockmar and I have worked out a course of lessons for you. If you do not already know why great care must be given to your education Mr Gibbs will explain to you. It will be necessary for you to work hard now. The time for play is over.'

'But Mr Birch ... he ... he is not going away?'

'Oh, Bertie,' said the Queen, 'don't you ever listen? Papa has just been explaining. You should be thankful to have such a good kind Papa who has your welfare so much at heart.'

'But ... I love ... Mr Birch. Mr Birch is a good man...'

Bertie's lips trembled. How could he explain to the cold man who was his father, to the bland obtuse woman who was his mother, what Mr Birch meant to him?

'Yes, we know that Mr Birch is a good man. Papa would not have chosen him as your tutor if he had not been. But a good man is not always the best tutor.'

Bertie could not speak. He was not afraid of his parents at that moment. He was only conscious of his misery.

'I think,' said the Queen severely, 'that you had better go to your room, Bertie, and Papa and I will see you later when you have controlled yourself.'

As Bertie went they looked at each other and sighed.

'Oh, yes,' said the Queen, 'it is certainly time there was more discipline.'

'One can trust the dear Baron to find the right solution,' said the Prince.

Meanwhile Bertie was lying on his bed, shaking with sobs. Suddenly he stopped and raising himself started to pummel his pillows furiously... As he did so he thought of his father's cold, unloving face.

When Mr Birch retired for the night he found a rather ill-spelt note on his pillow with a tin soldier impeccably dressed in the uniform of the pre-revolutionary French Army. Bertie wanted Mr Birch to have his best soldier. Bertie was very, very sad because they were going to send Mr Birch away.

Mr Birch read the letter and put it carefully

away with the soldier.

So he was to be dismissed. His rule had been too lenient. His efforts were appreciated, his scholarship was not in question, but the Prince of Wales had an unfortunate nature.

He wanted to protest. The Prince of Wales is a normal boy. He wants love and understanding. It is true he is not as clever as his elder sister, but he has gifts which she lacks. He may not be intellectual, but he is kind-hearted, fond of fun. He has an ability to make himself loved which should not be warped by severity.

But how could one explain? The Queen and the Prince might know how to govern a country (through their Ministers) but they did not know how to bring up a child.

They were a wretched three weeks while Mr Gibbs was taking over from Mr Birch. Bertie was very unhappy, he cried himself to sleep every night; he left notes on Mr Birch's pillow; and he hated Mr Gibbs, who soon made his views known, which were identical with those of the Prince and Stockmar.

The Baron had interviewed Mr Gibbs in the presence of Albert. They enumerated Bertie's weaknesses. His temper was fierce and ungovernable; he was lazy; he was frivolous; he would at moments stutter, although recently this was less pronounced; when addressed he was inclined to hang his head and look at his feet. It was the Baron's opinion that the cure for these faults was in renewed work and constant applications of the cane. The Baron did not criticise Mr Birch, who was a very learned gentleman, but his methods had been too mild – all very well when dealing with a clever child like the Princess Royal perhaps, but for such a miscreant as the Prince of Wales they were doomed to failure.

Mr Birch departed and the Prince of Wales watched him go, as well as his tears and a window steamed by his breath would let him.

Mr Birch had told him that the time would pass and he would soon escape from the schoolroom altogether; that was one of the great consolations of life. Nothing lasted for ever.

The carriage had gone. Desolation remained. Bertie was convulsed by his sobbing in which Alfred joined, for he too had loved Mr Birch and the fact that Bertie was broken-hearted meant that Alfred must be too.

Mr Gibbs' first task was to explain to the Prince the awful task ahead of him. It must be work, work, work, because one day when some dire event should fall – the death of his mother – he would be the King. Bertie was a little bewildered. His mother was the Queen but his terrifying father was not the King. He couldn't understand it.

His mother was the less terrifying of the trio which consisted of father, mother and Mr Gibbs. In fact there were times when she was quite different. When she laughed and showed her gums he forgot about her being on their side. And she could play games too, and when they did play it was fun. Then Papa would come and look on and spoil it, it was true, because he would say they weren't doing something as it should be done, and then he for one would forget his lines simply because Papa was there.

So when he was walking with Mama in the grounds of Buckingham Palace and Papa wasn't there, which seemed to make her more friendly, he asked: 'Mama, why are you the Queen?'

She always liked to talk about the family. 'Well, my Grandpapa was George III and he had several sons. The eldest of these was my uncle George who was George IV. He had a daughter, Charlotte, who would have been Queen but she died, so when George IV died his brother William IV was King. William had no heir so the next son was my father and as he had no children but me, I was the Queen.'

Bertie nodded gravely.

'And,' went on Mama, 'your dear Papa and I married and you are our eldest son. So one day you will be King. You understand that, don't you?'

'Yes. It was what I thought but...'

'Well tell me, Bertie, if there is something you don't understand.'

'Can you and Papa make the next sovereign?'

'What do you mean by that?'

'Can you say who it will be?'

'It is not for anyone to *say*. It is the next in line of succession.'

'Oh, I thought that it would be Vicky who was Queen and not me the King.'

'No. If there is a boy, it is the boy.'

'But I thought as you and Papa love Vicky so much you would want her to be Queen.'

Victoria was a little startled. She looked sharply

at Bertie but that was true bewilderment she saw in his eyes and she felt her conscience vaguely disturbed.

Her impulse was to tell him that parents loved all their children equally if they were good, but that was not true and she was too honest to deceive herself.

All the same she would have liked to have embraced Bertie and to tell him that she wanted to love him; but Albert would say that was bad for him. He must be aware of his responsibilities and severity would make him so.

Bertie was behaving badly. He refused to do his sums; he was disobedient; he was caught putting his tongue out at Mr Gibbs' back and he was inciting Alfred to behave as badly. His temper was in constant evidence; he called Mr Gibbs objectional names; he once threw stones at him.

All this was reported to Albert and Stockmar who congratulated themselves on having installed Mr Gibbs in time.

One could only get the attention of the Prince of Wales by story telling and play acting. For instance when Mr Gibbs had told the story of Robert the Bruce both Bertie and Alfred had sat listening entranced. Why could he not show the same interest in his studies?

When they did amateur theatricals Bertie was again amenable. He could learn his part as well as anyone, but when the children performed before their parents the Princess Royal so outshone him that he became rather sullen. The Princess, being so much bigger than her brother, played the masculine parts to perfection. 'How well Vicky looks in *her* costume,' the Queen was heard to say. 'Poor Bertie's *swamped* in his.'

Mr Gibbs must bring all possible accounts of Bertie's shortcomings to Stockmar and his father. The remedy, said the Baron, was harder work and more canings.

The younger children copied Bertie. He was an evil example. Even Vicky was not always a paragon.

But as the Queen said to Albert: 'Vicky was charmingly naughty.' She repeated the latest account of Vicky's charming naughtiness, when she was confined to her room in disgrace.

Albert, not feeling very well, had summoned a Windsor physician who was highly thought of in the neighbourhood instead of calling on Sir James Clark or one of the royal doctors. He was a Mr Brown and the Queen and Albert addressed him as Brown. The Princess Royal imitated her parents and referred to him as 'Brown' at which the Queen reprimanded her. He was *Mr* Brown, an eminent doctor, and the children must call him by his proper name.

Vicky, very conscious of her rank, which was partly due to her doting parents, addressed the doctor once more as 'Brown'. After he had left the Queen sent for her to tell her that this was very rude and she had already been told that she must call him *Mr* Brown. But the Princess Royal persisted in dropping the Mr, at which the queen said that if it happened again she would be sent to bed immediately. Mr Brown came again and Vicky said defiantly, 'Good morning, Brown.'

Then watching her mother's expression, she curtsied and went on: 'Good night, Brown, for I am now going to bed.'

So Vicky spent the rest of the day in disgrace and the Queen and Albert laughed uproariously about her charming naughtiness.

Meanwhile Bertie's conduct did not improve.

'The children are a great anxiety,' said the Queen, 'particularly Bertie who continues to plague his tutors and worry his father.'

Vicky's punishment for her charming misdeeds was always to be sent to bed. She didn't mind in the least. It was pleasant to be alone in her room with her books. She could read and then astonish them all with her cleverness. So they doted on her more and more.

## Chapter XX

## ALBERT'S EXHIBITION

It was the first day of May, and two important events were about to take place. First little Arthur's birthday, for he was just a year old, and secondly the opening of the great Exhibition.

Arthur was in his high chair with his table of presents beside him – his first introduction to what it meant to have a birthday. The children had all brought him gifts and what a pleasure it was to see him so excited. He wanted only Bertie to help him open his packages and it was a very happy family breakfast.

At eleven o'clock the royal party set out for Hyde Park and Victoria could see that, although he hid his emotions under a calm facade, Albert was as nervous and excited as he had been on his wedding day. She herself was reminded of her coronation. Everywhere she looked she could see crowds of people; and everyone was in festive mood. A few drops of rain fell as they were leaving the palace, then the sky cleared and the sun shone brilliantly as the royal procession passed down Rotten Row, and there, gleaming like a great crystal palace (which was what it was called), was the Exhibition – Albert's Exhibition, for his was the brain which had conceived it and she had seen him absolutely exhausted with the innumerable plans he had made for it. She remembered gleefully how all those stupid people who had decried it and tried to prevent its coming into being had been forced to admit their mistake. Albert was the one who should take the credit.

What a thrill to enter that great gleaming edifice! Bertie held her hand and Vicky clung to her father's. It was magical! The flowers and the fountains were beautiful. The organ was playing triumphant music and there was an orchestra with two hundred instruments and six hundred singers. When the music stopped the cheers broke out. Cheers for Albert. This was far more magnificent even than the coronation, and Victoria was deeply moved because it was Albert's creation.

The orchestra began to play *God Save the Queen* and the tears were in Victoria's eyes as she listened to those loyal voices. She then declared the Exhibition open. The trumpets sounded and the cheering was deafening.

How much happier was such a *peace* festival than these foolish riots which had been tormenting the country for some time, and worse still the fearful revolutions of Europe.

Everyone was loud in their praises of the exhibits and the wonderful Crystal Palace with its flowers and statues. The Queen had a word with Paxton, whose genius, guided by Albert, was responsible for the brilliant array. It was particularly wonderful that he had begun his career as a common garden boy.

The old Duke of Wellington put in an appearance. He was eighty-seven on that day and because Arthur had been born on his birthday the Duke had been one of his godparents. He asked permission to call at the palace later as he had some toys and a gold cup for Arthur and the Queen told him that he would be most welcome – not only by the fortunate Arthur who was to be the recipient of such gifts but by them all.

Oh, that was a happy day! To see Albert vindicated gave the Queen the greatest pleasure. She could even be charming to Lord Palmerston when he visited the Exhibition.

'Is it not a wonderful conception, Lord Palmerston?' she asked; and even he could find no fault with anything.

What a pleasure to return tired but happy to the palace to receive the Duke of Wellington when he called; and little Arthur, his namesake, was ready with a nosegay of flowers to present to his godfather.

And then to Covent Garden to see *The Hugue-nots* and be cheered by the audience.

When at last the day was over and the Queen and Albert were alone she said to him, 'This is the proudest and happiest day of my happy life.'

Hardly a day passed without the Queen's visiting the Exhibition. She greatly admired every section and made a great effort to understand the exhibits of machinery when they were explained to her. She drank in all the praise – and now everyone was praising. Royal relations came from overseas to see the wonders of which they had heard so much and among them the Prince and Princess of Prussia, with their son Frederick, who was known as Fritz – a charming young man. Albert was very inter-ested in him because he would one day be the King of Prussia and Albert had set his heart on Vicky's mounting that throne. If Vicky could not be Queen of England – and that throne *must* go to Bertie – then Prussia was the next best thing.

Prince Fritz found the Exhibition fascinating and, like the Queen, visited it frequently. He was ten years older than eleven-year-old Vicky so put himself in charge of her, Bertie, Alice and Alfred when they walked round the stands. He was most impressed by the intelligent questions Vicky asked; the others would often stroll off and leave them talking together.

It was the same in the gardens of the palace, Fritz and Vicky often walked together. Victoria and Fritz's mother were fully aware of this. 'Of course,' said the Queen fondly, 'Vicky is old for her age.'

'And there is no doubt that Fritz is taken with her.'

'If he should continue to be...' The mothers smiled at each other knowingly. The Queen had no qualms; she knew it was just what Albert was hoping for.

At the end of July the family went to Osborne for the heat of the summer, and this, as summer always did, passed too quickly. The Exhibition was to be closed on the 15th of October. The Queen had chosen this date because it was the anniversary of the day she and Albert had become betrothed.

On the 14th she paid her last visit to the Exhibition. It was so moving, particularly when the music played on the Sommerophone, an enormous brass instrument named after the man who had invented it, but of course sad to see the workmen already dismantling Albert's wonderful creations.

The next day it poured with rain and was, as the Queen said, appropriately wretched. She did not attend the closing ceremony as Albert had said that would not be fitting, so he went alone.

She was delighted to receive a letter from the Prime Minister in which he said;

*The grandeur of the conception, the zeal, invention and talent displayed in the execution, and the perfect order maintained from the first day to the last, have contributed together to give imperishable fame to Prince Albert.*

The Queen wept with joy when she read those words. Nothing, she declared, could have given her greater pleasure.

## Chapter XXI

## DEATHS AND BIRTH

The arrival of the Hungarian General Kossuth in October gave the Queen an opportunity for which she had long waited. Kossuth had endeavoured to free his country from the Austrian yoke and failing to do so had been obliged to escape to Turkey. While there he had decided that he would settle in America and the Americans had sent a frigate to convey him to his future home. On the way he called at Southampton where he was given a great welcome. He decided that he would like to see a little of England and did so, and because of his notorious bravery he was acclaimed wherever he went.

Victoria was uneasy. She admitted that Kossuth was brave; but he was a rebel who had been in revolt against his rulers. How could the Monarchy smile on that sort of behaviour? It would be an encouragement to the troublemakers in places like Ireland to rise up against their sovereign.

When she heard that Lord Palmerston admired Kossuth and was going to receive him she was furious and sent for Lord John Russell.

'I hear that Lord Palmerston is planning to

receive Kossuth in his house,' she said.

Lord Russell said that that was unfortunately so.

'I have told him that it is unwise,' said the Prime Minister, 'but he replies that he will not be told whom he shall invite as guests to his own house.'

'I will dismiss him if he receives Kossuth,' replied Victoria. 'I shall bring such pressure to bear that this is done.'

Lord Russell reported to Palmerston who, with his usual nonchalance, decided that after all he would not receive Kossuth.

The Queen laughed with Albert. 'He becomes more and more despicable,' she declared.

Another opportunity followed almost immediately, through relations with France. Louis Napoleon, the nephew of the great Napoleon, President of the Republic, arrested several members of the government and dissolving the Council of State and the National Assembly set himself up as Emperor Napoleon III.

The Queen was horrified. Members of the French royal family were in exile in England and hoping that the Monarchy would be restored; this would be a blow to all their hopes.

She was delighted when Lord John called to tell her that the Cabinet had decided at a meeting called to discuss these matters that a policy of non-interference had been decided on. But Lord Palmerston was a law unto himself. Calling on the French Ambassador in London he told him that he did not see how Louis Napoleon could have acted otherwise and this, coming from the

Foreign Secretary, could only mean that the new Emperor could hope for British recognition.

This was too much, not only for the Queen but for the Cabinet. The Queen declared that Palmerston must be dismissed without preamble, but Lord John Russell advised caution.

*Lord John Russell presents his humble duty to Your Majesty. Since writing to Your Majesty this morning it has occurred to him that it would be best that Your Majesty should not give any commands to Lord Palmerston on his sole advice. With this view he has summoned the Cabinet for Monday and he humbly proposes that Your Majesty should await their advice.*

Lord Palmerston when called to task tried to bluff his way out of the situation but he did not succeed in his usual manner. He answered that he was entitled to personal opinions and his attitude to the new Emperor was a matter of his own private feelings.

This was unacceptable and Palmerston was asked to resign.

In the midst of all this came news from Hanover that the King – Uncle Cumberland – had died. Strangely enough the Queen was shocked by the news. All her life this man had been the wicked uncle. In her childhood many had believed that he had tried to have her removed to make his way clear to the throne; and afterwards he had caused a great deal of trouble. Now he was dead and his poor blind son George was succeeding him. She could not help being saddened. Death was relentless. So recently they had lost poor dear Aunt Louise and she knew that Uncle Leopold mourned her deeply, as she did herself.

She was fortunate, she reminded herself. Her children were all healthy and so many of her family lost their babies or were unable to produce them like poor Aunt Adelaide, who had died recently.

But to return to Palmerston; this was great good fortune. Lord John and his colleagues decided that the Foreign Secretary had violated the confidence of his colleagues and was unsuitable for his office. To the Queen's delight even he could find no alternative to resignation and Lord Granville was appointed Foreign Secretary.

The Queen could not understand the public's objection to the departure of Lord Palmerston. Was it, the Queen demanded in exasperation of Albert, that people always admired the unworthy! Palmerston was an adventurer, bold and graceless, so people had to admire him.

The government's enemies were mounting, so there was nothing for Lord John to do but form a Coalition with the Peelites, while Palmerston went down to his country house of Broadlands and there gave himself up to the pleasures of the country. He hunted by day and in the evenings his wife gave dinner parties, when he entertained his friends with his amusing accounts of political life. Before long he had his revenge by moving an amendment to the Militia Bill in the House and so forcing such a show of lack of confidence that Russell had to resign.

'I've had my tit-for-tat with Johnny Russell,' laughed Palmerston.

When Lord Derby formed an administration he offered the office of Chancellor of the Exchequer to Palmerston. This he refused and the office fell to Benjamin Disraeli.

The family were in the Highlands when news came of the death of the old Duke of Wellington. The Queen was sad although she had never really liked him and had even refused at first to invite him to her wedding. Lord Melbourne had persuaded her against this but the old man had not supported Albert when he first came to England. He was however the great Duke and now that he was dead people were remembering Waterloo and calling him the saviour of England.

Everyone had become intensely patriotic; they spoke of the great Duke as though he were a god and he was to have a grand state funeral. Tennyson composed a poem to his memory; and Albert set about making the burial arrangements. All the pomp the people expected must be paraded before them to show proper respect for the great Duke; and on the gloomy November day when the Duke was at last laid to rest the Queen was on the balcony at Buckingham Palace watching the cortege pass while various bands played their dead marches as they went along.

She hated Death. It came and mowed people down. They had all gone – her own special friend Lord Melbourne, Sir Robert Peel, dear Aunt Louise, Aunt Adelaide, Uncle Cambridge, Uncle Cumberland – and now the Duke.

Shortly after the funeral Lord Derby's ministry came to an end and Lord Aberdeen became

Prime Minister. Palmerston accepted the Home Office and the Queen, although she deplored his return to the Cabinet, was at least relieved that he was not at the Foreign Office.

By this time, Victoria had become once more pregnant.

On a windy March night there was great alarm in Windsor Castle. One of the ladies had smelt smoke and on investigating found that a fire had started in the Red Drawing-Room. She rushed to give the alarm.

When the Queen and Albert were aware of what was happening Albert immediately took charge. The Queen was to go at once to the Green Drawing-Room and remain there with her ladies; he would superintend the extinguishing of the fire, which he did with his usual efficiency, coming in to her afterwards when it was all over with his coat and galoshes quite sodden.

The Queen was calm as she said she always was when she was actually in the midst of disaster. It was not knowing what was happening which worried her.

'Oh, Albert,' she cried, 'you must get those wet things off as soon as possible. You'll have another of your colds.'

Albert said: 'This should never have happened. I shall make an inquiry into how it did. There is still a great deal to be improved in the management of the household.'

'Yes, yes,' she said impatiently, 'but I am going to insist that you take off those wet things immediately.'

443

Albert complied but was soon suffering from one of his colds. She was uneasy about his health. He had so many colds, and after each one she fancied he was not quite as strong as he had been before.

'It is so tiresome of you, Albert,' she cried. 'You take little care of yourself. It causes me a great deal of anxiety and I think I should be spared that.'

Albert sighed. It was one of her bouts of 'pregnancy irritability' which he reminded himself he must bear stoically. The fire had upset her; she was touchy and anxious. Without telling her he sent for the midwife, Mrs Lilly, immediately although the birth was reckoned to be due in some three weeks' time.

'Mrs Lilly!' cried the Queen. 'But it is not yet time. Why have you arrived so soon?'

'Ma'am,' replied the nurse with dignity, 'I come when I am sent for and His Highness Prince Albert gave strict instructions to come at once.'

She stormed into Albert's study. 'Really, Albert, this is too bad. *I* should know when to send for Mrs Lilly. I will not have you sending for people without my knowledge. I was *astonished* when she arrived.'

Albert passed his hand wearily over his forehead.

'I see we have to deal with the Queen,' he said.

'You have to deal with a woman who is about to have a child and she begs to be allowed to say when the midwife shall be called. Any woman has that right ... but...'

'Yes, yes,' said Albert, 'but you are the Queen.'

'And it will be well if some people remembered it more often.'

'Some people?' asked Albert.

'Yes, Albert. *All* people.'

Albert stood up and bowed and was about to leave the study when she noticed how tired he looked and was filled with contrition.

'Oh, Albert,' she cried, 'I am *so* bad tempered. And I wonder how you forgive me. It is just that I so dread the ordeal and this makes me as I am.'

Albert embraced her and stroked her hair. 'I know,' he said.

'And you are so good and so calm always. Oh, Albert, please forgive me. I am so stupid.'

Then Albert murmured gently: 'Do not cry. All will be well.' And he added his favourite term of endearment: *'Gutes Frauchen'*.

'Oh, yes,' she cried, 'while we have each other all is well.'

Three weeks or so after the fire the baby was born. It was a boy and the Queen decided to call him Leopold after that beloved uncle.

Sir James Clark had talked to her before explaining to her the use of chloroform in childbirth. He could see no danger in its use and it could be given when the agony was extreme. If the Queen agreed he would call in Dr Snow, who was an expert in these matters.

The Queen, who had before the birth of Leopold undergone the ordeal of child-bearing seven times and who was always apprehensive when her time drew near, welcomed the idea.

She was delighted with its effect.

Many women were grateful to her, for arguments against the use of chloroform had been raging throughout the country. Many people – mostly men, and women who were past child-bearing age – deplored its use as 'going against nature'. If God had not meant women to suffer in this way He would not have made birth painful, therefore to alleviate pain was to go against God and nature. However, those to whom it could be useful were delighted that the Queen had come down on their side, for since Victoria had used it opinions changed. Chloroform was not merely, as the Queen had said, a 'blessed relief', it was fashionable.

The Queen recovered quickly from her confinement, not having to undergo such strain, but the child was smaller and more frail than his brothers and sisters and it was very soon discovered that he suffered from a strange disease. If for any reason he bled it was difficult to stop the bleeding.

The fact that she had produced a delicate child upset the Queen and because of this a fracas between herself and Albert would frequently occur. Albert remained patient and would calmly explain where she was wrong; he called her his 'dear child' which was meant to imply of course that she was somewhat fractious.

There was a great deal to worry about: Bertie's naughtiness, which made him sometimes quite violent; Leopold's fragility; and politics. A very unpleasant situation was blowing up between Russia and Turkey; Mr Gladstone was making himself tiresome in the House of Commons and Lord Aberdeen, finding himself unequal to the stresses all about him, wanted to resign.

Most alarming of all was Albert's health. He would go into moods of depression; he was so ready to believe the worst and was so worried about the situation in Russia and Turkey; he had constant attacks of a kind of nervous fever which Sir James Clark could not diagnose; and he caught cold easily.

How she longed for summer days at Osborne and long autumn holidays at Balmoral. Only in those dear homes was she really at peace; and now that they had purchased Balmoral and pulled down the original place and Albert had designed a castle, it was just the ideal place, which after all was his creation, and he really had a genius for designing royal houses. Look at Osborne – that other happy home. And up at Balmoral their privacy was respected and even if any of the Highlanders of the village met them on the road they knew they must pretend not to see them. In the house and on the estate they had their good loyal servants and their wonderful gillies who looked after them so magnificently when they went out into the countryside, the Prince to shoot or stalk and the older boys with him. She often said to the Prince that she did not know what they would do without people like John Grant and John Brown.

# Chapter XXII

## CRIMEA

The Queen was in despair. That which she had always dreaded was threatened. War! She believed fervently that at costs the country must keep out of war and there was one man who was trying to drag them into that unhappy state: Palmerston.

Palmerston was the man of the moment. The eyes of all Europe were on him. He was the strong man, not afraid to state his views, to offend the Queen and her husband, nor to give up office if need be. The people were convinced that Palmerston was the man to lead England.

No sooner had Sir John Russell insisted on his resignation than England's enemies were exulting, and Nicholas, Emperor of Russia, threatened to annexe Turkey. Lord Malmesbury, the new Foreign Secretary, had had little experience of foreign affairs and his great desire was to fall in step with the Queen and Albert; Aberdeen's policy was peace at any price. Only Palmerston, with the bulk of public opinion behind him, saw that the only way to prevent war was to take a firm hand and threaten it. If Russia believed that England would stand aside – which Palmerston fervently believed she could not without great damage not only to her prestige and status but to her commercial interests – Russia would swallow up Turkey and command not only the Black Sea but the Mediterranean.

Ever since the enforced resignation of Palmerston, Russia had been creeping nearer and nearer to Turkey and was poised ready to spring. The British lion stood up and growled at these onslaughts and then settled down again.

A climax came when Russia destroyed the Turkish fleet. Palmerston resigned, but the vacillating Aberdeen, while referring to Palmerston as 'that obnoxious minister', had at last seen that the policy Palmerston had suggested must be followed. Palmerston then withdrew his resignation.

Meanwhile the public, led by the press, had become aware of its weak government and Palmerston was the national hero.

*Punch* summed up the situation with a caricature of the Russian Emperor stuffing a Turkey into his pockets and saying: 'I don't mean any harm,' while policemen representing France and England stood by watching.

Why, asked the press, was England remaining aloof, blind to her own interests? Because the Queen was against it. And who guided the Queen and was trying to rule the country through her? The Queen's German husband.

If Palmerston had become the hero of the drama, Albert was chosen for the villain.

Cartoons, lampoons and libellous articles were published and all were directed against German Albert. He wanted to hand England over to his German family; that was why he wanted to see her brought low. He was in sympathy with Russia because he was related to the Russian royal family. He might be the Queen's husband but he was the country's enemy.

The people had always disliked Albert. He was a German; he spoke with a guttural accent; he was cold and aloof and there was no humour in him. How different from Lord Palmerston, who in his most serious moments could never resist a joke. Albert was a virtuous husband it was true, but how colourful was Lord Palmerston. There were stories about his gay past when he had been involved in many an amorous scrape, and then in later life he had married Lord Melbourne's sister with whom it was said he had been in love for years and now he had settled down to a life of domestic felicity with a wife whose sole purpose in life was to care for her husband and further his career.

The anger against Albert was great. It was said that he had a key to the Queen's Dispatch Box and opened it before it came into her hands. He altered the Foreign Secretary's dispatches and sent them to their destinations without further reference to the Queen or the Foreign Office. On Christmas Day he had dined off turkey and had drunk the health of the Russian Emperor. In short, Albert was a traitor.

The Queen was aghast at such perfidy. She wept with rage. It was only a short time ago that Albert had given them that wonderful Exhibition. Everyone had applauded it and said that there had never been such a clever, artistic and brilliant display. They had known that it was Albert's creation; and the very same people who were telling these lies about Albert were talking of Palmerston as though he were a hero whom she and Albert hated because he was the great patriot of the age. But there was nothing she could do to prevent the hysteria which was rising against the Prince.

A rumour was started that the Prince was to be sent to the Tower of London and crowds collected by the Traitor's Gate. When he did not arrive they dispersed, grumbling that he had tried to make the Queen share his fate and she had refused and that he had forced her to have the charges against him withdrawn.

The situation was becoming so ridiculous that responsible persons like Mr Gladstone realised that it must be stopped without delay or the mob would be so incensed that they might even attempt to assassinate the Prince. Mr Gladstone wrote to the *Morning Post* explaining the groundlessness of the accusations and the matter was brought up in the House of Commons where Lord John Russell so effectively defended the Prince and showed the calumnies against him to be so ridiculous and false that it halted the streams of abuse. But a great deal of gossip about the subversive activities of the Prince persisted: and when the Queen went to open Parliament the crowd hissed her and great precautions were taken because Albert was with her.

The French exiles were still at Claremont and this was another matter which was brought against the Queen and her husband. The French under Napoleon III were involved with England in the obligation to go to the aid of Turkey and the fact that the French royal family had found refuge in England was taken to indicate that Albert and Victoria were the enemies of Napoleon III, since they befriended the exiled King and Queen.

All these troubles had their effect on the Queen's temper, and when Albert said that he thought it unwise for them to visit Claremont her anger flared up.

'Let's wait until this storm has blown over,' said Albert.

'But don't you see, they will think you are not going because you are guilty?'

'I think it unwise to go,' said the Prince firmly.

'What will those poor exiles think if you don't?'

'My dear love, we have to think of our position.'

'It is cruel. So unjust!'

'Of course we know it is, but it doesn't help us to say it. We have to think and act wisely and with caution.'

'I think we should defy them and go.'

'I think we should not.'

She stamped her foot. She was the Queen. Who would believe that, by the manner in which her people treated her – or the manner in which Albert treated her!

She faced him defiantly and suddenly she saw how tired and wretched he looked and she began to cry.

He was all tenderness immediately, and she was comforted. Her determination was as strong as ever, but it had been diverted. It was not to go to Claremont but to make sure that Albert was appreciated by the people. They *must* be *made* to recognise his great good qualities. She would never rest until they did.

A few weeks later England had no choice but, with France as her ally, to declare war on Russia.

The Queen could think of nothing but the war. How could it be carried on to the best advantage, what could she do to help her brave soldiers? She longed for it to be over because the thought of death and destruction was abhorrent to her, but she was eager for the glory of her country and she was now convinced that war was the only action possible in the circumstances. The Tsar Nicholas had become the villain. He alone was responsible. Palmerston in the background was murmuring that the right action a year before could have prevented the war. It was because the Russians had believed that England was ineffectually governed – which it was – by short-sighted men – which they were – it could take advantage of the situation – which it had.

The people in the streets were enthusiastic for the war. It was far away; it was fought on foreign soil and they had not yet begun to realise what misery was involved. They began to call for Palmerston who stood by awaiting the moment to come forward. At least, he said, the country was taking some action now. It was belated but at last the Russians had been shown that we were not going to stand aloof.

Albert worked for long hours; he was indefatigable, said the Queen; when he came to bed red-eyed and weary she would tell him how anxious she was for his health and that he must not exhaust himself. But his sense of duty was strong. He had been reviled – he still was – but he saw his duty clearly and he would perform it at no matter what cost.

News was coming in of disasters at the front. The greatest killer was disease. Cholera raged; dysentery and fever were commonplace; there was only salt pork to eat and not much of that; the weather was bitterly cold and the men's moustaches froze to their faces. The hardship was terrible; there was the disaster of Balaclava and the terrible anxiety of waiting for good news which did not come. Men were dying in the Crimea and Miss Florence Nightingale had gone out to nurse them.

The war was no longer glorious and everyone was longing for its end.

England's government was weak. That much was certain. Lord Aberdeen had no stomach for war; he was almost ready to put into practice his policy of peace at any price. What the country needed was a strong man and it looked to Palmerston, who had prophesied that the war was inevitable months before the government had realised it, who had reiterated that had he been at the Foreign Office a firm line would have been taken with the Russians and war would have been avoided. He was a prophet; he was the strong man; the country called out for Palmerston.

Lord Aberdeen resigned and the Queen sent for Lord Derby but he could not form a government. Then she sent for Lord John Russell.

Lord John Russell shook his head. 'Your Majesty,' he said, 'it will have to be Palmerston.'

'No!' cried the Queen. 'Not … that man.'

Lord John lifted his shoulders. 'The people will only be satisfied with Lord Palmerston.'

She dismissed Lord Russell and went to Albert. She told him what Russell had said. Albert shook his head wearily.

'Albert, we could be firm. We could stand out. We could refuse.'

'We could,' said Albert, 'but we dare not.'

'Albert, I am the Queen.'

'Yes, my love, you are the Queen, but sovereigns rule by the will of the people, as the French royal family discovered. The country is desperate; the war is not going well, and the people want Palmerston.'

'They do not understand. He is an old man. I believe he *paints* his face to give himself a good colour. He is seventy-one and he has lived a very immoral life.'

'It is not only that the English want him. The rest of Europe fears him. If he were at the head of affairs there would be a change in opinion of us and that would be reflected in the progress of the war.'

'Albert, you too!'

'And you too, my dear. This is too big an issue for personal prejudices. You and I cannot like or admire this man but the world has made up its mind that he is the one to lead this country to victory.'

The Queen saw that she had no alternative. She was forced to sink her pride and send for Lord Palmerston.

He arrived jaunty as ever, knowing full well why

she had sent for him and what it had cost her to do so.

'Lord Palmerston, I have called you to ask if it is possible for you to form a Ministry.'

Palmerston was confident. 'Why yes, Ma'am,' was his answer. 'I could undertake with a fair prospect of success to form an administration which will command the confidence of Parliament and effectually conduct public affairs in the present momentous crisis.'

The news was out. Newsboys shouted it; the people in the streets called to each other, 'Have you heard?'

The cry went on: 'Palmerston is in. The war will now soon be over.'

They were right. Palmerston was the man who was needed. By the end of the year negotiations to end the war were in progress and a conference was being arranged to take place in Vienna to discuss them. This proved to be abortive but the change in the situation since Palmerston had taken over was apparent to all. The war dragged on but there was a new spirit of optimism. Cartoons showed Palmerston as a boy with a broom energetically sweeping away disorder. 'This is the greatest mess I ever saw at anybody's house,' ran the caption. And everyone believed this to be a fair comment. It was only people like Benjamin Disraeli – who had hoped for the premiership himself – who expressed dissatisfaction. He called Palmerston an imposter, 'ginger beer not champagne even at the height of his powers' and now an 'old painted pantaloon, very deaf, very blind, with false teeth' which were always on the point of falling out of his mouth. But no one was interested in the ravings of jealous politicians; people wanted the war conducted in such a manner as to bring it to an early end.

When the Emperor Nicholas died suddenly hopes soared. He had been killed by 'pulmonary apoplexy' it was said but many construed this as a broken heart. The war had not been the easy victory for which he had hoped. Lord Palmerston had changed everything. The Tsar had seen his beautiful cities laid waste and it had all been too much for him.

The Queen could not help shedding a tear. 'He was such a handsome man,' she said.

Albert would remember how he had visited them and had descended on them so suddenly without warning and she had been so put out because she was heavily pregnant with dear Alfred.

Albert remembered well.

'I remember what wild eyes he had. It was because you could see the white all round his pupils and his eyelashes were so light. Lady Lyttleton said they gave his eyes no shade. He certainly did look a little sinister – and so he turned out to be. But I remember he was charming to me.'

Another death! And although many rejoiced in this one she could not bear hearing of the deaths of people whom she had known.

At the back of her mind was the fear that it might happen to someone very near and dear to her. She was afraid that little Leopold might meet with some accident and they be unable to stop his bleeding; she would not face the fears she sometimes felt when Albert was ill.

After all she told herself, I am older than he is. Only three months it was true, but still they were both young and he *was* her junior.

The war progressed. The Queen reviewed her troops and distributed medals. She called the soldiers her *'dear brave* army'. 'I am so *proud* of them,' she said.

A new order was made – the Victoria Cross – and in the May of 1855 she awarded this to sixty-five heroes from the Crimea.

Then the Emperor Napoleon paid a visit to England with his beautiful Empress Eugénie. They were fêted everywhere and the Queen, who had been so much against them because friendship with them would have been so disloyal to the Orleans family, found them charming. The Emperor was so unaffected; his wife the Empress Eugénie so beautiful. She was tall and slender and when they were together the contrast between her and the Queen was almost comical, the Queen being so tiny and inclined to plumpness. Napoleon made the same contrast with Albert. Albert was tall and handsome, although his hair was thinning and he looked so pale and wan sometimes; the Emperor was very short and his head seemed too big for his body to support. He was very dashing, though, with his enormous moustaches and knew very well how to say the gallant thing to ladies, which of course Albert never did.

There was something rather scandalous about them both. There was a faint possibility that Lord Palmerston could have been Eugénie's father for he was very friendly with her mother just before her birth. So, it seemed, were several other members of the nobility. There was a story that the lady had responded to this scandal by saying sharply: 'Impossible,' and adding, 'the dates would rule that out.' As for the Emperor, before he had come to power he had lived in England in quite a humble fashion and had once waited with the crowds in the park to see the Queen ride by on her way to the Houses of Parliament.

The children were fascinated by the visitors. Eugénie seemed to Vicky the most beautiful creature she had ever seen. She declared that she wanted to be just like her. Bertie's admiration was for the Emperor. He could not take his eyes from the little man and the Emperor delighted in this admiration. He talked to Bertie as though he were one of his generals and Bertie confided that he wanted to be a soldier more than anything else on earth.

'You'll be a good one,' said the Emperor and added with a grin, 'I should like to have you in my army.'

Bertie thought of being in the Emperor's army and compared it with all the tasks that had to be completed under the unattractive Mr Gibbs, and of his own father and Baron Stockmar who were determined that he should have no spare time at all in which to enjoy life.

'I wish you were my father,' said Bertie.

Of course there must be a return visit and Victoria and Albert, taking with them the Prince of Wales and the Princess Royal, crossed in the royal yacht and visited Paris where they were received with great pomp by the Emperor and his Empress.

Bertie was delighted with everything he saw. Paris was the most enchanting city he had ever imagined; he loved the crowds of excited people and of course the Emperor was there.

They visited the Paris Exhibition and Napoleon's tomb; they watched the firework displays at Versailles and admired the flowers in the *Jardin des Plantes*. An exciting fairyland it seemed to the thirteen-year-old Prince.

The Queen was delighted too. It was such a pleasant way of doing her duty. The Emperor paid such delightful compliments and gave her such looks that secretly shocked her. He was a very worldly man, but he certainly made a woman feel beautiful and desirable and that was comforting. Not that she could ever think of any other man but Albert but it was pleasant to know that she was admired ... for Albert's sake of course.

The visit came to an end all too soon and they must return to England, to the political conflicts and preoccupation with the war. That fortunately was now in its last stages. There was a conference in Paris which was to end in peace.

The Queen could not help being grateful to Lord Palmerston because she had to admit that when he had come to office things had begun to change. She was even ready to admit that had he remained at the foreign office there might not have been a war at all.

'One must be just,' said the Queen. 'And it was a most unsatisfactory war.'

# Chapter XXIII

## A PROPOSAL FOR VICKY

As they walked in the gardens of Buckingham Palace arm in arm, Albert explained his plan to the Queen.

'I want you to ask Prince Frederick of Prussia here for a visit ... soon.'

'But of course, Albert. That will be delightful. I love having visitors.'

'This is rather more important than an ordinary visit,' explained Albert. 'I am thinking of Vicky.'

'Vicky. And the Prince you mean? Vicky is only fourteen.'

'It is very young,' said the Prince. 'Too young. But Fritz is twenty-four, which is not so young. I am afraid that if we wait too long a match might be made for him elsewhere.'

'His mother was very pleased at the idea of a marriage between him and Vicky.'

'Times change. Prussia has been aloof from the Crimean conflict. I should like to see Prussia and England close allies.'

'Of course.'

'I don't trust Napoleon. I don't trust the French.'

The Queen smiled at the memory of those delicious compliments Napoleon had whispered to her.

'*Don't* you, Albert?'

'They are frivolous. One can't trust them. The Emperor has tried to flatter us. I believe he should be watched. I am certain an alliance with Prussia is what we need. I want to see our Vicky on that throne.'

'But fourteen, Albert!'

'Oh, not yet, not yet. But why shouldn't there be some understanding?'

'A betrothal, you mean?'

'An understanding. And then perhaps in a year...'

'When she is fifteen.'

'Two years perhaps.'

'It's heartbreaking when one's children grow up,' said the Queen; but she thought, if Vicky were not here I should see more of Albert. And she was vaguely pleased because it was he who had suggested the marriage which meant the departure of Vicky. Sometimes his doting on the child did irritate her. It was as though he thought there was no one in the world like his eldest daughter.

'We will invite Fritz without delay,' she said.

When Fritz arrived at Balmoral both the Queen and Albert were delighted with him.

'He has not changed from that dear *natural* boy who took the children to your Exhibition, Albert,' said the Queen, 'except for his moustache which really makes him look so handsome and manly.'

Albert agreed; and it was so pleasant to be in the dear Highlands again with faithful servants like the head gillie John Grant, and John Brown

462

who had a sort of uncouth charm which was very appealing.

Fritz was determined to make himself popular. He went stalking with Albert and showed his skill by bringing down a fine stag; he talked affectionately of his family to the Queen and of the army to the Prince of Wales; he played games with the younger children who all thought him wonderful; but of course his attention was focused on Vicky. He always seemed to be at her side; he wanted to talk to Vicky, alone if possible; he was always telling her about the Prussian Court and there was no doubt that Vicky was very interested.

Vicky had always been inclined to be a little coquettish, the Queen reminded herself, and had now and then been detected trying to call masculine attention to herself. Vicky was in a way as rebellious as the Prince of Wales but charmingly so. And Albert had only had to show his displeasure – he was hurt rather than angry at Vicky's misdemeanours – for her to be immediately contrite. There was no doubt that the deep affection between Albert and Vicky was almost as strong on her side as on his; they had often been seen whispering together as though sharing some secret from which even the Queen was excluded.

Now Vicky was well aware that in Fritz's eyes she was the most attractive member of the household – and she was revelling in the knowledge.

As for Fritz, he found Vicky attractive but she was only fourteen and he being twenty-four and not unworldly, he felt he must know her a little better before committing himself to marriage. But Vicky had always been old for her age; that was why poor Bertie had suffered so much in comparison; and in a few days Fritz was of the opinion that in view of her gay personality and her unusual intelligence she would make a very satisfactory wife.

He decided to speak to the Queen and Albert and chose breakfast time when they were alone.

The Queen said: 'Well, Fritz, how are you enjoying Balmoral?'

Fritz said that he had never enjoyed a visit more. Then he plunged: 'I want to ask your permission to talk to you on a very intimate matter.'

The Queen glanced at Albert who appeared to be almost aloof but was in fact very alert.

'I have enjoyed being in the heart of your family,' went on Fritz. 'I should be very happy indeed if I might belong to it.'

The Queen's eyes were filled with tears; she leaned towards him and taking his hand pressed it warmly.

'My dear Fritz,' she said, 'it is a pleasure for us to welcome you into the family. Vicky is however only fourteen. There could not be any announcement yet.'

'She is very young indeed,' added Albert. 'Next year she will be confirmed. Perhaps after that there might be a proposal. But I think Vicky should not be aware of these plans just yet.'

Fritz said he well understood. He hoped that he would be invited to come again later on and then he would make his formal proposal to Vicky.

'That,' said the Queen, 'is what the Prince and I would desire more than anything.'

When they were alone together the Queen

464

noticed how despondent Albert was. He looked quite ill. His rheumatism was very painful and yesterday he had found it difficult to hold a pen. The wig he occasionally wore to keep his head warm now accentuated the pallor of his skin. He was grieved of course at the prospect of his beloved daughter's departure.

'Of course it is what we want,' the Queen reminded him.

'Of course,' said Albert sadly.

'Stockmar sees no reason why the marriage should not take place quite soon. He thinks this alliance between us and Prussia to be essential to the strength of Europe. So ... I suppose you agree with him.'

There was a little asperity in the Queen's tone. She disliked Albert's subservience to Stockmar. She could not bear Albert to care so much for people as he did for Stockmar ... and of course Vicky. She felt it took away from her some of the love which should be hers. In her heart she knew that Albert was the very centre of her life. All the rest of her family together could not mean to her what he did. She was constantly trying to hide little jealousies and that was why her anger flared up.

'Stockmar is one of the wisest men in the world.'

'Only *one* of them?' said the Queen ironically. 'Sometimes I think he is more concerned with politics than human feelings. If Vicky does not love Fritz then I should not agree to the marriage.'

'Do you think I would? My great desire is to see the child happy.'

'No, I didn't think so for a moment. You dote

on her. That's obvious. Perhaps that's why you have been so harsh with Bertie. The poor child can't help it because he is not Vicky.'

'My dear love, what *are* you saying?'

'Well you do favour her, don't you? And she has been just as naughty as Bertie. She has at times been quite rebellious and coquettish with some of the equerries. *I* have had to reprimand her. And you, Albert, who set yourself up as being so calm, have just turned a blind eye to Vicky's shortcomings. The child has been quite spoiled.'

'You have been stern enough with her.'

'Someone had to correct her. It's no wonder that she adores her dearest Papa and thinks Mama a little cruel now and then.'

'You are overwrought,' said the Prince. 'It is the thought of your daughter's growing up, becoming almost a woman.'

She looked at him tearfully. 'Yes, Albert, that is it.' She held out her hand and he took it. 'She will go away from us and this will no longer be her home ... only a place she will visit. It's sad, Albert.'

Albert was very sad. The idea of losing his beloved Vicky affected him more than it did Victoria. 'It is the way of life, my love,' he said mournfully.

'And whatever comes, Albert, we have each other.'

'That, my dear child, is something for which we must always be thankful.'

He smiled at her tenderly and happiness was restored.

Albert loved to organise the family whether it

was hunting moths and butterflies, reading, climbing or acting the plays they enjoyed so much. As he felt better and his rheumatism had subsided he thought that a ride to Craig-na-Ban would be enjoyable. All the family, apart from the very young children, including Fritz, were to set out on their ponies accompanied by John Grant and good John Brown. They would go up into the hills on their ponies and a carriage would pick them up at a point to be decided on by the Prince.

They set out, Victoria and Albert leading; it was soon very clear that Vicky and Fritz were going to straggle.

The Queen and Albert exchanged significant glances.

'As long as they are not out of sight,' murmured Albert.

Vicky and Fritz were talking earnestly.

'What a beautiful place,' Fritz was saying.

'Mama thinks it is the most beautiful in the world. Papa is enamoured of his Thuringian forest and loves this because he says it resembles it. Uncle Ernest said it was not in the least like Germany. What do you say?'

Fritz looked at her earnestly: 'I can only give my attention to one thing at the moment.'

'Fritz,' cried Vicky, 'you are not referring to *me* as a thing!'

Fritz laughed delightedly. She was bright and animated; who would believe she was only fourteen? She was almost ready for marriage – or would be in a year or so.

Fritz himself being twenty-four was impatient,

and he realised that Vicky was well aware of this.

'You will have to grow up quickly,' he said.

'I grew up at an early age,' retorted Vicky. 'And you know girls are said to mature earlier than men.'

'What is the equivalent age in a woman compared with that of a man of say ... twenty-four?'

Vicky pretended to consider. 'That would depend. Eighteen shall we say, sixteen, in some cases perhaps fourteen.'

Vicky pressed her heel against the pony's side and he trotted a little faster. Fritz came up to her and pressed a piece of white heather into her hand.

'I just picked it,' he said. 'I am told it means good luck.'

'Thank you, Fritz.'

'Your good luck,' he said soberly, 'will be mine.'

'Why?' demanded Vicky.

'Because,' replied Fritz, 'I hope that one day you will be my wife.'

Vicky opened her eyes very wide and stared at him. She had known of course why he had come and there had been many sly allusions from the members of the household. She was excited. Fritz was so handsome. And of course he would one day be King of Prussia.

'Well,' said Fritz, 'are you surprised, horrified, shocked or perhaps a little pleased?'

'Perhaps a little pleased would fit the case better than any of those other conditions you mentioned.'

Yes, thought Fritz, Vicky was certainly exciting. He was glad he had spoken and he did not think the Queen was going to be too displeased about that.

As soon as they returned to the castle Vicky went to her mother's room.

'My darling,' cried the Queen and embraced her.

'Oh, Mama, you know.'

The Queen smiled. 'My love, I was aware of *dear* Fritz's feelings for you. Papa and I had decided that he would be a good match for you. But you know that if you did not care for him we should never have forced you. He was not going to speak to you yet.'

'I know, but it slipped out. Perhaps I wheedled it out of him.'

The Queen laughed.

'Oh dear, dear Mama!'

'There must of course be no wedding for some time. You would have to be seventeen.'

'Oh, Mama, three years.'

The Queen laughed again so indulgently. 'It is not very long, my dearest.'

'Three whole years without Fritz!'

'Oh, you have progressed so far already, have you?'

'Well Mama, as soon as Fritz gave me the white heather I knew. I shall keep that piece of heather for ever.'

Albert came in. He must have heard Vicky's arrival.

Vicky flew into her father's arms and the Queen felt a twinge as she saw the tender expression in Albert's eyes.

'So, my love, you have forestalled us all, eh?' said Albert.

'Papa, *dearest* Papa. I have just thought of something dreadful. When I marry Fritz I shall have to leave you.'

'My love, it is the way of the world. A daughter must leave her parents and cleave to her husband.'

'But, Papa, to leave *you...*' There was a brief pause and Vicky seemed suddenly to be aware of her mother. 'And Mama...' she added.

'My dear,' said the Queen, 'you shall visit us often and perhaps Papa and I will visit you. But I have been telling her, Albert, that there can be no marriage yet. She seems to have forgotten that she is a child of fourteen.'

'You were very young when you married Papa.'

'Not fourteen, nor even seventeen. I was nearly twenty.'

'How old!' wailed Vicky.

'Your Papa and I were in love just as you and Fritz are. But of course I had great responsibilities, which you will have later. But you will have a husband to stand beside you. I had no one until your father came. And what a difference that made to me!'

'I can only hope,' said Albert, 'that you, dear daughter, will be as happy as your mother and I have been.'

Fritz left a few days later, already engaged to Vicky; and the two people behaved like a young couple deeply in love. There were tears at their parting and Albert sat down to tell his friend Stockmar all about it, knowing that the news

470

would cheer him greatly. It was always so pleasant when those for whom marriages had been arranged obligingly fell in love.

'The young people are ardently in love,' he wrote. 'An abundance of tears was shed at their parting.'

As for himself he was 'tortured and tormented by rheumatism and could hardly hold the pen'.

The Queen came in while he was writing.

'Writing to the Baron?' she said. 'Well, he will be delighted, and you are because he is.'

'I am glad that he will be pleased but chiefly I am glad for our daughter. I am sure this is the best possible match for her.'

'We can no longer treat her as a child. This has turned her into a woman overnight.'

'She is still the same little Vicky.'

'Oh, no, she is not. She is soon going to be a wife. I do hope she does not start having children too soon.'

'My love, that is a matter for the future.'

'I can't bear to think of our child being submitted to that ordeal too soon.'

'We shall hope that in due course she gives Prussia an heir.'

'But not too soon, I trust,' said the Queen.

'Oh, she will delight in children.'

'But not in bearing them. Men never understand what we have to suffer. I know, Albert. I do happen to have experienced it eight times. I don't really think I could endure it again.'

Albert could see that she was working herself up into a passion and did his best to soothe her.

'Perhaps you will not have to, my child,' he said.

471

She softened at the term of endearment. Dear Albert, she must not upset him; and he did look worn and wan. She knew that his rheumatism was very painful.

It was impossible to keep the matter of Vicky's betrothal secret. The press wanted to know what Fritz had been doing at Balmoral. Clearly his visit had had some ulterior motive; the Princess Royal was destined to marry a German – just as her mother had!

The Princess was confirmed and, thought her mother, looked so touchingly innocent in her pure white dress and she made her responses perfectly. Yes indeed, Vicky was no longer a child.

'It is always Germans,' said the press. And who was this Prince Frederick William of Prussia? The heir to a little German kingdom! It was obvious whose hand was in this. Once Germans had a foot in at the door they were ready to take charge of the house.

The Prussians resented the English attitude and there were comments in their press. Why all this fuss? Who was their future King marrying? The Princess Royal of England! They would first like to know what dowry was offered before they crowed too much about its being a good match, and if she married the Prince, the Princess Royal would have to come to Germany to do so.

When the Queen heard this she was furious.

'I suppose you agree with this!' she accused Albert. 'After all you are a German. And Stockmar too, I suppose he thinks it is right and proper for an English Princess to be overawed at the prospect of marrying into Prussia! If it is too much trouble for a Prince of Prussia to come over here to marry the daughter of the Queen of England, he had better not come at all.'

'Now,' soothed Albert, 'you are getting worked up again. There is no need to. Of course Fritz will come over here for the wedding.'

## Chapter XXIV

## MUTINY

The Prince of Wales provided a problem. Mr Gibbs' stern rule seemed to have profited him little and he had made scarcely any progress with his studies. He was deliberately wilful. Alfred had wanted to go into the Navy and although this was not Albert's original idea for his future, he believed that if the boy was so enamoured of the life he would probably do well at it. When he was sent to Royal Lodge there had been a terrible scene between the two brothers because they were to be parted. They had wept bitterly and although it was pleasant to see their affection, Bertie's behaviour afterwards was worse than ever. He had taken to teasing the younger children and there were often battles.

Leopold was also wilful and could be very naughty at times and sometimes in a fit of temper he would hurt himself and there would be those worrying haemorrhages. What could one do with

Leopold but whip him? The Queen's mother, who adored the children and spoilt them all, said that she hated to hear the children crying after a beating. It hurt her, she declared, as much as it did them and she simply could not bear it.

'I have too many of them to be upset by the tears of one or two,' said the Queen grimly. 'I daresay Feodora and Charles were good children and rarely cried, and as for myself I don't think I did much either ... not tears of anger in any case.'

'You had your storms,' said the Duchess. 'And little Leo is a good boy at heart. He's so delicate and that could make him peevish. In fact they are all good children at heart.'

'Even Bertie?' said the Queen.

'Even Bertie,' answered the Duchess firmly.

The Queen sighed. 'How I wish I could believe that!'

It was so easy for grandmothers; they had the pleasure of children without the anxieties they created.

And then to her dismay, the Queen was once more pregnant.

There was no end to trouble. It now came from the East because the Chinese had boarded a ship and after having arrested the crew as pirates had torn down the British flag. Although this particular ship was registered in Hong Kong it was not at all certain that it had a right to fly the flag, but no matter, the flag must not be insulted, so the British Plenipotentiary in Hong Kong saw no reason why reprisals should not be taken.

Admiral Seymour was given orders to destroy

certain Chinese forts and as a result there was an attempt to kill the Plenipotentiary in Hong Kong.

A dispute in the House of Commons arose about the manner in which the government had acted and there was to be a motion led by Cobden and Bright to censure it. Lord Palmerston was dubious about its outcome and felt it very probable that it would succeed. The thought of Lord Palmerston's being forced to resign threw the Queen into a panic.

She had almost forgotten that a short time ago she had been eager to keep Palmerston out at all costs. The manner in which the Crimean War had been brought to a conclusion had decided her that her old enemy was the strong man the government needed. It had been the same with Sir Robert Peel. She had hated him at first and had later been forced to admit his admirable qualities. Now this was the case with Palmerston.

'He cannot resign,' she cried. 'Oh dear, how tiresome these people are! When they have a strong man at the head they do their best to get rid of him. I cannot face a crisis now.'

Albert tried to soothe her. He was finding her pregnancies almost as trying as she did herself. The baby was due in a month's time and as she had put on weight considerably she was even more ungainly than usual; and she was aware of it.

'My love, a vote of censure might force the Prime Minister to resign,' said Albert.

'But he must be told that I do not wish it. I really cannot endure it at this time. Do these people realise that I have to face my ordeal in a few weeks' time? And to thrust this at me with all it entails! They must be made to *see*. Albert, I cannot face a crisis like this. I feel so humiliated. This will be the ninth time.'

'Will you leave this to me?' asked Albert.

'Oh, please, Albert, yes.'

Albert wrote to the Prime Minister:

*My dear Lord Palmerston,*
*The Queen has this moment received your letter giving so unfavourable an account of the prospects of tonight's division. She is sorry that her health impera-tively requires her going into the country for a few days... The Queen feels herself physically unable to go through the anxiety of a Ministerial Crisis and the fruitless attempts to form a new Government out of the heterogeneous elements of which the present Oppo-sition is composed, should the Government feel it necessary to offer their resignation, and would on that account* prefer any other alternative.

But Lord Palmerston could not be dictated to by the Queen's temporary physical disabilities. His government was defeated; he went to the country and was returned with a large majority. The Queen was delighted; and by that time she had given birth to her ninth child, a daughter, Bea-trice, and was once more helped through the birth by 'blessed chloroform'.

She had reason later that year to be glad that Lord Palmerston was in office. There were rumours of unrest in India. Many reasons were given for this. Discipline had been relaxed; there had been an effort to convert Indians to the Christian faith, and marriage for Hindu widows had been made legal.

British prestige abroad had waned in the last years because of difficulties in Afghanistan and the reverses of the war in the Crimea. It was said that what finally decided the Indians to revolt was the greasing of cartridges with the fat of cows and pigs which they considered sacred. The Mutiny had started.

When the Queen heard what was happening she was in despair. She wept when she heard of atrocities committed against women and children; she stormed at the incompetence which had allowed such carnage to take place. Why was not something done?

She sent for Lord Palmerston; she wanted to know why there was this *inactivity*.

Lord Palmerston presented the facts in his bland manner. It was deplorable. There was something wrong with their government of India and they must rectify it; but first they must have forces sent out to India; this revolt must be quelled with all speed. It must be realised that the British could not be treated in this way with impunity.

'You will do this! You will do that!' cried the Queen. 'But what *are* you doing? If I were in the House of Commons, Lord Palmerston, I would tell you what I think of some of you.'

'It is as well for those of us with whom Your Majesty does not agree, that Your Majesty is *not* in the House of Commons,' said Lord Palmerston with a smile.

But she knew that if there was a man who could deal with this horror that man was Lord Palmerston.

She wrote to Uncle Leopold:

*We are in sad anxiety about India, which engrosses all our attention. Troops cannot be raised fast enough. And the horrors committed on the poor ladies – women and children – are unknown in these ages and make one's blood run cold. Altogether the whole is so much more distressing than the Crimea – where there was glory and honourable warfare and where the poor women and children were safe...*

Lord Palmerston did not believe in leniency, which would be construed as weakness; and this seemed to be the case, for the Mutiny was suppressed.

The Queen was worried about Lord Palmerston. 'He is so old,' she said to Albert, 'and what shall we do without him?'

She scolded Lord Palmerston for not taking greater care of his health.

Whenever she did so a puckish look would be visible on that old painted face, and the Queen was fully aware of the time when she so disliked him that she wished him anywhere – dead if need be – anywhere to keep him out of the Houses of Parliament.

# Chapter XXV

## VICKY'S WEDDING

Ever since her engagement Vicky had been treated as an adult and that meant that on days when there were no guests the Queen and Albert sat down to dinner with only their eldest daughter for company. In the days before the engagement Vicky had been in the nursery with her brothers and sisters, but now she was soon to be a bride.

The Queen had recovered from the birth of Beatrice and could now give all her attention to Vicky's coming marriage. Her feelings were mixed. Sometimes she would look at the radiant young girl and think of herself on the point of marrying Albert. And almost immediately the babies had started to come. She trusted it would not be like that with Vicky. *She* must wait a while. A pity that she was marrying so young. On the other hand she did miss those meals she and Albert had taken *alone*. A third person could spoil the intimacy even though it was one's own daughter. Albert's devotion to Vicky and his deep interest in all her concerns did not help because she fancied he did not resent their daughter's presence in the least. On the contrary he could not have too much of her company.

Albert had designed a course of study for her. Nothing pleased him more than organization and

479

when it concerned his family so much the better. Vicky must study history; he would map out a course for her. With her intelligence she would find it all absorbing and it would be of inestimable value to her. They would talk in German together so that she would be perfect at the language; she was very good already, like all the children, having spoken it in the nursery.

It was small wonder that the Queen at these informal meals felt a little shut out.

'At least,' she said to Albert after Vicky had retired one night, 'when she is married I shall have you to myself for a while.'

'But I am always with you,' protested Albert.

'You are constantly at your desk or arranging things on committees.'

'My love, that is our work ... yours and mine.'

'And then,' she went on, ignoring the interruption, 'when we are together, you scarcely have a word for me because your attention is all for your daughter.'

'You will be thankful to be rid of her,' he said incredulously.

'Albert, how dare you say such a thing!'

'It seems so.'

'My daughter ... *my* child of whom I think constantly! I am afraid for her ... afraid that she will soon be having one child after another which has been my fate. Nine! Just imagine that. Beatrice is the ninth.'

'There is no need for me to imagine it,' said Albert calmly. 'I am fully aware of the number of children I have.'

'*You* have! Yes, but who has to bear them ... and

all the discomforts that go with them?'

'No one can bear your sufferings. That is something you yourself have to face. You should not brood on them so much.'

'I am sure if you felt some of my pains you would brood on them a little.'

Then she was sorry suddenly, for she remembered how worried she was about his health and she began to cry, which was the signal for Albert to comfort her.

The new year had come and the 25th of January was to be Vicky's wedding day. The family had gone to Windsor for Christmas but they must move back to Buckingham Palace for the wedding. The honeymoon was to be spent at Windsor – as the Queen's had been – and as she prepared to leave for London she was thinking of that happy time. If only Vicky can be as happy as her mother I shall ask nothing more, she told herself. Except of course I should not wish her to have to bring *nine* children into the world as I have done.

Vicky had only just passed her seventeenth birthday. 'She is too young,' said the Queen; and yet she could not stop thinking of returning to the intimacy of dinner with Albert alone. After all, Princesses had to marry. It was their duty.

She went to look at the apartments which had been set aside for the honeymoon and thought of her young innocent daughter.

Poor, poor Vicky!

Vicky came to her there and she saw the fear in her mother's eyes.

The Queen forgot her jealousy then; she forgot

everything but that this was her child, who such a short time ago had been a baby.

'Oh, Vicky, my darling child!' she cried.

And Vicky threw herself into her arms and they clung together. It was as though the child sought protection.

'Dearest child,' murmured the Queen; and she was thinking of marriage and what she called the shadow side. The weary months of waiting and the final agony. She prayed again that dear Vicky would not have to suffer *that* nine times.

'But my darling,' she said, 'you love Fritz.'

'Yes, Mama, but I can't stop thinking of leaving home and Papa ... and you.'

'You will be happy, my dearest child,' the Queen assured her.

The palace was full of royal guests. It was wonderful to see dear Uncle Leopold; and of course Fritz's parents were there. There were between eighty and ninety to dinner.

'Such a house full!' said the Queen to Albert.

Poor Albert, he was very sad. Victoria believed that if he could have done so conveniently he would have stopped the wedding because he could not bear to think of parting from Vicky.

Albert's brother Ernest came, which was a great comfort to Albert since he was what the Queen called 'beatdown'.

Ernest was as gallant as ever.

'Why,' he told the Queen, 'who would believe it is eighteen years since you were a bride? To look at you it seems incredible. You look far too young.'

It was comforting to be flattered; she loved compliments and Albert rarely paid them because he was so honest, but when he did give them they meant so much of course.

Besides the ball there were visits to the theatre and a very special performance of *Macbeth* at Her Majesty's Theatre which was quite wonderful.

The 25th was a Monday and on the previous Saturday Albert was to go and meet Fritz on his arrival in England and conduct him to the palace. Before he left the Queen walked with Albert and Vicky in the garden, their arms entwined, and she and Albert tried to cheer Vicky who was feeling very despondent at the prospect of leaving home.

'Bertie is so lucky,' said Vicky, 'when he marries his bride will have to come here.'

Poor sad little Princesses, thought the Queen, who were so young and must leave the nest. It would be Alice's turn next.

But when Albert returned with Fritz, and Vicky stood at the top of the staircase with Alice beside her, the radiance of her smile as she looked at her betrothed comforted the Queen.

The next day there was the great excitement of arranging the presents on tables; there were some magnificent diamonds and emeralds, and later Vicky and Fritz came in and went into ecstasies over them.

Vicky came to the Queen's room and said: 'Mama, I have a little gift for you.'

It was a brooch with a piece of her hair in it and Victoria remembered how often she and *her* mother had exchanged such gifts. Vicky said tearfully that she hoped she would be worthy to be the Queen's daughter, which moved Victoria deeply and she broke down and wept and demanded to know how she was going to get along without her darling Vicky.

Vicky's last night as an unmarried girl had come at last. Nothing would ever be the same for her again, thought the Queen. That sweet age of innocence was almost over.

She and Albert went with Vicky to the bedroom she was sharing with Alice. Dear Alice, who was going to miss her sister so much! Vicky seemed to be aware of the solemnity of the occasion because suddenly she turned to Albert and threw herself into his arms.

'Oh, Papa, dearest, *dearest* Papa,' she sobbed.

And Albert, who was usually so calm, broke down and said that his thoughts would be with her always and she must never forget that he loved her infinitely and if she needed him at any time he would be there.

The Queen wiped her eyes. It was so touching; and on such occasions how could she be jealous of the love between these two?

The sun was shining gloriously even though it was cold January. The Duchess of Kent, looking magnificent in purple velvet and ermine over white silk trimmed with purple, was in tears. The years had mellowed her considerably and she was now all that a devoted grandmother should be and the children all loved her. She had come to whisper words of comfort to dear Vicky, but Vicky did not seem to need them on this morning. Vicky was in love.

Crowds had gathered in the streets to see the procession pass from Buckingham Palace to the Chapel Royal at St James's. Victoria wondered if Albert was thinking of that day eighteen years ago when he and she had made their marriage vows. And now, she thought, I am even more in love with him than I was then.

In the chapel it was impressive. Lord Palmerston was present holding the Sword of State, and she was fleetingly reminded of Lord Melbourne. *Poor* Lord Melbourne whom she had once thought she loved before she knew what real love was.

Bertie and Alfred stood close to dear Vicky and the Queen kept Arthur and Leopold on either side of her.

Victoria felt the tears rush to her eyes as Vicky came forward walking between Albert and Uncle Leopold – three people, thought the Queen, who all mean so much to me. Vicky, she was delighted to see, seemed quite calm and dear Fritz so solemn and *tender*.

'Oh, may she be as happy as I have been,' prayed the Queen. 'May Fritz be only half as good as my blessed Albert and I shall be content.'

As soon as that part of the ceremony was over Vicky was embraced by Albert and the Queen and there was the Duchess of Kent waiting to kiss her. The Prince and Princess of Prussia then kissed Vicky and the Queen kissed Fritz. But the music of Mendelssohn's *Wedding March* was filling the chapel and they went to sign the register.

Then out into the streets where the crowds were immense. They cheered the Queen; they cheered

Vicky; they even cheered Albert and Fritz. Into the palace to stand on a balcony, to wave, retire and come out to wave again.

Who could believe that these were the people who a short time ago had hissed the Queen when she rode to Westminster?

After the wedding breakfast Vicky and her husband left for Windsor.

How lonely it seemed without their dear daughter! Albert was quiet and withdrawn and the Queen did her best to comfort him.

'At least they are deeply in love, Albert,' she reminded him, 'as we were. And that means so much. She is going to a new country which may seem strange. They will have their difficulties. Even we had those. But they love each other and that means all will be well.'

Albert pressed her hand, too moved to speak.

Two days later the Court went to Windsor. 'How like my own wedding and brief honeymoon!' sighed the Queen. It was a pity they could not have a little longer, but there were certain duties to be performed. Fritz for instance had to be given the Order of the Garter and after that it was necessary for the bridal pair to return with the Court to Buckingham Palace.

When they went to the theatre to see *The Rivals* the audience went wild with enthusiasm; and it was really affecting to hear the fervour with which they sang the national anthem.

'The people can always be won over by a royal wedding,' dear cynical *poor* Lord Melbourne had said; and he had been right.

But the separation was coming nearer.

The Queen and Albert tried to comfort themselves by continually commenting on the love between the young couple, but as the Queen wrote in her diary: the separation 'hung like a storm' above them.

Poor Vicky, in spite of her love, was at times in tears.

In a weak moment she clung to her mother and said: 'I think it will kill me to take leave of dear Papa.'

They wept together.

At last came the dreaded day. The 2nd of February. The Queen arose with a heavy heart. Such a wretched day – cold, dull and misty.

The Princess came to her parents' room and they desperately tried to talk brightly of anything but the departure, until the Princess had to leave them to get ready for the journey.

Albert had persuaded the Queen not to go to the ship. 'It will be too heartrending,' he said. 'You will not be able to contain your grief.'

She knew that it was true. So Albert would take Bertie and Alfred with him and the rest of the party.

In the audience room the Duchess of Kent, in tears, with the rest of the family, was waiting. It was so hard to say goodbye. Mother and daughter clung together.

Albert said: 'We must go now.' And he whispered to the Queen: 'I shall soon be back with you. It grieves me to see you like this.'

So to the sound of bands the party set off and the Queen ran to her room and throwing herself on the bed wept afresh.

It had started to snow. How dismal it was to stand at the window and look out on the falling flakes; the sky was heavy with more snow to come. But not as heavy as my heart, thought the Queen.

Alice brought little Beatrice to see her but even the baby could not comfort her mother.

'Yesterday,' cried the Queen, 'Vicky was playing with her.' In due course Albert came back with the boys, and told her that he had waited to see the ship sail.

They tried not to speak of Vicky but their thoughts were filled with her.

It was Albert who said: 'We have our child. She is not lost to us. Why, soon she will be preparing to visit us. What a day that will be!'

'Of course,' said the Queen; and took Albert's hand. 'I can bear anything,' she added, 'while I have you.' Albert went to his room and wrote to Vicky:

*My heart was very full when yesterday you leaned your head on my breast and gave free vent to your tears. I am not of a demonstrative nature, and therefore you can hardly know how dear you have always been to me and what a void you have left behind in my heart; yet not in my heart, for there assuredly you will abide henceforth, as till now you have done, but in my daily life which is evermore reminding my heart of your absence.*

# Chapter XXVI

## BERTIE'S PROGRESS

With Vicky married the pressing problem was the future of the Prince of Wales.

'Ah,' sighed Albert, 'if only Bertie had half the brains of his sister!'

'The trouble with Bertie is that he refuses to work,' replied the Queen.

There were continual complaints from Mr Gibbs. Bertie would not 'concentrate'. He seemed to 'set up a resistance to work'. 'Could do so much better,' was the continual report.

Baron Stockmar, who was back in England, was consulted. People who would not work must be made to work, was his verdict, but it was not easy to whip a young man of almost seventeen into submission.

Perhaps it was time to change Bertie's mode of education. He should no longer have a tutor but a Governor. A stern disciplinarian would be the best choice; someone who would stamp out the inherent frivolity of Bertie's nature. A course of study should be planned for him which would give him no opportunity of wasting time.

Having mapped out a stringent course for the Prince to follow, Stockmar declared that he must return to Coburg. His health, which had always been one of his major concerns, and the care of which had given him great enjoyment, was failing fast and he felt he must go back to his family to be nursed.

When Bertie heard that the old man was going, he was wild with joy. His immediate reaction was to seize Alice and dance round the room with her.

'You had better not let Papa see you do that,' she warned.

'What does it matter? Everything I do is wrong in Papa's eyes, so this can't be much worse than anything else.'

He would no longer have those cold eyes on him criticising everything he did, planning great working programmes (to complete which satisfactorily he would have to be a mathematician, theologian, historian and goodness knows what else), commenting on the way he did everything, discovering that he had a violent temper (what about Mama's?) and that he was in every way an unsatisfactory person.

It was all really a waste of time because his parents knew that already. But lots of people did not think so. His sisters and brothers for instance; some of the members of the household too, and old Lord Palmerston had winked at him once when his mother was telling him how her eldest son had failed to do this or that; and he had heard the Prime Minister say that he was of the opinion that the Prince of Wales was a very intelligent young man.

But of course it was those in authority over him who counted and it was very pleasant to contemplate that the disagreeable old Baron was about to depart.

Bertie watched him go with great glee while his parents wept and embraced the old fellow and told him how they would miss him. He must write regularly, said Albert; which made Bertie groan inwardly for he realised that Stockmar could be a menace from afar. Still he could do less harm in Coburg than in Buckingham Palace and Bertie had learned to be grateful for small mercies.

His seventeenth birthday arrived. Surely a day for celebrations. But not for him, it seemed; there on the table was a long account of the changes which would be taking place in his life. Mr Gibbs was going and Colonel Bruce was replacing him. The Colonel was known as a martinet and Bertie would have to report to him before he even left the palace; it would be like being under military command without any of the fun of being in the Army.

The long list of requirements ended with the words: 'Life is composed of duties. You will have to be taught what you may and may not do.'

Bertie was experienced enough to see that he was jumping out of an irritatingly restricting frying-pan into fire which was planned to envelop him like a straitjacket.

As if they had not enough to worry them without Bertie's intransigence there was trouble as ever at home and abroad. When Orsini had attempted to assassinate the French Emperor and Empress and it was discovered that the grenades had been manufactured and the plot hatched in England, a great wave of hostility swept across France towards their new ally. To placate them Palmerston introduced a bill making it a felony to conspire to murder and on this the government was defeated and Lord Derby, with his henchman Mr Disraeli, returned to office. Orsini was executed in Paris but one of his confederates, tried in London, was acquitted. An uneasy situation prevailed between England and France which was so disappointing after the great friendship the Queen had felt for the charming little Emperor and his beautiful wife.

The Derby Ministry was of short duration. When they tried to introduce an amendment to the Reform Bill they were defeated. A new difficulty presented itself when both Lord John Russell and Lord Palmerston were contending for the premiership and the Queen had no alternative but to send for Lord Granville. Fortunately he was unable to form a ministry and very soon Lord Palmerston, having succeeded in doing so, was back at the helm.

'It is comforting to know that we have a strong man at the head of affairs,' said the Queen.

But there was no real comfort.

Almost immediately after her marriage Vicky had become pregnant.

In the midst of all this political activity the Queen's mind was constantly with her daughter. No sooner had she discovered that she was pregnant than she was writing long letters of advice. She commiserated with Vicky, saying that now that Vicky had actually experienced marriage they could talk frankly as two women. Vicky was very quick to experience the 'shadow side' of the relationship between the sexes. It was wonderful to have children, and although they were quite ugly at birth they quickly grew charming (she must tell Vicky the latest sayings of Baby Beatrice who was a *great* comfort to them just now) but at the actual birth human dignity was lost and women were more like cows or dogs and their poor nature became quite animal.

Stockmar wrote protesting that the Queen's spate of letters was worrying the Princess. It was true that Vicky had a great deal to contend with. The schloss to which Fritz had taken her was very ancient, said to be haunted and bitterly cold; hot water had to be carried in buckets through draughty corridors to the bedrooms and was tepid by the time it reached them; there was some suspicion of the foreigner within their midst and although Fritz was kind and easy-going, Vicky missed home, particularly her father.

There was bickering between Victoria and Albert because of Stockmar's criticisms and Victoria retaliated by saying that Stockmar was an interfering old man.

Three months after Vicky had left England Albert decided that he must see her and paid a visit to Berlin. He spent only three days with his daughter but it was comforting to see that she was well and as happy as she could be in the circumstances.

When he returned Victoria said that while she had been waiting for his return she had decided that next time she would accompany him. She was longing to see Vicky and she thought they might go again *together* in August.

This they did and it was wonderful to see the beloved child again. The Queen wanted to carry her daughter off for cosy chats about how she should look after herself and discussions on the baby's arrival which were far from cosy.

'How I wish I could be here when the baby is born!' she cried. 'It is a mother's privilege to be with her daughter at such a time. Alas, I have to remember that I am the Queen.'

Vicky smiled in the old mischievous way and retorted: 'Well, Mama, as Papa says, you are the last one to forget that.'

But it was different talking with a young married woman from talking with a daughter whom one felt one had always to correct.

Vicky confessed to her that she had always loved her dearly, but she had been very naughty at times and disobedient, she knew. She had been thinking since the parting that because of this her mother might not think she loved her as much as she did.

'All children can be naughty,' said the Queen fondly.

'Then you understand, Mama?'

'Perfectly!' declared the Queen happily. 'Perhaps I didn't behave always as I should. That temper of mine would burst out. And I always felt that you children came between me and your father, and the greatest joy in my life was to be alone with him. You must understand that now that you have Fritz.'

Vicky said she could understand her mother's feeling for dearest Papa. 'Papa is an angel,' she added.

Victoria wept with pleasure. It was wonderful to think that her daughter had such understanding.

She was eagerly looking forward to the birth of her grandchild, she said, but Vicky must do everything her mother said. She would send a list of instructions.

'Oh, my darling,' she cried, 'how willingly would I bear your suffering for you.'

In January – a year after Vicky's wedding – her child was born. The birth was protracted and Vicky suffered far more than her mother ever had. At one time her life and that of the child were in danger. Fortunately the Queen and Albert did not know of this until the danger had passed.

Then they heard that Vicky had a son; he was to be called Wilhelm.

Bertie's worst fears were realised. He was practically Colonel Bruce's prisoner. He could not leave his apartments without his Governor's wanting to know where he was going and any sharp retort or the slightest protest would be reported to his parents. He must conform to the diet prepared for him; he was to have three meals a day at precisely the time laid down for them in the rules; and as Prince Albert did not believe in self-indulgence in any form, these meals must be light. Pudding might be served but it would be wiser not to take it or if the Prince of Wales did take it, it must be a small helping.

The Queen underlined this. She and his father had noticed that once or twice on holiday he had been sick through overeating, which should be a lesson to him.

When he heard that his father was considering sending him to Oxford or Cambridge, he was delighted. He had heard of the freedom undergraduates experienced there, and it sounded very pleasant.

But how different was the reality. The Prince of Wales was not to attend lectures; he was not to mix with other undergraduates; Colonel Bruce would choose the people who were to visit him. He was not to smoke and he would have a private tutor.

'Why do I have to go to Oxford?' demanded Bertie. 'It's no different from being anywhere else.'

'The only use of Oxford is that it is a place of study,' said his father. 'You seem to have the idea that you are going there to indulge in riotous living.'

The Dean of Christ Church, Henry Liddell, protested at the manner in which the Prince of Wales was being treated. If he were going to get the best from Oxford he should attend lectures, forget his rank and mingle freely with people of his own age.

Albert laughed this idea to scorn. 'The man seems to forget that Bertie is going there to work.'

Oxford under the governorship of Colonel Bruce was a bore and Bertie longed to escape from it.

There was great excitement at Windsor. Vicky was coming home for a brief visit. The change in Albert was remarkable. He seemed ten years younger. As for the Queen, she was so delighted at the prospect of seeing her daughter that she had been in a good mood ever since she had known Vicky was on the way.

And there she was – looking a little older, a little more mature, Vicky the mother.

'My dearest child!'

The tears, the embraces, the adoration for dearest Papa! Dear, dear Vicky, what a happy day that was, with the children all dancing round her and Alice trying to lure her sister away so that they could talk secrets.

Baby Beatrice, the darling, amused them all, because she was very bright and a little spoilt. Albert could only gaze fondly at his dearest daughter but there was no need for words to convey *their* feelings.

'I hope I shall see Bertie,' said Vicky.

'Bertie is at Oxford,' said the Queen, her face growing stern.

'I am sure he will enjoy that.'

'He is not going there to *enjoy*, my dear child,' said Albert tenderly, 'but to work. I hope he has realised that by now, for he had not when I last had news of him.'

'Poor Bertie!' said Vicky.

Later her father talked to her about Bertie. He was in despair, he said. The Prince of Wales grew more frivolous rather than less so and he thought that they would have to marry him early or there would be trouble. He did not wish to discuss this in front of the Queen who was apt to get over-excited about Bertie's shortcomings, but he was an anxiety. If Vicky would keep her eyes open for a suitable wife for Bertie it would be interesting.

If any visiting royalty came to Berlin she might have a chance of studying them. What Bertie needed was a serious young woman – a princess from the right Royal House, of course.

'Your mother and I have discussed this with Uncle Leopold and he has given a list of Princesses who might be suitable. I must show it to you.'

Albert was delighted to be able to treat this beloved daughter as an adult. He smiled as she looked down at the paper he handed her.

'Most of them are German, Papa,' she said.

'They are probably the best suited. German women and German men make the best spouses,' he added smiling.

'I have heard of this Danish Princess Alexandra. She is very beautiful.'

'Uncle Leopold has put her right at the end of the list.'

'Well naturally, Papa,' said Vicky with a laugh. 'She is not German.'

Albert said: 'And you, my dearest child, will keep your eyes open for some beautiful suitable German Princess for your brother.'

Vicky promised that she would.

Vicky sought an opportunity to be alone with her mother.

'Mama,' she said, 'I have something to tell you.'

The Queen smiled, ready for one of those cosy woman-to-woman talks which she enjoyed so much.

'Come and sit beside me, my love. There, now we can be comfortable. My dearest child, you know you can tell me *anything.*'

'I know, Mama, but it hurts me to tell you this.'

'Vicky, dearest, what is it?'

'It's the baby. You heard what a bad time I had.'

'Papa and I were almost frantic.'

'I'm so glad you were not there. It was so long, Mama, and so ... so...'

'I know, my dearest. You can't tell me anything about those horrors. Baby is my ninth child. To think I have endured that nine times!'

'Wilhelm's was a breech birth, Mama.'

'My dear, dear child.'

'His arm was dislocated as he was delivered.'

The Queen stared in horror.

'It has made a slight deformity. Apart from that he is a very healthy child.'

'Can nothing be done?'

'The doctors say no.'

'So he will go through life with this ... deformity.'

Vicky nodded. 'It may be so.'

'Oh, my darling! And you have only just told me.'

'I wanted to tell you myself, Mama. I didn't want to write it. But you must not fret. In every other way he is perfect.'

The Queen nodded.

Vicky said she must see Bertie so she arranged to visit him at the university. She took Lady Walburga Paget with her. Wally, as this lady was called, was the sister of the Countess Hohenthal, Vicky's lady-in-waiting; Wally was young, vivacious and very beautiful, and Vicky had found her friendship of great help in the gloomy haunted schloss.

Bertie's delight in seeing his sister and her very charming friend was obvious. He sat laughing and chatting with them and paying great attention to Wally, much to her and Vicky's amusement.

They were having a very merry time until Mrs Bruce, the Colonel's wife, came in and found them together. Her frigid manner showed her disapproval and when Vicky and Wally had left she told the Prince of Wales that she would have to report the matter to her husband who would no doubt wish to inform Her Majesty and His Highness Prince Albert what had happened.

'Good God!' cried the Prince, and the expression made Mrs Bruce wince, 'can't I see my own sister?'

Mrs Bruce had made a very alarming discovery. The Prince of Wales was not only lazy, unable to concentrate and below normal intelligence, but he was also fond of women.

When this was reported to Albert he was deeply concerned. It was something he had always suspected. Bertie's free and easy manner, so different from his father's, was a pointer. Albert too had noticed the manner in which some of the ladies of the household regarded Bertie.

A new danger was in sight.

They must be doubly watchful.

The manner in which the Prince of Wales was being treated was beginning to be one of the main topics in the press. He was not given the dignity due to his rank, it was said. He was treated like a schoolboy. The people wanted to see more of him. They had liked what they had seen.

It was decided that he should visit Rome. He was excited at the prospect until he learned what he might have suspected. A plan was laid out for him. Italian lessons in the morning, reading from eleven until twelve; after the midday meal he could visit art galleries and study architecture, then French lessons from five until six. It was inconceivable that he should have the evenings to himself. They were to be given over to private study, reading and music.

'Why should I go to Rome to do all that?' demanded the Prince. 'It's almost exactly what I do at home.'

He then went to Edinburgh University because, as the Queen said, the Scots would expect the Prince to have some education in their country. While there he had quarters in Holyrood House with the omnipresent Colonel preventing him enjoying life.

Once he tried protesting to the Queen. The result of this was the rejoinder: 'But, Bertie, your father has arranged this. Therefore everything he has ordered is for your good.'

What could he do? He could only endure until he was of an age to go his own way. And then? His eyes sparkled at the prospect.

Perhaps, said Albert, it would be a good idea, as some of Her Majesty's ministers seemed to think, if Bertie went to Canada and America. Bertie was nothing loth. There might be an opportunity of eluding his jailors there.

The Duke of Newcastle was to accompany him and here Bertie saw his chance.

501

They had a big schedule of public engagements, said the Duke. And when Bruce – now promoted to General – talked of lessons and the routine which had to be followed, the Duke cried; 'Impossible! There's no time for that.'

So Bertie attended all kinds of ceremonies; he was the centre of attraction at parades and levees given in his honour. On one occasion he had to make a speech. The Duke wrote it for him but when he gave it he ignored what had been written and said freely what came into his mind. It was a success. Bertie had discovered that he had a flair for making speeches, receiving attention, giving it – in fact after years of failure the ugly duckling had turned into a swan; he had become the perfect Prince of Wales.

Bertie was enjoying himself. Every time General Bruce approached him he would wave his hand and say, 'No time. Too many engagements!' and delightedly charm everyone with whom he came into contact.

The Duke of Newcastle was enthusiastic.

'Your Royal Highness knows just how to get along with people. This is good for our relations with these countries. Her Majesty will be grateful to you.'

Bertie glowed and prepared to spray his charm over the Americans as he had over the Canadians. This was even easier. They could not have enough of him.

A magnificent ball was given for him to which three thousand people were invited. Three thousand! There were many more than that number eager to see the Prince of Wales. They crowded into the ballroom in such numbers that the floor gave way. But it was all part of the pattern. Beautiful women thought Bertie 'cute' and wanted to dance and talk with him. The Duke thought that the Prince of Wales should not be persecuted in this way. 'Oh, I like this kind of persecution,' said Bertie.

General Bruce was fuming. If he had ever had a doubt that the morals of the Prince of Wales might be a little lax he was certain now.

After this there would have to be even stricter vigilance.

The Queen and Albert were delighted with the reports of Bertie's tour.

'It seems that for once he has done rather well,' said Victoria.

'We have General Bruce to thank for that,' replied Albert.

'Do you think we should reward him in some way?'

Albert thought it would be an excellent idea.

'The Order of the Bath for Services to the Crown, perhaps,' said the Queen. 'I will speak to Lord Palmerston about it.'

When Palmerston called she broached the subject.

'The North American tour has really been a great success.'

Palmerston agreed that it had been a spectacular success. 'His Royal Highness's talents are coming to light,' he added.

'We have to thank General Bruce for this. And the Prince and I thought that we should like to show our gratitude with some reward ... say the Order of the Bath, for instance.'

'But Your Majesty is forgetting that this is not Bruce's triumph. It was the Prince of Wales they liked, not the General.'

'Bertie did what he was told.'

'Your Majesty will know that there are ways of doing what one is told. It was not what was done but the manner of doing it. No, it is not Bruce to whom we should be grateful but to His Royal Highness the Prince of Wales.'

'I like to see services rewarded,' said the Queen severely.

'And I can happily say that I am in agreement with Your Majesty. And like Your Majesty I do not care to see rewards given where they are not merited. I hope to have the pleasure of congratulating His Royal Highness on the service he has done to his country but I do not think Your Majesty's Government would agree to bestow the Order on Bruce.'

'I shall expect a report on this,' said the Queen shortly.

Palmerston bowed.

He was laughing to himself as he left her. The Order of the Bath for that old spoilsport! Not if he knew it! He chuckled to think of Bertie's escape from the ridiculous restrictions they placed on him.

And, he said to himself, no ribbon for Bruce.

The Queen should have known that Lord Palmerston always had his own way.

So General Bruce was not rewarded for his services in North America.

Life at Cambridge, whither the Prince of Wales was sent after his return, seemed more than ever intolerable after the freedom he had enjoyed on his tour. He was getting so tired of General Bruce that on one or two occasions, he couldn't resist telling him what he thought of him. The Prince's outbursts of temper were reported in detail to his parents.

Was there no escape? Only time could release him and he longed for the day when he would be independent.

One day he was so bored with the hours of study, so weary of his jailors that he seized an opportunity and left the house. He had no idea where he was going, but decided that he would first go to London. Then perhaps he could go to stay with someone who would keep him hidden. When he was at Oxford he had been allowed to hunt and had there become friendly with two young men, members of the Oxfordshire Hunt, Frederick Johnstone and Henry Chaplin. They would be at Oxford. He might telegraph them and go there. They could keep him hidden. What a lark! And it would serve them all right.

These two young men had told him how the press laughed at the way he was being brought up. The press was on his side. He believed the people would be. This would show them.

When he arrived at the station two men came towards him; they stood on either side of him.

'The carriage is waiting, Your Highness,' they said.

'Carriage?' he stammered. 'What carriage?'

'General Bruce telegraphed the palace from Cambridge, Your Highness.'

There was the royal carriage. What could he do but get in and be driven to Buckingham Palace?

There he had to face his parents. It was the old question: Whatever can we do with Bertie?

At length they decided to send him to the Curragh Camp in Ireland.

## Chapter XXVII

## THE BETROTHAL OF ALICE

Disturbing news came from Vicky in Berlin. She was pregnant again. The Queen was angry.

'Oh, it is too soon,' she cried, and the Duchess of Kent agreed with her.

Victoria was inclined to be a little short with Albert. Men, she remarked to the Duchess, never really understood what a woman had to suffer. Even Albert was a little obtuse on the subject.

But when Vicky was safely delivered of a baby girl there was great excitement at Windsor. She called the family together and told them that they had become little aunts and uncles.

'Oh, Albert,' she said, 'how I should love to see darling Vicky and the babies! But the two of us together.'

Albert said it must be arranged. It was, and on a lovely September day the Queen and Albert with Alice and a suitable retinue left Gravesend to visit Vicky.

How they enjoyed travelling through Germany on the railway! The scenery was perfect – the river, the red-roofed houses nestling below mountains, the pine forests touched Albert so deeply that his eyes glistened with tears as he passed through his own country. He'd never quite recover from the homesickness which beset him from time to time.

At Frankfurt they found Fritz and his parents who had come to meet them, and at the Hotel d'Angleterre other relations were waiting to welcome them.

The next day they resumed their journey. Victoria was watching Albert; she could understand the appeal of this country which could be beautiful, inviting and forbidding all at the same time. Here were the homes of woodcutters and trolls, creatures of the forest who peopled the fairy stories which Lehzen had told her in the past and which Albert would consider too frivolous for their children. How exciting to see the vineyards and the little villages clustering round their churches, the faces of the people tanned by weather. The women wore handkerchiefs tied over their heads, which was a custom among the women of the Highlands. How moving to see their dearest daughter waiting to embrace them.

The Queen could scarcely wait to see the grandchildren.

As soon as they were refreshed they came down to the room which looked out over the streets of the town and the market place and Vicky said they must meet their grandson. Victoria was trembling at the prospect. How great was the deformity? Had Vicky understated it for fear of alarming her mother?

Little Wilhelm came in clinging to the hand of his English nurse. What a little love in his white dress with black bows (for they were all in mourning for Albert's step-mother, who had recently died). The Queen knelt down and embraced him. He smiled at her. He was plump as a child should be and had a beautiful white skin and sturdy shoulders. She did not want to look too closely at his arm, which a cleverly made sleeve partially disguised. If one did not look too closely it merely appeared that he was holding it rather awkwardly.

'Why,' she cried, 'he has Fritz's eyes and Vicky's mouth.'

They all agreed that this was so.

Once the Queen had trained herself not to look too closely at little Wilhelm's arm she was happy for Vicky. She must not have any more children just yet if that were possible, though.

She whispered: 'We have to stand together sometimes, my darling. It is a little in all clever men's natures to despise our poor degraded sex. They think that we poor creatures are born for their amusement. Even dear Papa is not quite exempt.'

She noticed that Vicky and Alice were often talking earnestly together; she hoped that Vicky was preparing Alice, for it was easier sometimes for a sister than a mother to do these things.

How pleasant it was to be abroad with Albert! These holidays had been the happiest times of their lives – and particularly holidays in Germany, that *dear* country with which, because of Albert, she felt so much in tune. She loved the forests, the red-roofed houses, the costumes of the women and the dear people generally. And Albert was always so happy there.

Stockmar came to see them. How he had aged! He talked of his latest symptoms and then he, Albert and the Queen discussed the subject of the Prince of Wales. Stockmar was a little depressing about this and the Queen was sorry for she could not bear that the visit should be spoilt.

It was wonderful to see Ernest and Alexandrine again, but Victoria noticed that Albert was a little depressed. He and Ernest went for long walks together.

During this Ernest told his brother that he was a little worried about his appearance. He was not looking well.

Albert replied that he had constant rheumatism and recurring bouts of fever in addition to colds. He felt very tired. There was a great deal of work to do. Moreover he worried about the children. The Prince of Wales showed 'wild' tendencies.

'I shouldn't worry about that,' said Ernest. 'It's natural in young men. We settle down. Let us sow our wild oats, Albert. It does us no harm.'

'I remember its doing you some harm at one time.'

Ernest shrugged. 'Poor Bertie!'

'Poor Bertie will one day be King of England. I wish he had not been the eldest.'

'Your English branch of the family are noted for quarrels between father and son. Don't conform to that pattern, Albert. Try to understand the boy.'

'My dear Ernest, what do you know of our position?'

'Well, I admit it's different from mine. But cheer up.'

'I confess to being depressed.'

'What, among our forests! Doesn't this remind you of those expeditions we used to take? Remember our trophies.'

'It reminds me, Ernest ... too well. I have a terrible premonition that I shall never see Coburg again.'

'Come. You need cheering up. What a pleasant creature Alice is.'

'Yes, she is more placid than Vicky. Not so clever though.'

'That's better. Now you're the fond father. What a lot you have to be thankful for, Albert. A fine family and a wife who thinks you're perfection itself.'

Albert smiled slowly and the deep depression passed.

Albert was being driven along in an open carriage with four horses when these took fright and the coachman was unable to control them. They came to a level crossing with the barrier up and seeing that a crash was inevitable Albert jumped out of the carriage. Though badly bruised he was able to get up and go to the help of the coachman to find that he was pinned under the carriage. One of the horses was badly hurt, the others had galloped back to the stables where they were seen, and help was immediately rushed to the scene.

When the Queen, who had been out visiting, came to the palace and was informed of the accident she was horrified. She rushed up to Albert's bedroom to find him lying in bed, his face covered in lint and looking, she noticed with alarm, very shaken.

Dr Stockmar, who was there with the resident doctor, told the Queen that the coachman was badly hurt and that one of the horses had had to be shot.

She could only think of what had happened to Albert and the miraculous escape he had had.

Stockmar was studying the Prince. He did not tell the Queen but it did occur to him that Albert was far from well and that if real illness attacked him he would have very little chance of fighting it.

Albert soon recovered from the accident and apart from a little stiffness, and cuts and bruises, was able to continue his journey. It was a great joy to be at Rosenau for dear Albert's birthday. It was always such a moving pilgrimage for him to walk in the familiar woods and meet old friends. They even visited Herr Florschütz who had been Albert's and Ernest's tutor in the past.

But it must come to an end of course and the sad part was leaving Coburg and Vicky and Fritz, and darling little Wilhelm.

'We must come again, soon,' said the Queen.

Albert merely smiled at her. He could not shake off the strange premonition that he had seen his home for the last time.

Later that year Prince Louis of Hesse came to England. It was not his first visit and when he had come previously he had taken a great liking to Alice and she to him. The Queen had first met him some fifteen years before, when she had been travelling on the continent; he had then been a boy of eight and she had described him as 'nice and intelligent'.

He had come specially to see them on their recent tour, much to Alice's pleasure, and the Queen and Albert had discussed the young people. Albert thought that Louis would be an excellent match for Alice.

And so soon following on their recent encounter here he was in England – and there was no question why.

Victoria smiled indulgently to see the young people together and one evening after dinner when there was some company present she saw them talking very earnestly by the fireplace, unaware of the rest of the company. She went over to them and Alice in some confusion said: 'Louis has just proposed to me, Mama. I want you to give us your blessing.'

The Queen pressed her daughter's hand firmly and whispered: 'Come to our room later.'

When Alice arrived, her parents were both there and Albert sent for Louis. The pair were embraced and told how happy they had made their parents, for the Queen had heard from the Prince and Princess of Hesse-Darmstadt that they knew Louis greatly admired Alice and were happy that this should be so.

When they had gone the Queen sighed deeply.

'So, Albert, we are to lose another daughter.'

'It is something to which we must reconcile ourselves,' said Albert.

'My love, as long as I have you I am content,' said the Queen. 'When I think of those horses running wild and what might have happened...'

'It did not,' said Albert, 'and I am still with you.'

The Queen smiled. 'I thank God daily for your escape,' she said. 'Oh, Albert, if the children all marry and leave us I shall not mind as long as I have you. You are my all in all.'

Albert smiled a little sadly. He had begun to wonder what would happen to her if he were no longer there.


## Chapter XXVIII

## A FATAL JOURNEY

In the middle of March the Duchess of Kent underwent a slight operation. She had a painful abscess under her arm which had been making her feel depressed and wretched so it had been decided to remove it. She had been recuperating satisfactorily in her home of Frogmore when suddenly she became seized by shivering fits.

A few days later Sir James Clark arrived at Buckingham Palace with the news that he was disturbed by the Duchess's condition.

'We must go to her at once,' cried the Queen, and she with Albert and Alice took the train to Windsor.

How long that journey seemed, and all the time

Victoria was thinking of the old days at Kensington Palace when she and her mother had had such 'storms'.

When at last they reached Frogmore the Queen went straight up to her mother's bedroom. The Duchess lay on a sofa, propped up by cushions and wearing a silk dressing-gown. She looked almost like her normal self but that was because the blinds were drawn and the room was so darkened.

Victoria knelt by the sofa and kissing her hand held it against her cheek. The Duchess looked at her daughter and Victoria saw with a pang of dismay and horror that she did not know her. She could not bear it. She went out of the room to give vent to her tears. Albert came in to comfort her.

'We will stay for the night,' he said.

Oh, blessed Albert! What would she do without him?

She would never forget that night. She lay sleepless, listening to every hour as it struck. At four o'clock she could bear no more, and she rose and went to her mother's room. The Duchess was breathing heavily and there was no sound but the ticking of the old repeater watch in its tortoiseshell case which had been her father's and had stood in the bedroom she had shared with her mother up to the time of her accession.

She stood looking at her mother and then went back to her room and tried in vain to sleep.

The next morning it was clear that the end was near. The Queen could not bear to look at that familiar face now so changed and suddenly she

514

was aware of Albert who lifted her up and carried her from the room.

'Is it all over, Albert?' she asked.

Albert, who rarely wept, was weeping then as he said: 'Yes, my love, it is all over.'

The death of the Duchess had a deep effect on the Queen.

She was filled with remorse, remembering those battles of the old days. The entries in her journal brought them all back too vividly for comfort. How unkind she had been to dearest Mama! She remembered the occasion when she had refused to see her and insisted that she had to make an appointment before they met. Her own mother!

There were the accounts of how she had considered herself a prisoner – Mama's prisoner. When all Mama had wanted to do was protect her. She and Baroness Lehzen had behaved as though the Duchess was their enemy. It was terrible. Not until Albert had come had she realised that. Albert had done that for her as he had done everything else.

She was overcome by a deep melancholy. If only Mama could come back and she could talk to her.

The Queen's melancholy was noted and so exaggerated that rumours persisted on the Continent hinting that she had inherited her grandfather's malady. Any member of the family only had to step out of the line of conventional behaviour for someone to remember the madness of George III.

Stockmar wrote urgently to Albert from Coburg. The Queen must understand what a situation her conduct was bringing about. She must stop mourning for her mother. She must be seen in public. These rumours must be quashed. They could be dangerous.

Albert realised this and remonstrated with the Queen.

He agreed that she had been an undutiful daughter before her marriage. But the blame for that must rest with the Baroness Lehzen who had influenced her so strongly. Had she not tried to make trouble between Victoria and her own husband?

Albert could always handle her. She saw his point. While she had him, she said, she had everything to live for.

She became gay again. The period of mourning was over.

But, alas, Albert's health did not improve.

Trouble came from an expected quarter.

Stockmar wrote to break news which, he said, perhaps not strictly truthfully, he would rather have kept to himself.

It was well known on the Continent that while he was at Curragh Camp the Prince of Wales had formed a liaison with an actress. This affair had gone as far as it was possible for such an affair to go. It seemed as though the Prince of Wales was fulfilling their doleful prophecies.

When Albert read the letter his first thought was: The Queen must not know.

She would be horribly shocked; this might

bring on that dangerous mood of depression. He must if possible keep this from her.

What could he do to a young man of nineteen? He thought of his brother Ernest and the evil which had befallen him. Bertie, it seemed, was going to be such another.

He must go to Cambridge and see Bertie. He must discover the truth of this matter. He had a streaming cold and he could feel the fever in his body; his frequent shivering was a warning, but it was his duty to go to Cambridge and when had he ever shirked his duty?

The weather was bleak, cold and damp, and although the symptoms which were affecting him warned him that he should stay in bed, he went off to Cambridge.

When Bertie saw how ill his father looked he was immediately contrite. He spoke naturally and without the embarrassment he usually felt in his father's presence.

'Oh, Papa, you shouldn't have come in this weather.'

Albert looked at him sadly. 'My son,' he said, 'it was my duty to come. You will know why, when I tell you I am aware of your conduct at the Curragh Camp.'

Bertie flushed scarlet.

'You may well be ashamed,' said his father. 'I confess I could scarcely believe it even of you. How could you behave in such a way?'

Bertie stammered that it was not really such an unusual way to behave. Other fellows...

'Other fellows! You are not other fellows. You

are the heir to the throne.'

Bertie cast down his eyes. He wanted to shout at his father that he was tired of being treated like a child; they couldn't go on robbing him of his freedom all his life. When he was twenty-one, he would show them.

But his father looked so ill. He had never seen him quite like this. His face was such a strange colour and the shadows under his eyes so deep; his eyes were unnaturally bright too.

'I'm sorry,' said Bertie.

Albert nodded. 'I believe you are,' he replied with a faint smile. Some of the reforming fire had gone out of him. He felt utterly weary and longed for his bed.

'Bertie,' he said, 'I want you to realise your responsibilities.'

'I do,' said Bertie.

'I want you to act in a way that will show that you do.'

Bertie's kind heart was touched by the pitiful looks of his father. He wanted to end this interview as quickly as possible so that his father could get back home and to bed where he obviously should be.

'I will try to in future,' he said. 'Papa, you are not well. You should be in bed.'

Albert held up a hand that was not quite steady.

'If you would mend your ways, try not to make your mother so anxious, remember that one day you will be King of England...'

'I will, Papa.'

Albert nodded. He did not love his son; he could never do that; but he did not feel that mild resentment and faint dislike which he had felt before.

'Bertie,' he said, 'I shall say nothing to your mother of this affair.'

'Thank you, Papa.'

Albert rose.

'You are going home now, Papa?' asked Bertie.

Albert nodded.

'You should be in bed.'

Albert smiled. It was the first time his son had ever told him what *he* should do. In the circumstances it touched him.

When he returned to the palace it was clear that he was ill. The Queen was worried and scolded him for going out in such awful weather.

'I had to go,' he said wearily.

'What on earth could be so important as to make you?' she demanded.

He said nothing and seeing how weary he was she stopped scolding and helped him to bed. She sat beside it watching him, holding his hand.

'You'll soon be well, Albert,' she said. 'I am going to insist on your taking greater care.'

He was a little better next morning and would not stay in bed; he sat in the bedroom in his padded dressing-gown with its scarlet velvet collar and went through state papers; but he could eat very little and the Queen was growing very anxious.

Sir James Clark was a little concerned. His colleague Dr Baly, the other royal physician, had been killed only a short while before in a railway accident. Sir James, never very sure of himself, now wished to call in further advice and suggested Dr Jenner, who was an expert on typhoid fever.

When Dr Jenner came and examined Albert it was his opinion that, although Albert was not a victim of the fever, there were signs that he might be affected by the germs. They must therefore prepare themselves for an attack of this dreaded disease.

When the Queen heard this she was terrified. People *died* of typhoid fever.

'The Prince would have every possible care,' said Sir James. 'And so far he does not have typhoid fever.'

Albert insisted on sleeping in a small bed at the foot of their big bed.

'I toss and turn so much that I should disturb you,' he said.

'Disturb me!' cried the Queen. 'Do you think I shall have any sleep? I would be afraid to sleep in any case. You might need me.'

She was up and down all night giving him cooling drinks.

'If I get this fever,' he said, 'I shall die.'

'You will not die!' she commanded.

And he smiled at her. 'Dearest little wife,' he said, 'I do not fear death. I only think of how you will miss me and how sad you will be.'

'Oh, Albert, don't. I can't bear it. *You* are my life. How could I go on if you were not here?'

'You must, dearest, you must.'

'I'll not have this talk,' she cried. 'You are here with me, and here you are going to stay. You haven't got the fever. You're not going to have it.'

'No,' he said, to soothe her, 'no.' And he

thought: Poor Victoria. Poor little Queen.

For five nights he tossed and turned in his little bed. She had scarcely slept at all. The Queen was desperate because he would not eat. When she tried to tempt him with a little soup, he only shook his head.

One day he seemed a little better and the Queen asked if he would like Alice to read to him. Vicky used to and when she had gone Alice took on the duty. He brightened a little. But when she came and started *Silas Marner* he shook his head. He didn't like it. She tried others but he did not want to listen to anything.

The Queen said brightly: 'We'll try Sir Walter Scott tomorrow, Papa dear.'

Albert smiled at her wanly.

Then he became irritable.

'I believe it's a good sign,' cried the Queen jubilantly.

His complaints were peevish, which was not like him. The Albert Victoria had known seemed to be replaced by a wild-eyed man.

Alice read to him again and he seemed to enjoy that for a little while.

'That's a good sign,' said the Queen. 'More like dear good blessed Papa.'

But a few hours later when she was sitting by his bed he said suddenly; 'Can you hear the birds singing?'

She could not and he added: 'When I heard them I thought I was at Rosenau.'

She went out of the room because she could not control her sobbing. She knew that he was very ill.

Dr Jenner wanted to talk to her. She looked at him anxiously. 'Your Majesty knows that all along we have feared ... gastric fever.'

Gastric fever! Bowel fever! She knew that these were kinder names for the dreaded typhoid.

'I know it,' she said. 'And now...?'

'I am afraid that this is what His Highness is now suffering from.'

She felt dazed. Typhoid! The dreaded killer!

'Vicky,' he said, 'Vicky.'

For a moment she thought that he was speaking to her, then she realised that he thought she was their daughter.

'Vicky is well, my darling,' she said. 'Vicky is in Berlin with her husband.'

He nodded. Alice sat on the other side of the bed.

He looked at her and was suddenly lucid. He remembered that Vicky was pregnant again and that he was worried about her. 'Did you write to Vicky?'

'Yes, dear Papa.'

'Did you tell her how I was?'

'I told her that you were ill, Papa.'

He shook his head.

'You should have told her that I am dying,' he said.

All the children were there. Bertie oddly enough was her greatest comfort.

'Oh, Bertie, what am I going to do?'

'I will care for you, Mama.'

'But he will get better. The doctors have been telling me. They never despair with fever. People get over it ... often.'

'Yes, Mama. He has every care. You must take care of yourself.'

'I tried to take care of *him*. He would go off. That awful November day he went off because he felt it was his duty. I never quite knew where he went. He was in such a hurry. He said it was so important and when he came back he was too ill to say anything. We could only think of getting him to bed. I'll never forgive those people who asked him to go wherever he went...'

Bertie had grown pale, but the Queen did not notice that.

She had thought he was a little better. He sat up in bed and arranged his hair, just as he used to when he was going somewhere.

Then she noticed that there was a dusky hue about his face which she had never seen before.

He seemed to be preparing himself – as though he were going on a journey.

She could not bear it. He must not see her distress. She got up and went out.

But she must be with him. She had a numbing fear that there might not be much time left. She went and sat beside his bed.

He was aware of her. '*Gutes Frauchen,*' he murmured.

All the children came in one by one and kissed him.

She did not know how she endured it, but she

controlled her grief because she could not bear that he should see it nor could she bear to leave him.

She bent over him. He looked at her wonderingly.

'*Es is kleines Frauchen*,' he said, and he smiled and kissed her.

She sat there holding his hand and suddenly all the pain and suffering seemed to fall away from his face and he was the young and beautiful Albert again at whom she had only to look to know that she would love him for ever.

Albert was dead.

# Bibliography

Argyll, The Duke of, *V.R.I., Queen Victoria, her Life and Empire*

Aubrey, William Hickman Smith, *History of England*

Creston, Dormer, *The Youthful Queen Victoria*

Davey, Richard, *Victoria (Queen and Empress)*

Duff, David, *Victoria in the Highlands, The Personal Journal of Her Majesty Queen Victoria, with Notes, Introductions and a Description of the Acquisition and Rebuilding of Balmoral Castle*

Esher, Viscount, *The Girlhood of Queen Victoria (A Selection of Her Majesty's Diaries between the years 1832 and 1840)*

Greville, Charles C.H. (edited by Henry Reeve), *The Greville Memoirs. A journal of the Reign of Queen Victoria*

edited by Philip Whitwell Wilson, *The Greville Diary*

Jerrold, Clare, *Early Court of Queen Victoria*

Jerrold, Clare, *The Married Life of Queen Victoria*

Longford, Elizabeth, *Victoria R.I.*

Martin, Sir Theodore, *Life of the Prince Consort*

Oliphant, Mrs, *Queen Victoria, A Personal Sketch*

Pike, E. Royston, *Britain's Prime Ministers*

Sitwell, Edith, *Victoria of England*

Smith, G. Barnett, *Life of Her Majesty*

*Queen Victoria*

Smith, G. Barnett, *The Prime Ministers of Queen Victoria*

Strachey, Lytton, *Queen Victoria* edited by Sir Leslie Stephen and Sir Sidney Lee, *Dictionary of National Biography*

Tooley, Sarah A., *The Personal Life of Queen Victoria*

edited by Christopher Benson and Viscount Esher, *The Letters of Queen Victoria, A Selection of Her Majesty's Correspondence between the years 1837-1861*

edited by Arthur Helps, *Leaves from the Journal of Our Life in the Highlands, From 1848-1861*

The publishers hope that this book has given you enjoyable reading. Large Print Books are especially designed to be as easy to see and hold as possible. If you wish a complete list of our books please ask at your local library or write directly to:

**Magna Large Print Books**
Magna House, Long Preston,
Skipton, North Yorkshire.
BD23 4ND

This Large Print Book for the partially sighted, who cannot read normal print, is published under the auspices of

## THE ULVERSCROFT FOUNDATION